SCANDINAVIAN CLASSICS

VOLUMES XV—XVI

. .
.

THE CHARLES MEN

BY

VERNER VON HEIDENSTAM

THE CHARLES MEN

BY

VERNER VON HEIDENSTAM

TRANSLATED FROM THE SWEDISH
BY CHARLES WHARTON STORK
WITH AN INTRODUCTION BY FREDRIK BÖÖK

TWO VOLUMES IN ONE

WILDSIDE PRESS

VERNER VON HEIDENSTAM

Author of " The Charles Men"

I

FOR more than five years the world has been full of strife and the clash of weapons, and still the last shot has not been fired or the last sword thrust into its sheath. Humanity finds itself in a situation recalling that in which Lucius Cary, Viscount Falkland, found himself during the English Revolution and Civil War; when Clarendon relates that he, "sitting among his friends, often, after a deep silence and frequent sighs, would, with a shrill and sad accent, ingeminate the word *Peace, Peace;* and would passionately profess that the very agony of the war, and the view of the calamities and desolation the kingdom did and must endure, took his sleep from him, and would shortly break his heart."

It is at this time that there is brought before the American public one of the most distinguished works of modern Swedish literature; a work devoted to the king who lived his whole life in the field and died in a trench, and who even in the days of Voltaire stood as the genius of war, the symbol of its desolating and misfortune-bringing might; a work that deals only with campaigns and battles, with slaughter and pillage, the wailing of the wounded, and the long, hopeless agony of the captives—with all that humanity would fain forget, and cannot forget. The moment might seem to be ill chosen; more than one, perhaps, may feel himself minded as Aeneas when, having barely escaped from the burning of Troy, the swords of the Greeks, and the terrors of shipwreck, Queen Dido asks him to relate the story of his life, and he answers with a shudder: *Infandum, Regina, jubes renovare dolorem.*

But as surely as it is the province of fiction to give us what we do not have in fact, and to make us forget what hurts and oppresses us, so surely does it also have the mission of helping us to understand what we have gone through, of looking with clearer and purer eyes on the struggles and experiences of life. Fiction frees from external reality, not only by taking us away to the lands of fantasy and the world of beautiful visions, but by animating the dead matter of events, by giving significance and substance to things, by showing us the confusing spectacle *sub specie aeternitatis.* From this point of view, *The Charles Men* is a timely work. The fall of the Swedish empire, the desperate contest of an inflexible ruler for what he believed to be true and right, the boundless suffering of an ill-fated people, the ravages of hunger which they endured, their growing despair and infinite fortitude, their inevitable ruin and eternal glory — such is the picture that appears before us in simple, majestic lines; a tragedy clear and compelling as one of the Greeks', composed by the very history of the world, and fitted to purify our hearts through terror and pity, as Aristotle taught. He who ponders the nature of war and the philosophy of history may win instruction from the epic which Swedish history and Swedish imagination together have formed about Charles XII and his men. It was no superficial romance of war, no rancorous and hypocritical chauvinism, that inspired Verner von Heidenstam. He saw before his eyes the misery and degradation of war; no pacifistic Barbusse has painted it in grimmer colors than he. He saw the problematic side of his hero; the rigid, petrified insensibility that misfortunes and spiritual torments wrought in the breast of the king. And yet he felt deeply the moral beauty, the human magnanimity, which these men of battle displayed, and which they gave to posterity as a noble, strengthening essence, extracted from withered herbs and crushed reeds, a *medicina mentis* for every one who must needs fight, endure, be vanquished and overpowered.

The highest praise one can give to *The Charles Men* is that this work, which was composed in deep-

est peace, has not lost its color and quality during
the World War. Verner von Heidenstam has come
forward among the pacifists side by side with Ro-
main Rolland; but he does not belong to the superficial, blind zealots for peace of whom Paul Elmer
More speaks in his profound and humane essay,
The Philosophy of War. He belongs with those who
have always seen mankind in all its contradictory
profusion and have laid to heart what the great
American critic writes: "Nor is war in itself wholly
bestial. There has grown up amongst us of recent
years a literature devoted to the propaganda of
peace, both in the form of fiction and of exhorta-
tion, which throws into vivid relief all the horrors
incidental to the battlefield, and slurs over and de-
nies the honor and exaltation that are also a part
of the soldier's life. That literature, I say boldly, is
as false and mischievous as its Nietzschean antago-
nist. There is an element of heroism in war which,
through all the waste and evil, has not been without
its salutary effect. Is it because he has passed his life
in a career entirely cruel and vile that the typical
soldier, in his later years of retirement, is a man so
true and honorable, often so gentle? Shall we, in
our imagination of peace, forget all that we have
felt in the reading of history, and slander our in-
stincts?"

True, honorable, gentle—that is the stamp of the Charles men: the prisoners in Siberia, as they are gathered around the Bible in their bitter poverty; and those that have returned to their native land, as they set the plough in the earth to build a new Sweden on the ruins of the old.

It is not, however, the affair of the Swedish critic to subjoin the reflections to which *The Charles Men* invites, but to tell of the author who wrought the work, and to make clear what we admire in it.

II

Verner von Heidenstam is by birth an aristocrat; he was born on the sixth of July, 1859, at the manor house of Olshammar in Närke. As a boy he was thought to have lung trouble, and for that reason did not follow the usual course of education; instead he was sent to the milder climate of southern Europe. His youth received, therefore, a different impress from that of most Swedish authors of the same age. The horizon of the Mediterranean surrounded it. He lived in Italy and visited Greece, Egypt, Palestine, and Asia Minor; while for nearly eight years he was away from Sweden. The attraction toward the Orient was very strong in his nature; one has the impression that it was found in all of his family, because at the end of the seventeenth century one of his ancestors was the Swedish Minister at Constantinople, and was actively interested in Turkish civilization; another travelled to Persia, and died in 1878 as *chargé d'affaires* in Athens, and branches of the stock are still flourishing in Cyprus and Smyrna. Heidenstam wanted to become a painter, and was in fact a pupil at the studio of Gérôme in Paris. But it gradually became clear to him that he was above all a poet; in 1887 he returned to Sweden, and in 1888 made his debut with the collection, *Pilgrimage and Wander-Years*.

In this we have the verse of a painter; strongly colorful, plastic, racy, vivid. In the bold, sometimes careless, form there is nothing academic; all is seen and felt and experienced, the observation is sharp and the imagination lively. The young poet-artist reproduces the Italian carnival, the French life of the streets, impressions of Attic landscapes; he tells stories from the *Thousand and One Nights*, and conjures up before us the bazaars of Damascus. He loves the ancient world: its clear beauty, its fresh joy of life; he showers ridicule and scorn upon the ugly, sad, nervous, bustling present. In the carefree indolence of the East he sees the last reflection of the old happy innocence, and for that reason he loves it. He is a reckless epicurean, who lets the Egyptian priests of Hator proclaim:

Wine, the kiss of a girl, and the daring jest that will startle
Senile women and men—to the gods above these are blameless.

And yet amid all the gay hedonism in *Pilgrimage and Wander-Years* is a cycle of short poems, *Thoughts in Loneliness*, filled with brooding, melancholy, and sombre longing.

In the year 1888 Heidenstam brought out a volume of travel descriptions, *From Col di Tenda to Blocksberg;* and in the novel *Endymion*, published in 1889, he displayed a picture of the East which is stifled to death in the embrace of the West. In a couple of brochures, *Renascence* (1889) and *Pepita's Wedding* (1890), the latter a rollicking *jeu d'esprit* executed in collaboration with the poet and literary historian, Oscar Levertin, he attacked the prevalent naturalism, the gray-weather mood in life and fiction. With the right of a strong, youthful temperament he craved an art that would move freely and boldly, unfettered by social doctrines and pseudo-scientific theories of the day; he wished to give back their dues to the imagination, to the love of beauty, and insisted upon the sovereignty of the artist. These writings took on a decisive meaning in the development of Swedish literature: during the decade of 1880 Sweden had been dominated by the "literature of indignation," literature with a purpose, by the naturalism of the positivists, and by methodized prose. Heidenstam turned the current: the decade of 1890 became lyrical and imaginative, the decade of free and sovereign poetry. Gustaf Fröding, Selma Lagerlöf, Per Halström, and Erik Axel Karlfeldt carried out the program that Heidenstam and Levertin had laid down.

But the joy of life and enthusiasm for beauty, which the young Heidenstam had proclaimed, soon gave place in himself to deeper moods. Even the great fantastic epic, *Hans Alienus*, which he completed in 1892, is a monument on the grave of his care-free and indolent youth. He discovered that beauty cannot satisfy the hunger of the soul; his hero, a pilgrim in the storied lands of the East, is a brooding Faust, who even in the pleasure-gardens of Sardanapalus cannot cease from his painful search after the meaning of life. He is driven back by his yearning to the snowy country of his fathers, far up in the Swedish forest of Tiveden.

In the collection, *Poems*, which Heidenstam brought out in 1895, the horizon of the Mediterranean has disappeared. The soughing fir-trees tell him stories different from those he listened to among dancers and camel-drivers. The love he now sings is that which a man's own effort has brought to birth, and which "flings arms of flame around

heaven and earth." The meagre land rises before
his glance with new beauty: it is the stretch of earth
which his fathers cleared with toil and self-denial.
No one has praised home more fervently and inti-
mately than the pilgrim and traveller, the restless
wanderer:

> *A home! 'T is like a fortress*
> *By walls securely shielded,—*
> *Our world, our own, the one thing*
> *We in this world have builded.*

Heidenstam's nationalism, which had its theoretical
expression in many of the essays which he collected
in 1899 under the title *Thoughts and Sketches*, is
above all born of a deep filial affection for the past.
Annals, monuments, ruins, and portraits become
living realities to the man of powerful imagination;
wherever he goes, the present moment unfolds and
lets us look into the ancient records; the dead sur-
round us like gigantic spirits, overshadowing our
thoughts. But despite this entering into the past,
which is so characteristic of Heidenstam, his tra-
ditional bent has never become an inflexible con-
servatism. There is a strong democratic current
throughout all of his markedly aristocratic nature.
Among *Poems* is included *Singers in the Steeple*,
where he celebrates the idea of brotherhood, and
makes the classes privileged as to power and gold

pour their treasures into a cup, on which is inscribed:

Not joy to the rich, to the poor man care;
Our toil and our pleasure alike we share.

The collection of poems that gives the strongest
expression to his passion for his country, *A People*
(1902), contains the lyric *Fellow-Citizens*, where he
takes up the cause of universal suffrage and thor-
oughgoing democracy.

The Charles Men, which appeared in 1897–98, is
Heidenstam's chief work in prose; to Swedish read-
ers it is evident that only verse allows his artistic
greatness to come to its full right. *The Charles Men*
forms the introduction to a series of historical descriptions: *St. Birgitta's Pilgrimage* (1901), which
sets before us the greatest religious personality of
Sweden in the Middle Ages; *Folke Filbyter* (1905)
and *The Legacy of Bjälbo* (1907), which render the
ancient and mediaeval times in pictures composed
around the Folkung family; *The Swedes and their
Chieftains* (1908–10), which makes all the Swedish
annals pass by in review. The last-named work is
written in the form of a reader for Swedish schools.
In the collections of tales, *St. George and the Dragon*
(1900), and the volume of sagas and stories which
he collected in 1904 under the title *Forest Murmurs*,

are to be found some of his most original and personal creations. His last book is *New Poems* (1915),
where the simple and compact form of the lyrics
expresses the noble, quiet humanism of the ripened
and matured man.

After his homecoming in 1887, Heidenstam sèt-
tled for a time on his ancestral estate of Olshammar, but in 1890 shifted to Djursholm near Stockholm, and in 1897 participated in the founding of
the great national-liberal newspaper, the *Svenska
Dagblad*, whose program was defence and reform.
In 1900 he settled at Naddö (near Vadstena), on the
shore of Lake Wettern, which he loved so deeply
and on whose strand was situated the home of his
childhood. In 1917 he departed thence, after his
third marriage, like both of those preceding, had
been dissolved by divorce, and in 1919 he betook
himself afresh to foreign travel. In 1910 he was
made an honorary Doctor of Philosophy by the
University of Stockholm; in 1912 he became a
member of the Swedish Academy, and in 1916 received the Nobel Prize for Literature.

III

The Charles Men is a poem in prose. Heidenstam's
technic has all the freedom, abandon, even caprice
that belongs to verse. There is no steady and clear

stream of narrative in his work; he leaps over what is inessential, and his imagination concentrates itself on the scene, the figure, the detail that strikes him as significant. This technic is in accord with the historical atmosphere. Uniform realism, methodical description, and painstaking motivation may be in place in a modern novel; if, on the other hand, it is a question of conjuring up visions from the past, the poet must not bring his figures out into the full daylight—that can only lead to destroying the illusion, as when masks go about in the sunshine. We must have a broad river of darkness, which contains all the mystery of the past, and against this black background the figures and scenes may glimmer forth—symbolic flashes of that life whose depth and scope one cannot define, but only surmise.

That Heidenstam dreamed at one time of becoming a painter, to this every page of *The Charles Men* bears witness. What a mighty composition is the picture of Stockholm's castle in flames which closes the first narrative, *The Green Corridor!* Heidenstam has rendered the picturesque element of Charles XII's history with the most finished art: not only the gloomy scenes in black, gray, and white from the wintry land in the North, but also the variegated and highly colored representations

of the wanderings in the war. The Queen of the Marauders among the Cossacks by the Beresina; the
march of Mazeppa, surrounded by drunken Zaporogeans; the flaxen-haired Stupid Swede in the
serail of the sultana, among gilded parrot-cages and
black cypresses — one could not draw a more mas-
terly contrast between the simple poverty of the
Charles folk and the exoticism of the Orient.

The artist reveals himself everywhere, but so,
too, does the aristocrat. The patriarchal idyl of the
country manor is immortalized in the airy *Midsummer Sport*. The gay, care-free spirit of adventure that
played through the centuries among the Swedish
nobility is incarnate in the indomitable Grothusen
who is always in debt; and when Rika Fuchs rides
in front of his regiment to make an estimate of his
property, every Swede must recognize the national
sense of humor. The joking spirit has undergone
an intimate union with a proud and taciturn sense
of duty. It is only in the solitude of the prison cell
that Gustaf Celsing gives words to the deep grief
that burns among these officers, humiliated, in-
sulted, trampled to earth in the service of their beloved master:

> *In alien places*
> *His men of proud races*
> *As beggars must crouch.*

Even when dispersed in slavery, they preserve their sense of order and responsibility; they keep up their muster-rolls and accounts, they are not a horde but a people, a state (*The General of Papers*).

Of the glittering conqueror, " King Charles, the youthful hero," illuminated by the sunshine of triumph and success, whom Tegnér celebrated a hundred years after, Heidenstam has not much to tell. Only for a brief second may we catch a glimpse of his boyish ardor as he steps ashore at Zeeland. It is in the time of adversity and defeat that he begins to interest Heidenstam. When the king feels himself to be alone, abandoned by God and man, the transfiguration of poetry falls over his form. He is a wholly tragic figure. The author himself has propounded his view of Charles XII in an essay: " A tragic problem comprises a duel between conflicting claims of right which appear so strong that it lies beyond human justice to reject either one of them entirely. Not only is it impossible to cut the blood-red thread that the logic of misfortune spins through the tragedy, but even in respect to the final moral judgment we cannot get further than a dim scrutiny. This awakens sympathy, if not a full and devoted admiration for the tragic hero; but it arouses, too, inquisitive reflection, the search for a possible solution, however impossible it may be to find. The tragic problem is therefore insoluble to mankind, and from that fact, first and last, comes the general confusion in contemplating Charles XII, the continual dissension between our admiration on one side and our moral demands on the other. If a solution were ever possible, it would mean that the king was not really tragic; but we need have no fear. What is tragic in the deepest classical sense, if not the strife between the claims of personal and of universal justice that fill his life as we behold it? He finds himself treacherously attacked and ensnared. He cannot escape from the single thought that he must get back what force is tearing out of his hands. The prudent and the exhausted cry out for him to make peace, but he cannot overlook the thought that at the first opportunity the enemy will again fall upon him, if he does not first strike them to earth for a long period. It is not he that has made the Swedish empire, but if it collapses, it is he that must bear the shame; and the more his honor weakens, the more ambition becomes his all-engulfing passion. In this manner he assumes in his person all of his people's demands for justice, and tragedy spreads its wings over millions."

The hero of this tragedy is, accordingly, not only the king, but the Swedish people as well. In *Poltava* Lewenhaupt says: "The wreath he twined for himself slid down upon his subjects instead." And in *A Hero's Funeral* Brother George answers the slanderers and revilers: "Are not your eyes opened yet so as to see that it was our own secret will and desire which he preserved against our own indecision, like a banner against a rebellious guard?"

The Charles Men, therefore, is not only a monument over the fall of the Swedish empire, but also a hymn on the beauty in its destruction, the hopeless magnanimity of obedience to duty, the poetry of sacrifice. It expresses Heidenstam's deeply tragic philosophy of life. The highest that a man can attain is to fall with honor, and such is the fate of the best. Happiness is common and superficial; suffering is holy and great.

None of the stories in *The Charles Men* is more deeply characteristic of Heidenstam than *The Stupid Swede*. The parks and pavilions of the Turkish serail, with their roses and jewels, symbolize the oriental doctrine of pleasure and beauty that he celebrated in his youth. But at the moment when the awkward and joyless Swedish thrall stands among the glittering, soulless dancing-girls, who know nothing more of earth than that it is lovely, and dream of nothing else than of a kiosk with red damask hangings and perfumed fountains, her form suddenly takes on an exaltation that none of the others possesses; and when she seizes the basket with the snake in order to fulfil her duty, it is she who is the most beautiful. Beauty of self-sacrifice, of misfortune, of the soul, causes her to shine more brightly than even the odalisque Evening Starlight.

Anatoie France has related a legend of the juggler of the Madonna who worshipped the Holy Virgin, and won her favor by the naïve piety with which he performed his tricks in her honor. *The Stupid Swede* is a legend of that soul-temper which transforms ugliness to grace and misfortune to harmony. That soul-temper is glorified in the concluding words of *The Charles Men*, where a benediction is called down upon the people who in their fall from greatness caused their poverty to be glorified before the world.

FREDRIK BÖÖK

Lund, Sweden, December, 1919

The translator wishes to express his gratitude to Mr. O. A. Linder of Chicago for his collation of the English text with the original, and to Mr. Edwin Björkman of New York for assistance in certain difficult passages.

THE CHARLES MEN

PART I

CONTENTS

Part I

The Green Corridor

IN the castle attic, where the fire-chief sold brandy and ale, a tall, narrow-shouldered customer had been thrust down the stairs and his empty pewter pot thrown after him, so that it rolled between his shoes. His worsted stockings were mended and dirty. He had tied his neck-cloth over his mouth and unshaven cheeks, and he continued to stand with his hands in his coat-tail pockets.

"Show out crazy Ekerot!" said the fire-chief. "He has spit tobacco plug into the ale, stuck Peter Painter with a bodkin, and is full of mischief all through. Then shut up the folding table! There is a command to bar the castle gates, for now it will soon be over with His Royal Majesty's life."

One of the wardens was Charles XI's faithful old servant, Hakon. He had a tranquil face, but walked so bowlegged in his stiff clothes that he looked as if he had just dismounted from a horse. He picked up the pot and stuck it good-naturedly under Ekerot's arm.

"I shall follow you, constable," he said, — "or lieutenant, or whatever I should call you."

"Lars Ekerot is a captain in His Gracious Majesty's battle fleet," answered Ekerot, "and travelled

and learned in tongues he is, too. Here in the castle
attic one sees no distinction between folk and folk.
I shall leave a report and complain of it, that I
shall. Have I not told you that soon fire shall rain
from heaven, and every rafter in this house break
out into bright flame? Mercenary councillors, un-
righteous judgments, execration, and lamentation,
—that has become our daily bread, and the wrath
of Heaven rests heavy on the land."

"Lieutenant—or captain—you need not spread
talk of worse misfortunes than those which God has
already given us to bear. Round about in the sub-
urbs has the fire made way, and for ten years we
have had failure of harvest and famine. Four bush-
els of rye already cost twelve rix-dollars in silver.
Soon fodder will run short even in the royal stable,
and the boats with imported grain lie frozen solid
out by the coast."

Ekerot went down the steps beside him and
looked around without fixing his small, restless
eyes on any definite object. Sometimes he stood
still, nodding and talking to himself in an undertone.

Through the loopholes came glimpses of the
castle grounds far below and the covered terrace
with obelisks and sentries who went back and forth
in the trumpeters' gallery. Beyond the snow-covered towers and roofs, small groups of people moved
on the frozen Mälar between King's Island and

Söder. The light of the March evening shone slanting through one of the halls in the western wing of the castle, so that it appeared as if light had been kindled in the chandelier.

"Yes, yes," mumbled Ekerot, "that shall all burn, all — all that which was our shame, all that which was our greatness. I have seen shining fellows in the heavens, and when I sit with my pipe at night, I see in the tobacco smoke wonderful planets, which show me that the old order of the world is upset. In Hungary and Germany rain down swarms of Arabia's grasshoppers. The fire-spurting mountains cast up glowing stones. Two years ago we had grass finger-high in the park in February and heard the birds of spring, but in September I picked strawberries at Essing. It is in such times that the Lord God opens the eyes of his elect so that they see what is hid."

"In God's name, do not talk so!" stammered Hakon. "Do you see your visions waking or asleep?"

"Between the two."

"I promise that I shall report every word to His Royal Majesty himself, if you, lieutenant, will recount for me quite veraciously all that you have seen and known. Do you see down below there the two windows where the shutters are closed? It isn't half an hour since I was in there. There His Royal Majesty sits in a chair made into a bed with covers and pillows, and he has become so small and dried up that he is only nose and lips. And he cannot raise his head. His poor Majesty, who has to endure such agony, though he is but some forty and odd years! Formerly, when he came limping through the door, I was most glad if I could slip out, but though I am only the least among servants, he can now put his arms around my neck and press me to him with streaming tears. I do not believe that he feels much more warmly for his son than he did for his wife. When he sends for him, he is brief of speech and mostly sits and looks at him. He speaks now only of his kingdom—and again of his kingdom. Up to a week ago I saw on his knee house-inspections and tariffs and such trifles, but now he has written down his secret instructions to his son and laid the letter in a sealed iron casket. As soon as any one steps into the room, it is as if both with his feverishly gleaming eyes and his words he stammered a constant: 'Help me, help me to uphold the kingdom, to make my son worthy and prudent. The kingdom, the kingdom!'"

Hakon passed his hand across his forehead, and they went on down the steps from loophole to loophole.

"In the room below us to the left is Her Majesty, the queen dowager. She has locked herself up during these last days, and not even Tessin slips in with his portfolios. No one knows just what she is about, but I can well believe that she does her best to banish her sad thoughts with a game of cards. There's a tinkling and jingling of watch-charms on the edge of the card table, and a crunching and a rustling and a frizzling of lace and ruffs—and a cane with a gold knob slips to the floor—"

"And the pretty Lady Hedwig Stenbock, who stands behind the chair, picks it up."

"That she certainly does n't, for she is long since ·married and old and ugly, and at her own home. You live only in that which was and that which is to be."

"That may be." Ekerot screwed up his eyes and pointed to the north wing of the castle, which had just been reared by Tessin, after the old one had been levelled to the earth. Some scaffolds were still standing with fir branches on the highest pinnacles.

"Well, who lives under that long box-lid? Fie! There lives no one at all—and neither will any one come to live there, that I know. Why could n't it be left to stand as it was? Devil take the Gottorp woman that put all this building nonsense into the head of His Royal Majesty! You see, warder, just as every man has his soul, so every old house has in it all sorts of spooks and other creatures of darkness, which are disturbed and uncomfortable when people come with pick-axe and trowel. Do you remember the Green Corridor which used to run under the section of the roof above the old castle church? It was there that for the first time I got my eyes opened. Oh, I 'll tell you all about it. I will tell you the whole story, warder, if you will follow me home and then keep your promise to relate every word to His Royal Majesty himself."

Having now come down to the entrance door, they went on the drawbridge across the castle moat. A courier with a leathern bag on his back was just about to dismount from his horse, and his answer to the many questions was heard through the trampling of feet and the orders.

"For six miles north of Stockholm seen only three human beings—They sat by the side of the road and fed on an animal that had died a natural death. In Norrland a pound of meal mixed with bark cost five rix-dollars in silver. Soldiers starving to death—Regiments hardly half their complement—"

Ekerot nodded assentingly, as if all this had been known to him long since, and he continued to walk beside Hakon with his pewter pot under his arm and his hands stuck in his coat tails.

When they had come up to his attic room at Trångsund he gave Hakon a mistrustful side-look, and when he stuck the key into the lock he ascertained carefully that the door had not been opened in his absence. The room was large and bare. In the window stood a cage with a squirrel, and on one wall was a medley of unlike pieces of money nailed up in rows. There were bright Elbing rix-dollars, small and large copper coins, a five-ducat piece of Reval, and even a couple of Palm-struch's old bank-notes, which had been worthless for thirty years. Ekerot advanced, inspected, and counted the money.

"A fool," he said, "sinks his possessions so deep that he cannot himself keep watch over them, but I want to have them under my eyes, so that I can easily count them into a sack, when the great fire comes."

Out of one corner, Ekerot carefully took five logs, which he put in the fireplace and lighted with a piece of tarred stick. Thereupon he and Hakon filled their pipes, and as there were no chairs, they sat on the floor in front of the blaze.

" Well, let us hear now," said Hakon.

Ekerot narrated:

Never have I seen anything so frightful as the Green Corridor. That was at the time when I was constable with the battle fleet. Now they have given me my little pension of two hundred and fifty dollars. Oh, to be sure. I was as good as driven from the service because people were afraid lest otherwise I should end as admiral-in-chief. And *that* Hans Wachtmeister wants to be himself. " The fellow is crazy!" he screamed on the deck, when I politely asked him to raise his hat before he ordered me into

the rigging. And so it was all up with me. Crazy
Ekerot I was called wherever I came and went. So
it keeps on. A poor journeyman carries a comrade
to the grave; then he carries his master to the grave;
and at last, for a groat, he carries one after another,
gets himself a glazed hat and a long black cloak,
and when he is in a hurry rolls of braid fall out of
his pocket—and children take to their heels and
weep and scream: "The corpse bearer, the corpse
bearer!" But though one may become such a bug-
bear, at the beginning we are, to be sure, all baked
of the same dough. Report that now, word for word,
to His Royal Majesty in person. Ah well, at that
time I was quite skilful in drawing and sketching.
A few days before that quarrel with Wachtmeister,
I therefore received a gracious command to take
with me another constable, who was called Nils,
and appear in the store-room above the old papist
church in the castle tower that stood by the river.
There we were to draw a broken lantern of a galleon, according to which the queen dowager wished
to have a new one made for her sloops on the
Mälar.

When we had sat there in that manner for a day,
gambling and worrying over the smashed lantern of
the galleon, which the devil himself could n't have
drawn, a merry fit came upon me, and I cried: "Nils,
have you ever seen a dog with five legs?"

When Nils shrugged his shoulders, I went on:

"I saw one just now in Iron Square. He walked on four legs, and the fifth he had in his mouth."

Nils got angry, and to provoke him I cried still louder: "Clever you are not. Let's see if you are brave. I'll wager you this pewter pint measure filled with good Spanish wine and with a ducat at the bottom that I shall go alone at guard-bell through the Green Corridor."

Nils replied: "I know that when you set your mind on anything it's no use trying to keep you from it, and I don't want that you should think me stingy of gifts. Therefore, my dear Ekerot, I take your wager as you desire, but I will not bear the responsibility to your old mother if any ill befalls you. Therefore I prefer to go home to my place. In daytime this splendid building is fine enough to see; but at night strange things are supposed to happen here, and I'd rather sleep in the wretchedest hole in the suburb."

I called him poltroon, and let him ramble off home. As soon as I was alone, I noticed that it had already begun to grow dark, and, in order to harden myself, I went up the two or three winding stairways to the Green Corridor and looked through the keyhole.

The green paint had fallen down in many places, so that the older bright red color shone out. Along the walls stood all sorts of household furniture that had been worn out and carried up there. I saw cabinets and chairs, and representations of dogs and horses, and in the far corner a bed with drawn curtains. On the sides were hidden recesses, where there was a dropping and dripping from the leaky roofing.

It was Walpurgis Night and therefore somewhat light, and this restored me to a certain feeling of security, so that I could sit down and wait, but I knew that wondrous beings had their resort up there under the roof. The warders called them night-goblins, because only at twilight did they lift up the dark boards and stick out their heads. They were not larger than a three-years' child, were brown all over, naked, and had the bodies of women. Often they would sit mounted on a cabinet and wave their arms, and he who happened to touch a night-goblin died within the year. They were wont to spring about in the attics, and sometimes they shrieked in the privies and clattered under the seats, so that the court ladies dared not go there, but rather lay in bed with colic all night.

As soon as I heard the guard-bell, I opened the door wide.

I took a step forward, but my terror was so great that I remained standing with hands on the doorjamb and only stared. Through a bare space in one of the chalked panes I looked all the way up to the tower at Brunkeberg, and that strengthened me so that I sprang right into the Green Corridor, in order that the ringing should not be still before I had got back. As long as it sounded, the creatures of darkness would have no power.

In about the middle of the corridor I suddenly saw something dark shoot forward along the curtain-bed and slink down in one of the armchairs to hide or wait. My left knee gave way of itself, and I heard the echo of my scream through the attics. It was from that time that my eyes were opened so that men called me crazy.

Against the light of the window, I saw that a man was sitting in the chair. He remained as motionless as I. All at once he seized me by the arm and whispered through his teeth: "*Figlio di un cane!* Spy? What are you? The queen dowager's warder?"

"God bless me!" I stammered, for now I understood that it was a fellow human being, and by the trembling and fumbling hands I comprehended that he was no less frightened than I myself. I even noticed that he was in his stocking feet, and had his shoes stuck in his bosom.

I summoned my wits and described my foolish enterprise, and finally I was believed.

"Such a damned, dilapidated old nest," growled the man, to excuse his own astonishment. "There are such drippings from the roof that my feet are wet through. As sure as I live, there shall be a new house here. My good man, if you can find the way, help me through this labyrinth of attics to the ballroom. Who I am is no matter."

"Very good," I answered, though I recognized the gracious Chamberlain Tessin.

He was silent, and took me by the coat tail, and so I turned and went before him. I imagine that at bottom we were both equally pleased at having happened upon each other. When we came down to the ballroom, he ordered me to stand outside the door, but I heard the night-goblins jumping in the dark behind us, and I kept my hand on the lock, so that I was instantly able to open the door again and steal in after him unnoticed. Through the window I saw the river, and within, around the walls, stood a multitude of leaning side-scenes, painted with trimmed trees and white temples.

Tessin stood in the middle of the hall and clapped his hands thrice.

A lady rose behind the side-scenes, and opened a little dark lantern. Who should it be but Hedwig Stenbock, the queen dowager's highborn lady-in-waiting! "Look, look, look," I thought, biting my lips, "has that foreign dandy there climbed so high already?"

"Hedwig, my dearest of all in the world!" said he. "Let us go directly to your room. No arguments, *ma chère!*"

Hedwig Stenbock was then nearly thirty-five, and she went so stiffly and rigidly to meet him that I should not have believed she had either heart or soul, had she not all at once become wholly transformed and showed the blood in her cheeks, when he embraced her.

Then I forgot myself, and burst out half aloud, "Aha, yes!"

Tessin turned around, but he was so hot that he only knitted his eyebrows and spilled out all his words in explaining my presence.

"We might have needed some assistant in any case," said he, "and Ekerot may be as good as any one else. If he knows how to keep silent, he shall not be without reward."

He then ordered me to take the dark lantern and go through the empty conference chambers — thanks for the favor! — and on, by a course which he described, to the corridor where the queen dowager's ladies dwelt — sweet sleep, my pretties! As soon as I had carefully ascertained that no flies in court dress were buzzing around there, I was to return and so report.

I had, however, something else to announce, when I did come back. I had heard the night-goblins clatter inside the door of the Art Room, and had seen them running with small sparks of fire in their hands down the stairs to the Archive Hall, where the affairs of the kingdom lay in the wall cabinets. Finally, in the aforesaid corridor I had come upon one of the queen dowager's warders, who sat asleep over his dark lantern with his back against the wall.

"He has been sent there since I left," said Hedwig Stenbock, and again she stood as stiff and straight as at first. "He does not suspect that the bird is already flown. But how to get back?"

She pushed Tessin's arms from her and became thoughtful.

"Long have I feared and suspected. To-night scandal has come upon us. Her Majesty is jealous."

Tessin clutched in the air with his hands as if toward invisible swords and daggers, and his eyes flashed and sparkled.

"Jealous! Of me? She is forty and grizzled, and she is somewhat hoarse and rough of voice like a man. Shall I never escape hearing that babble? With whom should I have laid my plans and sought gracious protection, if not with Sweden's Hedwig Eleonora?" He bowed. "Yet fear not, my dearest one, for no shame shall attach to your days, but this very night you shall follow me hence. A sleigh can always be had — and then — *addio!* In Italy I have friends."

"God in heaven knows," she answered, "that I will always follow you wherever you desire, and for men I care not at all, but will rather be by you than forsake you, yet we must first consider with a certain friend what is wisest. I am thinking of Erik Lindskiöld, who this evening sits and drinks with His Majesty. Ekerot shall go down across the courtyard to the king's little staircase and wait there

till Lindskiöld comes. Then—with many apolo-
gies—he shall entreat him to hurry up here—to
me."

Tessin made a dissuasive motion with his hand,
but I paid little heed to the cavalier, finding a
greater pleasure in obeying such a noble lady.

It had drawn far into the night when I came back
with Lindskiöld. He interrogated me fully about
everything. His peruke swayed, and he swore
kindly, guffawed, and was as noisy as if the whole
castle were his.

When he came into the ballroom, he bent one
knee, while he threw his hat into the air and cried:
"Are ye altogether staggering mad, my worthy
folk, who of love would partake and never forsake,
though all to hinder you watch and wake? Your
inclination gives more delectation than elevation.
Paff, poof! A poor master builder, who thrives by
adventure, though good luck bewilder, may not
without censure suppose himself worth, sir, a lady
of birth, sir. That day began mankind's vexation
when Adam awoke at Eve's creation and said, impelled by a new proclivity: 'Congratulations on
your nativity!'"

"Fiddlededilly, reeling—silly!" muttered Tessin to his lady. "That's what they call the Swedish
esprit. Lindskiöld is drunk."

"Only a trifle. He is in the most favorable
mood."

Lindskiöld did not hear them, but went on so
that the wide hall rang: "I have long suspected
this, and the titled class is likely to take it ill. But
travel to Italy! Ah, bah! Here the chamberlain has
a land that needs his genius. Let him look me in the
whites of the eyes, and say whether he can travel
from the designs for the royal castle that he has
spread out on my table, whether anything in the
world is as dear to him as his art."

Tessin became blood-red, and looked down in the
light of the lantern.

"I have determined to marry Chamberlain Tessin," said Hedwig Stenbock, "and that is how this
has happened."

Lindskiöld laid his hand on his heart: "Of
course, of course! says the royal widow. A wreath
will I twine, the best to be had, of flower and vine
from my Lindevad. I was born at no manor, with
chapel and banner, and my sire was a smith, but
they made him forthwith — aha, burgomaster of
Skenninge. Think if the chamberlain had sprung
from Skenninge. How would he have built then?
A new royal castle in the Skenninge style? A sight
for the city, or the devil may get me! What pride
would be his to be just who he is!"

Lindskiöld seized Tessin by the arm in a lofty,
threatening way, with a gesture as if he suddenly
threw off a spattered masquerade cloak.

"Let him calm his ardor for a moon or so. To

begin with, the chamberlain now kisses the hand of
his chosen one, goes three steps backwards, makes
a reverence, and then follows with me. Silent, when
I talk in the halls of the king! Ekerot goes back to
the dowager's warder, blows out his lantern, wakes
him with a sound and expressive box on the ear, and
throws his shoes after him when he runs, so that he
believes it is the night-goblins. Afterwards the gracious young lady returns unseen and tranquil to her
room. It is fully determined that she, in due time,
shall go along on a trip to Pomerania. Then the
chamberlain overtakes her, and marries her in all
secrecy. His Majesty I shall see to here at home.
The Gottorp misfortune— I mean the royal dowager—crafty woman— her the devil himself cannot
control, but the high-noble set, them I 've heard
assessed before the Royal Commission, and I shall
know them well enough to remind them what they
are worth. New times are at hand here. Ah, my children, my children, if you knew how the breast fills,
when one stands at the helm of state and steers according to distant beacons, whose name one dares
not once utter to His Royal Majesty himself. But
for the present, rely on my word. Here where we
now stand, the chamberlain shall build his immortality."

Confusedly Tessin drew his hand to his lips, and
when I had performed my errand with the warder, he handed me, with a supercilious grimace.

the two Palmstruch notes that hang there on the wall.

"There you have your promised reward, if you are silent," he said.

But then began my visions and misfortunes, and when I sat sick in my room at home, my ailments became a by-word in the square — gout, lung trouble, snuff disease, accidental bullets in the leg — and buzzing in the head. And when I pulled out the Palmstruch notes which the dishonorable villain stuck into my coat pocket, I found that they had lost all value many Lord's years before. Report that now to His Royal Majesty's person!

Ekerot would have related still more, but there was a violent banging on the door, and a messenger called Hakon to the king, who was worse.

Some days later, on the second day after Easter, people said that the king lay at the point of death, but Ekerot only nodded in his usual way as if it had all been known to him before. A crowd of men and maid-servants, who had been dismissed in the country because of the famine, stood homeless and despairing on the streets in the snow, and Ekerot went from group to group with his hands in his coat tails, and listened and nodded. By night he composed letters of prophecy, which he then presented to the court pastor superior, Wallin. "The unfortunate," he wrote, "are accustomed to see in the darkness, so that in the end they can discern that which is dim and hidden to those blinded by the light of prosperity."

One windy April day, when he had just stuck his last letter of prophecy under Wallin's entry door and come home to his room, he sat down at the window and prattled with the squirrel. Now and then he chewed at some dried pears, which he picked out of a drawer. Just as he was sitting so, he heard the tocsin and alarm, and when he stretched himself out through the window, he saw the castle roof enveloped in yellow smoke. Turning around to the room, he began to take down the coins from the wall, counting them accurately into his pocket. He trembled, and his teeth chattered, as, with the squirrel cage under one arm and the pewter pot under the other, he toddled down the stairs to the street.

He was jostled against the house wall, and stood staring up at the castle, where roaring streaks of fire already spurted forth under the dark rafters. Soon all three of the wings flamed like huge bonfires, and the thunderous noise of the conflagration drowned the tocsin and the trumpet flourishes.

"Look, look!" he said. "The night-goblins must out into the light of day. Look how they jump in rows along the roof-ridges with fire in their hands! Now they climb up on the tower roof and hop over the new Tessin addition, which disturbed their com-

fort. They want to burn themselves in it. This is
only the beginning. It will all burn—all."

Soldiers and warders thronged on the castle
bridge amid barrels of water and itinerant chairs,
cabinets, and paintings. Under the two lions that
held the coat-of-arms above the door of the gate
stepped forth Hedwig Eleonora, the mother of the
Charleses. Two courtiers supported and almost carried her, for she shrunk together, and constantly
wanted to stand still and look back. The wind raised
the mantilla over her silver-gray hair, and the next
moment drew it as a veil over her eyes red with
weeping, her proud aquiline nose, and thickly
painted cheeks.

"The pyre is burning under your son's body,"
shouted Ekerot, pointing. "And the throne on
which your grandson has ascended is burning, and
before you close your eyes his whole realm shall be
burned in ashes. Don't you remember that he was
born with blood on his hands?"

He made his way anxiously along the wall and
around the corner to Trångsund. Sparks rose to
heaven like stars, and beyond the churchyard wall
one saw the great castle tower called the Three
Crowns, which rose four full stories above the highest roof. With every story that the fire conquered,
the smoke burst out through the loopholes as from
cannon. That's the night-goblins, thought he, who
fire victory salutes, while the citadel of the Vasa

kings is burning. Again and again, the smoke enveloped the ancient arms of the realm on the spire
of the tower—and again, dizzyingly high, gleamed
forth the golden crowns, like three storm birds
resting on their wings. The ringers of St. Nicholas Church climbed up the steps to swing even the
great bell and the preliminary bell, but when they
heard the rumble, as the tower floors and vaulting
plunged down together, pulling the spire and arms
with them in the fall, they turned and fled. Smitten
with terror, children and women began to sob and
run, and it was told that people at the South Gate
saw an insane man steal out with a squirrel cage and
a pewter pot, singing in an undertone an old song
of penance.

A Sermon

IN Great Church the audience arose from their
pews and looked toward the armory, before
which Charles XII dismounted from his carriage.

He was a handsome, but slender and undeveloped boy. His hat, edged with plumes, sat comi-
cally in its smallness upon the great curly peruke,
and when the king stuck it under his arm, his gestures were nervous and embarrassed. He walked
trippingly, a trifle bent in the knees, as was the
fashion, and his eyes were lowered. His costume of
mourning was precious with ermine on the facings
and blonde lace around the gloves, and on his high-
heeled shoes of cordovan leather he had buckles
and ribbon rosettes.

Bewildered by the inquisitive glances, he took his
place in the royal pew, under the gilded crown up-
borne by genii. He sat stiffly, facing the altar, but
was unable to collect his thoughts around the sacred
ceremonies. When, at last, the minister stepped into
the pulpit and with an epigram and a vigorous blow
on the back of the book aroused a subdued murmur, the king reddened and felt himself caught in
the very act. Directly, however, his thoughts became the same rebels as they were just before, and
went their own ways. To cover his shyness, he began to pluck off the black points on the ermine.

" Look at un," said a woman in one of the bottom pews. "He still needs to wear out his father's rod. Has the devil bit un i' th' fingers?"

"That's for her to say, the dirty wench, who has traipsed into a higher pew than belongs to her!" answered a grand lady, and pushed her headlong out into the aisle.

The old man with a cane, who stood down by the door and had the office of going around and cuffing on the neck those of the congregation who went to sleep, tapped on the floor and menaced with his hand, but the scuffle was heard as far up as the pews of the nobility, so that the fine gentlemen turned their heads, and the preacher straightway interpolated the following words:

"Concord, I said, Christian concord! Whither does she repair with her mild sweet-gruel? To the populace, perchance? Hold her fast! In God's house or around His Royal Majesty's own person, perchance? Well for him who finds her! Therefore I say unto you, ye princes of the earth, seek diligently for concord and love, and lift not into strife the sword which God has placed in your hand, but lift it only for the defence of your subjects."

At this allusion the young king again blushed red and laughed shamefacedly. Even Hedwig Eleonora, the queen dowager, in the royal pew just opposite to him, nodded simperingly, but the young princesses beside her laughed most of all. Ulrica Eleanora sat tolerably stiff, but Hedwig Sophia leaned forward with her slim long neck. In happy consciousness that she wore gloves, so that her malformed thumbs were not visible, she held the prayer-book in front of her mouth.

The king now became bolder and looked around. In what a strange temple of the Lord he found himself on this day! The whole church was over-crowded with the furniture and objects of art which had been saved from the fire at the castle. Only the middle aisle was free. In the corner up by the altar stood, rolled up, Ehrenstrahl's representations of the Crucifixion and the Last Judgment, and behind the tomb of the Skyttes he recognized the plume-tufts and the green curtains from the bed on which his father, sitting crosswise and supported on pillows, had given up the ghost. The recollection of this, however, moved him not, since he had scarcely felt for his father anything but fear. He had seen in him rather the deputy appointed by God than the dear blood-relation, and in his thoughts as in his speech he preferred to call him plainly and simply, the *old* king. Like two questing bees, his eyes wandered over the numerous familiar objects, and tarried long at last on a coat-of-arms on the nearest pillar.

There, since several years, rested beneath the floor his teacher, Nordenhjelm, the good-hearted old Norcopensis whom he had loved with childish enthusiasm. He recalled hours of study early in

winter mornings, when he sat and learned the four
branches of ciphering, and poked at the wick with
the candle-snuffers, or when Nordenhjelm told stories of the heroes of Greece and Rome. Since the
old king's death he had walked in a dream. He
understood that he must not show gayety, that lamentation was the only thing he had license to claim,
but at the same time he saw that there were many
who were quite ready in private to court his favor
by amusing him though attracting as little attention
as possible, now with one prank, now with another.
Even His Excellency Piper could at the same time
dry his tears and beg the king not to forsake his
youthful sports but play a game of shuttlecock.
The gloomy, serious faces about him afflicted him
sometimes, so that the tears sprang into his own
eyes, but from the most secret depth of his boyish
soul rose the dizzying, triumphal intoxication of victory. The morose and stiff-necked old men whom
he had formerly feared and shunned, he had suddenly found humble and submissive. Sometimes at
table, while they were sitting with their most anxious expression, he had audaciously filliped fruit
seeds into their faces so as to see them laugh all at
once, and then go away again and range themselves
in a lugubrious ring around the queen dowager.
The burning of the castle, with its adventures and
dangers, had been for him a day of curiosity and
excitement. It had even been almost the jolliest

day he had yet had in his life, though he himself did not dare to think so. The affright of the others and his grandmother's faintings had only made that wild spectacle the more strange and extraordinary. Now all the old life was done. The old king was dead, and his stronghold in ashes. All the new, all, all that Sweden longed for, should now mount on high with him like a flame of fire — and there he sat, lonesome and fourteen years old.

It seemed to him next that Nordenhjelm stood at the pulpit behind the speaker and dictated the words. Only for an instant had the minister shaken the clown's staff with bells so as to make himself intimate with his listeners. Then he addressed himself to the king in sight of all the congregation, earnestly, strictly, yes, even commandingly. He required him, in the name of God, not to let himself be led 'to vanity and pride by sycophants and hangers-on, but to dedicate his actions unselfishly to the unselfish people of Sweden, so that when, in the fullness of years, he closed his weary eyes, he might be followed by the blessings of thousands, and might enter into God's glory.

The voice of truth sang and thundered beneath the arches of the church, and a lump rose in the young king's throat. He tried afresh to link his thoughts to other, indifferent things, but every word struck his upright childish heart, and he sat with bowed head.

It was a relaxation for him when the carriage took him again to Karlberg. There he bolted himself into his apartments, and not even the resolute summons of the dowager could induce him to go down to table.

In the room outside his sleeping-chamber lay the books which were used in his rarer and rarer lesson-hours. Already he liked to philosophize over the riddles of creation, and he was always fascinated by the sciences, but he began to despise books like a merry troubadour intoxicated with life. The uppermost work dealt with geography, and, after turning the page back and forth, he threw it to one side. Then, vehemently and at random, he drew out instead the bottom book. With it he remained sitting.

It was broken at the corners and severely worn, and the contents was only a few manuscript pages with the evening prayers that he had learned to recite as a child. Many sentences and words had already been frozen out of his memory, but as he now saw the familiar lines before him, he needed only to read them through two or three times to know them by heart.

In the evening he ate only a cup of beer-soup, and the warders then began to undress him. He bore his violent emotions with such propriety that they only thought he was tired, and when they lifted the peruke from his short-clipped and dark-brown, somewhat wavy hair, and he climbed up in his shirt into the great bed, he looked like a little girl.

The dog Pompey crept up by his feet, and below the foot of the bed a lighted candle was set in a basin of silver filled with water. The king was afraid of the dark, and it had therefore become the custom that the door to the outer room should be left open, and that a page or playmate should spend the night there. This evening, however, the king ordered with decision that the door hereafter should be closed. Only when they heard that did the warders begin to wonder and become uneasy, noticing that he was disturbed in spirit.

"Ah bah!" grumbled old Hakon, the faithful servant from his father's days, who obstinately continued to treat the king as a child. "To what shall that serve?"

"It shall be as I have said," answered the king. "And from to-morrow on the night-light is not necessary either."

The warders bowed as they went backwards from the sleeping apartment, but when Hakon had closed the door, he sat down on the threshold outside. One of the warders, who was named Hultman, also remained there standing. They heard how the king turned and threw himself on the mattress, and when Hakon finally stretched himself up to the keyhole, he saw indistinctly in the glimmer of the night-light that his young lord was sitting upright in bed.

Gusts of the night wind roared and rattled out on the castle terrace and in the lindens of Karlberg Park, but within doors it was already hushed and still. Yet Hakon thought, to his wonderment, that he could distinguish a muffled, almost whispering human voice, and even detached words. He became attentive and listened.

He heard then that the king recited with half-raised voice the prayers he had taught himself to pray in his earliest childhood.

"Teach me to control myself and not to be misled by flattering talk to presumption and self-will, and thereby to sin against the regard which I owe to God and men."

Old Hakon brought his knees together and clasped his hands for prayer, and, through the stillness and the soft rustle of the blast, he heard continually the words of the king.

"Though the son of a king and hereditary heir to a mighty kingdom, I yet would always humbly consider that these things are a special grace and blessing of God, on which account I must strive after Christian virtues and knowledge, so that I may become skilful and worthy in so great a calling. Almighty Lord, Thou who dost raise up kings and put them down, teach me ever to obey Thy commands, so that I may never to my own ruin and the oppression of others misuse the power that Thou lendest me. For Thy holy name's sake. Amen."

The Successor to the Throne

HOW dull it was! How long were the days at
the little court, where the black-clad councillors of state yawned in armchairs and stared in
front of them, as if they pondered how it was that
they were similarly shod on both feet, and had not
a jack-boot on one and a silken slipper on the other.
And so they yawned again—and out on the stairway the warders yawned, and down in the kitchen
the cooks tasted the viands with their fingers in
the grease, and said to one another: "Is that sour
enough, so that the great gentlemen will at once
make wry faces?"

The coachmen harnessed horses with black
plumes and ribbons in front of black carriages.
Black broadcloth was being cut out or sewed on
all the tables. In the church on Grayfriars' Island,
where the old king had been interred, the black
canopies and tapestries still hung, and the king's
funeral knell was heard far out into the country.
When, finally, the coronation train moved forth
over the snowy streets, all went in mourning, and
only the young king wore his purple. The echo of
the last festal salutes had hardly rolled over Tysk-
bagareberg, before the same intolerable dulness
again settled over the throne in the dark Yuletide
days.

Then, one sullen gray noon, the dowager's master cook stamped on the floor. In his hands he held a pot with boiled tomatoes.

"*Ach, du Lieber!* There's something to do here to-day. His Grace, the Duke of Holstein, who is to be expected here shortly, has sent us a costly gift. Her Majesty and Mistress Greta Wrangel have already tasted the fruit, and Tessin, who is a travelled man, is coming down into the kitchen himself to advise us in the preparation. Don't stand there gaping, boys. Dishcloths to the saucepans! Rub and polish!"

The remote little court in the outermost corner of the world had that day gotten something to think of. At table the talk was of nothing else than the tomatoes, and each and all had something to say about their smell and flavor. Meanwhile there was drinking, and the old councillors who had been invited, growing mellow, forgot their intrigues and said drolly agreeable things to one another.

After the meal the king took Councillor Lars Wallenstedt by the coat-button, and led him along to the window recess, like a panting grumble-bear with a ring through its nose.

"Tell me," inquired the king earnestly, "how should a prince sacrifice himself for his people? That sermon of last spring never leaves my mind."

Wallenstedt had the habit when he talked of puffing out his lips as if he were saying " Pooh! "

Accustomed to the king's precocious and pene-trating questions, he answered: "A prince should sacrifice all small misgivings, gather all power to himself, become his people's archetype and will. That was truly a pious discourse we heard that time in church, but does not the Most Reverend Bishop Spegel say that subjects should be as thralls to their lord? The councillors and nobles now quarrel but for their share of the power since the time of Your Majesty's revered father. And Oxenstjerna and Gyllenstjerna and—ah, well—they have their ears to the ground. But it was for that reason I always ventured to support Your Majesty's will that even at your youthful years you should shift the heavy weight of government from the shoulders of Her Majesty the queen dowager."

When Cronhjelm, the king's tutor, who stood in the recess, heard the words about the weight of government, he wrote with his finger on the moisture of the window-pane: "The old woman feels that burden as deliciously light as her head-dress."

"Yes, yes, my dear Wallenstedt," the king meanwhile answered. "I, too, have always felt within me that my will urged me in that direction. On Atland's throne a man must sit. It is a wondrous troublesome thing to will. How is that? To-day I feel that I will ride to Kungsör and hunt bears. But why? I might equally well will something else. Will is to me a fetter, a chain drawn tight around my breast, from which I cannot twist myself free. It is the master, and I am the servant."

Wax candles were already lighted when he stepped into his outer apartment. On the table stood the sealed iron box in which the old king had deposited his final secret and fatherly instructions. Many days had elapsed since the retiring guardians of the realm had let it leave their hands, but he had not yet been able to bring himself to open the lid. One night, to be sure, he had violently torn off the seal, but he had then shrunk back. This evening he felt that the will was come.

But when he set the key in the rattling iron, his old fear of the dark fell upon him. He saw before him the old king's coffin of tin, on which had just fallen the spadefuls of earth, and it came over him that now he was to stand eye to eye with the dead. He called in Hakon, and bade him lay wood on the fire. Meanwhile he turned the key, threw back the lid, and with chilly trembling unfolded the closely written paper.

"Take the power into your own hand," stood there, "and beware of the great lords who are about you, of whom many have French stomachs. Those who chatter most eagerly hanker only after their own interests, and the best at times keep their own counsel."

When he had read to the end the anxious and mistrustful warnings of the departed, he did not notice that Hakon had left the apartment.

Now he was lord over all the land of Sweden.

The high dignitaries had thronged outside his door to declare him of age. Did they even know themselves whether their words were dictated by the hope of favor or by pure intentions? Did they not love him more than they did their own sons or brothers? But nevertheless he could not talk familiarly with these old men, who weighed and adjusted their speech. And could he talk with those of his own age, a crowd of shyly courteous playmates, who knew naught of the affairs of the day? Alone he went about as never before, and alone he had to carry the old king's sceptre. Nothing could be greater than Sweden, and of all Sweden's kings he willed to be the foremost and best. Had he not received a token of it from the hands of Almighty God, in that he was exalted to be a ruler so young, with the many years of a long life before him? The old, which had brought down the wrath of God, was now passed away. Song rose on high, there was jubilation of drums and trumpets.

He arose, and his hand fell with a light blow on the edge of the table.

Piper was right. Piper had said that Sweden was a great realm with a little court in a small town at the world's end. There was to be no more of that. He had himself set the crown upon his head, and had ridden to church with it. Had he not already received it from God at the hour of his birth, on the June morning when the glittering star of the

Lion's Heart ascended above the rim of the east?
The floor-cloth on the streets, in which his horses'
hoofs had beaten holes, he had given to the peasantry for clothing, but the nobles had had to go on
foot, and the very councillors of state had borne
his canopy and waited on him like warders. Why
should he dissimulate, why should he confer honor
on men whom he did not honor in his soul? Had
he ever given a royal charter? The Estates, but not
he, had had to take oath. His kingly vow he had
sworn in silence before God, as he stood at the altar.
Now, now was he lord over all the land of Sweden!

He went to the hanging mirror, eyed compla-
cently the small pock-marks in his girlish skin, and
compressed with his fingers the stern furrow in his
brow.

Then he pointed into space, sat himself astride
on a chair, and galloped around the room.

"Forward, boys, forward for your king! Jump,
Brilliant, jump, jump!"

He imagined he was riding over a meadow
against the enemy and that hundreds of bullets
struck him on the breast, but fell flattened in the
grass. Round about on the heights stood spectators, and at a distance the very king of France came
on a white horse and waved his hat.

In the hall below, the old dignitaries still stood
in conversation. When they heard the racket, they
were still a moment and listened, but Cronhjelm

wrote in the moisture and grumbled half aloud: "That is only His Majesty who is occupied with the management of the realm. He is devising marks of favor for us in return for declaring him of age."

Wallenstedt blew out his lips and gave him a furious glance.

When the king had galloped all around his room, a sudden recollection struck him, and he went to the door.

"Klinckowström!" he cried, "Klinckowström, can you tell me why I have just now taken such a fancy for riding to Kungsör and hunting bears?"

Klinckowström, a merry page with red cheeks and a light tongue, answered: "Because it's pitch dark and infernal weather, and because no bear is started, so that hunting is impossible. Shall I give orders for horses and torch-riders?"

"Have you any better suggestion?"

"All other suggestions are better, but—"

"No, you are right. We must ride to Kungsör just because it seems impossible, and because we will it."

When, a little later, the king rode down Queen Street, he passed close to a suburban place which extended below St. Clare's churchyard to a yellow-painted house. There an old widow known as Mother Malin kept an inn. The grounds were fenced in with boards, on which the builders at work on the castle, when in summer they emptied their glasses at Mother Malin's, had painted arches of triumph and obelisks and dancing Italians. In one corner lay a pleasure-house having a fireplace and chimney. One window was on Queen Street, the other faced inward on plum trees and flower-beds, now covered with snow. For several weeks Mother Malin had daily carried food to the plea-sure-house, but no one of her old customers knew anything with certainty as to the guest she lodged within. At a sale of a noble family, whom narrowed circumstances had bowed to the earth, she had pur-chased for her guest a piano, and in the evenings behind the closed shutters were heard strange mel-odies, accompanied by a weak and delicate voice.

Just as the king's torch-bearers approached, Mother Malin was standing at a crevice of the planks, looking out upon the dark street.

"It's he himself," she burst out, and thumped on the door of the pleasure-house. "It's the king that's coming. Put out the light and peep through the heart in the shutter!"

At that moment the king dashed by in wild career.

"So handsome he is o' the cheeks, the gracious young lord!" she said, and went down again to her inn. "And pure and holy is his life, too. But why should he tempt God and set the crown on his head with his own hands? That's why he slipped on the way, and the box of sacred ointment thudded on the floor of the church."

The night went by, and so did month after month. In the garden the chestnut trees became green again, as well as the plum trees behind the barberry and currant bushes. The Maypole was raised, and the court drove by to Karlberg.

Beside the king sat the Duke of Holstein, who had come to marry his sister, Princess Hedwig Sophia, and make an end of the intolerable dulness. As they drove past the pleasure-house, he happened by accident to throw a glance through the wide open window.

In the evening came a man with his cape-collar up, who knocked stealthily at the inn, but Mother Malin regarded him mistrustfully. "Be off to the devil with your cape-collar!" said she.

He laughed loudly and talked broken Swedish.

"I lie here on one of the German galleons, and would but have a mug of berry juice in your garden. *Schnell!*"

He thrust a couple of coins into her hand and pushed her aside. She was near to giving him a blow, but, as it was, she counted her money and thought things over. She put the mug of syrup on the earthen bench in the garden, but she herself sat behind the half-closed shutters to keep the new customer under her eyes.

He sipped a little at the juice, wrote with his heel on the sand, and looked about him. When he had sat awhile and thought himself unobserved, he arose and turned down his collar. He was a young, handsome gentleman, of a daring and merry appearance, and he walked slowly along the path.

"Impudent villain!" muttered Mother Malin. "I vow he's going to knock at the door of the pleasure-house."

When the door remained shut, he shrank several paces aside to the open window, and stuck his hat under his arm in knightly fashion. Then he sat on the window-sill and spoke softly and eagerly.

With that Mother Malin's patience gave way, and she went out. She walked on the sand path, twisting a thread of yarn between her fingers and holding her head slyly bent forward. Meanwhile she meditated on the abuse which she should utter. But when she had gone a little way, the young gentleman flew from out the barberry hedge, and roared with the most disrespectful wrath, "Ha, you crone, march! I am the Duke of Holstein. But not a word of this!"

Mother Malin was so astonished that she could only turn completely around and smite herself on the knee. Again, when she went back into the house, she smote her knee, and could not comprehend that it was she, precisely, in her little abode, who had come to experience anything so great and extraordinary.

It then happened often in the bright, summer evenings, when the chestnuts stood without showing a breath of wind, that the duke came to the place. The door of the pleasure-house was never opened, no matter how insinuatingly he rapped, but he sat on the window-sill; and Mother Malin, who had meanwhile got a shining ducat in her kirtle-pocket, served there both syrup and wine, and once even a raisin-cake, on which she had written with white of egg: "No prince on earth has nobler worth."

On this particular evening the duke tarried longer than at other times, and within the pleasure-house the piano sounded.

As he finally rose to go, he said: "Power, power? Why to be sure, all cry out for it. Why should you alone be silent? Consider that your father has played away his last sovereign. Adieu, adieu! If you fail with the lion, you bid fair next to hold the door open for the wolf."

The duke stood before the window. It was hushed and still, for down at the inn all had by now gone to bed.

"You do not answer," he continued. "Is it shyness? Then answer with a sign. One stroke on the piano means Yes, but if you trill with your little finger-tips it means No, irrevocably No."

He went lingeringly down the path. The night heavens were bright, the ground without shadow, and he felt about in a gooseberry bush without being able to find any fruit. Then a chord sounded softly from the piano. He pressed his hat down on his head, drew his cloak about him, and hastened from the garden with cheerful steps.

After that night, Mother Malin went about in vain waiting to open the gate at dusk for the great lord. In ill humor, she began at last to draw from her pocket and count over the ducats, and she cursed herself because she had not at the right time known how to entice to her yet more.

Meanwhile, one evening, a barber's widow had been buried in the churchyard of St. Clare, and after the twelve torch-bearers had gone, two journeymen remained to keep watch. They sat on planks by the grave and spoke ill of the house of mourning.

"They ought to smart for it. The old hag lay covered in a cambric bonnet with crape ribbons, like a noble, and both spice-cakes and preserves stood on the table, but here to us they have n't even sent a stoop of small beer."

"I see across the wall that light is shining through the heart in Mother Malin's shutters. Should n't we go there and knock?"

They went out on the street to the yellow wooden house and thumped on the tin.

Mother Malin set one of the shutters ajar.

"You come just in the nick of time, lads," said she, when she recognized them. "No one has treats to offer in these days, but you can earn a pretty penny."

She pushed open the shutter still further and lowered her voice.

"Here you have each of you a whole Charles-piece. Yes, look at it, you noisy lads; it'll stand taking hold of. Within here stands a royal page, who is soon coming down to you. At dawn, as usual, some night-cuckoos from the court are to ride by here. Pretend then to trip up and thrash the young gentleman, and afterwards take to your heels. That's all."

"That seems right enough," said the journeymen, and thumbed the coins. "The hardest thing will be not to lay on in the excitement so that it cuts."

They went back to the churchyard gate and waited, and they heard Mother Malin whispering with the page up in the room.

The time grew long. A star flamed over the dead-house in the summer heat, the fire-watch called on Brunkeberg, and the dawn drew near.

There was a creaking and squeaking on Mother Malin's steps, and the page, walking with knees somewhat turned in and arranging the buttons of his coat, came down to the journeymen.

In the alley off Queen Street was heard roistering and trampling of horses. First rode Klinckow-ström, who was so drunk that he had to hold himself on by his horse's mane. Behind him could be seen the king, the Duke of Holstein, and some ten

other riders. All had blades in their hands, and all
but the king were in only their shirts. He was mad
with drink, and with his sword knocked in window-panes, lifted off signboards, and cut at wooden
doors. There was no one now in the whole world
whom he need obey. He could now do anything
whatever that occurred to him, and no one would
have a single word of reproach. Let them but dare!
At supper he had struck the dishes from the pages'
hands and thrown fragments of cake on his comrades' clothes, so that they had white marks as from
snowballs. The intolerable old was now done with.
The old men might yawn and clear their throats
by their snuff-jars as they pleased. They had no
longer anything to attend to but to be fools. He
dedicated his old kingdom of bears to joy and the
spirit of youth. The whole of Europe should be
amazed. Now he was lord over all the land of
Sweden!

Meanwhile the unknown page had laid himself
on the ground in the churchyard gate, and the journeymen pinched and beat to their heart's content,
and clutched at his throat.

"Who's there?" shouted the king, and set upon
the journeymen, who straightway fled between
grave-mounds and crosses. He was close at their
heels, and stabbed one of them several times in the
left arm, so that the blood dripped. At last, in defence, they lifted one of the planks by the half-

filled grave of the barber's widow. Then the king
laughed and rode back to the wicket gate.

"One of ours?" he inquired of the unknown,
who had picked himself up again. "What, are you
so tipsy that you don't even know our password:
Snuff on all perukes? No matter. Sit up behind our
friend Klinckan, and hold him fast on his Wallach.
Forward!"

Singing and hallooing, the shirt-clad band dashed
on along street and hillside, waving and making
long noses at the sleep-dazed folk who came to the
gates. When the panes tinkled about Chief Marshal Stenbock, that most worthy old man went
himself to the window in his dressing-gown and,
bowing, began to lament that, at last, it was necessary for him to flee the realm. But the king tore
his wig from him, and cut it in two halves with his
sword.

"This is life!" shouted the Duke of Holstein.
"Hats in the air! If we could only take along all
the royal lady wooers who sit and peep in their
bed-chambers. Wigs in the air! Rise in your stirrups and piddle over your horses' heads! Soho,
boys! Devil take you. *Vivat Carolus*, king of Sweden and of scandals!"

Shirts were fluttering out; hats, wigs, and gloves
lay on the street; hoofs struck sparks, and the
horses rushed forward as in a fire.

When the wild riders had come back to the

castle, they sprang from their saddles, and let the horses run as best they could. Upon the stairs they broke the lampshades and fired pistol shots at a marble Venus.

"*Vorwärts!*" shouted the king, as he stormed with all his following into the chapel, and slashed amain at the pews. "They shall get splinters in their breeches here o' Sunday."

The duke pounded on the floor demanding silence, and Klinckowström, who had set to throwing dice in the circle of the altar, held his hand over his mouth so as to keep still.

"Dearly beloved listeners!" began the duke. "Nothing could make this earnest occasion more solemn than if my exalted and charming brother-in-law in this morning hour would give us, his faithful servants, a hint as to the choice of his heart. Let us speak of ladies that woo! Let us think of the baggage from Bavaria who scampered all the way hither with her sweet mother, though there was hardly any lodging for her after the castle was burned. Oohoo! says the owl. Only eight little tulip-red summers older than Your Majesty. Or of the Princess of Wurtemburg, who already showed her amorousness by paying suit to Your Majesty's father of most blessed memory, and who is sickly in the chest. Don't cough during the ceremony! Or of the Princess of Mechlenburg-Grabow, who with her mother is also supposed to be climbing into her travelling-coach. Or of the Prussian princess, who is only two never-so-little sugar-grain years older; or the Danish princess, the tooty-tooty little pink-and-gold bird, who is only five small rose-leaf years older. All of them are bent upon wooing, and sprucing themselves up, and beautifying their pictures, because their love afflicts them full sore."

The king became abashed and replied, "Have I not always said that surely no man need think of being married before he is forty?"

As the duke noted his embarrassment, he winked at the page from the inn and pounded anew on the floor.

"Very good. His Majesty of Sweden will not parcel out his glory and the love of his subjects in anything else than manly courage and joy. Snuff on all wigs! Were I the monarch of the Swedes, I should therefore frighten the old fellows out of their wits by summoning the prettiest ladies and minxes to my festivities. *Potztausend!* They should sit before us on the saddle and stay with us till the cock crowed the third time. But, as if I would talk any longer! Set your knees to the pew-ends! Hey! Beat and break, snap and crack! Stamp on the floor!—*Herr Gott*, bring water! The king is sick. Water or wine—just wine—wine!"

The king had grown pale, and put his hand to his forehead. It was nothing to him that the others were flaming red and reeled about. At bottom, perhaps, he loved none of them deeply. What did it matter if they called one another drunken? But never should any such thing be said of him, the chosen of God.

"That's enough now, boys!" he said, trying to thrust his sword into the scabbard, whereupon he noticed that he had lost it. Instead, therefore, he very calmly stuck the weapon through the skirt of his coat, and walked with resolute step toward the door.

The duke seized the unknown page by the arm, whispered, and made signs with his hands. The page hurried immediately after the king, opened the door for him, and followed him upstairs.

"Never shall I taste wine again!" thought the king. "I could not bear if people said that I stuttered in my speech and held pages to my breast. Why should I after that be respected more than they? And wine does not taste so much better than small beer. That depends on habit. A really wise man drinks water."

They went together along the stairs and corridors, and came, at length, to his sleeping apartment. Here Wallenstedt and a couple of other high nobles were already waiting. Wallenstedt puffed up his lips.

"Six o'clock in the morning," he began, "is the usual time for us to consider the affairs of government."

"If it concerns a criminal matter, yes," answered

the king; "otherwise I will receive no counsel, but will regulate and decide as seems to me right."

He did not pick up the poker, as did his father. He was as wakefully solicitous about his dignity as a nobly-born young lady about court propriety. Smiling and bowing, he went straight up to the gentlemen, so that they had to leave the room backwards.

"That is our return for setting a boy on the throne," they dinned maliciously into the ears of Wallenstedt.

The page, however, had already locked the door behind them with a subdued bang. That pleased the king. He stood leaning against the end of the high bed beside the casket in which his father had gathered together jewels and valuables of all sorts, and which had now been fetched up from the treasure-vault known as the Elephant.

"What is your name?" he asked the page. "Why don't you answer?"

The page breathed hard, fumbling and plucking at his clothes.

"Well, but answer me, boy! You know your own name, I suppose. You stand almost with your back to me so that I cannot see you."

The page now stepped forward into the middle of the room, lifted the peruke from his head, tossed it on the night-table, and answered: "My name is Rhoda— Rhoda d'Elleville."

The king saw that it was a very young girl with dark-pencilled eyebrows. Her yellow hair was crisply curled with a curling-iron, and a lightly shadowed line trembled around her mouth.

She sprang forward, threw her arms about his neck, and impetuously kissed him on the left cheek.

For the first time the youth of sixteen lost his self-command. Flames rose before his eyes, his cheek became grayish-white, and his hands hung impotent. He only saw that the page's coat was unbuttoned over the breast, so that lace was hanging from it. She continued to hold him fast in her arms, and pressed a long kiss upon his mouth.

He neither responded to it nor made resistance. He only raised his hands little by little and lifted her arms back over his head like a ring. Then, stammering, and bowing deeply and ceremoniously, he moved aside.

"Pardon, mademoiselle!" He scraped with his foot, clicked his heels, and, bowing again with each step, moved still further away. "Pardon, mademoiselle, pardon!"

How thoroughly had she not studied beforehand every word she meant to say! But now she remembered nothing. She spoke at random and without herself any longer knowing what she said.

"Mercy, sire! The good God may be excused if He punishes such presumption as mine."

She bent her knee to the carpet.

" I have seen you on horseback, sire; I have seen
you from my window. In imagination I have seen
you, before I made the long journey up here, have
seen my hero, my Alexander."

At once he went forward to her, took her under
the elbows, and conducted her in precocious cavalier fashion to a chair.

" Not so, not so. Sit, sit!"

She kept hold of his hand, and wrinkled her
brow a little, as she looked him brightly in the eyes
—and then she burst into a ringing laugh of relief.

"Ah, well, you are human after all, sire. Not a
trace of the preacher. You are the first Swede I have
met who understands that the eyes of virtue look
inward and do not evilly squint at others. Your
favorites drink and throw dice and pay attentions
to women without your saying anything about
it. You barely notice it. Let us speak of virtue,
sire."

Perfume, the scent of her hair, of a woman, tortured him so violently that he was near to vomiting.
The contact, the feel of her warm hand, nauseated
him like touching a rat or a corpse. He believed
himself offended and defiled both as the king, specially chosen of God, and as a man in that a stranger
had touched his clothes and face and hands. Another, and that a woman, had taken hold of him
as of a prey, a conquered captive. The person who
had touched him straightway became an enemy,

with whom he wished to fight, whom he wished to strike down in punishment of lese-majesty.

"When I was yet but a child," she continued, "my confessor fell in love with me. He wrung his hands and strove with himself and babbled prayers, and I played with the madman and made a fool of him. Sire, how different you are from him! You never strive with yourself. You are wholly and completely indifferent, sire. That is all. Virtue with you is so innate that"—she laughed playfully—"I do not know if I can even call it virtue."

He tried to twist his hand free, and exerted his strength more and more. How had not the duke, the pages, and the warders dinned in his ears about lady wooers and pretty mamselles in the last weeks! Was this, too, a game behind his back? Should he, then, have no peace?

"Pardon, mademoiselle!"

"I know, sire, that for whole hours you can sit and turn over Tessin's etchings, and that you look especially at pictures with tall young ladies. That is perhaps only the esteem for art which you have inherited from your noble lady grandmother; but will it always remain so? I am no dead representation, sire."

Though bowing constantly, he now tore himself free with such vehemence that at the same time he jerked Rhoda d'Elleville up from the chair.

"No, you are a live page, mademoiselle, and the

page I order to go down into the chapel and send the comrades to the east anteroom."

She saw at once that the game was hopelessly lost, and the shadowed expression around her mouth became deeper and more weary.

"The page must obey," answered she.,

When the king was left alone, he became again tranquil as before. Only at times there passed over his thoughts a flash of indignation. The unexpected adventure had chased the wine fumes from his head, and he wished not to go to rest like a weakling after the pranks of the night, but to continue them hour after hour.

He threw off his coat. In his shirt-sleeves, with sword in hand, he went out to his comrades in the east anteroom.

This room was sprinkled with dried stains of blood. The boards of the floor had been drenched and embrowned with pools of blood, and by the portraits on the wall, whose eyes were poked out, hung lumps of hair and of long-congealed blood.

In the room outside a lowing was heard. A calf was led in and brought forward to the middle of the floor.

The king bit his under lip so that it grew white, and with a single whistling blow struck off the calf's head. With blood oozing under his nails, he then threw the head through the broken window down on the passers-by.

Outside the door, meanwhile, the duke whispered hurriedly with Rhoda d'Elleville.

"So no one is likely to get my exalted brother-in-law out of his stiff-neckedness. Old Hjärne of the funny face talks of cooking a love potion, but that's likely to be of little avail. Had he not inherited his father's coldness, he would with his bravado have become a Swedish Borgia. If he can't soon get to be a demi-god, he'll become a devil. When such a bird does n't find flapping-room for its wings, it breaks apart the walls of its own nest. Hist! Some one's coming. Don't forget! This evening at nine at Mother Malin's. Have on hand some figs and raisins!"

Behind them on the stairs came faithful old Hakon, leading two goats. He stood still, threw his hands aloft, and sighed anxiously:

"What have they made of my young lord? Never has such a thing been seen in the home of Sweden's kings. Almighty God, have pity and give us yet greater misfortune than before, because the quiet that has now come upon us can be borne neither by the Swedes nor by such a prince!"

Midsummer Sport

TWO little girls stood in a pasture with a sieve, and near by, on a mossy stone, lazy and half-asleep, sat their brother, Axel Frederick, who to-day completed his twentieth year. His intended, the frightened little Ulrica, who had come to the place on a visit, bent down juniper twigs over the sieve and cut at them with her sickle. The little girls spread their hands to hold the twigs and help all they could, and melting snow dripped from the birches and alders.

"Oh, oh, even grandfather has come out in this heavenly weather," said Ulrica, pointing down at the great house.

The little girls then began to shout and hop. They took the sieve between them and went off to the great house, while they swung the sieve in time and warbled:

> *The birds of springtime, they sing so well.*
> *Come little goat-girls, come!*
> *To-night we 'll have music and dance in the dell.*

On the other side of the fence, where the neighbor's land began, Elias, the farm-servant, brought down the last load of wood from the forest. The water dripped from his wooden shoes, and the two red oxen, Silverhorn and Yeoman, had sprigs of rowan in their yoke as a protection against witch-craft. Elias, too, began to join in:

The birds of springtime they sing so light.
Come, my goat, oh, come!
The flowers will push through the turf to-night.

But with that he broke off and, bending over the fence, said to Axel Frederick, "Powder smells ill when people shoot, and soot falls from the chimneys, so surely the thaw will last."

The entry of the great house was covered with a snowy thatch of turf, where in summer a goat was wont to browse among the house-leeks and lime-wort. Below on the bench sat grandfather in his gray frock coat with pewter buttons, and Ulrica led forward the little girls so that they might greet him. They were clad in basted-up smocks, which were home-dyed with whortleberry juice, and every time the little girls curtsied, they made lilac circles on the wet steps of the stairs.

Grandfather patted Ulrica on the cheek with the back of his hand.

"You will grow up in time no doubt, little one, and become a help to Axel Frederick."

"If I were only quite certain of it, grandfather. It is so big here, and there is so much to manage that I am not accustomed to."

"Ah, yes. And pity it is for Axel Frederick that he lost both father and mother so early, and had no one but his aunts and his old grandfather. But still we have looked after him in every way, and you, little one, must of course learn to take our place.

The hardest thing is his frail health, the fine boy.
— Ah, dear children, God be thanked for this day
of spring and for blessed years of peace!"

Grandfather felt of the cut juniper and praised
it because it was moist, so that it would take up a
great deal of dust.

Behind him in the kitchen window stood the two
aunts, cooking a mash of castoreum and laurel berries for a sick heifer. Both of them had plain black
clothes and ice-gray hair combed back.

"Why is n't Axel Frederick with you?" they
asked of Ulrica. "Remember that for supper he is
to have his favorite dish, honey-pudding dipped in
syrup, and there is to be pork with shallot."

"Yes, yes," said grandfather; "and then let the
servants have a rest for to-night."

Ulrica hastened into the maids' room, where the
servants were picking tow, but she had not taken
many steps before her timid and undeveloped little
face again took on an anxious and listening expression.

"But, Ulrica!" called grandfather. "I don't understand this, Ulrica! Come here, Ulrica!"

She hung the bunch of keys she had just taken
up behind the door-post in the entry, and went
out.

"Is n't that a rider coming off there?" asked
grandfather. "Three months now I've been spared
from letters. I grow so full of dread when I get a

letter. Look at him, look at him! He digs his paw
into his bag."

The rider came to a standstill a moment by the
steps, and delivered a sealed and folded paper.

The aunts elbowed their way forward on both
sides of grandfather, and reached him his spectacles, but his hands trembled so that he could
hardly break the seal. They all wanted to read
the writing at the same time, and Ulrica forgot herself so far that she leaned over grandfather's arm,
pointed along the lines, and spelled aloud before
the others.

At last she struck her hands together and stared
in front of her, while tears mounted to her eyes.

"Axel Frederick, Axel Frederick!" she cried,
and ran over the sanded court to the pasture. "For
heaven's sake!"

"What the mischief is the matter with you now?"
answered Axel Frederick, throwing away the withered fern which he was chewing. He had a full, pink
face and an agreeable, careless voice.

She did not come to a halt before she had taken
his hand.

"Axel Frederick, you don't know! There's an
order that the regiment shall hold itself in readiness to gather under the flag. It's on account of the
Danes' invasion into Holstein."

He followed her back to the great house, and
she squeezed and squeezed his wrist.

"Dear children," stammered grandfather, "that I must needs live to see such a visitation! We have war upon us."

Axel Frederick stood and pondered.

Finally he looked up and answered, "I won't go."

Grandfather tramped around on the steps, and about him the aunts went back and forth.

"You are already enrolled, dear child. The only thing would be if we could perhaps hire some one else."

"One can surely do that," replied Axel Frederick indifferently.

He went into the house, and Ulrica sprang up the stairs with her apron before her eyes, and threw herself on her bed.

In the evening, when the honey-pudding was eaten, and they all sat around the table, grandfather wanted, as usual, to work on a hundred-mesh net, but he trembled too much.

"It has gone ill up there in Stockholm," said he. "Ballets, masquerades, streets covered with carpets, comedians and conjurers of all sorts—that has been the daily food with our new 'King Christina.' I've heard all about it. When the money ran out, he began to give away the crown jewels. Now our gracious lord must spell out another lesson."

Axel Frederick moved back his candlestick, and sat leaning indolently forward with his elbows on the table, while the aunts and Ulrica, her eyes red with weeping, cleared the table. Grandfather nodded and coughed and went on with his talk.

"In all these years of peace there has been nothing but greed and extortion, and the very worst fellows have pushed themselves nearest to the throne. Now these fatted oxen are behaving ill, I fancy. Ha-ha! You should but have seen the old times when grandfather was young, and was called to the nobles' banner. The king's standard that was kept in the royal wardrobe was unfurled, and the horse with the kettledrum was equipped in its long saddle-cloth with crowns in the corner, and then we assembled in our tight, braided coats, while the trumpets began to play."

Grandfather took the yarn and tried to tie it, but threw it aside again and rose.

"You should only have seen, Axel Frederick. Even in the moonlight, as we stood drawn up on the icy ground and sang psalms before the advance, I recognized the Närkingers' red uniforms with white facings, which were like striped tulips; and the yellow Kronobergers, and the gray boys from Kalmar, and the gay blue Dalecarlian regiment, and the West Gotlanders, who were yellow and black. That was a feast to behold, but quiet as in the Lord's house. Well, there have come other men and other coats. Everything now is to be severe and simple."

There was silence in the room awhile.

After that Axel Frederick said, as if to himself, "If my togs and gear were in good order, there might be merry times in a camp."

Grandfather shook his head.

"You are frail in health, Axel Frederick, and it will be hard to march down through the whole kingdom to Denmark."

"Yes, march I won't, but I might, though, have Elias with me and the brown long-wagon."

"That you may of course have any time, but you have no cloth tent with stakes and ridge-tree and pegs and whatever else there ought to be now."

"Elias could very well purchase that for me on the way. As to uniform, I 'm passably well off."

"Let 's see now, let 's see now." Grandfather became eager and toddled off over the floor to open the wardrobe. "Ulrica, come here, Ulrica, and read how it stands there in His Royal Majesty's" (he bowed) "edict which lies on the table! Here we have the cloak with brass buttons, lined with smooth Swedish baize. That is right. And the vest is here, too. Read now about the coat!"

Ulrica trimmed the tallow candle, and sat down at the table with hands over her brow, while she read monotonously, spelling out the words, in a loud voice: "Coat of blue unstretched cloth, red collar, lined with madder-red baize, twelve brass buttons in front, four above and three below the pocket-flap, and one button on each side, three small on each sleeve."

"Eight—twelve—that's right. Now we come to the breeches."

"Breeches of good buckskin or deerskin with three buttons covered with chamois."

"They are fearfully chafed. There will soon be eyes in the seat. However, Elias could very well see to getting you a new pair on the way. But the hat and gloves. Where are the hat and gloves?"

"They're lying in the chest in the entry," said Axel Frederick.

Ulrica read: "Gloves with large gauntlets of yellow shamozed ox-leather, stiffened and reinforced, with the grip of buck- or goat-skin. Shoes of good Swedish wax-leather with straps cut in one piece. Bottom of an insole and a middle-sole. Shoe-buckles of brass."

"The shoes and wax-leather boots are here, and are fairly good. You can have my spurs. You shall be a fine-looking Swedish soldier, my dear boy."

"Neckcloth: one of black Swedish wool-crepon two-and-a-half feet long and a full nine inches wide with a leather cord half a yard long at each end, and two of white."

"That Elias must get for you at Örebro."

"Pistols: two pairs. Holsters of black leather with tops of gathered broadcloth."

"You must take mine. And my broadsword is in

excellent condition with calf-skin sheath and sword-band of elk-leather. That's how a Swedish warrior ought to look. We must now think, too, of equipping Elias and putting in haversacks and all."

Axel Frederick stretched his arms.

"It's surely the best thing for me to go up and lie down and take a good rest beforehand."

There was now noise and commotion in the great house. There was nailing and battering every day, there was flaming and sputtering in the fireplace, and by night the candle was burning. The one room that stayed dark was Axel Frederick's.

On the last night no one but Axel Frederick went to rest, and when the dawn had come on so far that all lights could be put out, the aunts waked him and gave him something warm to drink in bed with drops of *aqua fortis*, for they had heard that he coughed in the night.

When he came down into the hall, the others were gathered there already, even the maids and the men-servants, and the table was spread for all in common. They ate without saying a single word, but when the meal was over, and they arose, the Bible was brought to grandfather, and Ulrica read with choked voice. When she had ceased, grandfather clasped his hands and spoke with eyes closed:

"Like as my forefathers have done, even so will I now in the hour of departure lay my hands upon

you, my daughter's son, and bless you, for many
are my years, and who knows when the hour-glass
has run out? God, the Most High, I invoke from
my lowly dwelling, that He may lead you to honor,
and that the heavy trials which await us may only
exalt our little nation to be greater and more glorious."

Axel Frederick stood at the corner of the table,
fingering and balancing the plate, until from outside was heard a clatter, as the brown long-wagon
was driven up.

All now went out, and Axel Frederick sat up beside Elias, wrapped in grandfather's wolf-skin coat
and much heated, for in the spring weather the
water was dripping from roof and tree.

"Here is the butter firkin," said the aunts, "and
here the bread sack. Hearken now, Elias! In the
seat-box are the curd-cake and the flask with the
aqua fortis. If the strain and peril are too hard, dear
Axel Frederick, never forget that the way home is
short."

But grandfather pressed in among them and
stuck his hands down in the back of the wagon.

"Is the chest tied on right? And let's see now!
Here is the sprinkling-brush and the whisk-cloth
and the scraper—and here we have the fodder-bag
and the water-bottle. That's as it ought to be. The
lead-mould, bullet-cutter, and casting ladle are in
the chest."

Ulrica stood behind them without any one noticing her.

She said very softly, "Axel Frederick, when it
is summer, I shall go out some evening and bind
joy-threads and sorrow-threads on the rye, to see
which has grown highest the next morning—"

"Now it's all ready," broke in grandfather, who
had not heard her; "and God be with both you and
Elias!"

Round about on the side of the road stood the
farm-folk and the day-laborers.

But just as Elias raised his whip, Axel Frederick laid his hand over the reins.

"This journey may turn out ill," said he.

"Still it would look badly," answered Elias, "to
unharness and unsaddle now."

Axel Frederick stuck his hand back into the
sleeve of his coat, and between the lines of silent
people the wagon rolled away.

.   .   .   .

The weeks passed, and the trees blossomed. It
was a slow march with the Närke regiment through
the wilds of Sweden, and Axel Frederick sat in his
coat and slept beside Elias, warm on the brow and
with his gloves of goat's-hair very moist. A little
way from Landskrona, the brown long-wagon had
fallen behind the regimental baggage, and the horse
stood in the blaze of the sun, and browsed beside

the ditch. Both master and man fell asleep, shoulder
to shoulder.

The horse whisked at a gad-fly, the water purled
in the ditch, and a couple of vagrants threw their
bad language at the sleepers; but they continued to
sit in the same untroubled repose.

Then there came behind them at a gallop a shab-
bily dressed rider with a large flaxen peruke, who
pulled up his horse beside the wagon.

Elias nudged Axel Frederick, and picked up the
reins, but Axel Frederick, unwilling to open his
eyes, only said: "Yes, drive on, Elias! I need to get
a good rest before my hardships."

Elias gave him another nudge in the side.

"Rouse yourself, rouse yourself!" he whispered.

Drowsily Axel Frederick opened one eye — but
in that instant he grew blood-red over all his
face, he rose, and saluted from the middle of the
wagon.

He recognized at once from pictures that it was
the eighteen-year-old king himself. Yet what a
transformation! Was this majestic and commanding youth, who had grown up so quickly, the same
that a few months before beheaded calves and broke
windows? He was not above middle height, and his
face was small; but the brow was high and noble,
and from the large deep-blue eyes beamed an en-
chanting radiance.

" The gentleman should throw off his coat, so

that I can inspect his uniform," he said deliberately. "The earth is green long since."

Axel Frederick panted and struggled to get off his grandfather's accursed pelisse, and the king surveyed coat and buttons, fingered them, pulled at them, and counted.

"That is fair," said he with a precociously earnest expression; "and now we shall all become entirely new men."

Axel Frederick stood dazed and erect, looking fixedly at the wagon wheel.

Then the king added slowly, "In a few days we may perhaps have the fortune to stand before the enemy. I have been told that in battle nothing is as hard as thirst. If the gentleman should some time meet me in the tumult of the strife, let him step forward and lend me his drinking-flask."

The king once more gave his horse the spurs, and Axel Frederick sat down. He had never loved or hated, never been worried or carried away with enthusiasm, and he pondered the king's words.

The pelisse came to lie between him and Elias. When at dusk the wagon clattered into Landskrona, the regiment had already pitched their tents. Axel Frederick looked about for the covered drinking-table of which he had dreamed. Instead he found only taciturn comrades, who pressed one another's hands, and looked away in crowds across the Straits of Oresund, where the waves were rushing under the cloudy summer heavens, and where flags and pennons fluttered over the forest of masts of the Swedish fleet.

Next morning Elias put the horse and wagon into a barn, because the Crown had taken over all vessels, and only on the day after the fleet had sailed could he follow on a fishing-boat to Zeeland. He remained standing on the shore, almost out in the water, when the monstrous anchors, dripping with mud, were hoisted up by the creaking cables. On mast after mast rose the swelling sails, and the sunlight glittered on the lanterns and glass windows of the poops. The billows danced and shot by, mirroring in flaming coils the lofty, swaying forms of the galleons, which with their laurel garlands and tridents pointed out across the sea to the unexplored land of wonder, toward adventure and achievement. The masses of cloud, after resting long on the waves, had sunk into the sea, and the atmosphere was blue as in a saga.

Then the king forgot himself; the boy in his soul conquered so that he began to clap his hands. He stood in the poop just in front of the lantern, and around him the gray-haired warriors of his father's time smiled, and also began to clap. Even His Excellency Piper sprang up the ladder as nimbly as a ship's-boy. There were no longer any old and decrepit men or greedy bickerers; it was an army of youths.

As if at a mysterious sign, music and drums began to sound at the same moment, swords flew from their sheaths, and, rising above Admiral Anckarstierna's words through the speaking-trumpet, a hymn was sung from the nineteen warships and the hundred smaller vessels.

Elias recognized Axel Frederick, who sat on grandfather's pelisse, hemmed in by the cargo of gabions, sacks for earth, and trench entanglements. But when Elias saw that he, too, slowly rose and drew his blade like the others, and saw how the fleet gradually vanished on the water, he passed his hand over his eyes, shaking his head.

He returned toward the barn, muttering, "How will he look after himself with his fragile health till I can catch up?"

A few days afterward Elias came alone with his longwagon on the Småland roads. Peasant women, who recognized him from the time he had driven past with the sleeping officer, set their entry doors ajar, and asked if it was true that the Swedes had landed at Zeeland, and that the king had thanked God on his knees for the victory, but had stammered from embarrassment.

He nodded assentingly without replying.

Day after day he drove northward, step by step, walking with the reins the whole way beside the wagon, which was covered with a piece of an old sail.

When at last, one evening, he came to the hedge in front of the great house, all immediately recognized by the noise that it was the brown long-wagon, and the horse neighed. Amazed, they went to the window, grandfather himself came out on the steps, and Ulrica stood in the middle of the courtyard.

Elias walked as slowly as ever with the reins in his hands, and at the steps the horse stood still of itself.

Then Elias carefully drew the sail from the wagon, and there stood a long, narrow, nailed-up coffin, with a yellowed wreath of beech-leaves on the lid.

"I brought him home with me," said Elias. "He received a shot in the breast as he sprang forward and handed His Royal Majesty his drinking-flask."

Gunnel the Stewardess

IN a vault of the fortress at Riga, Gunnel the stewardess, an old woman of eighty, sat and spun. Her long arms were veinous and sinewy, her breast was lean and flat like an old man's. Some thin white wisps of hair hung down over her eyes, and she had a cloth knotted about her head like a round cap.

The spinning-wheel whirred, and a trumpeter lad lay on the stone floor in front of the fire.

"Grandma," said he, "can't you sing something while you are spinning? I've never heard you do otherwise than nag and scold."

For a brief moment she turned towards him her tired and wickedly chilling eyes.

"Sing? Perhaps of your mother, who was set on a wagon and carried to the Muscovites? Perhaps of your father, whom they hanged at the chimney of the house on the bridge? Curse will I the night when I was born, and myself will I curse and every human being I have met. Name me a single one who is not even worse than his repute."

"If you sing a song, you'll be cheerful, grandma, and I should be so glad to have you cheerful, this evening."

"He whom you see playing or laughing is only a master of deception. Misery and shame is all,

and it is for the sake of our sins and our baseness
that now the Saxons have come and besieged our
city. Why don't you go in the evening and do your
duty on the wall as at otherwhiles, instead of lying
here in your laziness?"

"Grandma, can't you say a single pleasant word
to me as I go?"

"Thrash you I should, if I were not so infirm
and bent with my years that I no more can lift my
countenance to heaven. Do you not want me to
tell your fortune? Do they not call me the Sibyl?
Shall I tell you that the crooked line over your eyebrows signifies an early death? I see years ahead
into the future, but as far as I see I find only evil
and low purposes. You are worse than I, and I am
worse than my mother, and all that which is born
is worse than that which dies."

He arose from the floor and stirred the logs.

"I will tell you, grandma, wherefore I sat myself by you this evening, and wherefore I asked
of you a kindly word. The old governor-general
has ordered to-day that before the following night
all women, young and aged, sound and sick, shall
go their way, so as not to consume the bread of
the men. Those who refuse shall be punished with
death. How can you, who in ten years have never
gone further than across the castle courtyard to the
storehouse, now be able to range about in wood and
waste in the midst of the winter cold?"

She laughed and trod the spinning-wheel faster and faster.

"Haha! I have been waiting for this after I tended so faithfully the noble lord's storeroom and all that was his. And you, Jan? Aren't you worried at having no one any longer to bake for you at the oven and make your bed on the folding-bench? What other feeling is there in children? Praised be GOD, be GOD, Who at the end casts us all under the scourge of His wrath!"

Jan clasped his hands about his curly brown hair. "Grandma, grandma!"

"Go, I tell you, and let me sit in peace and spin my tow, till I open the door myself and go out of it to be quit of this earthly life!"

He took a few steps forward toward the spinning-wheel, but thereupon turned about and went out of the vault.

The spinning-wheel whirred and whirred, until the fire burned out. Next morning, when Jan the trumpeter came back, the vault stood empty.

The siege was long and severe. After divine service had been held, all the women went out of the city in the snowy days of February, and the feeble or sick were set upon litters and wagons. All Riga became a cloister for men, who had nothing to give to the flocks of begging women that now and then stole out in front of the wall. The men had scarcely bread for their own necessities, and the starved

horses tore each other to pieces in the stalls, or de-
voured the mangers, and gnawed great holes in the
wooden walls. Smoke hung over the burned sub-
urbs, and at night the soldiers were often wakened
by warning tocsins, and took down their broadswords from the ceiling.

In the evenings, however, when Jan the trumpeter came home to the vault which he and his
grandmother had had as a living-room, he almost
always found the folding-bench made up as a bed,
and a bowl with mouldy meat beside it on a chair.
He was ashamed of saying anything about it to
the others, but he was really terrified. He believed
that his grandmother had perished in the snow-
drifts, and that now, remorseful over her former
hardness, she went about again without rest. In his
fright he shook as with ague, and many a night he
preferred to sleep hungry in the snow on the wall.
After he had strengthened himself with prayer,
however, he became easier, and finally he felt himself more surprised and anxious when he now and
then found the folding-bench untouched and the
chair empty. Then he would seat himself at the
spinning-wheel and, treading it very softly, would
listen to the familiar whirring which he had heard
day after day since his birth.

Now it happened one morning that the governor-
general, the celebrated Erik Dahlberg, a man of
seventy-five, heard violent shooting. He rose with

impatient anger from his sketches and fortification models of wax. As a reminder of his bright youthful excursions in the service of beauty, splendid etchings of Roman ruins hung on the wall, but his formerly mild countenance had become wrinkled with melancholy, and an expression of harshness stiffened around the narrow, compressed, almost white lips. He adjusted his great spliced wig, and tremblingly ran his nails over his thin moustache. When he went down the stairs, he struck heavily on the stones with his cane, and said:

"Ah, we Swedes, we blood-kindred to the Vasa kings, who in their old age could only find fault and quarrel and at the last sat in their own rooms afraid of the dark, — we have in our soul a black seed, from which with the years is raised a branching tree filled with the bitterest gall-apples."

He became bitterer and harsher in spirit the farther he went, and when he finally stood at the wall, he spoke to no one.

Several battalions had been drawn up with flags and music, but afterwards the shooting had quieted, and through the gate returned scattered bands of weary and bleeding men who had just repulsed the enemy's attack. Last of them all, came a thin and feeble old man, who had himself a red sabre wound on the breast, but who painfully carried in his arms in front of him a wounded boy.

Erik Dahlberg raised his hand over his brows to

look. Was not the fallen boy Jan the trumpeter, the lad from the castle? He recognized him by his curly brown hair.

At the arch of the gate the exhausted bearer sank down against the stone pillar, and remained there sitting with his wound and with the dead boy on his knee. Some soldiers, bending down to examine the wound, slit up the bloody shirt above the breast.

"What!" they shouted, and stepped back. "It's a woman!"

Wondering, they bent down still lower to look at her face. She had sunk her head sidewise against the wall, and the fur cap slid down, so that the white locks of her hair fell forward.

"It's Gunnel the stewardess, the Sibyl!"

She breathed heavily and opened her dulling eyes.

"I did n't want to leave the boy alone in this world of evil, but after I had put on men's clothes and served night and day among the others on the wall, I thought that I was eating a man's bread without wrong."

Soldiers and officers looked dubiously at Erik Dahlberg, whose commands she had transgressed. He continued to stand there, reserved and harshly gloomy, while the stick in his hand trembled and tapped on the stone paving.

Slowly he turned to the battalion and the thin lips moved.

"Lower your colors!" he said.

French Mons

A HIDE–COVERED field wagon had stuck in one of the swamps of Poland, and the horse had already been unhitched. On the wagon stood a young man who had just come to the army to work his way up. His comrades called him French Mons, because as tutor he had followed some distinguished lords to France, and had there filled his chest with all sorts of odd things. Captain Olof Oxehufvud and several subalterns and soldiers waited alongside in the mud, and the snowstorm struck them in the face.

"The wagon and chest must be left behind," said Oxehufvud.

French Mons opened the chest, and pulled out as much as he could carry.

"What a pied dressing-gown with all that needlework and tassels!" exclaimed Oxehufvud and the subalterns. "What miserable little slippers! And false calves! And a bonnet!"

"That's a *cadeau* from ma—"

"Kick it into the slush!"

"—From mama."

"Look at the little peruke!"

"And the medium peruke!"

"And the great spliced peruke!"

Oxehufvud could now control himself no longer, but took him by the leg.

"Kick the damned stuff into the slush, I say!"

The delicate blonde countenance of French Mons flamed up, and he struck his hand on his sword.

"Master Captain, such an import—"

"Such an important person as you can freely hold up the march, you think?"

"No. Such a victorious army, I would say, surely need not go in shabby clothes, with dressing-gowns from the time of King Orre."

"Stuff and nonsense! Little schoolmaster! Consummate ass!"

"The captain treats me like a menial, yet I have had education, have travelled in France, yes, have stood eye to eye with Vauban himself."

"Well, what did Vauban say?"

"What did he say?"

"Just so."

"'Get out!' he said, for it was at his own gate, and I was in his way."

"Lord! Lord! Get down from the wagon and be quick about it! Come here, two of you fellows, and take this beggar in lady's chair style!"

French Mons rolled up the slippers and wigs in the dotted dressing-gown and took it on his back, while he held a lorgnette before his eyes.

When he had been carried to the bank, Oxehufvud stood in front of him, tall and slim, with brilliant red cheeks and small dark moustaches.

"Hark now, monsieur, what do you want in the field? Do you want to work up?"

"Though not of noble rank, I aspire to it. Who knows if perhaps even I may not sit some time with a certificate of nobility in my pocket?"

"You may ennoble yourself in fools' hell! In this army no one says a word about nobility, but every one must work his way up the best he may."

Oxehufvud had now abused him so long as leader that his comradely heart began to thaw, and he added grumblingly in a somewhat milder tone, "Behave yourself gallantly, and you may get your officer's commission to start with! We have already broken so many Swedish dandies of your sort and made men of them. There by that little wood you see a large house with a white stairway. Since we are in all no more than five-and-twenty men, I can't afford to leave you a single soldier. Reconnoitre and spy diligently on the enemy, so that no one falls on us from the rear!"

Oxehufvud marched off with his little band, and French Mons went up to the house with his bundle on his back.

No human being was visible, and he stationed himself irresolutely in the lee of the wall. He was cold and wet through, but above all he was troubled by the dirt and mud on his boots. Would he not be able to keep equally good watch from one of

the windows? A well-made bed with a silken coverlet and a foot-muff was exactly what he longed
for.

Transversely under the house went a dark car-
riage-door, and thither with great caution he slunk
along the wall. When he had dried his moist lorgnette, he leaned forward and looked in with stealthy
alertness.

There was a stamping and clattering, and he distinguished two gleaming eyes. With throbbing heart
he took a step back and drew his sword. A black
horse rushed out and ran back and forth in the
courtyard, while it threw the snow high in the air
with its hind feet.

" I won't catch that black fellow," thought French
Mons. "If a soldier sits on such a wild horse, the
dead owner will rise from the swamp, jump up
behind, and pull him from the saddle. They tell
of such things in the evening by the camp-fire."

He threatened the horse with his sword, and
went in, pushing the door open on the other side
so that the light would be better. He saw now that
the door to the house was walled up.

Snorting and stamping, the horse came back, but
French Mons chased him out again. Then he went
out and called up to the window. A gray-haired
serving-woman stuck out her head.

" Does a friend of King Stanislaus or of the
Saxon drunkard dwell here?" he asked.

"Here dwells an old recluse, who is no one's enemy and no one's friend."

"Good. Then he cannot deny shelter to a frozen Swedish soldier."

The serving-woman vanished and finally returned after a time with a ladder, on which he climbed in.

The room was large, and the ugly but clean wooden chairs stood in a stiff row along the bare walls. When he chanced to push back one of the chairs with his scabbard, the serving-woman hastened at once to move it back to its proper place. Two girls dressed in blue, with pale faces and curled hair, came and went without saying a word. As soon as one got a few steps behind, she ran anxiously forward to the other's side. They rubbed against each other and groped with their long fingers, and though it was still bright daylight, they carried two lighted lamps.

When the serving-woman had rubbed the mud from his boots and sufficiently dried the wet places that the soles had made on the floor, she quietly and carefully opened the door to the next room.

"Don't walk too roughly!" she whispered.

There stood a man of middle age in a dressing-gown and with the most impudent and pointed nose, but no one had ever worn a more elegantly curled peruke, and on his white fingers gleamed rings with jewels.

French Mons set down his bundle, and eyed him

with his lorgnette. Much pleased with his venerable exterior, he thereupon made a wide gesture with his arms, and bowed to the floor.

"My intentions are courteous," he said, "and humbly I beg the favor of knowing with what nobleman I have the good fortune to speak."

"Sit down, my good sir. I am nothing but a forgotten old recluse, but since you are a man of quality, I shall at once explain various things that may seem remarkable."

The two gentlemen sat down stiff and straight with hands on their knees.

"Formerly I was a merry companion, and my coat of brocade was the talk of all Warsaw, but on my thirtieth birthday, when I sat drinking with my comrades, I lifted my glass and spoke somewhat in this fashion: My friends, with every year your eyes become harder and your hearts more shrunken. One believes in King Stanislaus of the white cheeks, and the other in King August with the big belly. Afterwards you forge your plots accordingly, and seek for appointments and rewards. I will not go to the grave with the horrible recollection that each of my brothers was at the last a Cain. I set friendship much higher than love, because it is a bond exclusively between souls, and therefore to-day I say unto you farewell, while we are all still young. Of me you shall never hear anything further, but such as I now see you, you shall still go about me

in my room before my eyes and keep me company,
when I sit alone and old. When the serving-woman
outside the door hears that I prattle half aloud, she
will say: 'Now the old man is talking with the
friends of his youth.'"

"And after you had so bade them farewell?"

"Then I went home and had the door walled up.
My servants have to get themselves out and in as
best they may."

"With a host of such delicate sensibilities a guest
will surely get on well."

"Get on well? What are you thinking of? My
twin daughters who walk about the room here with
their lamps are insane. Their mother was an abducted
nun. No, a guest would not get on in the least."

"You mean, perhaps, that my coming disturbs."

"Ah well, I won't exactly say that. But there are
ghosts here."

His nostrils rose at the corners, and he got up
and rubbed his hands in satisfaction.

"I consider it my duty as host to tell the truth as
well first as last. There is a dead lackey who goes
about again, and whose name is Jonathan. He
stands in window-recesses and behind doors in
brown livery with black braid. His servant zeal so
sticks to the poor fellow even after death that he
watches over and serves guests when they least expect it. Fortunately guests are rare here. Tell me,
are you a count?"

"I? No."

"Are you a baron?"

"No, I'm not a baron yet."

"Are you not at least a plain nobleman?"

"Is it my lord's intention to insult?"

French Mons flushed with embarrassment. "The certificate has been my dearest dream," he thought, "and would to God I carried it already in my coat pocket. Then no one any longer should cry, 'Little schoolmaster!' Then it should be: 'I saw the marks of nobility on that man long before he got his certificate.'"

"How can such a simple question wound you?" exclaimed the recluse, with yet more enjoyment.

"Of course I am noble. My family is extremely old."

"That would be another thing. That's very good. Though Jonathan had a Christian burial and all that, he is such an out-and-out aristocratic lackey that he starts all sorts of malicious tricks as soon as he has before him a parvenu or a plebeian."

French Mons stroked his small moustache with the nail of his little finger and swung his lorgnette uncomfortably.

"Is my lord a connoisseur of Syracusan wine?" he asked.

"No."

"I too think much more of a glass of Frontignac. My favorite dish is ragout with mushrooms, though I shall never speak ill of a *haché* of lamb with thyme. Much in this part of the world depends on the sauce. Oh, I do not long to be back home with oatmeal and pitchy darkness."

"Pitch darkness? Are you thinking of the summer nights?"

"They are bright."

"And winter evenings are bright, too, for then you have snow. If you are afraid of pitch darkness, never travel southward again! Have you in your land any great artists and scholars?"

"We have not and never shall have."

"You do not over-value your countrymen."

"I have seen a little of the great world, my lord. I have travelled in France a good two months, my lord. I have even been a whole evening with *roi Soleil.*"

"You? Have you been with Louis XIV?"

"That I have—at the theatre—though I only got a wretched standing-place in the parterre. Since Augustus there has not lived so majestic a sovereign. Only look at his style of bowing!"

"The king of Sweden is a man, too."

"That he is, for he makes us noticed in foreign countries, but how poor for all that!"

"Mightily poor in Warsaw lately. When Stanislaus stepped into the church for coronation with his spouse, who is always frightened and tremulous, he not only got as a present from the Swedes the

newly wrought crown, sceptre, apple, sword, ermine, belt, and shoes, but also a banner, tapestries
on the church walls, the plates on the table, coronation money to be scattered about, and soldiers who
kept guard and fired the jubilation salute — and
at the last he thanked His Excellency Piper and
kissed his hand. — Are you poor yourself?"

"Poor? I?"

French Mons thought of the two wretched
Charles-pieces that were sewed under the lining of
his coat, and were all he possessed, but he rapped
his lorgnette on the table and hastened to say: "My
expenses are enormous — and play amuses me — I
never go without ten louis d'or in my purse."

"Will you lend me five louis d'or?"

French Mons looked up at the ceiling.

"Just to-day, unluckily, I forgot my purse in a
coat on my tent-post. But I shall deem myself
happy to have the trifle sent you at the first opportunity. My lord, do not regard us awkward Swedes
as any *grands seigneurs*. However high I mount, still
Mons always peeps out between the seams."

"You were mightily awkward lately at our Polish
election, when Arvid Horn sat with his note-book
and registered all who voted against the Swedish
orders, and when our land-marshal broke his staff
in despair. — But now consider my house as your
own. The tobacco pipe lies by the flask of scented
water, the scented water on the powder-box, the

powder-box on the tobacco keg, the tobacco keg on the commode. That you must hunt out as time goes on."

With these words he took up a leather-bound book and sat down to read.

"I beg you to trouble yourself no further," answered French Mons, looking at him sidelong through his lorgnette with wakening mistrust. Within his soul he thought: "Just wait till I'm sitting with my certificate in my big state carriage! Then it will be: 'That gentleman is our newly made knight, Magnus Gabriel.'"

The two girls every now and then pattered past through the room, and threw the light of their lamps upon him, and every time he rose and bowed. As the recluse meanwhile continued to read and gradually appeared to forget his presence entirely, he finally took his bundle and went back into the outer room.

"It's getting dark," he said to the serving-woman, "and I am too tired to keep company longer."

"We have arranged the gentleman's bed here to the left in the great hall. That is the only room that has a fire."

The hall was whitewashed and long, with inhospitable rows of chairs and a couple of rough folding-tables. Just by the door stood a bed with curtains of Holland linen. The old woman lighted the four candles in the sconces and left him alone.

Chilled, he looked about him and laid his sword on the table. Then he unpacked his bundle. Three of the candles he blew out, and on them hung the little peruke and the medium peruke and the spliced peruke, but with the fourth he threw the light under the bed and in the window recesses and then set it back in the socket.

"Impudent pack!" he muttered. "I'd rather have stood outside in the snow, but since I'm now inside here, it's a matter of keeping awake, peeping about, and going often to the window to listen and spy."

He tried to lock the door from inside, but it was without both bolt and key. After he had worked in vain for a long time to get off his wet boots, whose musty smell annoyed him, he put on his dressing-gown and lay down in his boots on the bed.

At times he heard a muffled stamping and snorting from the wild horses in the carriage entrance under the floor of the hall, but after a while it grew more quiet, and he began to think that the candle did not light sufficiently, because all the corners and recesses were dark. He raised his lorgnette, sharpened his gaze, and turned his eyes on all sides, but otherwise lay quite motionless.

Then he saw by the door-jamb close behind the curtain at the head of his bed a tall, thin lackey in a brown coat with black braid.

A cramp-like dread caught him by the throat, he

grew dizzy, but he thought: "It is only the good
God who wishes to try me because I am dreaming
of distinctions and certificates."

Softly and almost imperceptibly he caught hold
of both sides of the bed so as to control his shud-
dering body, and then he stuck his right leg out
between the curtains.

"Jonathan," said he, "pull off my boot!"

The lackey grinned so that his dark mouth
twisted itself up to his ears, but he did not move
from his place.

French Mons chattered his teeth, but he did not
draw back his leg.

"Jonathan, is this the way you serve folk of the
nobility?"

The lackey grinned still worse, and made a dis-
dainful gesture of refusal with his hand.

French Mons now understood that the lackey
had seen through his deception and treated him as
a parvenu and a plebeian, and his terror grew so
great that he panted and moaned softly, but his leg
he held continually outstretched.

"Pull off my boot, Jonathan!"

His voice was now barely a whisper.

The lackey rubbed his hands on his hips and
grinned, but remained standing by the door-jamb.

At that moment the horse down below in the carriage entrance neighed long and piercingly, and far
off in the snowstorm many horses answered.

French Mons threw himself from the bed.

"I'm neglecting my duty," he cried. "That's the enemy!"

He sprang forward to the table to grasp his sword, but the lackey walked beside him with long steps and stared him in the eyes.

Then he again grew paralyzed and stood still. Meanwhile the lackey took the sword with one hand, stretched out the other over the candlestick, and with two fingers lifted the great spliced wig on high and then drew it as an extinguisher over the burning candle.

"Good God in heaven!" stammered French Mons. "I have seldom gone into Thy house and have rather pampered myself and played with all sorts of vanity, but help me for this one time so that I do not neglect my duty and become a disgrace! Then Thou may'st punish me eternally."

Neighings were heard ever nearer and nearer, and the wild horse rushed stamping and snorting from its retreat.

Then French Mons bent down with his clenched hands over his head, and threw himself in the dark upon the lackey.

"You spook of Beelzebub!" he shouted.

He pulled the sword to him and struck on all sides in the dark, and chairs fell to the floor. He could nowhere lay hold on Jonathan, but at last he struck his hands against the wall, and the door opened. The two sisters with their lamps and their pale, wide-eyed countenances entered in only their chemises, without the wit to feel any embarrassment about it. They only rubbed against each other and stared at the stranger who had waked them with his racket. On this occasion he did not give himself time to bow, but shoved up the window and hopped to the ground. In his dressing-gown, with sword in hand, he ran along the house and heard behind him a harsh voice from the window, but he did not know whether it was that of the recluse or of Jonathan, or whether they were both one and the same.

"I said that you were a fool," cried the voice, "a great fool, a fool without peer, and I wanted to be even with you. But if the horsemen get to see you, and there is a hand-to-hand fight, my house, my home, my nook will be an ash-heap before the cock crows."

Without looking back, French Mons sprang in among the trees, thinking all the while: "Now's the chance for an officer's commission! And then the certificate, the certificate!"

The moonlight shone through the snowstorm, and he saw Polacks with waving plumes flit by like shadows. When they came too near, he threw himself down beside a heap of twigs or set himself behind a tree trunk.

At last he discovered an old snow-covered barricade. Behind the logs a soldier rose and asked in a whisper: "Who goes there?"

"God with us! Good comrade!" answered French Mons, and climbed into the triangle. "The enemy is upon us!"

"I have long thought I heard hoofs," said Oxehufvud softly. "Perhaps it would be wisest to run down and occupy the house."

"Captain, do not command me to show the way! I was received there as a guest; I am a chevalier and would rather be shot."

"And how were you treated there?"

"Like an excellency."

"We shall see. It seems to be too late now. Take aim! Fire!"

A swarm of Polacks galloped forward and struck with their spears across the logs, but the first volley threw them from the saddle.

"Oohaho! oohaho!" rang through the wood. Riding shadows and long lines of men on foot gathered as far as the eye could see. In the half light they resembled the dark bushes that swayed in the wind.

"I fancy we're going to have a pretty party with the enemy," said Oxehufvud. "We are five-and-twenty men, and around us stand fully three battalions."

"Now we are only twenty-four," answered

French Mons as he took the musket from a fallen soldier.

"Now we are only nineteen," said Oxehufvud after a time.

Shot rained over the triangle and killed man after man. As soon as the riders shrank back, the Swedes stopped shooting, but when the silence once more enticed the Polacks and inspired them with the belief that there was no longer any man living behind the barricade, they were met at once by shot and swords and stones and boughs of trees. So the raging strife continued hour after hour.

Oxehufvud stole along the stockade and counted half aloud: "Eight, ten, thirteen — we're not many now. A sorry number."

He, too, had taken a musket, and on his knees was picking up the ammunition from the cartridge-box of one of the fallen.

"Comrade," said he, and without rising he drew French Mons to him in his dressing-gown. "I gave it to you rough, comrade, at noon on the swamp."

"Now we are only seven," answered French Mons, loading and firing. "But soon we shall have held out three hours."

"Comrade, you are not the first who has shown me that the Swedes should not always laugh at their dandies. You see, comrade, it happens sometimes in this world that he who begins with a great peruke may end with a great deed."

"Now we are only two."

"Hardly two, for I have got mine already," answered Oxehufvud, and sank back against the logs. "Hardly two."

French Mons now stood alone among the dead. He tore up his dressing-gown and twisted some rags about his left arm, which was bleeding violently. His waistcoat, too, he cast away, and the lorgnette he stuffed into the leg of his boot. Then he lay down among the others as far in among the branches and twigs as he could creep.

The next time the Polacks galloped forward, all was still.

They vaulted over the logs with a wild cry and began to plunder, but when they saw him, bloody and half undressed, they let him lie, and at daybreak they went away.

"Now," thought French Mons, "now I have my officer's commission. The certificate comes later."

He crept out between the logs, and up by the house in the snow he happened upon the peruke, which had been thrown after him from the window.

"The wretch!" he whispered. "That's my thanks for saving his nest."

All day he went through the woods with his peruke under his arm, and only late in the even-

ing was he challenged by the outposts of the Swedish camp.

Tents and cabins of brush were set up in the
woods without any sheltering entrenchments. On
wagons or before their huts the women sat on a
separate lane and cradled their children on their
knees or whispered gently and quietly with their
soldiers. Round the fires the clay pipes puffed in
scarred hands. There Cornet Brokenhjelm and the
dauntless Lieutenant Pistol related their adventures. Lieutenant Orbom let his neighbor feel with
his fingers the shot from Klissov which still remained behind his right ear after having gone in
under his left eye and through his head. Per Ad-
lerfelt, the dancing-master, lamented that the enemy always, as at Duna, shot so low that at last
they would mar his handsome legs. There the lively
Dumky jested, still wearing on his arm the garter
which as a page he had got from a Silesian duch-
ess. Svante Horn, who was being bandaged by his
faithful servant, Lidbom, muttered that he could
never charge without immediately getting a Cossack spear or sword in his body. Before him stood
the genial gray-haired surgeon, Teuffenweisser, who
continually put on and took off his spectacles, and
always required a dram before he attended rich
patients. All conversed of the fortune of war, which
allowed one man to grow gray under hardships and
honors, but let another fall by the first shot in the

spring of his days. No drinking-songs rang out,
but the king had kettledrums and oboes play merrily all night. It was a camp where that soft noise
was like the murmur of a clear forest brook under
leafage dewy with June.

Against the wish of the king, his bodyguards
had wound his tent with hay and on that had laid
sod, so that it was like a charcoal-kiln. It stood,
not in the middle of the camp, but on the outermost edge and almost in darkness. Within, by the
tent-pole, they had built a fireplace of stones and
had brought there time and again a red-hot cannon-
ball. There was a wash-basin of pure silver, and on
the table, beside the Life of Alexander the Great
and the gold-bound Bible, stood a little silver-plated
image of the dog Pompey, which had died. But the
light blue silken brocade on the chair and field-bed
was already worn and spotted. In the middle of the
tent crouched the dogs, Turk and Snuffler, but the
king lay among the fir-twigs on the ground. The
small beer was done, and the lackey Hultman had
had nothing but a glass of melted snow and two
slack-baked biscuits to offer him for supper. After
that he had spread his cape over him and put on his
embroidered nightcap. There now, at the midday
height of his victories, slept the king of the Swedes,
and his narrow head was turned toward the lan-
guishing gleam of the last glowing cannon-ball. It
was long now since he had read the evening prayer

which he had formerly stammered out in his room while the wind raged in the lindens of Karlberg Park. His god had gradually darkened into the thunderous god of the Old Testament, to the avenging Lord of Sabaoth, whose commands he heard in his soul without needing to pray for them; and it was Thor and the Asar who drove around this camp in the rumbling of the nocturnal storm, and who with their trumpets hailed their youngest-born on earth.

Then the dogs began to whimper and growl, and the half-grown Max of Wurtemberg, the Little Prince, came, overjoyed and beaming, to the opening of the tent.

"Your Majesty," he cried, with his ringing boyish voice, "awake, awake! Five-and-twenty Smålanders have been out and played with the enemy."

Behind him stood French Mons, propped against the gallant Captain Schmiedeberg, who himself still went on a crutch after an engagement over the baggage, where he with twelve men had fought against three hundred Polacks.

French Mons had never carried his head more proudly and contentedly, though he reeled with weariness; but when he heard that he was standing before the king's tent, he stopped short in anxiety. He stooped and tremblingly wiped the bloodstains from his hands. His hat, the medium peruke, and the little peruke he threw upon the ground, and

without considering the regulations, put on the
great spliced peruke. When he got himself in order,
he extended his arms along his sides and told his
story stammeringly with chattering teeth.

The king, who continued to sit on the fir-twigs,
then slowly repeated it, investigating every word
so as not to miss a single detail of the adventure.
He rejoiced as a child would at a wonderful saga.
Finally he gave him his hand.

"Oxehufvud spoke rightly," he said. "The gentlemen have had a pretty party with the enemy. It
has been quiet enough here in camp, and I should
myself have gladly been along. Since the Polish recluse begged in jest the loan of five louis d'or, I
will leave him ten, and the gentleman shall go back
and throw them in to him through the window."

French Mons went backward through the tent
door, and Schmiedeberg caught him around the
waist and conducted him into a ring of inquisitive,
expectant comrades. There were ensigns and lieutenants and captains, who were his equals in age,
but who had already risen higher in rank than he.

"French Mons," they murmured, "now no one
any longer dares laugh at your lorgnettes and your
wigs. But how did it go with your commission and
certificate? The certificate!"

"Quiet, quiet!" said Schmiedeberg. "There are
other rewards for the poor fellow. If His Royal
Majesty might prevail, he would give no rewards,

but would wish that each and all should fight and fall for honor alone."

No one dared contradict Schmiedeberg, and dropping the arm of his new-found charge, he limped on his crutch a few steps nearer the fire.

"Did n't you see?" he whispered — "did n't you see that His Royal Majesty took him by the hand almost as an equal?"

"There I got my certificate for time and eternity," said French Mons.

In his dripping spliced wig and ragged shirt he stood all the while upright with arms at his sides, and he still stammered in his speech and chattered his teeth.

"And your charter as baron," answered Schmiedeberg softly, "you get when you fall."

The Queen of the Marauders

THE tocsin in the church tower at Narva had ceased. In a breach of the battered rampart lay the fallen Swedish heroes, over whose despoiled and naked bodies the Russians stormed into the city with wild cries. Some Cossacks, who had sewed a live cat into the belly of an innkeeper, were still laughing in a circle around their victim, but the gigantic Peter Alexievitch, the czar, soon burst his way through the midst of the throng on street and courtyard and cut down his own men to check their misdeeds. His right arm up to the shoulder was drenched with the blood of his own subjects. Weary of murder, troop after troop finally assembled in the square and the churchyard. Under the pretext that the churches had been desecrated by the misbelievers who lay buried there, bands of soldiers began to violate and plunder the graves. Stones were pried up from the floor of the church with crowbars, and outside the graves were opened with shovels. Pillagers broke the copper and tin caskets into pieces, and threw dice for the silver handles and plates. The streets, where at the first mêlée the inhabitants had thrown down firebrands and tiles, and where the blood of the slain was still running in the gutters, were for many days piled up with rusty or half-blackened coffins. The hair on some of the bodies had grown so that it hung out between the boards. Some of the dead lay embalmed and well preserved, though brown and withered, but from most of the coffins yellow skeletons grinned forth from collapsed and mouldered shrouds. People who stole anxiously among them read the coffin-plates in the twilight, and now and then recognized the name of a near relative, a mother or a sister. Sometimes they saw the ravagers pull out the decayed remains and throw them into the river. Sometimes, again, protected by night, they themselves succeeded in carrying them off and burying them outside the city. So in the dusk one might encounter an old man or woman who came stealing along toilsomely with children or serving-maids, carrying a coffin.

One night a swarm of pillagers bivouacked in a corner of the churchyard. Hi! what fun it was to pile up a bonfire of bed-slats and bolsters and chairs and coffin-ends and what the devil else could be dragged forth! Flames and sparks blazed up as high as the attic window of the parsonage. Round about stood coffins propped one against another. The bottom of one of the uppermost had been broken, so that the treasurer, of blessed memory, who was inside it, stood there upright with his spliced wig on his head and looked as if he thought: "I pray you, into what company have I been conducted?"

"Haha! little father," the robbers called to him, as they roasted August apples and onions at the flames; "you surely want something to wet your whistle, you there!"

The glow of the fire lighted up the living-room of the parsonage, and the sparks flew in through the broken panes. In the rooms stood only a broken table and a chair, upon which sat the parson with his head propped on his hands.

"Who knows? Perhaps it might succeed," he mumbled, and raised himself as if he had found the key to a long-considered problem.

His silver-white beard spread itself all over his breast, and his hair hung down to his shoulders. In his youth, as chaplain, he had gone in for a little of everything, and he had never pushed back a cup that was offered him. Afterwards, as a widower in the parsonage, he had worshipped God with joy and mirth and a brimming bowl, and it was bruited about that he did not reach first for his Bible if a well-formed wench happened to be in his company. He therefore even now took misfortune more bravely and resignedly than others, and his heart was as undaunted as his soldierly body was un-bowed by years.

He went out into the entry and cautiously pulled out the five or six rusty nails that held down a couple of boards above a little narrow recess under the stairs. Then he lifted the boards aside.

"Come out, my child!" he said.

When no one obeyed him, his voice grew somewhat more severe, and he repeated his words: "Come out, Lina! Both the other maids have been bound and carried away. It was verily at the last minute that I got you in here. But it is almost a day since then, and you cannot live without meat and drink. Eh?"

When he was not obeyed, he threw back his head in annoyance, and he now spoke in accents of harsh command: "Why don't you obey? Do you think there is food here? There's not so much as a pinch of salt left in the house. You must be got away, you understand. If it goes ill with you, if a plunderer gets you on the way, I can only say this: clasp your arms about his neck and follow with him on his horse's back wherever it carries you. Many a time in the rough-and-tumble of war have I seen such a love, and then I have slung the soldier's cloak over my priest's frock and waved my hat for a lucky end to the song. Don't you hear, lass? When your late father, who was a tippler—if I must tell the truth—was my stable-boy and pulled me out of a hole in the ice once, I promised for the future to provide for him and his child. Besides, he was Swedish born, as I was. Well, have n't I always been a fatherly master to you, or what has Her Grace to object? Have her wits deserted her, eh?"

Something now began to move in the pitch-black recess. An elbow struck against the wall, there was a rustling and scraping, and with that Lina Andersdaughter stepped out, barefooted, in nothing but her chemise and a torn red jacket without sleeves but with a whole back to it, over which hung the braid of her brown hair.

The light of the fire fell in through the window. Squatted together, she held her chemise between her knees, but her fresh, downward-bent face with broad, open features was as merry as if she had just stepped out of her settle-bed on a bright winter morning in the light of the dawn.

The blood ran impetuously enough through the veins of the white-haired chaplain, but in that moment he was but master and father.

" I did not know that in my simple house folk had learned such a ceremonious feeling of delicacy," said he, and gave her a friendly pat on the bare shoulders.

She looked up.

"No," she said, "it's only because I'm so wretchedly cold."

"Ah, well, that's natural. That's the way I like people to talk in my house. But I have no garments to give you. My own hang on me in tatters. The house may burn at any time. I myself can maybe sneak out on my way unaccosted, and I have a Riga rix-dollar in my pocket. Who asks about a ragged old man? It's another affair with you, Lina. I know these wild fellows. I know but one way to get you off, but I myself shrink from telling it. Naturally, you are afraid."

"Afraid I'm not. It will go with me as it may. To be sure, I am no better than the others. Only I'm perishing of cold."

"Come here to the door, then, but don't be frightened. Do you see out there in the doorway the rascals have set a little wooden casket. It cannot be very heavy, but I think you will have room in it. If you dare lay yourself in the casket, perhaps I can smuggle you out of the town."

"That I surely dare."

Her teeth chattered, and she trembled, but she straightened herself up a little, let the chemise hang free, and went out on the stones in the doorway.

The pastor lifted off the moist lid, which was loose, and found nothing in the plundered casket but shavings and a brown blanket.

"That was just what I needed," she shivered. She pulled up the blanket, wrapped it over her, stepped up, and laid herself on her back in the shavings.

The pastor bent over her, laid both his hands on her shoulders, and looked into her fearless eyes. She might be eighteen or nineteen years old. Her hair was stroked smoothly back to the braid.

As he stood so, it came over him that he had not always looked on her in the past with as pure and fatherly feelings as he himself had wished and as he had pretended to do. But now he did so. His long white hair fell down as far as her cheeks.

"May it go well with you, child! I am old. It matters little whether my life goes on for a while still or is destroyed in the day that now is. I have been in many a piece of mischief and many an ill deed in my time, and for the forgiveness of my sins I will also for once have part in something good."

He nodded and nodded toward her and raised himself.

There outside the clamor sounded louder than ever. He laid on the lid and fastened in as well as he could the long screws that had been left in their places. Then he knelt, knotted a rope crosswise around the casket, and with strong arms lifted the heavy burden on his back. Bending forward and staggering, he strode out into the open air.

"Look there!" shouted one of the pillagers at the fire, but his nearest comrade silenced him with the word: "Let the poor old man alone! That's only a miserable beggar's casket."

Sweat trickled out over the old man's face, and his back and arms ached and smarted under the heavy weight. Step by step he moved forward through the dark streets. Every now and then he had to set the casket down on the ground to take breath, but then he stood with his hand on the lid in constant fear of being challenged and hustled away or of being stabbed by some roving band of soldier revellers. Several times he had to step to one side because of the heavy wagons, loaded with men and women, who were to be taken hundreds of miles into Russia to people the waste regions. The great conquering czar was a sower who did not count the seeds he strewed.

When finally the old war-pastor reached the town gate, and the watch came to meet him, he roused his strength to the utmost with all the collected will-power of his anxiety. With a single arm he held the casket in place on his back, while with his free hand he drew the Riga rix-dollar from his pocket and handed it to the sentry as a bribe.

The soldier motioned to him to go on.

He wanted again to move his foot forward, but now he was unable. Through the town gate he saw the river glimmer on the open plain, but then it grew dark before his eyes. Still afraid for his burden in his helplessness, he softly and cautiously lowered the casket beside him on the stone flagging. Thereupon he fell forward and died.

The other men of the watch sprang forward and began to curse and complain. No casket could remain standing there in the door of the gateway.

The officers, who were sitting and gambling in a room of the casemate, now came likewise to the spot. One of them, a little dry, weather-beaten figure with rectangular spectacles, who was more like a clerk than a soldier, took a lantern, came forward, and held the lid slightly ajar with his scabbard.

First he drew back his head precipitately, nearly dropping the lantern. The next time he bent down and looked in, he dwelt on the action longer and more searchingly, and afterwards passed his hands over his whole face to hide his thoughts. Then he unhooked his spectacles and stood pondering. When he bent the third time, he sent the light back and forward through the crevice, — and there inside lay Lina Andersdaughter quite calmly, screwing up her eyes at him in the lantern's light without herself knowing what was going on.

"I 'm hungry," she said.

He laid aside the lantern and went a couple of paces up and down through the door with hands crossed behind his back. There came then into his frigid expression a sly and merrily vibrating life, and unnoticed he took some August apples and thrust them into the casket. Thereupon he began to give commands.

"Come here, boys! Let eight men take the casket to General Ogilvy, salute him, and say that this is a small gift from his humble servant, Ivan Alexievitch. Eight of you others who have just come from working on the walls go after it, and roll up your leather aprons like trumpets in which you are to blow the regimental march. But in front of all, two men are to go with rushlights. Forward, march!"

The savage soldiers looked open-mouthed at one another and obeyed. Laughing, they lifted the casket on their muskets. Two long stalks, tarred and twisted about with straw, were brought forward from a corner of the gateway and lighted at the lantern; and as the procession set itself in motion into the field toward the camp, the musicians tooted the march in their aprons:

> *O you, who have chosen a gun to bear,*
> *You care not for lodging or bed, lad,*
> *You feed like a prince on the finest fare,*
> *Of girls and of lice you've enough and to spare,*
> *But when will you ever be paid, lad?*

When they came to the camp, the soldiers rushed together around them in the torchlight. General Ogilvy, who was sitting at table, came out of his tent.

"Beloved little father," said one of the bearers, "Lieutenant Ivan Alexievitch humbly sends you this gift."

Ogilvy grew pale and bit his lips under his bushy gray moustache. His face, wrinkled and strained to harshness, was at bottom good-natured and friendly.

"Is he out of his right mind?" he thundered with pretended wrath, though in reality he was as frightened as a boy. "Put down the casket and break off the lid!"

The soldiers pried it open with their blades, and the dark lid rattled to one side.

Ogilvy stared. With that he burst out laughing.

He guffawed so that he had to sit down on an
earthen bench. And the soldiers laughed, too. They
laughed down through the whole lane of tents, so
that they reeled and tottered and had to support
themselves one against another like drunkards.
Lina Andersdaughter lay there in the casket with a
half-eaten apple in her hand and made great eyes.
She had now become warm again, and was as blooming of cheek as a doll.

"By all the saints," Ogilvy burst out. "Not even
in the catacombs of St. Anthony has man seen such
a miracle. This is a corpse that ought to be sent to
the czar himself."

"By no means," answered one of his officers.
"I sent him two little fair-haired baggages day
before yesterday, but he cares only for thin brunettes."

"So it is," answered Ogilvy, and turned himself,
bending, toward Narva. "Salute Ivan Alexievitch
and say that, when the casket is returned, there
shall lie in the bottom of it a captain's commission.
— Hey, sweetheart!"

He went forward and stroked Lina Andersdaughter under the chin.

But at that she sat up, took hold of his hair, and
gave him a resounding box on the ear, and after that
another.

He did not let it affect him in the least, but continued to laugh.

"That's the way I like them," he said; "that's the way I like them. I will make you Queen of the Marauders, my chick, and as token thereof I give you here a bracelet with a turquoise in the clasp. A band of our worst rabble stole it just now from the casket of Countess Horn in Narva."

He shook the chain from his wrist, and she caught it eagerly to her.

When, later in the evening, the cloth was laid in the tent, Lina Andersdaughter sat at the table beside Ogilvy. She had now got French clothes of flowered brocade, and wore a headdress with blonde lace. But what hands! She managed to eat with gloves, but under them swelled the big, broad fingers, and the red shone between the buttons.

"Hoho! hoho!" shouted the generals. "Those hands make a man merrier than he would get with a whole flask of Hungary. Help! Tighten our belts! Hold us under the arms! It will be the death of us!"

Meanwhile she filled her plate, munched sweet-meats, and sat with her spoon in the air. If anything tasted bad, she made a face. Eat she could. Drink, on the contrary, she would not, but only took a swallow in her mouth, and then spurted the wine over the generals. But all their curses and worst expressions she picked up, while she sat ever alike blooming and gay.

"Help! help!" shrieked the generals, choked

with laughter. "Blow out the light so we can't see her! Hold our foreheads! Help! Will you have a little puff of a tobacco pipe, mademoiselle?"

"Go to the deuce! Can't I sit in peace?" answered Lina Andersdaughter.

There was one thing, though, that Ogilvy skilfully concealed, so that the laughers should not turn to him and nudge him in the ribs and pull his coat tails and say: "Oho, little father, you 've got into water too deep for your bald head. Bless you, little father, bless you and your little mishap!"

He pretended always to treat her with slightly indifferent familiarity, but he never sat so near her that his dog could not jump up between them. He never took hold of her so that any one saw it, and never when no one saw it either, for then he knew that her hand would catch him on the face, so that the glove would split, and the red shine out in all its strength. It was a fact that, notwithstanding, she now and then gave him a slap in the middle of the face, and no one did she snub worse than him. But at all this he only laughed with the others, so that never before had there been in the camp such a clamor and bedlam.

Sometimes he thought of knouting her, but he was ashamed before the others, because everything could be heard through the tent, and he feared that they then would the more easily guess how things stood, and how little he got along with the girl.

"Wait," he thought, "we shall be sitting alone sometime behind locked doors. Just wait! Till then things may go on as they do."

"Help, help!" shouted the generals. "That's how she carries her train. We must take hold of it. Lord, Lord, no; but just look!"

"Take it up, you," said she. "Take it up, you. That's what you are for."

And so the generals were cuffed and bore her train, both when she came to the table and when she went.

Then it happened one evening, when she sat among the drinking old men, that an adjutant stepped in, hesitating and embarrassed. He turned to Ogilvy.

"Dare I be frank?"

"Naturally, my lad."

"And whatever I say will be forgiven?"

"By my honor. Only speak out!"

"The czar is on his way out to the camp."

"Very good, he is my gracious lord."

The adjutant pointed at Lina Andersdaughter.

"The czar has a fancy for tall brunettes," said Ogilvy.

"Your Excellency, in these last days he has changed his taste."

"God! Call the troops to arms—and forward with the three-horse wagon!"

Now the alarm was struck. Drums rolled, trum-

pets blared, weapons clattered, and shouts and trampling filled the night. The drinking party was broken
up, and Lina Andersdaughter was set in a baggage
wagon.

Beside the peasant who was driving a soldier
sprang up with a lighted lantern, and she heard the
peasant softly inquire of him the purpose of the
flight.

"The czar," answered the soldier in a mono-
tone, and pointed with his thumb over his shoulder
at the girl.

At that the peasant shrunk together as at a frost-
cold breeze, and whipped the small, shaggy horses
more and more wildly. He hallooed and beat and
urged them into a thundering gallop. The lantern
light fell caressingly on the fir bushes and the burnt
homesteads; the wagon banged and tottered among
the stones, and creaked in its joints.

Lina Andersdaughter lay on her back in the hay,
and looked at the stars. Whither was she carried?
What fate awaited her? She wondered and wondered. On her wrist hung the bracelet as a talisman,
a pledge for the accomplishing of Ogilvy's wonderful prediction. Queen of the Marauders! It sounded
so grand, though at first she had but gradually discovered what the word really betokened. She
stroked and plucked at the small silver rings. Then
she sat up and scanned the stony road in the lantern's light. Cautiously she moved further and fur-

ther out. Unnoticed, she climbed slowly over the wagon-sill and lowered her feet to the ground. Would she be crushed and left lying? For a few steps she dragged along. Then she lost her hold, stumbled, and fell lacerated among the bushes.

On thundered the baggage wagon with its three galloping horses, and the lantern light vanished. Then she got up and wiped off the blood from her cheeks, while she wandered forth into the trackless woods.

When she met barbarous-looking fugitives, and they saw her pretty face, they at once picked berries and mushrooms for her and followed along. She got a whole court of ragamuffins, and she treated them so ill that they scarcely dared to touch her dress, but sometimes they stabbed one another. Finally she took service with a skipper's wife, who was to sail with her husband to Danzig. Scarcely had it begun to grow dark when the ragamuffins came out one after another and took service for nothing. The skipper sat on his cabin in the moonlight, blew his shepherd's pipe, and congratulated himself on having got such a willing crew. And never had the old woman seen a stronger serving-maid. But hardly had they put to sea when Lina Andersdaughter sat herself beside the skipper with her arms crossed, and all the ragamuffins lay on their backs and sang in tune with the pipe.

"Do you think I 'll scour your bunks?" said she.

"Beat her, beat her," cried the old woman, but the skipper only moved nearer, and blew and blew on his pipe. Night and day the vessel rocked on the bright waves with slack sail, and the skipper played for Lina Andersdaughter, who danced with her ragamuffins; but down in the cabin sat the old woman, crying and lamenting.

When they came to Danzig, the skipper stuck the pipe under his arm and slunk off the vessel at night with Lina Andersdaughter and her ragamuffins. They guessed now that she thought of going to the Swedish troops in Poland and compelling the king himself to give her his hand.

When she with her followers stepped, humming, in among the Swedish women of the camp, there was uproar and alarm, because for two days they had sat by their wagons without food. The last provisions had been delivered to the sutlers and divided among the soldiers. Then she stepped forward to the first corporal she happened on and set her hands on her hips.

"Are n't you ashamed," said she, "to let my women starve, when in spite of all you can't get along without them?"

"*Your* women? Who are you?"

She pointed to her bracelet. "I am Lina Andersdaughter, the Queen of the Marauders, and now take five men and follow us!"

He looked toward his captain, the reckless Jacob

Elfsberg; he looked at her pretty face and at his men. How the line surrounded her with their muskets, and the women armed themselves with whip-handles and pokers! At night, when the light of the camp-fire tinged the heavens, the king, inquisitive, got into his saddle. As the wild throng came back with well-laden wagons and oxen and sheep, the troops cheered louder than ever: "Hurrah for King Charles! Hurrah for Queen Caroline!"

The women thronged about the king's horse, so that the lackeys had to hold them back, and Lina Andersdaughter went to him to shake hands with him. But he thereupon rose in his stirrups, and shouted over the women's heads to the corporal and the five soldiers: "That's well maraudered, boys!"

From that moment she would never hear the king named, and whenever she met a man, she flung her sharpest abuse right in his face, whether he was plain private or general. When Malcomb Björkman, the young guardsman—who, however, was already famous for his exploits and wounds—held out his hand to her, she scornfully laid in it her ragged, empty purse; and she was never angrier than when she heard General Meyerfelt whistling as he rode before his dragoons, or recognized Colonel Grothusen's yellow-brown cheeks and raven-black wig. But if a wounded wretch lay beside the road, she offered him the last drop from her tin flask and lifted him into her wagon. Frost and scratches soon calloused her cheeks. High on the baggage wagon she sat with the butt of a whip and commanded all the wild camp-followers, loose women, lawful wives, and thievish fellows that streamed to them from east and west. When at night the flare of a fire arose toward heaven, the soldiers knew that Queen Caroline was out on a plundering raid.

Days and years went by. Then, after the jolly winter quarters in Saxony, when the troops were marching toward the Ukraine, the king commanded that all women should leave the army.

"Teach him to mind his own affairs!" muttered Lina Andersdaughter, and she very tranquilly drove on.

But when the army came to the Beresina, there was murmuring and lamenting among the women. They gathered around Lina Andersdaughter's cart and wrung their hands and lifted their babies on high.

"See what you have to answer for! The troops have already crossed the river and broken all the bridges behind them. They have left us as prey to the Cossacks."

She sat with her whip on her knee and with high boots, but on her wrist still gleamed the silver chain with its turquoise. All the more violently did the terrified women sob and moan around her, and from the closed baggage wagons, which were like boxes, crept out painted and powdered Saxon hussies. Some of them, none the less, had satin gowns and gold necklaces. From all sides came women she had never seen before.

"Dirty wenches!" muttered she. "Now at last I have a chance to see the smuggled goods that the captains and lieutenants brought along in their wagons. What have you to do among my poor baggage crones? But now we all come to know what a man amounts to when his haversack is getting light."

Then they caught hold of her clothes, and called upon her as if she alone could seal their fate.

"Is there no one," she asked, "who knows the psalm, 'When I am borne through the Vale of Death'? Sing it, sing it!"

Some of the women struck up the psalm with choked and nearly whispering voices, but the others rushed down to the river, hunted out boats and wreckage from the bridges, and rowed themselves across. Each and every one who had a husband or a beloved in the army had hoped that even at the last she would be taken along and hidden; but all the worst women of the rabble, who belonged neither to this man nor to that, stood with their rags or their tasteless, ridiculous gowns in a ring around Lina Andersdaughter. Meanwhile swarms of Cossacks, who had crossed the river to snap up any straggling marauders, were sneaking up through the bushes on their hands and knees.

Then her heart failed her, and she stepped down from the wagon.

"Poor children!" she said, and patted the hussies on the cheek. "Poor children, I will not desert you. But now—devil take me!—do you pray to God that He will make your blood-red sins white, for I have nothing else to offer you than to shame the men and die a hero's death."

She opened the wagon chest and hunted out from among her plunder some pikes and Polish sabres, which she put into the hands of the softly singing women. Thereupon she herself grasped a musket without powder or shot, and set herself among the others around the cart to wait. So they stood in the sunset light on the highest part of the shore.

Then the women on the river saw the Cossacks rush forward to the cart and cut down one after another of them with the idea that they were men in disguise. They wanted to turn their boats, and soldiers sprang down from their ranks to the water and opened fire.

"Hurrah for King Charles," they cried with a thousand intermingled voices; "and hurrah—No, it's too late. Look, look! There is Queen Caroline dying a virgin in the midst of the harlots with a musket in her hand!"

Mazeppa and His Ambassador

IN a splendidly decorated sleeping apartment stood a high bed with plumes at the corners. Behind the half-drawn bed-curtain lay an old man of sixty-three with the coverlet pulled up under his beard, his long white hair spread over the pillow. His whole forehead was hidden under a plaster. It was Mazeppa.

Beside the bed, among cups of medicine on the carpet, lay several books of Latin and French poetry, and at the door a little wizened priest carried on a whispered conversation with two green-clad messengers from Czar Peter.

" He scarcely comprehends your words," whispered the priest, giving a painfully searching look toward the sick man. "He even lies speechless for long periods. Who could have imagined that the old man with his joy of life would suddenly lie on his death-bed?"

"Ivan Stefanovitch," one of the strangers said with raised voice, approaching the bed, "our magnanimous czar, your lord, sends you greeting. Do you remember? Those three Cossacks of yours who stole off to him and related that you secretly planned a rebellion against his over-lordship, he has had them fettered and returned to you as gifts of friendship. Ivan Stefanovitch, he relies on your loyalty."

Mazeppa's eyes opened feebly and his lips moved, but he was only able to utter an unintelligible whisper.

"We understand you," cried the messengers, speaking all at once. "We understand you. You greet him and thank him for his favor, and we are to say to him that you are bowed under your years and that you have already turned all your thoughts to that which is not of this world."

"I fear," murmured the priest to them aside, "that here it will soon be over."

The messengers nodded sadly, and backed out of the sleeping apartment.

As soon as they were out, the priest bolted the door.

"They have gone," he said.

Mazeppa sat up and tore the plaster from his brow, throwing it far across the carpet. His dark wide-open eyes gleamed and twinkled. A flush rose and paled on his cheeks, and under the handsomely curving nose shone teeth as white and fresh as a youth's. He tossed away the coverlet and, fully clad from tip to toe in long-coat and boots with spurs, he sprang from the bed, and jestingly pinched the priest in the ribs.

"You little rascal priest, you! You vagabond! This time we did n't manage badly. In Moscow they will believe that old Mazeppa is lying helpless and harmless. God be gracious to his pious soul! Haha-hey! You little rascal priest, you! You arch-hypocrite!"

The priest laughed dryly. He was a deposed bishop from Bulgaria, and his round head with its short nose and deep-sunken eyes was like a skull.

Mazeppa grew still livelier.

"Mazeppa dying! Ay, ask his mistresses! Only ask them! No, my great Muscovite czar, you, now I am going to live and be quits with you."

"The czar suspects you, my lord, but he wishes to disarm you with magnanimity. He can be like that."

"And I should have been conquered by it, if one night at table, when we were drunk, he had not struck me on the ear. I value my ear as he does his, and an insult I can never forgive. It sticks in the soul and frets and gnaws. If I am not a king by birth, I am one in soul. And what does he want with his German coats on my splendid Cossacks? Now to business! Relate your adventures, you liar!"

"My lord, dressed as a mendicant monk, I went forth on my way to the Swedish headquarters. Sometimes I set a tavern lass on my knee and a can on the table corner, but when I peeped down and saw the toes sticking out of my ragged shoes, I thought to myself: This is Mazeppa's ambassador!"

"Very good, but how did you find the dandy?"

"The dandy?"

"To be sure. His Swedish Majesty, King Carolus. Don't you believe he dandifies as much with
his grimy rags as any French prince of scented
water with his silk stockings? And he possesses that
wonderful Northern recklessness which continually
snaps a riding-whip and cries: 'Rubbish! that's
nothing! It's no matter!'—He has never been able
to grieve for a misfortune longer than overnight.
That has been the secret of his power. Woe to him
and his fate when he sits up night after night without sleep! I am curious to see him. I long for it.
But tell on!"

"First I found him in wig and armor on the
tavern lass's neckcloth or pinafore, and on the
glass from which I drank, and on the icing I ate,
and on table-cloths and chest-lids and tobacco-boxes
and market-booths. No one spoke of anything else
than of him, and the children arranged themselves
and played at Swedish divine service. The old peasants called him the sword-pope of the Protestants
chosen by God Himself, and took off their hats in
speaking of him."

"Ah yes, but how did you find him himself,
when you came to headquarters?"

"I warn you. I predict misfortunes. I saw an omen.
I found him puffed up and haughty of spirit."

"As a great personality of whom the world begins to disapprove."

" Marlborough, after an audience in Saxony, left his camp with a shrug of the shoulders, and sovereigns begin to laugh at him behind his back. His own generals have grown weary."

" He has become a hero of the rabble, you think. Well, even then, that's the sort of man I need to gather the wild hordes. If you do not assure me that you have seen him eat and drink, I cannot believe that he is a living human being. Then I should have to say : The young prince of the Swedes fell in the tumult of victory at Narva, but his shade rides ever on before his troops. Snow falls and falls, and drums rattle and rumble, and the thinning battalions do not know and do not understand whither he leads them. When the enemy recognize him in the powder-smoke, they lower their muskets in superstitious awe and dare not shoot, and he does not notice that sometimes he cuts down men who are making ready to fall on their knees. Hired assassins throw down their weapons at sight of him and give themselves up—and he lets them go unpunished. Don't talk to him about states and treaties! He does not fight for possessions as men do; he wields the sword of God to revenge and reward. What did he require just now as the reward of victory at the conclusion of peace? Money? Land? Of Austria he required a councillor who had slandered him at table and a swarm of Russian soldiers who had fled in over the border—and free-

dom of conscience for the Protestants. Of Prussia
he demanded the imprisonment of a colonel who
had given counsel to the czar, and banishment for
a writer who had cavilled at his stipulations against
the Pietists. Of Saxony he demanded Patkull and
all Swedish renegades, but freedom for the Princes
Sobieski and all Saxons who had gone over to the
Swedes. King August himself he compelled to pack
up the old Polish regalia in a velvet trunk and send
them to King Stanislaus. And now, since he has deposed King August in Poland, he wants to depose
the czar or challenge him to a duel, but their crowns
and governments he would not even take as a gift.
Since antiquity no stranger man has held a sword
or a sceptre."

Mazeppa, while he was speaking, grasped one
of the bedposts so hard that the plumes of the
silken canopy shook.

But the other lifted three fingers and replied:
"I have warned you. Everything that he touches
he dedicates to misery and death. Yet he is the pa-
tron saint of adventurers. He has raised adventure
to stability and greatness. You too, my lord, are an
adventurer, and I myself am the worst adventurer
of you all. Therefore I will be compliant."

He lowered his hand and drew near with disrespectful familiarity. "You, Ivan Stefanovitch!
Have you never wondered that I directed my steps
to your particular door?"

"You were driven from your episcopal see because of your unfaith and your pranks."

"It really amounted to a little pilfering of small import. There were on the ikon-stand a couple of emeralds—"

"Which you replaced with bits of glass and in all secrecy sold, so that you might live more bountifully and in a manner more worthy a servant of the church."

"Let us say no more about it!—So I heard of Mazeppa, the former page at Johann Casimir's court, who in his powdered wig was attentive to the wayward sex so long that a jealous husband at last bound him naked on a horse's back and drove him forth into the wilderness. And there he built up a kingdom of adventurers. Saint Andrew guarded you, Mazeppa. I needed a little master who would be ashamed to strike off a good head, who would let me read my Greek and my Machiavelli in peace, and to whom I might say: 'Agreed, old fellow! It's all a shadow play, even this that you are lord and I servant.' Therefore I came to you. My adventurer's blood cannot bear to sit still, and I weary of your wine mixed with water, for you are a great miser, Mazeppa; but as you are now pondering a financial transaction in musket-balls, I follow you. And as the Swedish king no longer listens to his generals or to the beseeching letters from his grandmother and his people, and comes hither by the most perilous and impossible roads, he wishes to accept your offer of an alliance. With you and your Cossacks he will march against your lord. Here are the papers."

The priest shook off his cope and stood in Cossack dress with pistols in his girdle, and from his bosom he drew forth some folded papers.

Mazeppa grew pale, seized them, and held them pressed long to his mouth, while he sank his forehead and bowed as before the invisible image of a saint.

"Drums, drums!" he stammered in agitation.

But when the priest had got to the door, he checked him.

"No, don't let the drums strike up before tomorrow."

Thereupon he went to a plain wooden table in a little side-room, and sat down over his account books. He had his bailiffs summoned, and calculated and calculated, and prescribed greater economy in the milk department. Half a merry knight of the roads and half a learned but thrifty proprietor of lands, he finally superintended the packing of his many trunks and boxes. Sometimes he bent down and helped. Last of all, next morning he put on an old-fashioned and much-adorned Cossack costume. Impetuous and active, he sprang up from his chair as soon as he had sat down, but he remained standing before the mirror for some little time, now and then running his delicate, small white hand through his beard.

As soon as the music was heard, he mounted to the saddle and kept his charger constantly at a gallop.

.   .   .   .

When, after a time, he had come to the Swedes and was riding one morning through a flurry of snow in the king's retinue, the priest, as if by accident, pulled up his horse alongside him. Round about the troops marched past, sprinkled with grime, their weapons and cannon covered to prevent rusting. Baggage wagons clattered along with their weight of provision sacks and sick men, and sometimes with a covered coffin. Last were driven massed herds of cattle. Drunken Zaporogeans, prancing Cossacks, and eagerly drumming Polish Wallachians rode in green and red cloaks and with high brass helmets on which bells were tinkling. Some were brandishing tufted spears and bows or long flint-locks inlaid with silver and ivory. Others played on a sort of wailing wooden pipe. It was a colorful, legendary sort of march, that went over untrodden and unknown forest paths, over frozen marshes, and under snowy fir trees toward the mysterious East.

"Mazeppa," the priest began in a low voice, "you promised to come to the Swedes with thirty thousand Cossacks, but hardly four thousand followed you."

Mazeppa kept his roan at a gallop, and nodded in silence, and the priest never wearied of his gibes.

"Day before yesterday half of these went off. Yesterday more still. Soon you will have barely a couple of hundred fellows, barely the servants who watch over your trunks and the two barrels with your money. Your uprising was betrayed, your cities are burned, your few faithful men nailed on boards and thrown into rivers. Soon you will be nothing but a gorgeous knight in the train of the Swedish king."

As Mazeppa was still, the priest continued: "To-day I too will abandon you, because the small beer of the Swedes tastes sour to me, and my toes stick out too far from my shoes. Your ambassador needs a richer lord. Farewell, Ivan Stefanovitch!"

Mazeppa replied, "As long as I have still my head and my philosophy, I remain Mazeppa. While my Cossacks turned and broke away, I had the hetman staff and mace carried before me, and I rode on to the king as if I had come in front of Xerxes' millions. And he, with his impoverished realm, his discontented generals, and his sinking sun, came toward me like the most fortunate among princes. What does it trouble him and me how many ride behind us? He has had enough of kingly honor, and wishes also to be a chosen man of God. He thinks of history as a man in love does of his sweetheart: he would not win her favor by his birth but by his person. If we two, he and I, should one day be the last survivors and sit in an earthen hut on the steppe, we should still continue to talk philosophy and treat each other as at a coronation dinner."

"You speak of his sinking sun. You have seen the omen, even you! He can no longer talk without boasting like a baggage driver."

"It is easy to be modest as long as everybody praises."

Mazeppa threw back his white-haired head with lofty contempt, and galloped forward to the king, who raised his hat and bowed and bowed again in his saddle.

Round about several of the generals joked as loudly as possible so that the king might hear them.

"When I come to Moscow," said Anders Lagerkrona, "I shall mend the seat of my trousers with the czar's night-cap."

"Pshaw!" answered Axel Sparre. "There is an old prophecy that a Sparre will some day be governor at the Kremlin."

"This way!" cried the ensigns. "Shoot down any one who dares to hinder such a great and exalted prince from marching forward wherever he chooses."

The king smiled and hummed: "Russia must run, Russia must run." But when the speakers were no longer within his hearing, they were transformed and became absent and melancholy.

"Your Majesty!" cried Mazeppa in crisp Latin and with kindling eyes, "Your Majesty's conquering arms go on so far that one fine morning we shall have hardly eight miles more to Asia."

"As to that the authorities used to disagree," answered the king, moved, but hunting for the Latin words, his gaze fettered by Mazeppa's white and pleasingly mobile hands. "If the border is not far off, we must go there, so that we can say we were also in Asia."

The voices died away, and the priest reined in his horse.

"Asia!" he muttered, "Asia does n't lie in the middle of Europe. But ride on, ride on with you, my adventurous lords! I have changed my name and dress so many times that none of you Swedes will ever notice what I was. But do not forget that it was the ragged monk, the vagabond, Mazeppa's ambassador, who by his cunning negotiations laid his blue-frozen finger on your and your demi-god's fate and directed you into the wildernesses. You are right, King Carolus, and you, Mazeppa. Everything depends at the last on individual men."

It snowed and snowed, and he sat motionless on his lean horse, while the battalions marched by, silent and impatient. When the last soldiers turned and looked back at the solitary, unknown rider, and saw his little compressed death-skull head, they were seized with fear and hastened their steps.

Fifty Years Later

WHEN the porridge had been eaten and the branch candles of tallow which shone on both sides of the pewter dish stood more than half burnt out, the chairs were drawn close to the fire. The manor-house was one of the smallest and poorest in the district, but in the evening no poverty was visible there. The straw lay soft as a carpet over the floor planks, fresh juniper had been set beside the dark and streaming windows, the gleam from the open fireplace tinted with yellow the whitewashed wooden walls. Recently, too, a goblet of sherry had been offered about. All knew, furthermore, that the most festive time of the evening was now come. Even the two servant-girls, who wore to-day their best holiday jackets, cleared the table as slowly as possible and hid themselves, waiting, by the door, for now old Captain Höök, a Charles man, brought out his tobacco-box and drew in the chair of honor to the middle place before the fire. It was, however, only after he had unlaced his brogans and laid his crossed feet with their thick white stockings on the fender to warm them thoroughly that he seemed to feel himself fully at ease. To be sure, he alone had carried on the conversation almost all the evening, and now at last spoke of Ehrencrona, who had received the Order of the Sword from King Frederick and never could wear it otherwise than in a

snuff-box. But in the same moment he became stern
and reflective, and slipped into a new history. It
was, indeed, alleged that he generally lied roundly,
but nobody cared about that, for the principal thing
was that he should keep on with his tales.

He was already an elderly man with a frost-bitten
lump of a nose. Both his hair, which was brushed
forward, and his moustaches, which were twisted
youthfully, had always been so light that nobody
noticed whether the years had made one or another
strand still whiter. And he sat on the chair in his
scanty, buttoned-up coat as upright as formerly.
Without any transition he began in his usual way.

Yes, the autumn when I went astray in the woods
I was certainly badly off. I mean the autumn down
in Severia. Lewenhaupt had just made us destroy
our last wagons, and was leading us along the Soza
River to find a ford, so that when on the other side
we might be able to grope our way forward to the
king's army; but many foot-soldiers had stopped to
plunder the wagons. I was an ensign at that time.
Together with several others, I was sent back by
Major-General Stackelberg to master the fellows,
but the Russians were already among them, and I
scarcely knew in the darkness how I could manage
to save myself across the river. When, dripping with
water and mud, I stood in the heather on the farther
bank, I stumbled on a dragoon private. He was

from my own regiment, and we called him Long
Jan, because he was one of the tallest and slimmest
lads that ever lifted a Swedish blade. His chest was
narrow, but his hands were large. His arms and legs
seemed to have hardly a single muscle, and there
was not a particle of down on his lean and simple
face — a face any one would know again by the
slanting eyes and the thick under lip. — God knows
why he had ever been taken along. — But in that
moment I was as glad to get sight of that lanky
spectre as if I had met a sweetheart, and at random,
but still as fast as we were able, we turned our steps
into the forest.

At the start we leaped along so as to get warm
and dry our clothes, and not until dawn did we lie
down to sleep.

For many days after, we struggled on through
the woods and swamps, and our clothes were still
as wet as before. Once we took them off and hung
them on a branch, but in the misty autumn air this
helped but little, and we were only so much the
colder when we succeeded, with great difficulty, in
pulling them on again. As to our boots, there was
no talk of getting them off. They dried temporarily
during our progress, but soon became as completely
soaked in a marsh, and one shower of rain followed
another.

I had with me a bit of meat and a piece of black
bread, which I divided with my silent and, as it

seemed, submissive brother in misfortune, and after that we chewed leaves and twigs and anything we could find. Hunger, though, was not nearly such a gnawing plague as the continual chilly dampness, which made our teeth chatter even in our sleep. As our strength failed, our joints stiffened, so that we could not move them without pain.

One evening we heard an unexpected barking, and for a moment I realized that I flushed with joy, but immediately after came hesitation, with thoughts of danger. I turned to the opposite direction, and Long Jan followed me, silently as always, but when we had walked awhile, I noticed that we only came much nearer to the barking. Then I took the soldier by the arm and turned again toward the other side, but, similarly drawn by an irresistible inner attraction, we kept walking so that we came nearer and nearer to the dog. When I finally let go of Long Jan's arm, he still went on.

"Halt!" I called after him, excruciated with the damp and yet little minded to go straight into a hostile place where most likely axes would be the first things to greet us.

"Halt, halt!" repeated Long Jan obediently, but in spite of that continued to go on.

Then I raced up to him and caught him by the belt. As long as I held him, he stood quite straight and motionless, but as soon as I let go my hold, he went on.

" Halt! Stand!" I thundered, raging as if I had
found myself under fire, and dumbfounded at such
an abrupt and insubordinate obstinacy in a soldier
who had learned our iron-hard discipline. " Will you
not obey your own ensign, fellow? "

" Halt! Stand!" he repeated, but continued on as
before, as though no longer master of his own feet.

"Come on, then, in Jesus' name!" I burst out;
"we can't get it worse than it has been already. But
now you have made yourself an ensign, though you
are barely one of the rank and file, and me a common soldier. Be so good as to lay that up in your
memory!"

Long Jan answered nothing, neither perhaps did
he hear me. I resigned myself to following him, and
after a few minutes we came out on a level clearing
with many barns and houses. Right beside us stood
a great wooden building with many stories. The sunset glittered on the raindrops which hung on the
cementing moss between the rough logs of the wall,
and the window-panes glimmered as if lighted by
countless chandeliers; but the door was locked, and
no smoke came from the chimneys. The house was
as a corpse with closed mouth and without breath,
but with eyes hideously lighted by a cold gleam
from without. Tied to a stake behind a straw-stack
that had crookedly collapsed, a lean dog crept back
and forth along the ground and wagged his tail
when he saw us.

Long Jan went straight forward to the door and banged on it, but no one opened. Then he drew his blade and smashed in the nearest window with the hilt. At that moment we heard from within a frightened woman's voice shouting again and again to some one who was called Varvara. The broken glass fell tinkling, the leaden frame was bent on all sides into long hanging strips. Then running steps were heard in the house. The next moment the door was opened by a well-grown and stately serving-maid with a broad, light braid of hair down her back and a multitude of jingling silver pieces on her black hood and red and green bodice. In her hand she held an unlighted lantern, which in her terror she had presumably seized from habit.

"We'll do no harm," I said, trying as well as I could to explain myself in the bothersome speech. "Heaven forbid such a horror, most gracious young lady! But we are nearly starved and above all we require—"

"Dry clothes," broke in Long Jan, shivering.

That was the first time in the long wandering that I had heard this peculiar chap utter anything of his own accord, and then he had had the impudence into the bargain to take the word out of my mouth. When the girl turned around and left the door half open, he did indeed stand aside to give me place, but I remarked irritably: "The Herr Ensign will surely go first."

"God deliver me from any such thing," he answered, and smacked his boot-heels together. But, partly cheered by the peaceful reception, partly still angry, I added in such a sharp tone of voice that he could not doubt my seriousness: "Or else devil take the ensign!"

Then he dragged his long legs in through the door ahead of me and, as the house had no entry, we found ourselves at once in a large hall, where a heating-stove of variegated porcelain rose like a tower to the middle of the ceiling. Along the walls, which consisted entirely of rough-hewn logs caulked with moss, stood several black-varnished chairs, and on a shelf gleamed pots of pewter.

The serving-maid ran away and called Varvara, who finally appeared, dazed and frightened, in the farthest corner of the darkened hall. There the two girls tarried, whispering anxiously.

After a while, however, they grew easier; and they could not keep from giving each other a look and feeling more accommodating when I unexpectedly called them "gracious young ladies," and accordingly feigned not to understand that they were poor serfs. That was a drop of warm oil on the hard wax, and they now told us that the noble masters had gone away two weeks ago at the report of the Swedes' approach. They separately assured us that in the whole house, yes, in the whole place, there was nothing left of any value whatever, but that

they would gladly do their best to serve the strangers.

Varvara had pretty teeth, but she was too small
and fat and black-fleeced, and after a while she let
out such a piercing laugh that I was annoyed. The
yellow-haired girl, who was called Katarina, on the
other hand, I could not keep from pinching on the
ear in fun, when she brought in wood to the stove.
Meanwhile Long Jan had, without further ceremony, pulled off his tattered blue coat, and as he
had neither shirt nor vest, he soon stood naked to
the waist in all his miserable leanness, so that no
one could keep serious any longer — no one but
himself. Never had I seen a cheerful twitch pass
over that stolid face. After we had each of us got a
sheepskin coat and stilled the worst hunger with
a little mashed turnip and kvass, we laid us down
by the stove with broadswords between our knees,
and I ventured to order the Herr Ensign to watch
with me alternately, in case any one could possibly
have any evil in mind. I also forbade the two serving-maids to leave the hall, and reading my prayers
aloud in Swedish, entrusted us to the Almighty.

But! — The Almighty lets us human beings now
and then give each other surprises. When no one
addressed me, I went on sleeping for hours, till I
was waked by a piercing warmth, which at other
times I should have called a pain, but which now
at least reminded me that I was no longer a wan-

dering skeleton, but a living man again. And still,
who will not understand my terror when I saw the
heated hall dark and empty, and heard shrieks and
clamor from the room adjoining.

I at once took my broadsword and sprang to the
door. There I saw a blazing cook-stove, and before
it stood Long Jan in a checkered dressing-gown of
bright silk and high-heeled shoes. Obviously the
rascal had also skill in foraging, for a fowl sat already on the spit, and in a bubbling pot he threw,
higgledy-piggledy, everything he could gather from
the half-sobbing girls. In the midst of this he took
out of a broken cupboard one splendid glass after
another, smashed it to pieces on the edge of the fireplace, and threw the fragments on the floor. I went
forward and took the lanky loon around the body,
but was not in a condition to remove him from the
spot. His incredible obstinacy gave a giant's strength
to his slim body, and I was still exhausted by all the
sufferings we had gone through. When he turned
his face toward me, his eyes were glassily fixed, but
I noticed a whiff of wine. Quite taken aback, I now
let him go. He was drunk.

The yellow-haired Katarina, who really seemed
much more amused than frightened, meanwhile
came up to me and told me in her soft voice — ho!
old Captain Höök was young in those days and a
pretty fellow — . . . Where were we now? Oh, yes,
she said that he had gone from room to room,

hunted through everything, and broken the vases and clocks. Finally, in the cellar he had searched through all the vaults except one—except one—one—one, to which the key was lost, she added hurriedly.

"But you, poor fellow, may also need something," she said to me, and pushed me into another room, which might have been called palatial. Around the walls hung woven greenish tapestries, on which Diana hunted a deer. The most splendid garments lay spread out over the slippery and shining floor; the armchairs were gilded, and beside a dish in the middle of the table stood mugs which were not filled with sickening kvass, not even with ale, but with a clear, yellow wine.

I, too, now lost my reason at the vision of all this magnificence, and my mistrust was somewhat eased because the two girls themselves seemed heartily delighted at having the chance to waste and destroy. They, too, felt themselves on hostile ground in the house where they had formerly had to go about as obedient and humble thralls. It was for them a moment of victory to be able to destroy the delicacies which they had never tasted, to throw themselves into proud reclining-chairs before which they had been forced to bow to the floor, and to trample on the costly garments which they had been scarcely deemed worthy to touch. They selected for me a coat of stiff cloth-of-silver, which had tails spread out with whalebone so that they were like a swelling skirt; and I got stockings and red shoes on the feet from which that evening I had ripped the boots with difficulty. Just the same, I did not dare to throw off the broadsword from my body, because I could not altogether put aside all doubts as to an ambush.

With the wholly childlike frankness of a little heart-subduer Katarina clapped her hands, which in fact were neither white nor soft, and confessed that she felt really jolly, since with me, who was of the same class, they could be as they chose; whereas before the ensign, who was a fine gentleman, they always had to be careful.

I sat down to the table in one of the armchairs, which was nearly buried under my glittering coat tails, and on either side I invited one of the girls, and clinked glasses with them and drank.

"The Herr Ensign is of very high extraction," said I. "He will end as, it may be—yes, a councillor of state."—That was up to then my most unseasonable remark, because people who wield the pen— "But the gracious young ladies know that the highborn sometimes, by an unlucky hap, may be born both foolish and simple-witted, and it is therefore that I regard myself obliged sometimes to screw up his wits a little into the right groove, so to speak."

I have always had a fault as a soldier. I have

been able both to hack and to hew at the right time, but in the very act I have been too good-natured and accommodating. Therefore, too, I let Long Jan rummage in the kitchen however he chose, while I myself ate and drank to my heart's content. But with every gulp I felt how the wine kept on taking away my wits. That I did not become more forward than I was toward my merry hostesses depended less on the virtue with which the Almighty has sometimes wisely endowed beauty than on the hardships I had gone through, which quickly enough changed the wine into a sleeping potion. Reflection told me that I should push the mug aside, but, in addition to the distress of the last days, the wine was irresistible. I fell asleep sitting with hands crossed over the pommel of my sword.

"Now I hear tiptoeing steps," said I to myself in my dreams. "They are coming yet nearer behind my chair. Now I must draw steel. But what's that! I can move neither hand nor foot, though I am so much awake that I can see Diana and her greyhounds on the tapestry. All the air is dancing vapor, which rustles around the faces of the prattling girls and the flames of the waxlights. I am helplessly drunk. Of that there is no doubt, but now I am asleep again, and there's a tiptoeing behind my chair. A hidden serf stands there with his axe. Even now he's lifting it. The next instant I shall feel it as a lightning-flash through my head—and then all's over. Why won't the chair stand still? I can't hold myself on, if you jump. Whoa, there, Whiteface! I'd have you know there's nothing in the world that can scare me. But to hold myself on, sitting backward on the loins of one of the king's galloping chargers—that I can't. . . . Bang! Look there! Now I'm lying there in the middle of the stone pavement. . . . Fie! What are you laughing for? And then the vault in the cellar. . . . Why did you say just now that there was one . . . one . . . one two, one two, one two, lads in blue, two three, in grief and glee, three four, their land adore, four five, and boldly strive, five six, for Carolus Rex."

Finally I raised myself on my aching elbow and sang the whole of Psalm Number Six from the first to the last verse, and that with such a powerful voice that it seemed to me as if everything evil must have shrunk away in terror.

Many times have I treated myself to a booze, but never one that gave me worse agony. When I awoke in the morning, I sprang at once from the floor, where I was lying at full length on my back by the chair. I was still so sure of an ambush that I was wholly surprised when I found both the girls sleeping on a sheepskin under the table, on which a light was burning in the socket. Out in the kitchen I heard strange voices and came there upon an old

one-eyed witch who was called Natalia, and a shaggy
serf who was called Makar, and who to the smallest
detail resembled the man of whom I had dreamed.
They confessed that they had kept themselves hidden in the attic, but had now crept out when they
noted that we intended no harm. They related that
in the neighboring village there had also been several families during the night, but that at the report
of our coming these had straightway loaded their
belongings on a wagon and driven off at a gallop.

For the first time now I could honestly feel myself free from all apprehension, and with joy I went
back to the hall, bent over the girls, and kissed
Katarina both vigorously and long.

She woke up and laughed and turned over on
her side to sleep further, but I kissed her yet again,
and then she defended herself and jumped up, brisk
and cheerful.

"You are a fine girl, Katarina, and I don't need
to mistrust you any longer," said I. "Fetch me a
little fresh water now and some salt."

While she came and went to set out my breakfast I often took her about her none too slender
waist, and kissed her. At last she kissed me back,
too, and leaned against the cloth-of-silver on my
breast, and cried and laughed alternately. We went
back and forth through the many rooms, but at a
certain door she always checked herself, because
back of it the ensign had been pleased to go to rest

in one of the noble master's own down beds. Finally
we sat down in a yellow reclining-chair, and I took
her on my knee and wound her thick plait about
my wrist. It was no falsehood either when I whispered into her ear that my hardened soldier's heart
had seldom beaten more warmly.

I think with regret of the happy days that followed, and rather than recall them hour by hour,
I leave it to you, especially to the young ones, to
make use of your imaginations. Still, I always set
Makar every evening as a guard before the house
and never left off my broadsword. Sometimes Katarina in play would pull it from me, hold it out with
both hands on the hilt, and go tramping through
the rooms, while the autumn rain beat on the window-panes. The loosely suspended tapestries were
set in motion by the draught she made, so that the
pictures seemed to breathe and bow. There was an
echo every time when, with her black hat pulled
down like an old-fashioned morion, she shouted her
"Forward!" Then I built barricades of tables and
gilded leather chairs, until in the midst of the assault
I leaped forth and overpowered both the amazon
and her weapon. I had no longer any thought of my
comrades, who meanwhile were perhaps hungering
and bleeding, and my only wish was always to stay
where I now found myself.

Katarina always smelt of lavender. We had
barred off a corner room for our share of the house,

and thither she carried her big chest, which was
entirely plastered over with blue-checkered paper.
This contained her clothes and other belongings,
and it never was opened without filling the room
with lavender scent. It was her favorite diversion to
lie on her knees in front of the chest, pull out all
her garments with a multitude of small boxes and
receptacles, and then pack them in again with the
greatest care. When I found that too tedious, or the
room sometimes grew too cold, I persuaded her to
go out with me to the great hall, where we sat down
by the stove. Then I tried to fasten her attention
by telling the life history of my long broadsword,
which I did not shorten by a word. I knew for sure
that it had the death of eleven men on its conscience,
and on my arm I could show scars both of bullet-
grazes and cuts. But she did not ask much about
them. If I told the saga of Prince Gideon of Maxi-
brander, she grew impatient. "That is something
that never happened," she said, and began eagerly
to sew together green and red scallops of cloth on
two fur boots, which were clearly intended to become a masterpiece of their kind.

The Herr Ensign lived in a continual booze
and showed for the women the most open disdain.
Katarina found this, too, very fortunate, she confessed, because it was so hard for a person in her
class to reprove so high a gentleman, if he became
attentive. One morning, in the midst of this, Herr

Ensign called to mind the locked vault down in the cellar, which we had both forgotten. He went straightway there, and Katarina grew so beside herself with alarm that she could not conceal it. Pressing both my hands, she begged and prayed me to hold him back, and so completely was I then the prisoner of my heart that, although all my previous doubts awoke to life again, I let myself be forced to seek help for her.

We went down after Herr Ensign into the lighted cellar, where he was already absorbed in breaking open a locked wooden door.

"Let that alone!" I commanded him, and he assented, but kept on, nevertheless, with his immovable stubbornness, breaking and prying.

Then I excused myself before my wailing followers with the plea that a common soldier such as I could not command an officer—and at that moment the door gave way.

Within the vault a lamp burned under a gilded Russian Madonna, and beside a table with various sorts of food stood a made-up bed. Between the bed and the wall moved something round and dark, which, when we went nearer, showed itself to be the bent back of an old man. When the old man saw himself unearthed, he crept forward, embraced Herr Ensign's knees, and begged and conjured him to give pardon. He admitted that he was the mas-

ter of the house and that he had concealed himself
after he had sent away his family, but promised to
be our most humble servant if we had pity on his
life.

"Be easy!" answered I, and helped the tottering old fellow up from the ground. "But then you
shall be our drummer when we go to table."

When we ate that evening in the great hall, Herr
Ensign as usual had the splendid chair, and beside
him sat I and Katarina. At a table a little to the left
stood the white-bearded and trembling master of
the house with a brass mortar, and Makar with two
pot-lids. They made their cooking utensils thunder
in time to the melancholy folk-songs which ugly old
Natalia sang, as she sat between the two on the edge
of the table.

I don't know why, but her wailing voice gradually robbed me of all my brisk gayety, and I began
to think of my thousands upon thousands of absent
comrades. I had between my vest and shirt a whole
packet of letters which anxious relatives had written
to their dear ones in the field, and which they had
begged me to deliver to them, if I ever should get
on to the king's camp. I drew the letters from my
bosom. They were not secret, for I had received
many of them unsealed on my last evening at Riga.
I pushed the candlestick nearer, eyed by chance a
letter written in uncertain style, and read:

Give this into the hands of John.

My dere son:—

Receive thy father's blessing, though separated from him by both land and watter, and right nere the heathenish parts of the urth, where crocodiles, scorpions and other harmful crawling things strike fere. . . .

I drew a wry face, mayhap, but I felt my sacred responsibility, and my mind grew all the heavier. I noticed that Katarina pressed my foot more energetically than usual, but I pressed back and thought that it was only a love token. When at last I had laid the letters together, I discovered that she sat quite pale, and could not take any wine or food. I bent a little to one side, so that she might be able to whisper, but the old gentleman at the table stared at her unexpectedly, while he the more eagerly let his blows ring on the brass mortar, which he held out like a bell.

I remained in doubt and did not know rightly what trick I should invent. Then I trumped up the excuse that I was freezing. I went into the sleeping-room and, after pretending to search in the dark awhile, called, "Katarina, my girl, where have you put the sheepskin coat?"

When she came in, she rushed straight up to me and threw herself on my neck with stifled sobbing.

"You didn't hear," she whispered, "that Makar just now in the midst of the noise told the master that he had got together more than sixty of the serfs, and that, as soon as he gives them a signal by breaking the window in the great hall, they are coming in to cut down both of you."

I remained fairly cool and sought to console her, but, choked with weeping, she told how she herself at the beginning was with the rest in wanting to entice us into a trap, but that she now no longer believed she could live on a day without me.

I pressed her to me hard and kissed her burning mouth and throbbing temples, and yet in that moment a strange repose fell upon my soul. My acquaintance with her became all at once nearly as something in the past. I have since, in my gray years, regretted this bitterly and wondered at myself, who at that especial moment had so little to give her. Reading the letter, the sudden danger . . . I don't know fully which was most to blame. To be sure, it depended on both.

"If I could take you along," I stammered.

She shook her head, as I could very clearly perceive in the half-light from the open door, and drew me instead to the window, where she begged me to steal off. Then I lashed myself into a sort of pretended anger, threw her from me over the polished floor, and cried with raised voice, "For whom do you take me, lass?"

With that I drew my broadsword and went out into the great hall, and when Herr Ensign got sight of me so, he rose from the table directly and also drew.

Then the master raised the mortar to throw it at the misty window-pane, but we stood right in front of him with our weapons, and his shaking knees became all the more bowed. He grew shorter and shorter, and the pestle rang between his fingers. Natalia crossed herself in silence, and Makar, who saw his master ready to sink, supported him from behind under the elbows and let the pot-lids fall clattering to the floor. Every now and then he tried to snatch the pestle to throw it at the window-pane, but then the old man shut his hand around the shaft without daring to let it go.

So we stood a long while facing one another, and we heard the kettle purr in the kitchen.

But soon we heard also the tap of steps, for the serfs had spied through the window from without and seen all. The kitchen door was filled with dirt-gray sheepskin coats, on which a bright button glinted here and there. Then a shot rang out and blew the smoke over the shaggy hides.

Now I wholly forgot our ensign game and shoved Long Jan aside so as to go at them for life and death, but just at this moment, even better than at any other time, was I to learn whom I had for a comrade. He stood still, obstinate as ever, seized me around both arms and swung me aside with the irresistible strength which his thin limbs gathered, I don't know from where.

"Ensign," said he, "if you have made yourself a private and me the ensign, then you ought also to know our custom in war that an officer goes first into the firing."

Like a thunderbolt he burst in among the sheepskin coats, and with his great flat hands held the blade that with one blow cut the lintel over his neck and with another peeled off the poor wretches' hides and clothes. I heard yet another shot, and saw axes and hay-forks. His right arm twitched and grew bloody, and he could now only wield his weapon with the other, but I was at his side, hewing and thrusting.

We were forced into one corner of the kitchen, and my inflated fool's mantle of cloth-of-silver was cut to pieces so that the black stubs of whalebone stuck out through the holes. Blackened with smoke so that he was unrecognizable, Long Jan tottered against my shoulder, and I took him by his uninjured hand and squeezed it in brotherly fashion with the words, "Now I've learned what you amount to, Jan, and if we get out of this, we shall nevermore leave each other."

He answered nothing. One eye was shut, the other was staring wide, and he fell heavily in front of me to the floor.

That was the last time I saw Long Jan, at whom
I had so often laughed, and who had so often vexed
me, but to whom I was now glad to offer the respectful grasp of a friend and an equal.

For a moment I sought involuntarily to defend
his body, but gradually I perceived it would be
useless in that last forlorn hope. A moment later
I was groping around once more amid underbrush
and mud, wet through with rain, and with a wound
over one dexter finger.

I had, however, the luck to stumble upon a detail
of twenty other wandering Swedes, and climbed up
in a fir-tree to get with my eye to the kernel of the
far-stretching glow that tinted the lowering sky
above the wood.

"What do you see?" asked my comrades.

"I see pitch-black darkness. But if I shut my
eyes, I see still more. Then I see before me a hostile camp. Below me I see the soggy turf, which
sucks hard about our feet, greedy for the honor of
being the death-bed of a few poor wretches. Behind me I see the miles on miles of wilderness,
where our brothers' corpses grow yellow beneath
the fallen October leaves, where no hens cluck
before the burnt homesteads, and no horse can find
any food except the bark of twigs. But still farther
away lies the sea, and beyond that I see a long
road with tumble-down fences that climbs up to
an old red-painted homestead. Within there, the

turnips have just been taken from the table, and while the venerable old man opens his leather Bible, where a black cock's feather lies as marker to the first chapter of the Book of Revelation, he falls into musing and wonders if we perchance have by now got ahead with reinforcements to the king's camp, and if his dear boy may now be reading by the fire his half illegible letter."

Certainly I did n't say all this at that time, but I know that I thought it. Katarina was already an almost silenced memory.

"What do you see now?" asked my comrades. "You have climbed higher up."

Across the trees I saw beacons or camp-fires hanging within the yellow mist like lumps of melted iron, and as I strained my eyes, the row of gray tent-roofs in the light of the pitch beacons reminded me of a misty coast-line.

"That glow," I whispered to my comrades, "is a great apple with many kernels, and we need to have our swords ready. But wait! that was not Russian. Did n't you hear the two outposts who called to each other? As sure as I live was not that our own beloved mother-speech? If I did n't seven times hear 'devil,' may the devil take me!"

How did I come down from the fir? That I hardly remember. On all sides I shook outstretched hands and moved between blue and yellow coats from embrace to embrace. How many longed-for

embraces did I not have to give, how many adventures to describe! I went about ever further into
the camp, sometimes carried, sometimes dragged,
sometimes met with ringing laughter, as they got
sight of my ragged fool's-mantle, round which the
projecting whalebones shook with every motion.
Within me was a roar of joy.

"I have a letter to Captain Bagge," I shouted.

"Shot long ago."

"I have also a letter to Cederstjerne, Lieutenant."

"Shot."

I stumbled over a dead horse, which with its
stiffened grin was almost scorched by a smoulder-
ing fire of logs. The rain had quenched the flames,
and in the illuminated smoke behind the embers I
saw a seated circle of grim-looking officers. Among
them lay on the ground at full length a man with
a fur hood drawn down and a cape collar over his
face. I wanted to step over him and waved my
packet of letters, but a hand seized me by the shoulder and I was harshly stopped short by the words,
"Are you out of your wits? Don't you see it is His
Majesty?"

Then I struck my heels together as I raised the
hand with the packet to my head, and the tears that
burst forth ran down my cheeks.

Captain Höök arose and finished his story as he

bade good-night, but when he went out into the entry, the others heard that he remained standing on the winding stair.

Then one of the servant-girls drew her holiday jacket about her and loosened the last stump of one branch candle from the round table. As she carried it, she held one hand underneath, so that no grease should fall on the straw. Thereupon she went out carefully to light the captain, for they all knew that he, a Charles man, was so afraid of the dark that he never dared go alone across the attic.

The Fortified House

SURPRISED by the winter cold, the Swedes in crowded confusion had taken up their quarters behind the walls of Hadjash. Soon there was not a house to be found that was not filled with the frost-bitten and the dying. Cries of distress were heard out in the street, and here and there beside the steps lay amputated fingers, feet, and legs. Vehicles stood fastened to each other, so tightly packed from the city gate to the market-place that the chilly-pale soldiers, who streamed in from all sides, had to crawl between the wheels and runners. Buckled in their harness and turned away from the wind, the horses, their loins white with frost, had already stood many days without food. No one took care of them, and several of the drivers sat frozen to death with hands stuck into their sleeves. Some wagons were like oblong boxes or coffins, where from the chink of the flat lid stared out mournful faces, which read in a prayer-book or gazed longingly with feverish delirium at the sheltering houses. A thousand unfortunates, in muffled tones or silently, cried to God for mercy. Under the sheltered side of the city wall dead soldiers stood in lines, many with red Cossack coats buttoned over their ragged Swedish uniforms and with sheepskins around their naked feet. Wood-doves and sparrows, which were so stiff with frost that they could be caught with the hand, had fallen on the hats and shoulders of the standing corpses, and fluttered their wings when the chaplains went by to give a Last Communion in brandy.

Up at the market-place among burnt areas stood an unusually large house, from which could be heard loud voices. A soldier delivered a fagot to an ensign who stood in the doorway, and when the soldier went back into the street, he shrugged his shoulders and said to whomsoever cared to hear him: "It's only the gentlemen quarreling in the chancellery."

The ensign at the door had lately arrived with Lewenhaupt's forces. He carried the fagot into the room, and threw it down by the fireplace. The voices within ceased immediately, but as soon as he had closed the door, they began with renewed heat.

It was His Excellency Piper who stood in the middle of the floor, his countenance wrinkled and furrowed, with glowing cheeks and trembling nostrils.

"I say that the whole affair is madness," he burst out, "madness, madness!"

Hermelin, with his pointed nose, was constantly twitching his eyes and his hands, while he sprang back and forth in the room like a tame rat; but Field Marshal Rehnskiöld, who, with his handsome, stately figure, was standing by the fireplace, only whistled and hummed. If he had not whistled and hummed, the quarrel would have been finished by this time, because for once they were all fully agreed; but the fact that he whistled and hummed instead of being silent or at least speaking, that could be endured no longer. Lewenhaupt at the window took snuff and snapped shut his snuff-box. His pepper-brown eyes protruded from his head, and it looked as if his comical peruke became ever bigger and bigger. If Rehnskiöld had not continued to whistle and hum, he would have controlled himself to-day as yesterday and on all other occasions, but now wrath rose to his brow.

He shut his snuff-box for the last time, and mumbled between his teeth, "I do not ask that His Majesty should understand statesmanship. But can he lead troops? Does he show real insight at a single encounter or attack? Trained and proved old warriors, who never can be replaced, he offers daily for an empty bravado. If our men are to storm a wall, it is considered superfluous that they bind themselves protecting fagots or shields, and therefore they are wretchedly massacred. To speak freely, my worthy sirs, I can forgive an Uppsala student many a boyish freak, but I demand otherwise of a general in the field. Truly it avails not to carry on a campaign under the command of such a master."

"Furthermore," continued Piper, "His Majesty does not at present incommode you, general, with any particularly hard command. At the beginning, before one man had succeeded in distinguishing himself more than another, it went better; but now His Majesty goes around mediating and reconciling with a foolish smile so that one could go crazy."

He raised his arms in the air with a wrath which had lost all sense and bounds, notwithstanding he was altogether at one with Lewenhaupt. While he was still speaking, he turned about and betook himself impetuously to the inner apartments. The door slammed with such a clatter that Rehnskiöld found himself yet more called upon to whistle and hum. If he only had chosen to say something! But no, he did not. Gyllenkrook, who sat at the table and examined departure-checks, was blazing in the face, and a little withered-looking officer at his side whispered venomously into his ear: "A pair of diamond earrings given to Piper's countess might perhaps even yet help Lewenhaupt to new appointments."

If Rehnskiöld had now ceased to whistle and hum, Lewenhaupt would still have been able to control himself, to take up the roll of papers he carried under his coat and sit down at a corner of the table; but instead, the venerable and at other times taciturn man grew worse and worse. He turned about undecidedly and went toward the entrance door, but there he suddenly stood still, drew himself up, and smacked his heels together as if he had been a mere private. Now Rehnskiöld became quiet. The door opened. An icy gust of wind rushed into the room, and the ensign announced with as loud and long-drawn a voice as a sentry who calls his comrades to arms: "Hi–s Majesty!"

The king was no longer the dazzled and wondering half-grown youth of aforetime. Only the boyish figure with the narrow shoulders was the same. His coat was sooty and dirty. The wrinkle around the short, protruding upper lip had become deeper and rather morose. On the nose and one cheek he had frost-bite, and his eyelids were red-edged and swollen with protracted cold, but around the formerly bald vertex of his head the combed-back hair stood up like a pointed crown.

He held a fur cap in both hands, and tried to conceal his embarrassment and diffidence behind a stiff and cold ceremoniousness, while bowing and smiling to each and all of those present.

They bowed again and again still more deeply, and when he had advanced to the middle of the floor, he stood still and bowed awkwardly toward the sides, though with somewhat more haste, being apparently wholly occupied with what he was about to say. Thereupon he remained a long while standing quite silent.

Then he went forward to Rehnskiöld and, with a brief inclination, took him by one of his coat buttons.

"I would beg," he said, "that Your Excellency

provide me with two or three men of the common soldiers as escort for a little excursion. I have already two dragoons with me."

"But, Your Majesty! the country is overrun with Cossacks. To ride in here to the city from Your Majesty's quarters with so small an escort was already a feat of daring."

"Oh, nonsense, nonsense! Your Excellency will do as I have said. Some one of the generals present, who is at leisure, may also mount and take one of his men."

Lewenhaupt bowed.

The king regarded him a trifle irresolutely without answering, and remained standing after Rehnskiöld hastened out. None of the others in the circle considered it necessary to break the silence or to move.

Only after a very long pause did the king bow again to every one separately, and go out into the open air.

"Well?" inquired Lewenhaupt and clapped the ensign on the shoulder with a return of his natural kindliness. "The ensign shall go along! This is the first time the ensign has stood eye to eye with His Majesty."

"I had never expected he would be like that."

"He is always like that. He is too kingly to command."

They followed after the king, who clambered over

wagons and fallen animals. His motions were agile, never abrupt, but measured and quite slow, so that he never for a moment lost his dignity. When he had finally made his way forward through the throng to the city gate, he mounted to the saddle with his attendants, who were now seven men.

The horses stumbled on the icy street, and some fell, but Lewenhaupt's remonstrances only induced the king to use his spurs yet more heartlessly. The lackey Hultman had read aloud to him all night or had related sagas, and had at length coaxed him into laughing at the prophecy that, had he not been exalted by God to be a king, he would for his whole life have become an unsociable floor-pacer, who devised much more wonderful verses than those of the late Messenius of Disa on Bollhus, but especially the mightiest battle stories. He tried to think of Rolf Gotriksson, who ever rode foremost of all his men, but to-day it did not please him to bound his thoughts within the play-room of a saga. The restlessness, which during the last few days had struck its claws into his mind, would not let go of its royal prey. At the chancellery he had just seen the heated faces. Ever since the pranks of his boyhood he had been wrapt in his own imaginary world of the past. He had sat deaf to the piercing cries of distress along the way, while he became distrustful of each and all who exhibited a more sensitive hearing. To-day, as at other times, he hardly noted that they offered

him the best-rested horse and the freshest cake of
bread, that in the morning they laid a purse with
five hundred ducats in his pocket, that the horsemen at the first *mêlée* would form a ring about him
and offer themselves to that death which he had
challenged. On the other hand, he noticed that the
soldiers saluted him with gloomy silence, and misfortunes had made him suspicious even of those
nearest to him. The most cautious opposition, the
most concealed disapproval, he made a note of without betraying himself, and every word remained and
gnawed at his soul. Every hour it seemed to him
that he lost an officer on whom he had formerly
relied, and his heart became all the colder. His
thwarted ambition chafed and bled under the weight
of failure, and he breathed more lightly the farther
behind him he left his headquarters.

Suddenly Lewenhaupt came to a stand, debating
within himself how to exercise an influence upon
the king.

" My heroic Ajax!" said he, and patted his steaming horse, " you are indeed an old manger-biter, but
I have no right to founder you for no good cause,
and I myself am beginning to get on in years as you
are. But in Jesus' name, lads, let him who can follow
the king!"

When he saw the ensign's anxious sidelong look
toward the king, he spoke with lowered voice:
" Be faithful, boy! His Majesty does not roar

out as we others do. He is too kingly to chide or bicker."

The king feigned to notice nothing. More and more wildly over ice and snow he kept up the silent horse-race without goal or purpose. He had now only four attendants. After another hour one of the remaining horses fell with a broken fore-leg, and the rider out of pity shot a bullet through its ear, after which he himself, alone and on foot, went to meet an uncertain fate in the cold.

At last the ensign was the only man who was able to follow the king, and they had now come among bushes and saplings, where they could proceed but at a foot-pace. On the hill above them rose a gray and sooty house with narrow grated windows, the courtyard being surrounded by a wall.

At this moment there was a shot.

"How was that?" inquired the king, and looked around.

"The pellet piped nastily when it went by my ear, but it only bit the corner of my hat," answered the ensign, without the least experience of how he ought to conduct himself before the king. He had a slight Småland accent, and laughed contentedly with his whole blond countenance.

Enchanted by the good fortune of being man by man with him whom he regarded as above all other living human beings, he continued: "Shall we then go up there and take them by the beard?"

The answer pleased the king in the highest degree, and with a leap he stood on the ground.

"We'll tie our steeds here in the bushes," he said, exhilarated and with bright color on his cheek. "Afterwards let us go up and run them all through as easily as whistling."

They left the panting horses and, bending forward, climbed up the hill among the bushes. Over the wall looked down several Cossack heads with hanging hair, yellow and grinning as those of beheaded criminals.

"Look!" whispered the king, and smote his hands together. "They're trying to pull shut the rotten gate, the fox-tails!"

His glance, but recently so expressionless, became now flickering and anon open and shining. He drew his broadsword and raised it with both hands above his head. Like a young man's god he stormed in through the half-open door. The ensign, who cut and thrust by his side, was often close to being struck from behind by his weapon. A musket-shot blackened the king's right temple. Four men were cut down in the gateway, and the fifth of the band fled with a fire-shovel into the courtyard, pursued by the king.

Then the king wiped off the blood from his sword on the snow, while he laid two ducats in the Cossack's shovel and burst out with rising spirits, "It is no pleasure to fight with these wretches

who never strike back and only run. Come back
when you have bought yourself a decent sword."

The Cossack, who understood nothing, stared
at the gold-pieces, sneaked along the wall to the
gate, and fled. Ever farther and farther away on
the plain he called his roving comrades with a dismal and lamenting "Oohaho! Oohaho!"

The king hummed to himself as if chaffing with
an unseen enemy: " Little Cossack man, little Cossack man, go gather up your rascals!"

The walls around the courtyard were moulder-
ing and black. From the wilderness sounded an
endlessly prolonged minor tone as from an aeolian
harp, and the king inquisitively shouldered in the
door of the dwelling-house. This consisted of a
single large and half-dark room, and before the fireplace lay a heap of blood-stained clothing, which
plunderers of corpses had taken from fallen Swedes.
The door was thrown shut again by the cross-
draught, and the king went to the stable-buildings
at the side. There was no door there, and a sound
was now heard the more plainly. Within in the darkness lay a starved white horse bound to an iron ring
in the wall.

A lifted broadsword would not have checked the
king, but the uncertain dusk caused the man of
imagination to stand on the threshold, fearful of
the dark. Yet he gave no sign of this, but beckoned
the ensign. They stepped in down a steep stairway

to a cellar. Here there was a well, and at the arm
of the creaking windlass that brought up the
water, a deaf Cossack, wholly unaware of danger,
was driving around with whip and reins a human
figure in the uniform of a Swedish officer.

When they had loosed the rope and had bound
the Cossack in the place of the prisoner, they recognized the Holsteiner, Feuerhausen, who had
served as major in a regiment of dragoon recruits,
but had been cut off by the Cossacks and harnessed
as a draught animal for hoisting water.

He fell on his knees, and stammered in broken
Swedish: "Your Majesty! I gan't pelief my eyes
. . . My gratitude — " . . .

The king cheerily interrupted his talk, and turned
to the ensign: "Bring up the two horses to the
stable! Three men cannot ride comfortably on two
horses, and therefore we shall stay here till a few
Cossacks come by, from whom we can take a new
horse. Do you, sir, stand guard at the gate."

After that the king went back to the dwelling-
house, and shut the door after him. The horses
which, desperate with hunger, had been greedily
gnawing the bark from the bushes, were meanwhile
led up to the stable, and the ensign mounted guard.

Slowly the hours went by. When it began to
draw towards dusk, the storm increased in bitterness, and in the light of sunset the snow whirled
over the desolate snow-plain. Deathly yellow Cos-

sack faces raised themselves spying above the bushes, and borne in the wind sounded the roving plunderers' "Oohaho! Oohaho! Oohaho!"

Then Feuerhausen stepped out of the stable, where he had sat between the horses so as not to get frost in his wounds from the ropes with which he had been bound. He went forward to the barred doors of the dwelling-house.

"Your Majesty!" he stammered, "the Cossacks are gathering more and more, and darkness is coming soon. I and the ensign can both sit on one horse. If we delay here, this night will be Your Mightiest Majesty's last, which Gott in His secret dispensation forbit!"

The king answered from within, "It must be as we said. Three men do not ride comfortably on two horses."

The Holsteiner shook his head and went down to the ensign.

"Such is His Majesty, you damt Swedes. From the stable I heard him walk and walk back and forvart. Sickness and conscience-torture will come. Like a *pater familiae* the Muscovite czar stands among his subjects. A confectioner he sets up as his friend, and a simple servant-girl he raises to his glorious imperial throne. Detestable are his gestures when he gets drunk, and he treats women *à la françois;* but his first and last wort always runs, 'For Russia's goot!' King Carolus leafs his lants as smoking ash-heaps, and does not possess a single frient, not efen among his nearest. King Carolus is more lonely than the meanest wagon-drifer. He has not once a comrade's knee to weep on. Among nobles and fine ladies and perukes he comes like a spectre out of a thousant-year mausoleum — and spectres mostly go about witout company. Is he a man of state? Oh, haf mercy! No sense for the public. Is he a general? Good-by! No sense for the big masses. Only to make bridges and set up gabions, clap his hants at captured flags and a couple of kettledrums. No sense for state and army, only for men."

"That may be also a sense," replied the ensign.

He walked vigorously back and forward, for his fingers were already so stiff with cold that he scarcely could hold his drawn blade.

The Holsteiner shifted the ragged coat-collar around his cheeks and went on with muffled voice and eager gestures : " King Carolus laughs with delight when the bridge breaks, and men and beasts are miserably drownt. No heart in his breast. To the deuce wit him! King Carolus is such a little Swedish half-genius as wanders out in the worlt and beats the drum and parades and makes a fiasco, and the parterre whistles, Whee!"

"And that is why the Swedes go to death for him," answered the ensign; "that is just why."

"Not angry, my dearest fellow! Your teeth shone so in a laugh when we first met."

"I like to hear the Herr Major talk, but I'm freezing. Will not the major go up and listen at the king's door?"

The Holsteiner went up to the door and listened. When he came back, he said, "He only walks and walks, and sighs heavily like a man in anguish of soul. So it always is now, they say. His Majesty nefer sleeps any more at night. The comedy-actor knows he is not up to his part, and of all life's torments wounded ambition becomes the bitterest."

"Then it should also be the last for us to jest at. Dare I beg the major to rub my right hand with snow; it is getting numb."

The Holsteiner did as he desired, and turned back to the king's door. He struck his forehead with both hands. His gray-sprinkled, bushy moustaches stood straight out, and he mumbled, "Gott, Gott! Soon it will be too dark to retreat."

The ensign called, "Good sir, I should like to ask if you would rub my face with snow. My cheeks are freezing stiff. Of the pain in my foot I will not speak. Ah, I can't bear it."

The Holsteiner filled his hands with snow. "Let me stand guard," he said, "only for an hour."

"No, no. The king has commanded that I stay here at the entrance."

"Och, the king! I know him. I will make him cheerful, talk philosophy, tell of gallant exploits. He is always amused to hear of a lover who climbs adventurously through a window. He often looks at the beautiful side of womankint. That appeals to his imagination, but not to his flesh, for he is witout feeling. Ant he is bashful. If the fair one ever wishes to tread him under her silken shoe, she must herself attack, but pretent to flee, and all the others must strive against the *liaison*. The most mighty lady, his grandmother, spoiled everything with her shriek of 'Marriage, marriage!' King Carolus is from top to toe like the Swedish queen Christina, though he is genuinely masculine. The two should have married each other on the same throne. That would haf been a fine little pair. Oh, pfui, pfui! you Swedes. If a man gallops his horses and lets people and kingdom be massacred, he is still pure-hearted and supreme among all, if only his bloot is too slow for amours. Oh, excuse me! I know pure-hearted heroes who were faithfully in love with two, three different maidens or wives in one and the same week."

"Yes, we are so, we are so. But for Christ's pity you must rub my hand again. And excuse my moaning and groaning!"

Just inside the gate, which could not be shut, lay the fallen Cossacks, white as marble with the hoar frost. The yellow sky became gray, and ever nearer and more manifold in the twilight sounded the wailing cries, "Oohaho! Oohaho! Oohaho!"

Now the king opened his door and came down across the court.

The pains in his head, from which he had begun to suffer, had been increased by his ride in the wind and made his glance heavy. His countenance bore traces of lonely soul-strife, but as he drew near, his mouth resumed its usual embarrassed smile. His temple was still blackened after the musket-shot.

"It's freshening up," he said, and producing from his coat a loaf of bread, he broke it in three, so that every one had as large a piece as he did. After that, he lifted off his riding-cape, and fastened it himself about the shoulders of the sentinel ensign.

Abashed over his own conduct, he then took the Holsteiner forcibly by the arm and led him up through the courtyard, while they chewed at their hard bread.

Now, if ever, thought the Holsteiner, is the time to win the king's attention with a clever turn of speech, and afterwards talk sense with him.

"The accommodation might be worse," he began, at the same time biting and chewing. "Ah, good old days! That reminds me of a gallant adventure outside of Dresden."

The king kept on holding him by the arm, and the Holsteiner lowered his voice. The story was lively and salacious, and the king grew inquisitive.

The coarsest allusions always lured out his set smile. He listened with a despairing and half-absent man's need of momentary diversion.

Only when the Holsteiner with cunning deftness began to shift the conversation over to some words about their immediate danger did the king again become serious.

"Bagatelle, bagatelle!" he replied. "It is nothing at all worth mentioning, except that we must behave ourselves well and sustain our reputation to the last man. If the rascals come on, we will all three place ourselves at the gate and pink them with our swords."

The Holsteiner stroked his forehead and felt around. He began to talk about the stars that were just shining out. He set forth a theory for measuring their distance from the earth. The king now listened to him with a quite different sort of attention. He broke into the question keenly, resourcefully, and with an unwearied desire to think out new, surprising methods in his own way. One assertion gave a hand to another, and soon the conversation dwelt on the universe and the immortality of the soul, to return afresh to the stars. More and more of them flickered in the heavens, and the king described what he knew about the sun-dial. He stood up his broadsword with its scabbard in the snow and directed the point toward the Polestar, so that next morning they might be able to tell the time.

"The heart of the universe," he said, "must be either the earth or the star that stands over the land of the Swedes. No land must be of more account than the Swedish land."

Outside the wall the Cossacks were calling out, but as soon as the Holsteiner led the talk to their threatened attack, the king was laconic.

"At daybreak we shall betake ourselves back to Hadjash," said he. "Before then we can hardly secure a third horse, so that each of us can ride comfortably in his own saddle."

After he had spoken in that strain, he went back into the dwelling-house.

The Holsteiner came down with a vehement stride to the ensign, and pointing at the king's door, he cried out, "Forgif me, ensign. We Germans don't mince words when a wount oozes after a rope, but I lay down my arms and gif you, sir, the victory, because I also could shed my bloot for the man. Do I lofe him! No one efer understands him that has not seen him. But, ensign, you cannot stay any longer out in the weather."

The ensign replied, "No cape has warmed me more sweetly than the one I now wear, and I lay all my cares on Christ. But in God's name, major, go back to the door and listen! The king might do himself some harm."

"His Majesty would not fall on his *own* sword, but longs for another's."

"Now I hear his steps even down here. They are getting still more violent and restless. He is so lonely. When I saw him in Hadjash bowing and bowing among the generals, I could only think, How lonely he is!"

"If the little Holsteiner slips away from here alife, he will always remember the steps we heard to-night and always call this refuge Fort Garten."

The ensign nodded his approval and answered, "Go to the stable, major, and seek rest and shelter awhile between the horses. And there through the walls you can better hear the king and watch over him."

Thereupon the ensign began to sing with resonant voice:

O Father, to Thy loving grace . . .

The Holsteiner went back across the court into the stable and, his voice quavering with cold, intoned with the other:

In every time and every place
My poor weak soul would I commend.
O Lord, receive it and defend.

"Oohaho! Oohaho!" answered the Cossacks in the storm, and it was already night.

The Holsteiner squeezed himself in between the two horses, and listened till weariness and sleep bowed his head. Only at dawn was he wakened by a clamor. He sprang out into the open air, and beheld the king already standing in the court, looking at the sword that had been set up as a sun-dial.

By the gate the Cossacks had collected, but when they saw the motionless sentry, they shrank back in superstitious fear and thought of the rumors concerning the magic of the Swedish soldiers against blow and shot.

When the Holsteiner had gotten forward to the ensign, he grasped him hard by the arm.

"What now?" he asked. "Brandy?"

At the same instant he let go his grip.

The ensign stood frozen to death with his back against the wall of the gate, his hands on his sword-hilt, and wrapped in the king's cloak.

"Since we are now only two," the king remarked, drawing his weapon out of the snow, "we can at once betake ourselves each to his horse, as it was arranged."

The Holsteiner stared him right in the eyes with reawakened hate and remained standing, as if he had heard nothing. Finally, however, he led out the horses, but his hands trembled and clenched themselves, so that he could hardly draw the saddle-girths.

The Cossacks swung their sabres and pikes, but the sentry stood at his post.

Then the king sprang carelessly into the saddle, and set his horse to a gallop. His forehead was clear, his cheeks were rosy, and his broadsword glimmered like a sunbeam.

The Holsteiner looked after him. His bitter expression relaxed, and he murmured between his teeth, while he too mounted to the saddle and with hand lifted to his hat raced by the sentry: "It is only the joy of a hero in seeing a hero's noble death.—Thanks, comrade!"

A Clean White Shirt

PRIVATE BENGT GETING had got a Cossack's pike through his breast, and his comrades laid him on a heap of twigs in a copse, where Pastor Rabenius gave him the Holy Communion. This was on the icy ground before the walls of Veperik, and a whistling norther tore the dry leafage from the bushes.

"The Lord be with thee!" whispered Rabenius softly and paternally. "Are you prepared now to depart hence after a good day's work?"

Bengt Geting lay with his hands knotted, bleeding to death. The hard eyes stood wide open, and the obstinate and scraggy face was so tanned by sun and frost that the bluish pallor of death shone out only over his lips.

"No," he said.

"That is the first time I have heard a word from your mouth, Bengt Geting."

The dying man knotted his hands all the harder, and chewed with his lips, which opened themselves for the words against his will.

"For once," he said slowly, "even the meanest and raggedest of soldiers may speak out."

He raised himself painfully on his elbow, and ejaculated such a piercing cry of anguish that Rabenius did not know whether it came from torment of soul or of body.

He set down the chalice on the ground, and spread a handkerchief over it, so that the leaves which were tumbling about should not fall into the brandy.

"And this," he stammered, pressing his hands to his forehead, "this I, who am a servant of Christ, shall be constrained to witness, morning after morning, evening after evening."

Soldiers crowded forward from all sides between the bushes to see and hear the fallen man, but their captain came in a wrathful mood with sword drawn.

"Tie a cloth over the fellow's mouth!" he shouted. "He has always been the most obstinate man in the battalion. I am no more inhuman than another, but I must do my duty, and I have a mass of new and untrained folk that have come with Lewenhaupt. These have got scared by his wailing, and refuse to go forward. Why don't you obey? I command here."

Rabenius took a step forward. On his curled white peruke he had a whole garland of yellow leaves.

"Captain," he said, "beside the dying the servant of God alone commands, but in glad humility he delivers his authority to the dying man himself. For three years I have seen Bengt Geting march in the line, but never yet have I seen him speak with any one. Now on the threshold of God's judgment-seat may no one further impose silence upon him."

"With whom should I have spoken?" asked the

bleeding trooper bitterly. "My tongue is as if tied and lame. Weeks would go by without my saying a word. No one has ever asked me about anything. It was only the ear that had to be on guard so that I did not fail to obey. 'Go,' they have said, 'go through marsh and snow.' To that there was nothing to answer."

Rabenius knelt and softly took his hands in his.

"But now you shall speak, Bengt Geting. Speak, speak, now that all are gathered to hear you. You are now the only one of us all who has the right to speak. Is there a wife or perhaps an aged mother at home to whom you want me to send a message?"

"My mother starved me and sent me to the troops, and never since then has a woman had anything else to say to me than the same, 'Get away, Bengt Geting, go, go! What do you want with us?'"

"Have you then anything to repent?"

"I repent that as a child I did not jump into the mill-race, and that, when you stood before the regiment on Sunday and admonished us to go patiently on and on, I didn't step forward and strike you down with my musket. — But do you want to know what causes me dread? Have you never heard the wagon-drivers and outposts tell how in the moonlight they have seen their comrades that were shot limp in crowds after the army and hop about on their mangled legs and cry, 'Greetings to mother!'— They call them the Black Battalion. It's into the

Black Battalion that I'm to go now. But the worst is that I shall be buried in my ragged coat and my bloody shirt. That's the thing I can't get out of my mind. A plain trooper doesn't want to be taken home like the dead General Liewen, but I'm thinking of the fallen comrades at Dorfsniki, where the king had a coffin of a couple of boards and a clean white shirt given to each man. Why should they be treated so much better than I? Now in this year of misfortune a man is laid out as he falls. I'm so deeply sunk in misery that the only thing in the world that I can be envious of is their clean white shirts."

"My poor friend," answered Rabenius quietly, "in the Black Battalion — if you believe in it now — you will have great company. Gyldenstolpe and Sperling and Lieutenant-Colonel Mörner already lie shot on the field. And do you recall the thousand others? Do you remember the friendly Lieutenant-Colonel Wattrang, who came riding to our regiment and gave an apple to every soldier, and who now lies among the Royal Dragoons, and all our comrades under the meadow at Holofzin? And do you remember my predecessor, Nicholas Uppendich, a mighty proclaimer of the Word, who fell at Kalisch in his priestly array? Grass has grown and snow fallen over his mould, and no one can point out with his foot the sod where he sleeps."

Rabenius bowed yet deeper, and felt the man's forehead and hands.

" In ten or at most fifteen minutes you will have ceased to live. Perhaps these minutes might replace the past three years, if you sanctify them rightly. You are no longer one of us. Don't you see that your spiritual guide is lying on his knees by you with head uncovered? Speak now and tell me your last wish; no, your last command. Consider but one thing. The regiment is disorganized on your account, and meanwhile the others go forward with glory or stand already on the storming-ladders. You have frightened the younger fellows with your death-wound and your wailing, and you alone can make it good again. Now they listen only to you, and you alone have it in your power to make them go against the enemy. Consider that your last words will be last forgotten, and perhaps sometime will be repeated for those at home, who sit and roast their potatoes behind the oven."

Bengt Geting lay motionless, and a shadow of perplexity passed over his glance. Then he gently raised his arms as if for an invocation and whispered, " Lord, help me to do even so ! "

He gave a sign that now he was able only to whisper, and Rabenius laid his face to his so as to be able to hear his words. Then Rabenius motioned to the soldiers, but his voice trembled so that he could hardly make himself heard.

" Now Bengt Geting has spoken," he said. " This is his last wish, that you should take him between you on your muskets and carry him with you in his old place in the line, where he has stubbornly marched day after day and year after year."

The drums now struck up, the music began, and with his cheek on the shoulder of one of the soldiers Bengt Geting was carried forward step by step over the field toward the foe. Around him followed the whole regiment, and ever with bared head Rabenius went behind him, and did not notice that he was already dead.

"I shall see to it," he whispered, "that you get a clean white shirt. You know that the king does not regard himself as more than the humblest soldier, and it is so that he himself wishes sometime to lie."

Poltava

O N the first of May Field Marshal Rehnskiöld gave an evening dinner, and Colonel Appelgren became heated about the forehead and inquisitive; he rolled bread-crumbs with his fingers and looked cross-eyed.

"Can Your Excellency say why Poltava has to be besieged?"

"His Majesty wants to have amusement till the Poles and Tartars come with reinforcements."

"And nevertheless we know that neither of them is coming. Europe begins to forget our court *à la* Diogenes with riding ministers of state, fighting chancellor's clerks, chamberlains falling in battle, seats of honor on tree stumps . . . and with palaces of tent-cloth, and pancakes and small beer on the royal table."

"His Majesty wishes to practise fortifications now, and is getting the habit of camping out for the rest of his life. So we have time ahead of us. Poltava is a little flea fortress, which will probably surrender when the first shot cracks."

The field marshal became abruptly silent, and dropped his fork.

"I believe those fellows in the town have gone crazy, and are going to defend themselves."

He sprang out and threw himself into the saddle. All arose and heard a continuous firing.

The Russian sentries around the walls had the
custom of shouting long and noisily in the darkness, "Good bread, good drink!" During this
screaming, Colonel Gyllenkrook, without any one
being able to hear his approach, had begun to open
trenches, and had set up a cover, but at that moment the king ran over the field, and shouted aloud
something to his adjutant-general. The fact that he
held his drawn broadsword prevented him from
looking ridiculous as he ran. Gyllenkrook asked
him not to cry out so loud so as not to alarm the
enemy, but even while he was speaking, the outposts
were silent, and began instead to light their port-fires
and shoot. Fire-balls that rose aloft threw their light
over the hills and meadow-land, and were reflected
in the hurrying waters of the Vorskla. Gyllenkrook's
laboring Zaporogeans then sprang back from their
spades and gabions, and the Swedish soldiers, who
thumped on their leather coats with the flat of the
sword, at last began themselves to flee or to lie
down on the ground.

In that way the shooting had begun.

"Look there!" said Gyllenkrook, who stood behind a tree with the king and the Little Prince. "A
small cause may bring about such a big confusion,
and for the last time I dare propose that the whole
siege be given up. In my prayers unite the tired
troops and all the unhappy subjects at home. Why
were we not commanded hither in the winter, when

the town might have been easily taken? Now the garrison is strengthened every day, and the enemy's whole army is on the advance. We have barely thirty cannon left, and the powder, which has many times been wet and dried again, only casts the shot a little way from their muzzles."

"Nonsense, nonsense! Why, we 've shot away many a log thicker than a scaling-post."

"But here we need to shoot away many hundreds."

"If we can shoot away one, we can shoot away hundreds. We must perform just what is extraordinary, so that we get reputation and honor from it. Now we shall let the Zaporogeans see that they can work here without the least danger."

The king stuck his broadsword under his arm, and went out into the rain of shot on the field. Behind him followed the Little Prince, pale, erect, festal as a youth in an ancient procession to a sacrifice at the temple.

Two thick logs were driven down like two gate-posts close to the open trench, and there the king took his stand behind a fallen fire-ball, whose daylight brilliance exposed him to the enemy. The Little Prince gave him a hesitating side-look, and felt up and down his sword-hilt with his hand, which trembled a little. After that he climbed up on one of the logs and took a position with his arms at his side. Then a junior officer, who was called Mor-

ten Preacher, stepped up on the other log. He
had a face brown as leather, black hair, and brass
rings in his ears. Motionless as two painted wooden
statues in some Catholic country district, the two
guards stood in this way behind their king, and the
furious Russians directed their catapults and field-
pieces and muskets at the remarkable spectacle. No
one wished to humble himself and descend first, and
for that reason they had to stay. There was whistling and swishing as of whips and rods, as of storm-
gusts and pipes, while cannon-balls, striking near,
threw gravel and clods on high. It lightened and
thundered, the ground trembled like a frightened
horse, and splinters and bits of stone whirled
by.

"The king is there! Now he'll be shot!" cried
the soldiers, rushing forward and driving the Zaporogeans among them. Again they seized the spades,
and again the Zaporogeans tore up the turf and
opened the earth, so that they could lie down and
get shelter.

In the light of the burning pitch stood the monarch of the generals and dignitaries, the comrade
of the soldiers, at once knight errant, king, and philosopher. All day long dark memories had slunk in
his footsteps. He recalled Axel Hård, whom he
himself had killed by accident, and Klinckowström,
the friend of his youth, shot dead. He felt the loss
of neither, but he could not forget their bloody

clothes. All the heaven-storming gayety of boy-hood, however, awoke to life and silenced the heavy thoughts, when one heard the bullets. He had drained the cup of warlike adventure to the bottom, and the drink needed to be spiced more strongly every day to have relish. He began to see the great clamorous victories in a colder light as they became rarer. To be sure he could still sometimes talk about ruling great states, but that was mostly so that these should provide him daily with a hundred more gal-lant guardsmen. He never forgot that any moment might be his last, but the years of misfortune were come. How sweet would not repose be after a glori-ous death! To will, to know he had the power, but yet to fail and become a mockery, because the others could no longer follow — that was the breath of frost from the autumn of life. He wished to prove, he wished to show, that he was still the exceptional man under God's protection. If he were not that, then he wished to fall like the plainest soldier.

Morten Preacher meanwhile grew so excited that he could not hold himself motionless on the pillar, but shifted the musket from his back. Who did not know Morten Preacher, the sharpshooter, who could make even the king clap his hands? Either an infantryman or a cavalryman he could bring down in full career. He muttered and laughed, laid the weapon to his eye, and shot at a shadow that climbed in the farthest cherry-tree. Struck by the ball, it tumbled down among the blossoming twigs like a bird. Then a hunter's enthusiasm came over Morten Preacher, and he hopped down and sprang to the spot.

There lay an old man, shot dead, and beside him stood a little girl of nine years.

"That 's father," she said without crying, and looked at Morten Preacher. "We were out picking nettles, and on the way home—"

"Well, on the way home—?"

"We heard shooting, and then father climbed up to look around. That is father's cherry-tree."

Morten Preacher shook his head, took off his hat and tore at his hair, and sat down.

"God forgive me—the old man has never done me any harm. Dear child—you cannot understand this. But I have a ducat in my pocket. Take it! You see, my child, I'm a hunter, you understand, a regular old expert hunter. Formerly I had my cottage and my sweetheart, who quarrelled and struck at me because I never moved my spade—you know what a spade is?—but only sat in the woods and listened to the blackcock's song. Hearken now! Then one morning I took my musketoon and my dog and went my way out into the world."

The girl turned over the ducat in the light of the fire, but he drew her to his knee, and stroked her softly on the cheeks.

"When I had gone along so the first day, I shot

the dog. When I had gone another day, I gave the gun to a forester who showed me the way. After that I had nothing."

"Can one buy coppers for it?"

"Surely, surely. So when I joined the army like that and got me a war musket, then, as you may believe, I became a hunter again. But Heaven have pity!—You shall come here every evening in the dusk, and then you shall get half of my day's rations and all I can pick up."

She stared at the musket in the grass, so he rose and went, leaving it there.

"The girl can't know that it was I who fired the shot, and she shall never get to know it.—You are a Judas, who has robbed an innocent man of life.— Thou shalt not kill! Thou shalt not kill!"

He held his forehead and tottered away over the field. Then he came to d'Albedyhll's Dragoons, who lay around a log fire and read prayer-books, and there he sat down to read, until finally he began to pray aloud and preach.

"What news?" the soldiers asked next morning of Brakel's red-haired sutler, a little knowing West Gotlander, who stood in his gray blouse among the pots and hung-up clothes.

"News? Morten Preacher must have had a sunstroke in the middle of the night and become ripe for the fool's locker. He goes bare-headed down to the river and shouts. When the preacher's fever sets in on him, he always says he has been out and shot somebody."

In gloomy silence the soldiers received tin bowls hardly half full.

"Bread or dead. Why don't we go ahead and storm before it's too late?"

"The king is working with ditches, and Gyllenkrook has to stand by the work night and day. Just listen to Morten Preacher now down by the water! Here has been praying and psalm-singing lately so that it makes one warm at heart to hear the field marshal go on the rampage."

At dusk Morten Preacher slunk away to the cherry-tree, where the little nine-year-old stood already waiting with her smooth flaxen, almost white hair and her serious face.

He had with him his day's rations, and he gave her his last kopek for the promise that he might kiss her on both cheeks.

"Is your mother living?"

She shook her head.

"What's your name?"

"Dunya."

He wanted to kiss her again on the cheeks, but she moved away.

"Give me a kopek first!"

He went back to the camp—and begged kopek pieces of all whom he met.

"I will watch over her when there is a storming.

She is like a little, little princess. I will lay by from
my pay, so that one day she will have something
to get married on. — Why should she not get married?—Surely, surely! I have, to be sure, my wife
at home, and I have a sweetheart in the baggage-
train, too. And it seems I'm a murderer. Surely a
little princess shall marry!"

He had made a copy of St. John's Gospel and,
sitting down, he read aloud from it to d'Albedyhll's
Dragoons.

All the plants of spring flamed up over the hilly
meads down to the yellowish banks of the Vorskla,
but the soldiers looked only toward Poltava, which
shone out through clumps of forest with its white
cloister walls, its wooden towers, palisades, and ramparts, on which young and old men, women, and
children had thrown up a breastwork of sacks filled
with earth, of wagons, bundles of twigs, and barrels.

"What's the news? Will they never lead us
against the foe?" the soldiers inquired of the sutler.

"The foe is so kind as to come to us instead,"
he answered, and dried his forehead with his blouse.
"In the night I heard how he rolled his field-pieces.
The heavy firing is not from the Swedes, for we
have no other cannon-balls left than those which
the Zaporogeans pick up out of the ground. It's
the czar's whole army that's already standing on
the other side of the river."

Then came Major-General Lagercrona, spurring

his horse and shouting that the king was wounded in the foot. Beside the royal litter the field marshal pointed out the situation of the seventeen redoubts which the enemy had already begun to throw up at the village of Pietruska.

"What's the news?" muttered the soldiers daily around the sutler.

"If there's nothing else that any one offers, then I'm the richer," answered he, and pointed with his ladle around the verdant landscape. "The king has got mortification in his wound. The brandy is done. The bread is done. I've a little porridge for you to-day—but then that's done. The enemy has barred us in and disputes our retreat. Oh, the devil, the devil! It's only the Swedes that can stand such bitter days."

He stamped on the turf, put the ladle to his eye, and aimed like an assassin at the king's battered cabin, but the heroic, frost-bitten heads around him lowered their eyes.

"Thou shalt not kill!" whispered Morten Preacher with upraised arms.

So passed the month of May, and the heat of June shone in through the tent-cloths. The soldiers sat in a row and twined wreaths for midsummer-poles, but did not talk. They thought of the pastures at home, of the cottages, of the wide, wide moors.

On Sunday, a little before evensong, Morten

Preacher slipped to the grove, where little Dunya, in return for some kopeks, handed him a basket with the first half-ripened cherries. He ate them along with her, patted her small hands, and played with her, carrying her like a child, but he could not get her to smile. For his last kopek he was allowed to kiss her three times on the cheeks.

When he came back there was clamor and unrest. Officers inspected the soldiers' equipment and thumped on their swords, which here and there were so ground that they were like worn scythes. Brakel's sutler pulled together his empty pans. The king had resolved to deliver battle.

On the grassy banks outside the king's window the generals and colonels were already sitting to receive their divisions and written instructions. There sat the melancholy Lewenhaupt with his great clear eyes and a little Latin pocket lexicon stuck between the buttons of his coat. There sat the gallant Creutz with hands crossed over the pommel of his sword, and Sparre and Lagercrona carried on a noisy conversation in loud tones. Colonel Gyllenkrona stood by the table, bent over his fortification drawings, with which he appeared to be so fascinated that he did not notice the others in the least, but occupied himself instead with carefully and slowly flicking the grains of sand from his beloved sketches. Leaning back a little by the door, in the worst of tempers, stood the field marshal himself with his pointed,

somewhat turned-up nose and his puckered, pur-
ple-red girl's mouth.

.   .   .   .

In the dusk began the march with furled banners
and without music, and the king's litter was set
down for a while in a grove in advance of the life-
guards. From the field were heard sounds of the
enemy knocking and hammering on their palisades
as upon waiting scaffolds. The band of Charles
men, once so proud, had now so little shot and
powder that they could not bring along to the encounter more than four poor field-pieces, and now
when they heard hammer-blows so near, many
among the scarred warriors were seized with corporal fear and vainly offered a ducat for a swallow
of brandy. It was the wane of the moon. The
horses stood saddled, and the men had their muskets or carbines at their side. From one of the infantry regiments was heard murmuring and whispering, as the chaplain distributed the Communion,
and he had to grope with his left hand in the darkness to put the chalice to the mouths of the kneeling
soldiers. Around the litter, beside which the king
had stuck his broadsword into the earth, the generals had lain down for a moment in their cloaks,
and Piper sat on a drum with his back against a
tree. To break the force of gloomy thoughts and
avoid one another, they began a philosophic dis-

course with the king. He sat in a circle of ponderers and taught like a master in his school, and Lewenhaupt, the honest old Latinist colonel, recited Roman verses.

When he ceased, he took a burning torch from the attendants and threw the light on the king, whose head had slid to one side. Piper and all the generals arose and forgot their spite, so beautiful appeared to them the aspect of the sleeper. His hat lay on his knee, and the coverlet was folded about the hurt and bandaged foot. The emaciated and fever-wasted countenance with the frost-bites on nose and cheek had become even smaller than before, and harder and more set. Yellowish and humid, it was already shadowed by a premature old age, but there was a drawing and twitching of the lips. It looked as though he was dreaming.

The king of the Charles men dreamed that he saw an endless line of giggling and tittering folk, who went hurriedly past and held their hands before their faces to hide how they laughed at him. Sometimes they were bright green or blue, and they shone like lighted lanterns. Finally, on a sweating bay, there came a tall man who was completely clad in dusty silk taffeta. "Begone! you bald and lame Swede," he cried, guffawing from the back of his horse. "In this very place, three hundred years ago, the hordes of Tamerlane cut down the united armies of the West. What would you do to me and my ocean of

men with your last thinned-out regiments and your
four field-pieces? My men are thieves and drunken
miscreants, and are of less use to me than nails in
a plank, but I make good use of such nails. I am
building at a great ship to sail the centuries, and I
myself am still the same to-day as when I stood at
my trade, a simple carpenter in Saardam. Millions
upon millions shall bless my work."

The king would have answered, but he found
that his tongue was paralyzed.

Lewenhaupt knelt with bared head, and touched
him on the shoulder. "My most gracious lord, day
is dawning, and I call down God's protection over
your noble person and actions."

The glow of morning already burned between the
tree trunks, and the king opened his eyes. Straightway he grasped his broadsword. As soon as he
noted the many men who stood around him and
the bearded cavalry chaplain Norberg and all the
attendants, his expression changed, and he nodded
with his usual chilly friendliness — but the dream
still stood out clear in his thoughts. It seemed to
him that the others, too, must have seen it.

"What is a kingdom?" he said. "An accident,
a far-stretching estate with fortresses at the outly-
ing farms. Battles and negotiations move the bound-
aries. And yet, czar, supposing you have power over
millions but not over yourself? The Lord God may
so ordain that men shall one day inquire less con-

cerning states, but all the more concerning individuals. If I conquer you, your whole ship takes fire and becomes ashes, but if you cut down me and my men, you only fulfil thereby the victory of my achievements."

Lewenhaupt gripped Creutz by the arm, and whispered mournfully: "Dear brother, dark forebodings will not slip from my mind. Shall we all ever again stand together under God's free heaven? Hark how the field marshal swears and curses behind the Upplanders. Gyllenkrook won't even go forward to him and ask for orders. You are holding back, too. And look how haughtily Piper is glowering after us!"

"The Swedes always look haughtily at one another. For that reason they will some day be undone, and their name erased among peoples. Our children in the tenth or twentieth generation will see the time. To-day is only the beginning."

"The Lord pardon your words! Never did I see more glorious champions of God than the Swedes, and never a people so wholly free from the self-assurance and rough hands of a despotic will. The king is now too ill to hold us together longer, though he pretends to be as confident as a young cornet. He was given at birth the recklessness which the gods lend their favorites, but now—"

"Now?"

"Now he has got the impenetrable and over-

mastering delusion to which the favorite's recklessness hardens when the gods abandon him."

Lewenhaupt pressed his hat on his head and
drew his sword, but turned yet again to Creutz and
whispered: "Perhaps men such as I with my care
for the rank and file, and Gyllenkrook with his com-
pass-case and all his redoubts adorned with 'palisades, have never all this time understood him
rightly. You with your broadsword have blindly
obeyed. May it be granted us all to-day to fulfil
his mission with him, for I foresee that he who survives the evening will envy the brothers who by then
have entered into eternal blessedness."

The riders now sprang into the saddle. Lewenhaupt went to his foot-regiments, and in the light
of daybreak they saw before them the expectant
field. It was black. It was already burnt. It was a
heap of ashes, which without flower or grass-blade
vanished between clumps of trees into the barren
steppes. It was so level that a cannon-carriage could
easily be driven back and forth.

Out in front of the largest Russian redoubt came
a red-clad rider, who fired off his pistol. Then the
enemy let all their drums beat behind the outworks,
on which appeared innumerable troops of soldiers
and standards and catapults and field-pieces. Immediately the Swedish music answered throughout
all the regiments.

The indomitable Axel Sparre and Karl Gustaf

Roos rushed in front of the army with their battalions, and stormed the field redoubts. Horses
snorted, harness creaked, swords and carbines clattered, and ashes and dust fell over the clumps of
trees so that the green was quenched on the leafage.

The king sent Creutz with the left wing after the
conquering Sparre, and behind the captured entrenchments the enemy's cavalry rushed in flight
toward the swampy meadows by the Vorskla. On
the other side Lewenhaupt advanced with his infantry, occupied two redoubts, and disposed himself
to attack the enemy's camp from the south with
the bayonet. There the confusion was so great that
women began to harness horses to the baggage
wagons, but the czarina, a tall woman of some twenty
years with a high bosom, white forehead, and deeply
colored cheeks, still stood out by the wounded
among her bandage-strips and water-flasks with an
almost haughty tranquillity.

Meanwhile the generals collected around the
Swedish king's litter, which was borne along not
far from the East Gotland infantry regiment and
set down by a bog. Here a halt was commanded,
and a crowd with deep bowing and taking off of
hats began already to congratulate His Majesty and
wish for further progress. While the lackey Hultman was filtering water and catching it in a silver
goblet, the king said: "Major-General Roos has

been surrounded, and the field marshal has therefore checked the other troops, but Lagercrona and
Sparre have been sent back to help Roos on, and he
is likely to come here soon."

Thus the army remained standing there awhile,
but soon Sparre came up, sprinkled with drops of
blood, and related that he could not get through
on account of the enemy's superior numbers. The
troops now marched back and forth for a long time
without the officers' knowing where they should lead
them, and during the wasted time the Russians got
fresh courage. Then Lewenhaupt suddenly put
himself in motion, marched to the stretch of woods
where Creutz' squadrons had taken position, and
there drew up the infantry in line against the enemy.
No one knew from where the command for this had
been given out, and, beside himself with wrath, the
field marshal galloped forward to the king's litter,
which went beside the Guards.

"Is it Your Majesty who commanded Lewenhaupt with the infantry to draw himself up against
the enemy?"

The disrespectful tones took the king aback, and
as if by the light of a dark lantern that has been
suddenly opened, he saw how wearily and coldly
even his closest favorites in the circle were staring
at him.

"No," he answered reluctantly, but became blush-
ing red, and all understood that he lied.

Then in the furiously raging field marshal every last glimmer of respect and trust was quenched. He gave voice to the spite and despair which all had nourished for days and months. The king, acclaimed for his love of veracity, had all at once been humiliated to the level of a wounded soldier, had behaved himself churlishly, and tried to exculpate himself with rude prevarications. Rehnskiöld did not reflect. The moment of retribution had come. He lost control of himself. He wanted to take revenge and punish and humiliate. He could not pretend that he believed in the lying. He could not even use the customary form of address.

"Yes, yes," he shouted from his horse, "that's what you always do. Would that you would leave it to me!"

With that he turned his back on him.

The king sat motionless on the litter. He had been shamed before the whole troop, and his diffidence and disinclination for bickering had befooled him into an unpremeditated and pitiful trick. His own men had heard him lie like an interrogated baggage-driver. He could not take back his words without still more exposing his shame. The degradation he had brought upon himself as man was for him harder to endure than if he had lost his crown. He wanted to spring up, throw himself on a horse, and take along with him the deep ranks, *his* men, who still believed that he was the chosen of God.

But the pain in his foot and a great lassitude restrained him. His cheeks still glowed, but it was the heat of fever, and for the first time the broadsword trembled in the hand which he was now barely able to raise.

"Take the litter before the front!" he shouted. "Take the litter before the front!"

"The cavalry have not got forward yet," burst out Gyllenkrook with vehemence. "Is it possible that the battle shall begin so soon?"

"They are marching now," answered the king with vexation, "and the enemy is coming out of his lines with the infantry."

Then Gyllenkrook commended the king to God's protection, and seated himself on his horse beside the Guards, who straightway advanced and gave the first volley.

The battle-token was a straw fastened on the hat, and through the noise of shots and trumpets and oboes and drums and cavalry kettledrums sounded the battle-cry of the troops: "God with us! God with us!" In the throng and farther out on the field old war-comrades and near relatives, who had aforetime sat merrily together at home at wedding and christening, met and shouted to one another a last greeting. Where there was more space, captains and lieutenants and ensigns marched before the battalions, pale as corpses, in time with the music, as if they had filed up to a parade in the citadel square by the old

Three Crowns; but the soldiers clenched hands over their empty cartridge-boxes. Through the midst of the fire from the redoubts the Life Guards went in a stubborn line with muskets on shoulder, but when they came to close quarters with the enemy, they shook their clicking weapons savagely and grasped their bayonets. Dust and dirt soon begrimed them all, so that the green coats of the enemy could no longer be distinguished from the blue, and Swedes lifted musket butt against Swedes. In front of Kruse's dragoons Cornet Queckfelt tumbled from his horse with a bullet in his body and the banner against his breast. Major Ridderborg, who in the morning had seen his gray-haired father fall among the troopers by the king's litter, was dragged unconscious from the hand-to-hand struggle. In front of the Nyland regiment fell Colonel Torstenson, and Lieutenant Gyllenbögel stood with shot-wounds in both cheeks, so that one could see the daylight through them. In a thicket behind the Scanian Gentleman-Dragoons reeled Captain Horn, badly wounded in the right leg, and his faithful servant, Daniel Lidbom, held him around the body and dried his forehead. Cavalryman Per Windropp sat dead on his horse, in his hand the tatters of a company flag that had been torn to pieces, and Lieutenant Pauli, who believed him only wounded, offered him his canteen. In front of the Kalmar regiment dropped Colonel Rank, struck in the heart; Major Lejonhjelm lay with his leg shot off; and by the corpse of Lieutenant-Colonel Silversparre Ensign Djurklo fought with broken sword to save the banner, until he sank down dying. Around him lay half the non-commissioned officers and half the men as a hero's watch. The Jönköping regiment, which was nearest the redoubts, carried along their wounded colonel, and after Lieutenant-Colonel Night-and-Day and Major Oxe had fallen in their blood, Captain Mörner took command. Beside him lay prostrate in the ashes on the ground Ensign Tigerskiöld with his face hidden in his hands, propped on his elbows and bleeding from five wounds. Scarcely a fourth of the regiment could still bear arms.

At this moment the field marshal came riding, and cried out to Mörner with untimely warmth: "Where the deuce have the regiment's officers gone off to?"

"They are lying wounded or dead."

"Why the thousand devils aren't you lying there with them?"

"No, my old mother's supplications have called down God's protection over me, and therefore I'm alive and have the honor of commanding this regiment, which has done and will do its duty as true warriors.—Stand, boys, stand!"

Colonel Wrangel lay already dead and unrecognizable, and his recruits sought in vain to prop him up under the arms. Colonel Ulfsparre, who went

before the West Gotlanders, fell with his hands
pressed to his heart, and his major, the dauntless
Sven Lagerberg, was struck down backwards by a
musket-ball. The whole hostile army went over
him. He heard the horses and the cannon-carriages.
He was trampled and kicked and rolled in ashes
and dirt among stiffening corpses and moaning
wounded, till a wounded dragoon finally took him
on his horse, and mercifully conducted him to the
baggage-train.

The beloved old banners, shot into strips, were
still fluttering in goodly numbers over the human
sea, but they wavered and tottered, they were torn
and snapped, and at last they sank and vanished one
by one. The Uppland regiment, which drew most
of its men from the heart of Sweden, from the ancient home of the Svea at Mälardale, was annihilated. Flags with the cross-surmounted apple in the
corner were twisted from the clenched hands of the
fallen, and amid Cossack pikes and butts and sabres
Colonel Stjernhöök was stretched on the ground,
as he stammered: "Now is the time when we may
cry: Father, it is finished!" Lieutenant-Colonel von
Post and Major Anrep fell almost side by side. Captains Gripenberg and Hjulhammar, and Lieutenant
Essen, and the three boyishly slender and beardless Ensigns Flygare, Brinck, and Düben already
lay in the throes of death. "Stand, boys, stand!"
shouted officers and soldiers, and fell over one an-

other, so that of corpses and rags, of clothing and
sod and sand, was built a mound which served the
living for a breastwork. Whistling grapeshot and
musket-balls, grenades and exploding canister,
rained over the fighting and the dead, and the air
was so saturated with dirt and smoke that men could
see only a horse's length ahead.

Then the troops began to waver. Lewenhaupt
drew a pistol from the holster and pointed it at his
own men. He threatened and struck. "Stand, boys,
in Jesus' holy name! I see the king's litter." "If the
king is here, we'll stand," answered the soldiers.
"Stand, boys! halt, stand! God with us!" they
shouted to themselves, as if to control their limbs,
that trembled and dripped with sweat and blood.
But step by step they yielded, and the riders reined
in their horses, until, with slashed faces and hands,
they finally wheeled about in wild flight, man after
man, and trampled one another down. Under the
rising clouds of smoke they saw the king, who amid
fallen troopers, bearers, and attendants lay on the
ground without a hat, supported on his elbow, with
the injured foot propped on the crushed litter, over
which had been spread the clay-spotted cloak of the
slain trooper Oxehufvud. The stiffened face was
raven-black with grime, but the eyes kindled, and
he stammered: "Swedes! Swedes!"

In the yielding ranks many stood still when they
recognized the voice, because it seemed to them that

even if they could save themselves now, they must sometime on their death-bed hear across the pillow that timid and lonely voice. He had not the strength to raise himself, but they lifted him on their crossed pikes like a doomed and helpless invalid. Again and again, though, the bearers were shot down, and yet in that instant, when the bleeding men succumbed, they stretched up their arms to support him so that he should not be hurt in the fall. Then Major Wolffelt lifted him on his horse, and afterwards fell himself under the weapons of the pursuing Cossacks. The foot, which was laid over the horse's neck, bled violently, and the bandage dragged in the dust. A cannon-ball from the entrenchments struck off the horse's leg, but Trooper Gierta lifted the king upon his charger and, himself wounded, mounted on the three-legged and bleeding horse. The cavalrymen who had made a ring about the king could hardly hold back the pursuers.

Meanwhile Gyllenkrook rushed over the field, and exhorted the straggling soldiers to rally, but they answered him: "We are all wounded and our officers dead." He then met the field marshal, and now upon the day of retribution there was no longer any deference.

Gyllenkrook shouted to him offensively, "Does Your Excellency hear that the volleys are still sounding on our left wing! Here are a mass of

squadrons that have sat down. Order them to go
somewhere!"

"Here everything is mad! Here to be sure some
obey me with their haunches, but few with their
hearts," answered the field marshal, and rode further and further to the left. At the same time Gyllenkrook saw Piper with his men of the chancellery
ride off to the right. Had the two Excellencies
spoken together? He shouted after them that they
were betaking themselves straight toward the enemy, but they did not turn about. Then he struck his
hand on the pommel of his saddle, and understood
that now the wine of patience was drunk, that now
there remained only captivity or death.

There lay behind him no longer a field. There
grew from the earth a boundless wood, but the
trunks were men and the boughs weapons. It
broadened out. It filled the whole landscape, and
constantly, constantly spread forward over the
bleeding and dying. It was the czar's army, that
marched on to take possession of its land and dedicate its empire to future times. Ever nearer and
nearer was heard an uncanny and dull-sounding
religious hymn. Slowly, step by step, as in a funeral
procession, between swinging thuribles and high
over the heads of thousands upon thousands, was
borne the giant standard. On the cloth appeared
the czar's ancestral tree, surrounded by saints, and

above, under the Trinity, was his own likeness.

The Swedish fugitives gathered around the king by the baggage, where the Swedish Nobleman-Guards and some other regiments kept watch. Having bound up his foot and tolerably wiped off the grime, he now sat in a blue wagon beside the wounded Colonel Hård.

"Where is Adlerfeldt, the chamberlain?" he asked.

Those who stood around him answered, "He fell by a cannon-shot close to Your Majesty's litter."

At that moment the Dalecarlian regiment came past, shattered and in great disorder.

"Dalecarlians," inquired the king, "where is Siegeroth, your Colonel, and Major Svinhufvud, and where is the merry Drake, who is said to have fought so valiantly at the redoubt that he shall get a regiment?"

"They are shot, all of them."

"Where, then, are the Little Prince, and Piper, and the field marshal?"

Those around him shook their heads and looked at one another. Should they once for all tell him the whole truth? Should they on that day of judgment expose all his loneliness? Should they tell him, too, that Hedwig Sofia, his favorite sister, had lain for half a year in her coffin—unburied? There was none who dared to do that.

"Captured," they answered reluctantly.

"Captured? Captured among the Muscovites? Better go among the Turks, then. Forward!"

He paled, but he spoke calmly and almost triumphantly with the unalterable smile on his lips.

A grizzled soldier among the Dalecarlians whispered to the comrades, "Truly I have never seen him so youthful and happy since the day at Narva, when he went with Stenbock. This is a day of victory to him."

The wagon rolled away, and the king of the Charles men, in front of his disordered, fleeing army of haughty ragamuffins, swearing baggage crones, cripples moaning loudly, and limping horses, marched with flying banners and resounding music as from his greatest victory.

.   .   .   .

By two o'clock the last volleys were fired, and then stillness had spread itself over the battle-field, where Mazeppa's last Cossacks and countless Zaporogeans were impaled alive on stakes. Homesteads and mills stood burned, trees shot asunder, and the fallen heroes lay with dust and ashes blown over them, all with eyes wide open, as if they had stared back from another world on the past years and on the living. A few captured priests and soldiers roamed about, seeking for their countrymen and sometimes opening a shallow grave, over which the

words of burial in the speech of their far-off homeland were softly whispered out into the dusk of the
June evening. After that the grave was again shut,
to be overgrown with sedge grass and rough thistles.
For centuries after, they have rustled to the winds
of the steppes on the gloomy bogland to which the
Russians gave the name of the Swedes' Cemetery.

When one of the priests found Lieutenant-Colonel Wetzel, who had fallen, together with his two
sons, he picked up the empty covers of the prayer-
book which lay beside him, adorned with the family crest.

"You are the last of your family," he said; "and
how many a stock has been extinguished on this
field! Galle, Siegeroth, Mannersvärd, Rosenskiöld,
von Borgen. As I now tear apart the crest on this
cover and strew it to the winds, I also in the name
of my afflicted, my annihilated father-folk, shatter
the coats-of-arms above you all."

A multitude of bodies were thrown together in
a heap outside of the field entrenchment where the
day's conflict had been hottest, but the others remained strewn about. The air was filled almost at
once with a stale vapor and with countless flapping
crows. But darkness descended silently with all the
more solemnity over the wide city of graves, though
the wounded still cried for water. Those most
pitiably mangled prayed that some one in mercy
would finish them with a sword-thrust, or they

dragged themselves to a horse that had been shot, pulled the pistols from the holsters, and took them-selves from the light of day, after they had on tremulous knees called down a blessing over all at home and recited the Lord's Prayer. Then a mor-tally wounded dragoon began to speak words of power and to thank God for his glorious death-wounds. Over himself and his comrades he uttered the burial words and thrice took earth with his hands and cast it upon his breast. "Out of earth are we come, to earth we shall return." After that he preached with ecstasy of the Resurrection, and finally with a loud voice took up a funeral hymn, and twenty or thirty voices answered far off in the dark under the star-bright heavens.

Morten Preacher, who stole around on the plain without feeling any terror of the fallen, contin-ued the psalm when the dragoon was silent. Then he caught sight of an old woman, who came with a torch. After her followed a line of peasants with long, rude carts, on which they loaded clothing and all manner of plunder. A fallen cornet, who was not yet dead, defended himself with his hand and would not let go from him a necklace with a little silver cross, but they thrust him down with a hay-fork.

Then Morten Preacher sprang forward. "Thou shalt not kill! Thou shalt not kill!" he whispered. Among the plundering women he recognized his

nine-year-old Dunya, his little princess. His whole
countenance changed, and he stretched out both
hands to her, half like a father, half like a bashful
lover. She stared at him, and burst into a silly
laugh.

"That's the wicked Swede," she cried, "who
bribed me so as to get cherries and kiss me on the
cheeks."

She sprang upon him like a cat and tore the earrings from him, so that the blood ran down the sides
of his neck. He fell backwards, and the women
seized him and struck him and tore his clothes from
him. They came upon his transcript of St. John's
Gospel, and strewed the leaves around like feathers
from a plucked fowl. They pulled off his flap-boots
and ragged stockings, but when he saw his little
Dunya clutch at a hay-fork, he wrenched himself
loose with the strength of upflaming hate and fled
in his shirt over wounded and dead.

"Not even trust in a guileless heart is left us
more," he muttered, and clambered up on a lame
horse which had attached itself to him in the darkness. "God has abandoned us. This is the judgment. All is over, and the whole world is dark."

He rode for two nights and two days, and
wounded stragglers pointed out the road. He found
the fleeing Swedes on a peninsula between the
Vorskla and the bright Dnieper, which spread itself out like a lake between banks overgrown with

reeds, underbrush, and bushes. The Russians were close behind them on the landward side, but when the outposts saw Morten Preacher in his bloody shirt, riding bare-back on the lame horse, they sprang to one side in terror and only shot after him when he was already past.

The sun burned hot as fire. The wounded and those with camp-fever were bedded under bushes by the water. The generals stood in conversation, and Lewenhaupt turned mournfully to Creutz.

"If the king is taken, the men of Sweden will abandon their houses and leave their last wisp of hay for his ransom. The responsibility is ours. This war is a game of chess, where everything is decided by taking the kings. On my knees I have prayed him to have himself rowed across the river, but he pushed me away, and said he had serious matters to consider."

"My dear brother, you talk to him as to a gouty statesman. You should never talk to him as to a man, but as to a youth who is proud of being challenged to show his manhood."

Creutz went forward to the king's wagon and swung the gloves in his hand with such violence that it seemed as if he meant to strike Charles on the forehead, but he was at once confounded by his radiant glance.

"Your Majesty is in perplexity?"

"I fight ill with the pen—that's what I'm thinking of. I wish to draw up my will and arrange for the succession. Then we'll set the guns cracking! If I'm left on the field, I wish to be buried in my shirt like a common soldier on the place where I fall."

Creutz twisted and squeezed the gloves; he was cowed and lowered his head, like the others.

" Most gracious lord, I am not of those who pray God to spare their life, because full well do I understand the highest longing of a hero. If Your Majesty should get your bullet . . . well, so be it, in Jesus' name! But to-day Your Majesty can no longer stay in the saddle. God forgive my words, but Your Majesty has got to the point of being carried around helpless, and when the last of us has lost his life, there will be left only Your Majesty — a prisoner!"

"A man should not only stand one against five, he should also be able to stand one against all."

"True, true. But — devil take me! — we common fellows in uniform are not fit for that. One against all? That means one against the whole world. For that are needed men of quite a different sort, for we are such pitiful wretches that we have nothing to defend ourselves with but our blades. Now that I have described the situation plainly, I therefore beseech Your Majesty to stay with us and not cross the river, because then Your Majesty would set yourself one against all. Then it would be: What an Alexander to run away and leave his troops to the Russians! What a heartless,

disgraceful dolt! Look, look! And he took the plate
and money-barrels from Saxony along instead of
leaving everything to the Russians. Oho, yes, hahaha!
— We poor honest subjects can never allow that
Your Majesty should set yourself as one against the
whole world in that way, to expose your high person to the mud-flinging that ignorance and stupidity will not spare either to the field marshal or
Piper or Lewenhaupt or the rest of us. When did
stupidity ever learn to understand misfortune? Your
Majesty wants to die, and therefore it is no sacrifice and no achievement to die — that we old war-
dogs know; but pride, pride, Your Majesty, to offer
up that for your subjects is a sacrifice that the subjects cannot consent to. That the men cannot be
taken over is clear. We have no barges, no anchors,
no spikes, not enough logs, no carpenters. Therefore I require that Your Majesty remain and do not
defy the world."

"Get the boats ready!" ordered the king.

Mazeppa, the gallant landed proprietor, had
collected his trunks and his two barrels of ducats,
and was already sitting on his wagon far out in the
water. Zaporogeans and swarms of soldiers tied
their clothes on their backs, took wagon-lids and
branches of trees under their arms, and sprang into
the waves. At midnight the king's wagon also was
lifted on two boats tied together, and Gyllenkrook,
who stood at his feet, dumbly surrendered to Lew-

enhaupt the battle-plan, pasted on a board. No one spoke. The night was starry and quiet, and the oar-strokes of the troopers died away on the shining river.

"We two shall never see him again," muttered Creutz to Lewenhaupt. "His eyes were so wonderful just now! There is still oil in the lamp, but I am gazing curiously at his future. How will he be when he is conquered, ridiculed, old?"

Lewenhaupt answered, "The wreath he twined for himself slid off upon his subjects instead. It will lie forever on the forgotten graves up there in the marshes.—So we must thank him for all he has made of us."

Far off through the darkness of the night was heard the lamenting voice of Morten Preacher: "'And men have made of me a by-word before the world,' saith Job. 'And I am become a mockery, and mine eyes are wasted with grief, and my limbs are all a shadow. Unto corruption I say: thou art my father, and unto worms: ye are my mother and sister. And where then is my hope? It goeth down to the gate of death, when I and it shall rest in the earth.'"

Day came on, and Morten Preacher in his bloody shirt rode from group to group, examining the men in the Catechism and Biblical knowledge. The soldiers stood in silence by the empty tent of the king, but when the shout was raised that they must sur-

render, and when the Russian general Bauer, tanned
by the sun, ascended the hill to receive the trophies,
Morten Preacher stepped down and wrung his
hands.

Round about, with their brazen helmets , and
pikes, sat the Cossacks on their tired and panting
horses, and before them on the ground were laid
kettledrums and bass-drums and horns and muskets
whose thunder had rolled over battalions, and the
well-known flags to which once mothers and wives
had waved farewell from door and stairway and
window. There was gleaming and sparkling on the
heather. Sullen old under-officers embraced each
other sobbing. Some cut off their bandages and let
the blood run, and two battle-brothers quenched
each other's lives with their swords at the same
time that they threw them down before the conquerors. Dumb and threatening, the cripples advanced. There came youths with frost-bitten cheeks,
and without nose and ears, so that they were like
dead men. Ensign Piper, not yet full-grown, who
had lost his heels, stumbled up on crutches. There
came the courtier Gunterfelt, who lacked both hands,
and had got in France two others of wood, black and
shining, which fingered up and down on his coat.
There rattled wooden legs and canes and litters and
ambulance-wagons.

Morten Preacher stood with hands clasped.
Sparks leaped before his eyes. There was a roaring

and moaning within, and the old preaching-spirit
came so violently over him that he himself heard
how his voice at one time was choked and hoarse,
but the next grew so strong that it seemed to him
as if he were borne away on the wings of it and
were changed to a flame of fire.

He reeled forward to the arms that had been
laid down and pointed to the empty tent of the king.

"*He* alone is the offender. You, mother or
widow, clad in mourning, turn his picture to the
wall! Forbid the little ones to mention his name!
You, little Dunya, who with your playmates will
soon be picking flowers on the graves, build his
monument with skulls and horses' heads! You, crip-
ple, knock with your crutch on the hollow earth and
summon him to a meeting there below, where thousands whom he sacrificed await him!—And yet I
know that one day before the judgment seat of righteousness we shall all limp forward on our wooden
legs and crutches, and say: 'Forgive him, Father,
as we have forgiven him, because our love was both
his victory and his destruction.'"

When no one replied, but all stood bent forward
and dumb as if they had answered the same, his despair was yet more vehement. He covered his angu-
lar face with his hands.

"Tell me by the grace of God that he lives!"
cried he. "Say that he lives!"

With his black wooden fingers Gunterfelt raised

his hat from his head and answered, "His Majesty is saved."

Then Morten Preacher bowed his knee, and trembled, and recovered himself.

"Praised be the Lord of Hosts!" he stammered. "If the king is saved, then I will bear whatever burden fate shall lay upon me."

"Yes, yes, praised be the Lord of Hosts!" repeated the Swedes mumbling, and all slowly lifted their hats from their heads.

Behold My Children!

CORPORAL ANDERS GROBERG stood with his canteen on Saracen's Heath. Around him reeled and marched the last band of fleeing Swedes and Zaporogeans, and on wagons lay those who had been wounded at Poltava. The whole night and morning Anders Groberg had endured thirst so as to spare the last drops of water to the utmost, and the torture had now become overpowering. But in the very moment he lifted the canteen to his lips, he lowered it again.

"My God, my God!" he stammered, "why should I alone drink, when all the others are thirsting? If Thou hast led us forth into the wilderness and the steppes, it is that Thou shouldst sometime be able to say: 'From your poverty-stricken country of snow I let you go forth into the world with musket on shoulder to be hailed as heroes and conquerors, but when I read your hearts and saw that they remained pure, that ye were my children, then I tore your clothes in pieces and set crutches in your hands and wooden legs under your bodies, so that ye should no more hanker after domination over men, but should be gathered among my saints. Such greatness did I grant unto you.'"

Anders Groberg stood awhile longer with the canteen before him. Then he went on, and handed it to the king, who lay in burning fever among the sacks of hay on his wagon. The king's lips adhered to his teeth; they split and bled when he opened them.

"No, no," he whispered, "give the water to the wounded! I have just had a glass."

Anders Groberg knew well that the king had had no water. He himself was the only man who had taken thought for the morrow and saved it up, and neither spring nor bog had they found for many a mile. But now, as he turned away from the wagon, weakness and temptation once more came over him. He hung the canteen back at his side and continued to march and march without handing it to the wounded. He squeezed the stopper and strove in his soul, but every time he raised the canteen to his mouth, he let it fall again and had not the heart to drink of the water.

"Perhaps," he thought, "I might refresh myself with a clearer conscience, if as an offset I should humiliate myself in something else."

At noon, when the sun burned most hotly, he saw a gray-haired subaltern who went almost naked with unbandaged wounds on his shoulder. Thereupon he tore up his shirt, bound the other's wounds, and gave him his coat; but as soon as he shut his hand on his canteen again, his unrest of conscience woke anew. Then he gave his boots to a sick driver lad, who limped along with bare and bleeding feet, but when he still could not swallow the water with an easy mind in the midst of all the other thirsty

men, he became embittered and hard. He pointed
with derisive curses at the money-barrels which, full
of gold and silver, clattered as they were taken along
on two of the wagons, but which could not provide
the unfortunate soldiers with a spoonful of brackish
bog-water.

"Whip the horses!" he shouted, "whip the
horses, so that the money-barrels shall not be left
behind! Whip the men, too!"

The soldiers answered nothing, because now they
recognized him again as he used to be formerly,
when in the years of success he had gone in front
of the line, bitter and abusive. They did not notice
that he had hardly heard his own voice before he
bent his head and began again to cudgel his brains
and whisper to himself.

"Must I then of necessity offer up just the one
thing that has now any worth for me?" he thought.
" Haha! May we also some day roll the money-
barrels on the grass and nevermore touch them
with our fingers! My God, my God! Once at Veperik I heard the dying soldier Bengt Geting speak
with envy of the fallen who had received a clean
white shirt. My longing dares not rise so high. I desire so little . . . ah, only this, not to be left lying
behind the others on the heath, only to be laid in
the ground, to have earth and grass over me — and
a couple of words on the muster-roll. Now it will
stand: Anders Groberg, his fate unknown."

Towards dusk a halt was made to bury those who had died during the day, and a couple of Zaporogeans had already stuck their spades in the ground. In the reedy grass grew a few low bushes with cherries which, meanwhile, officers and soldiers picked and divided among them as a bounty bestowed from God's own hands. Anders Groberg slunk behind the bushes to drink the water unseen by the others. But just then the trumpets began to blow as a sign that the pursuing Russians had again become visible against the heaven on the farthest waves of the parched desert of grass.

Anders Groberg opened the tin stopper, but the longer he inhaled the moist smell, the harder beat his heart, and in the nearest wagon the dying Börje Köve, a soldier in charge of the silver, raised himself and stared at him.

Anders Groberg tried to meet his look, but could not, and yet again he pushed the draught of refreshment from him.

"Blessed are those that hunger and thirst after righteousness," he said.

Like an acolyte who gives the sacrament, he bore the canteen in front of him and held it to the mouth of the soldier, and the dying man drank the water to the last drop.

Anders Groberg held on tight to the tail-board, but when the wheel rolled on again, his hand slipped off, and he tottered to his knees on the grass.

"There is no place for me on the wagons," he said, and pulled a spade to him. "Though I'm hardly thirty years old, I am as weary and infirm as a man of ninety. But leave me one of the spades, so that, if my strength stays by me, I may at least be able to open the earth and lay me down in my last abode. All my unrest has now fallen sweetly to sleep, and a voice calls at my ear: 'Behold my children!'"

Once more the soldiers around the shaking wagons began their wandering, and the trumpeters turned in the saddle. Flocks of storks with outspread wings hovered in the dusk over the darkening tracts, and out on the steppe Anders Groberg still knelt with the spade in his hands.

Since then no one has learned anything of his fate.

At the Council Table

IN the ante-room of the Council Chamber already stood the secretary, Schmedeman, with the address to the chiefs of the provinces, which was now to be signed, and in which new levies were required from impoverished Sweden.

The lords began to assemble, and old Frölich, who with crossed hands was groaning and snoring in a corner beside the sick Falkenberg, suddenly awoke.

"We must hand over to the king the whole bank with the money and the patents," he said without lifting his reddened eyelids.

Then Arvid Horn started forward with such vehemence that his chair fell back on the floor, and shouted with his arms lifted toward the ceiling: "Keep yourself to your heavenly revelations and seasons of prayer with sister Eva-Greta and do not make thieves of us out of mere good intentions toward His Royal Majesty!"

"Satan, Satan!" retorted Falkenberg, and rapped with his colorless fingers on the arm of the chair. "Here is blackguarding and maligning from day to day. No Swede any longer respects the honor of another, but no one has the courage for an honest word against him who alone is responsible for it all. Yes, don't you sit down again, you Horn, for people are most of all incensed about your yacht in the Mälar, and assert that with the powder smoke from your salutes you want to win the same gallant favor with Princess Ulrika Eleonora which Creutz had with Princess Hedwig Sofia of most blessed memory. — Yes, yes, yes, don't talk any more about the person of the king. Read his letter instead! Do that! Is there a single line of it that is worthy of the leader of an unfortunate people?"

"Bah! Don't talk about the letter either!" answered Horn, picking up his chair and sitting down. "A little prattle for women, evasions, and indifferent matters! Don't ask that a person who never exposes himself in a conversation shall set himself down in a tent and pour out his soul on a sheet of paper! But I may well admit that sometime an after-reckoning will follow on all this misery."

"Sometime, say you!" continued the invalid Falkenberg, and raised himself on his trembling arms. "Sometime! Have the Swedes then become cringers and hypocrites? Neither Christian the Tyrant nor Erik XIV has done us so much harm as this man, and therefore he belongs to the devil. Since our men have fallen in the field, only old-woman souls are left alive, and those are they that now begin to propagate the Swedish people."

The venerable Fabian Wrede stood up among the speakers, and his voice was wondrously faint and quiet.

"The session is beginning," he said, and pointed

to the open doors. "I'm no cringer. I was never
of those who jostled around the young master to
make him of age, and I am in disfavor. My native
land, that is everything to me — father and mother,
home, memory, all, all! I know that now my native
land is bleeding to death. I know, too, that sometime retribution will follow. But the present is not
the time to waste thought upon that. When God
sets on us the crown of thorns, that man is not
greatest who most conveniently puts it off, but he
who himself presses it on all the tighter and says:
'Father, here stand I to serve Thee.'— And I say
to you that never, never amid the victory-banners
in former years has our little people come nearer
to imperishable greatness than to-day."

Horn went into the assembly hall, but on the
way he turned to Falkenberg with lowered voice:
"My mother had many sons besides me. They
have got their bullets. Shall I be worse than they?
You talk about the king. If a single man can lure
a whole people to so many sacrifices, must not that
man be superior to other men?"

Wrede took Falkenberg gently by the shoulders,
and added in an undertone: "And the people who
have borne so much — would you to-day forbid
that people to press fast the crown of martyrdom?"

The lords entered the hall, but, propped on his
stick, Falkenberg continued to wander back and
forth in the ante-room. When he at length sat down

at the Council table, the secretary had already read
out the long address, and the signatures were desired.

No one asked leave to speak. Falkenberg sat
huddled together in his armchair. His eyes were
moist and dim. Forgetful of precedent, he fumbled
with his hands on all sides and whispered, "A pen,
a pen!"

In the Church Square

BROAD-SHOULDERED Jöns Snare of
Mora was eating porridge with his peasant
neighbors, Mons and Mathias. He was so stingy
that he lay and slept all winter in a shutter-bed to
save lighting. His large, flat, beardless face, which
glowed in the light from the round window, was
uglier and more wrinkled than a troll's, and he
talked slowly with a hollow and rumbling voice.

"I predict," said he, striking his hand on the
table, "that days of bark-bread are coming. To-
morrow I kill my last cow. Every year brings new
levies and conscriptions, and now they want to take
from us the church bell, the money for the Communion wine, and the grain in the church storehouse."

"It's truly spoken, that," said Mons.

He scratched his gray cheeks and took another
pinch of salt on his porridge-spoon, because it was
the Sabbath. At other times Mons was so stingy
that he went around among the neighbors and
counted the pinches of salt on the porridge and the
sticks of wood under the pot.

Mathias, on the contrary, leaned forward over
the table, shrivelled and ugly, with black teeth and
two small shining gray vipers for eyes. He was,
however, the stingiest of the three. A more cov-
etous peasant never lived in the parish. He was

so stingy that he went into the sacristy to the priest
and ordered him on week days to wear wooden
shoes like the common folk.

" My opinion simply is," he droned, "that God
set us peasants to keep our thumbs on the nation's purse. Not a copper will I lay in the bailiff's
fist."

" But steal my fish-net," answered Jöns Snare,
"that you could."

" It's truly spoken, that," said Mons.

Mathias sneered, and broke a loaf with the back
of an axe: "What's a man to do when he's starving?"

Jöns Snare shook his long and straggling yellow
hair and got up, and his speech could be heard far
outside the cabin.

" Ay, sluggard, then do you take your father's
old blunderbuss from the wall, pick off the bailiff
and the tax assessor, and hide them in the hayloft.
And before you are done for or come to the gallows,
you shall go with me to Stockholm to teach the
great gentlemen peasant wit. Peace we demand,
and peace it shall be!"

" It's truly spoken, that. We'll go with you,"
said Mons and got up, swaying in the knees.

Even Mathias got up and gave Jöns Snare a
hand-shake.

" To begin with, let's go on to the church and
talk to the common folk," he said, with his whin-

ing voice. "We must hold by our ancient rights and liberties!"

"I'll talk, sure enough I will," answered Jöns Snare; "and peace it shall be. We demand it."

They went out of the cabin, and on the way talked with wives and servant-maids and old men and boys. When they came to the church square, they had a good twenty or thirty following with them.

The autumn sun shone cold and clear over woody ridges and lakes and. on the long white church. On the square in front of the stable-building the people murmured between wagons and carts, but the children of the confirmation class, who had sat by the altar, had as yet got no further than the threshold of the church porch. The shaggiest old men, who came down from the woods and who had already put on their fur coats, began to cry out and make a racket when they recognized Jöns Snare, because they all regarded him as the most stiff-necked and powerful peasant in the parish. The other Dalecarlians, as well, with bright, open features and white shirts that gleamed out between leather breeches and vests, turned toward him, for it seemed to them that nothing in the world had more weight than his slow and obstinate words.

"You are great church-goers, you," he shouted to them. "I suppose it's to learn the new church prayer about the subject's duty of patience."

No one gave himself leisure to answer. All thronged about him.

"The king is taken!" they shouted. "The king is taken! The king is taken!"

"Is the king taken?" Jöns Snare stood with his hands clenched and looked inquiringly from one to another.

"It's truly spoken, that," said Mons.

"Be still, you fellow! What do you know about it?" roared Jöns Snare, and lifted his clenched hands half up so that all edged away and left him space.

He sat down on a bench before the stables, but the Dalecarlians would not leave him, and the circle around him became closer. No one wanted to lose a single word.

"Is the king taken?" he asked afresh.

"So it's being told from one to another. A smith from Falun has said that the king is taken among the heathens."

Mathias moved up nearer and bent himself and stretched out his long fingers.

"What do you think about these tidings, Jöns Snare, I simply ask?"

Jöns Snare sat with hands on knees, and the sun shone upon his wooden, motionless forehead and hard lips. He looked down at the ground.

"What do you say?" murmured the Dalecarlians. "In Stockholm one of the councillors is giving his own money to the Crown, another his plate, and

the third proposes that every well-to-do subject shall
give all he has and hereafter possess no more than
the poor man. There is only the Queen Dowager
who wants her allowance undiminished, the stingy
trollop, and people on the street are breaking the
windows of Piper's countess."

"And we," said Mathias, "we ought to take the
blunderbuss from the wall, Jöns Snare says."

"It's truly spoken, that," confirmed Mons.

Jöns Snare was still silent, and it now became so
still around him that nothing else was heard than
the ringing of the bell.

"Yes," he answered after a time, and his voice
rumbled more deeply and bitterly than ever before,
"we ought to take the blunderbuss from the wall
and leave the house. By God! you good men of the
Dale, if the king is taken, then we demand that they
should lead us against the foe, so that we may get
him home."

Mathias remained in thought, but his brow became bright, and his gray eyes twinkled slyly.

"Look you, that is a demand that belongs to our
ancient rights and liberties."

"It's truly spoken, that," said Mons.

"Yes, yes, that's a demand that belongs to our
ancient rights and liberties," murmured the Dalecarlians, and lifted their hands in affirmation. Then
there was such a clamor and uproar that the bells
could no more be heard.

Captured

FAR out in the wastes of Småland and Finnved wondrous portents appeared in the air, and since work lost all worth and the morrow all hope, people either went hungry or ate and drank with riot and revel amid half-stifled curses. At every farm sat a mother or a widow in mourning. During the day's occupation she talked of the fallen or the captives, and at night she started from her sleep, and thought she was still hearing the thunder of the hideous wagons on which teamsters in black oil-cloth cloaks carried away those who had died of the plague.

In the church of Riddarholm the body of the Princess Hedwig Sofia had lain unburied for seven years from lack of money, and now a new coffin had been laid out for the old Queen Dowager Hedwig Eleonora, the mother of the Charleses. Several sleepy ladies-in-waiting were keeping the death-watch, and wax-lights burned mistily around the dead, who lay wrapped in a simple covering of linen.

The youngest lady-in-waiting arose, yawning, went to the window, and drew back the black broad-cloth to see if dawn had not appeared.

Limping steps were heard from the ante-room, and a little man of a gnarled and rugged figure, who in every way tried to subdue the thump of his wooden leg, advanced to the coffin and with signs of deep reverence lifted aside the drapery. His fair, almost white hair lay close along his head and extended down his neck as far as his collar. From a flask he poured embalming liquid into a funnel, which was set in the royal corpse between the kirtle and the bodice. But the liquid was absorbed very slowly, and, waiting, he set down the flask on the funeral carpet and went to the lady at the window.

"Is it not seven o'clock yet, Blomberg!" she whispered.

"It has just struck six. It's an awful weather outside, and I feel in the stump of my leg that we're going to have a snowstorm. But then it's a long while since one could foretell anything good in Sweden. Trust me, not this time either will there be enough money for a decent funeral. It was only the beginning when the sainted Ekerot prophesied misery and conflagration. And perhaps the fire didn't go on over the island in front of the castle! Over the plain of Uppsala it threw its light from cathedral and citadel. In Vasterås and Linköping the tempest sweeps the ashes around the blackened spaces devastated by fire — and now there's burning in all quarters of the kingdom. Forgive my freedom, gracious mistress, but to tell the truth is in the long run less dangerous than to lie. That's my old maxim that saved my life once down there by the Dnieper River."

"Saved your life? You were then a surgeon in

your regiment. You must sit down by me here and tell the story. The time is so long."

Blomberg spoke resignedly and a trifle like a priest, from time to time lifting his dexter and middle fingers with the other fingers closed.

Both cast a glance at the corpse, which slept in its coffin with gracefully disposed locks, and wax and rouge in the deepest of the wrinkles. Thereupon they sat themselves on a bench in the window-nook outside the hanging broadcloth, and Blomberg began whispering his narrative.

I was lying unconscious in the marshy wilderness at Poltava. I had stumbled along on my wooden leg and got a blow from a horse's hoof, and when I came to, it was night. I felt a cold, strange hand fumble under my coat and pull at the buttons. An abomination before the Lord are the devices of the wicked, I thought; but gentle words are pure. Without becoming frightened, I seized the corpse-plunderer very silently by the breast, and by his stammered words of terror I perceived that he was one of the Zaporogeans who had made an alliance with the Swedes and followed the army. As surgeon I had tended many of these men, as well as captured Poles and Muscovites, and could make myself tolerably understood in their various languages.

"Many devices are in the heart of man," said I

meekly; "but the counsel of the Lord, that shall abide. No evil can befall the righteous, but the ungodly shall be filled with misfortunes."

"Forgive me, pious sir," whispered the Zaporogean. "The Swedish czar has left us poor Zaporogeans to our fate, and the Muscovite czar, whom we faithlessly deserted, is coming to maim and slay us. I only wanted to get me a Swedish coat so that in a moment of need I could give myself out as one of you. Do not be angry, godly sir!"

To see if he had any knife, I searched out flint and steel while he was speaking and made a fire with dry thistles and twigs which lay at my feet. I noted then that I had before me a little frightened old man with a sly face and two empty hands. He raised himself as vehemently as a hungry animal that has found its prey, and bent in the light over a Swedish ensign who lay dead in the grass. Thinking that a dead man might willingly grant a helpless ally his coat, I did nothing to hinder the Zaporogean; but as he drew the coat from the fallen one, a letter slipped from the pocket. I saw by the address that Falkenberg was the name of the boy who had bled to death. He lay now as fairly and peacefully stretched out as if he had slept in the meadow by the house where he was born. The letter was from his sister, and I had only time to spell out the words which from that hour became my favorite maxim: "To tell the truth is in the

long run less dangerous than to lie." At that moment the Zaporogean put out my light.

"With your wise consent, sir," he whispered;
"do not draw the corpse-plunderers hither."

I paid little attention to his talk, but repeated
time after time: "To tell the truth is in the long
run less dangerous than to lie. That is a big saying,
my old fellow, and you shall see that I get along
further with it than you do with your disguise."

"We may try it," answered the Zaporogean,
"but we must promise this, that the one of us who
survives the other shall offer a prayer for the
other's soul."

"That is agreed," I said, and gave him my hand,
for it seemed as if through misfortune I had found
in this shaggy-bearded barbarian a friend and a
brother.

He helped me up, and at daybreak we fell into
the long line of stragglers and wounded that silently
tottered into Poltava to give themselves up as prisoners. They willingly tried to conceal the Zaporogean among the rest. His big boots with their
flaps reached up to his hips, and his coat tails hung
down to his spurs. As soon as a Cossack looked
at him, he turned to one of us and cried with raised
voice the only Swedish words he had learned in the
campaign: "I Shwede. Devil-damn!"

My Zaporogean and I, with eight of my comrades, were assigned quarters in the upper story of

a big stone house. As we two had come up there
first, we picked out for ourselves a little separate
cubby-hole with a window on an alley. There was
nothing else than a little straw to lie on, but I had
in my coat a tin flute, which I had taken from a
fallen Kalmuck at Starodub, and on which I had
taught myself to play a few pretty hymns. With
that I shortened the time, and soon we noticed that,
as often as I played, a young woman came to the window on the other side of the alley. Possibly for that
reason I played more than I should have otherwise
cared to, and I know not rightly whether she was
fairer and more seemly than all other women, or
whether long sojourn among men had made my
eye less accustomed, but I had great joy in beholding her. However, I never looked at her when
she turned her face toward our window, because I
have always been bashful before women-folk, and
have never rightly understood how to conduct
myself in that which pertains to them. Nor have
I ever sought fellowship with men who go with
their heads full of wenches and do nothing but
hanker after gallant intrigues. " Let every one keep
his vessel in holiness," Paul saith, "and not in the
lust of desire as do the heathen, which know not
God; also let no one in this matter dishonor and
wrong his brother, because the Lord is a powerful
avenger in all such things."

I recognized, however, that a man should at all

times bear himself courteously and fittingly, and
as one sleeve of my coat was in tatters, I always
turned that side inward when I played.

She usually sat with arms crossed above the
window-sill, and her hands were round and white,
though large. She had a scarlet-colored bodice
with silver buttons and many chains. An old witch
who often stood beneath her window with a wheel-
barrow and sold bread covered with jam called her
Feodosova.

When it grew dusk, she lighted a lamp, and
since neither she nor we had any shutters, we could
follow her with our glance when she blew on the fire,
but I found it more proper that we should turn
away, and I therefore set myself with my Zaporogean on the straw in the corner.

Besides the prayer-book, I had a few torn-out
leaves of Müller's Sermons, and I read and translated many passages for my Zaporogean. But when
I noticed that he did not listen, I gave it over for
more worldly objects, and asked him of our neighbor on the other side of the alley. He said that she
was not unmarried, because maidens in that country
always wore a long plait tied with ribbons and a
little red tuft of silk. More likely she was a widow,
because her hair hung loose as a token of sorrow.

When it became wholly dark, and we lay down
on the straw, I discovered that the Zaporogean
had stolen my silver snuff-spoon, but after I had

taken it back and reproached him for his fault, we slept beside each other as friends.

I was almost ashamed, when it was morning again, at feeling myself happier than for a long time, but as soon as I had held prayers with the Zaporogean and had washed and arranged myself sufficiently, I went to the window and played one of my most beautiful hymns.

Feodosova was already sitting in the sunlight. To show her how different the Swedes were from her fellow countrymen, I instructed my Zaporogean to clean our room, and after a couple of hours the whitewashed walls were shining white and free from cobwebs. All this helped me to drive away my thoughts, but as soon as I set myself again to rest, my torments of conscience awakened that I could be happy in such misery. In the hall outside, my comrades sat on floor and benches, sighing heavily and whispering about their dear ones at home. In due turn, two of us every day were allowed to go out into the open air to the ramparts, but when I laid myself on my straw in the evening, I was ashamed to pray God that the lot next morning should fall upon me. I knew very well within myself that, if I longed for an hour's freedom, it was only to invent an errand to the house opposite. And yet I felt that, if the lot really fell upon me without my prayer, I should still never venture to go up there.

When I came to the window in the morning, Feodosova lay sleeping in her clothes on the floor with a cushion under her neck. It was still early and cool, and I did not have the heart to set the tin flute to my mouth. But as I stood there and waited, she may have apprehended in her sleep that I was gazing at her, for she looked up and laughed and stretched her arms out, and all that so suddenly that I did not manage to draw back unnoticed. My brow became hot, I laid aside my flute, and behaved myself in every way so clumsily and unskilfully that I never was so displeased with myself. I pulled and straightened my belt, took my flute again from the window, inspected it, and pretended I was blowing dust out of it. When finally the Russian subaltern who had.charge over us unfortunates informed my Zaporogean that he was one of the two who were to go out into the city that day, I drew the Zaporogean aside into a corner and enjoined him with many words to pick a bunch of yellow stellaria such as I had seen around the burned houses by the ramparts. At a suitable opportunity we should then give them to Feodosova, I said. She appeared to be a good and worthy woman, who perchance in return might give us poor fellows some fruit or nuts, I said. The miserable bite of bread that the czar allowed us daily did not even quiet our worst hunger, I said.

He was afraid to show himself out in the sunlight, but neither did he dare to arouse mistrust
by staying in, and therefore he obeyed and went.

Scarcely was he out of the door, though, when
I began to regret that I had not held him back,
because now in solitude my embarrassment grew
much greater. I sat down on the bed in the corner,
where I was invisible, and stayed there obstinately.

Still the time was not long, for thoughts were
many. After a while I heard the Zaporogean's
voice. Without reflecting, I went to the window
and saw him standing by Feodosova with a great,
splendid bouquet of stellaria, which reminded one
of irises. First she did n't want to take them, but
answered that they were impure, since they had
been given by a heathen. He pretended that he
understood nothing and that he knew only a few
words of her speech, but with winkings and gestures and nods he made it intelligible that I had
sent the flowers, and then at last she took them.

Beside myself with bashfulness, I went back into
the corner, and when the Zaporogean returned,
I seized him behind the shoulders, shook him, and
stood him against the wall.

But scarcely had I let go my grasp when he
with his thoughtless vivacity stood at the window
again, made signs with his hands, and threw kisses
on all five of his fingers. Then I came forward,
pushed him aside, and bowed. Feodosova sat pick-

ing the flowers apart, pulling off the leaves and letting them fall one by one to the ground. Vehemence helped me so that I took courage and began to speak without stopping to consider how it would be most polite to begin a conversation.

"The lady will not take amiss my comrade's pranks and unseemly gestures," I stammered.

She plucked still more eagerly at the flowers and answered after a time, "My husband, when he was alive, often used to say that from heel to head such well-made soldiers as the Swedes were not to be found. He had seen Swedish prisoners undressed and whipped by women, and had seen that the women at the last were so moved because of their beauty that they stuck the rods under their arms and sobbed, themselves, instead of those they tormented. Therefore have I become very curious these days. . . . And the love songs which you play sound so wonderful."

Her speech pleased me not altogether, and I found it little seemly to answer in the same spirit by praising her figure and white arms. Instead I took my flute and played my favorite hymn: "E'en from the bottom of my heart I call Thee in my need."

After that we conversed of many things, and though my store of words was small, we soon understood each other so well that never did any day seem to me shorter.

At mid-day, after she had clattered about with jugs and plates and swung a palm-leaf fan over the embers in the fireplace, she lifted down from the ceiling a landing-net with which formerly her husband had caught small fish in the river. In the net she put a pan with steaming cabbage and a wooden flask with kvass, and the handle was so long that she could hand us the meal across the street. When I drank to her, she nodded and smiled and said that she did not regard it as wrong to feel pity for captured heathens. Toward evening she moved her spinning-wheel to the window, and we kept on conversing when it was dusk. I no longer felt it as a sin to be happy in the midst of the sorrow that surrounded us, because my intent was innocent and pure. Just as I had seen the stellaria shining over heaps of ashes among the burned and desolate houses by the ramparts as a song of praise to God's goodness, so seemed to me now the joy of my heart.

When it became night, and I had held prayer with my Zaporogean and yet once more reproached him that he had stolen my snuff-spoon, the garrulous man began to talk to me in an undertone and say : " I see clearly, little father, that you are in love with Feodosova, and in truth she is a good and pure woman whom you may take to wife. That you never would enter upon any love-dealing of another sort I have understood from the first."

"Such stuff!" answered I, "such stuff!"

"Truth is in the long run less dangerous than lying, you used to say."

When he struck me with my own maxim-staff, I became confounded, and he proceeded.

"The czar has promised good employment and wages to every one of you Swedes who will become his subject and be converted to the true faith."

"You are out of your wits. But if I could steal off and take her home with me on horseback, I would do it."

Next morning, when I had played my hymn, I learned that to-day it was my turn to go out under the open heavens.

I became warm and restless. I combed and fixed myself up even more carefully than at other times, and changed to the Zaporogean's ensign coat, so as not to wear my torn one. Meanwhile I deliberated with myself. Should I go up to her? What should I say then? Perhaps, though, that would be the only time in my life when I could get to speak with her, and how should I not repent thereafter even to my gray old age, if out of awkwardness I had missed that one chance! My heart beat more violently than at any affair with the enemy, when I had stood with my bandages among the bullets and the fallen. I stuck the flute into my pocket and went out.

When I came down on the street, she sat at the window without seeing me. I would not go to her without first asking leave, and I did not know rightly how I should conduct myself. Pondering, I took a couple of steps forward.

Then she heard me and looked out.

I lifted my hand to my hat, but with a long, ringing burst of laughter she sprang up and cried, · "Haha! Look, look, he has a wooden leg!"

I stood with my hand raised, and stared and stared, and I had neither thought nor feeling. It was as if my heart had swelled out and filled all my breast, so that it was near to bursting. I believe I stammered something. I only remember that I did not know whither I should turn, that I heard her still laughing, that everything in the world was indifferent to me, that freedom would have frightened me as much as my captivity and my wretchedness, that of a sudden I had become a broken man.

I remember vaguely a long and steep lane without stone pavement, where I was accosted by other Swedish prisoners. Perhaps, even, I answered them, asked after their health, and took some puffs out of the tobacco pipes they lent me.

I believe I disturbed myself over the fact that it was so long till night, so that I had to return the same way and pass her window in brightest daylight. By every means I prolonged the time, speaking now to one man, now to another, but shortly the Russian dragoons came and ordered me to turn about to my place.

As I went up the lane, I persuaded myself that

I would not betray myself, but would salute in a quite friendly manner before the window. Was it her fault that so many of the Swedish soldiers, of whom she had had such fine dreams, were now pitiful cripples on wooden legs?

"Hurry up there!" thundered the dragoons, and I hastened my steps, so that the thumping of my wooden leg echoed between the walls of the houses.

"Dear Heavenly Father," I muttered, "faithfully have I served my earthly master. Is this the reward Thou givest me, that Thou makest of me in my youth a defenceless captive, at whom women laugh? Yea, this is Thy recompense, and Thou wilt abase me into yet deeper humiliation, that thereby I may at length become worthy of the crown of blessedness."

When I came under the window and carried my hand to my hat, I saw that Feodosova was away. That gave me no longer any relief. I stumbled up to my prison, and at every step heard the thumping of my wooden leg.

"I have talked with Feodosova," whispered the Zaporogean.

I gave him no reply. My happiness, my flower, that had grown up over the heaps of ashes, lay consumed; and if it had again shone out, I myself, in alarm, would have trampled it to death with my wooden leg. What signified to me the Zaporogean's whisperings?

"Ah!" he went on, "when you were gone, I reproached Feodosova and said to her that you were fonder of her than she realized, and that, if you were not a stranger and a heathen, you would ask her to be your wife."

In silence I clenched my hands and bit my lips together, to lock up my vexation and embarrassment, and I thanked God that He abased me every moment more deeply in shame and ridicule before men.

I opened the door to the outer hall and began to talk to the other prisoners:

"As wild asses in the desert we go painfully to seek our food. On a field that we do not own we must go as husbandmen, and harvest in the vineyard of the ungodly. We lie naked the whole night from lack of garments, and are without covering against the cold. We are overwhelmed by the deluge from the mountains, and from lack of shelter we embrace the cliffs. But we beg Thee not for mitigation, Almighty God. We pray only: Lead us, be nigh unto us! Behold, Thou hast turned away Thy countenance from our people and stuck thorns in our shoes, that we may become Thy servants and Thy children. In the mould of the battle-field our brothers sleep, and a fairer song of victory than that of the conquerors by the sword Thou dost offer to Thy chosen ones."

"Yea, Lord, lead us, be nigh unto us!" echoed all the prisoners murmuringly.

Then out of the darkest corner rose a lonely, trembling voice, which cried: "Oh, that I were as in former months, as in the days when God protected me, when His lamp shone upon my head, when with His light I went into the darkness! As I was in my autumn days, when God's friendship was over my tent, while yet the Almighty was with me, and my children were about me! Thus my heart cries out with Job, but I hear it no longer, and I stammer forth no longer: Take away my trials! With the ear I have heard tell of Thee, O God, but now hath mine eye beheld Thee."

"Quiet, quiet!" whispered the Zaporogean, taking hold of me, and his hands were cold and trembling. "It can be no one else than the czar who is coming below in the lane."

The lane had become filled with people, with beggars and boys and old women and soldiers. In the middle of the throng the czar, tall and lean, walked very calmly, without a guard. A swarm of hopping and shrieking dwarfs were his only retinue. Now and then, turning, he embraced and kissed the smallest dwarf on the forehead in a fatherly way. Here and there he stood still before a house, and was offered a glass of brandy, which he jestingly emptied at a single gulp. It could be nobody but the czar, because one saw directly that he alone ruled over both people and city. He came so close under my window that I could have touched his green cloth cap and the half-torn-off brass buttons on his brown coat. On the skirt he had a great silver button with an artificial stone and on his legs rough woollen stockings. His brown eyes gleamed and flashed, and the small black moustaches stood straight up from his shining lips.

When he caught sight of Feodosova, he seemed as if smitten with madness. When she came down on the street and knelt with a cup, he pinched her ear, then took her under the chin and lifted up her head, so that he could look her in the eyes.

"Tell me, child," he inquired, "where is there a comfortable room in which I can eat? May there be one at your house?"

The czar had seldom with him on his excursions any master of ceremonies or other courtier. He took along neither bed nor bed-clothes nor cooking utensils; no, not even a cooking or eating vessel; but everything had to be provided in the turn of a hand wherever it occurred to him to take lodging. It was for this reason that there was now running and clattering at all the gates and stairs. From this direction came a man with a pan, from that another with an earthen platter, from yonder a third with a ladle and drinking utensils. Up in Feodosova's room the floor was strewn deeply with straw. The czar helped with the work like a common servant, and the chief direction was carried on by a hunchbacked dwarf, who was called the Patriarch. The dwarf every once in a while put his thumb to his nose and blew it in the air straight in front of the czar's face, or invented rascal tricks of which I cannot relate before a lady of quality.

Once when the czar turned with crossed arms to the window, he noticed me and the Zaporogean, and nodded like a comrade. The Zaporogean threw himself prostrate on the floor and stammered his "I Shwede. Devil-damn!" But I pushed him aside with my foot and told him once for all to be silent and get up, because no Swede conducted himself in that fashion. To cover him as much as possible, I stepped in front of him and took my position there.

"*Dat is nit übel*," said the czar, but at once fell back into his mother speech, and asked who I was.

"Blomberg, surgeon with the Uppland regiment," I answered.

The czar scanned me with a narrowing gaze, so penetrating that I have never seen a more all-discerning look.

"Your regiment exists no longer," he said, "and here you see Rehnskiöld's sword." He lifted the sword with its scabbard from his belt and threw it on the table, so that the plates hopped. "But for certain you are a rogue, for you wear a captain's or ensign's uniform."

I answered, "'That is a hard saying,' saith John the Evangelist. The coat I borrowed after my own fell in rags, and if that be ill done, I will yet hope for grace, because this is my maxim: To tell the truth is in the long run less dangerous than to lie."

"Good. If that is your motto, you shall take your servant with you and come over here, so that we may prove it."

The Zaporogean trembled and tottered, as he followed behind me, but as soon as we entered, the czar pointed me to a chair among the others at the table, as if I had been his equal, and said, "Sit, Wooden-Leg!"

He had Feodosova on his knee, without the least consideration of what could be said about it, and round them stamped and whistled the dwarfs and a crowd of Boyars who now began to collect. A dwarf who was called Judas, because he carried a likeness of that arch-villain on the chain around his neck, seized a handful of shrimps from the nearest plate and threw them to the ceiling, so that they fell in a rain over dishes and people. When in that way he had made the others turn toward him, he pointed at the czar with many grimaces and called quite coolly to him: "You amuse yourself, you Peter Alexievitch. Even outside of the city I have heard tell of the pretty Feodosova of Poltava, I have; but you always scrape together the best things for yourself, you little father."

"That you do," chimed in the other dwarfs in a ring around the czar. "You are an arch-thief, you Peter Alexievitch."

Sometimes the czar laughed or answered, sometimes he did not hearthem, butsat seriousand meditative, and hiseyes moved meanwhile like two green-glinting insects in the sunlight.

I called to mind how I had once seen the most blessed Charles the Eleventh converse with Rudbeck, and how it then came over me that Rudbeck, for all his bowings, amounted to far more than the king. Here it was the other way about. Although the czar himself went around and did the waiting, and let himself be treated worse than a knave, I saw only him—and Feodosova. I read his purpose in the smallest things. I recognized it in the forcibly curtailed caftans and shaven chins at the city gate.

There was a buzzing in my head, and I knelt humbly on the straw and stammered: "Imperial Majesty! To tell the truth is in the long run less dangerous than to lie, and the Lord said to Moses: 'Thou shalt not hold with the great ones in that which is evil.' Therefore I beseech that I may forego further drinking. For behold, I am soon done with the game, and my gracious lord—who is both like and unlike Your Imperial Majesty—has in the last year turned me to drinking filtered marsh water."

A twitching and trembling began in the czar's right cheek near the eye.

"Yes, by Saint Andreas!" said he. "I am unlike my brother Charles, for he hates women like a woman and wine like a woman, and offers up his people's riches as a woman her husband's, and abuses me like a woman; but I respect him like a man. His health, Wooden-Leg! Drink, drink!"

The czar sprang forward, seized me by the hair, and held the goblet to my mouth, so that the Astrakan ale foamed over my chin and collar. As we drank the prescribed health, two soldiers entered in brownish yellow uniforms with blue collars and discharged their pistols, so that the hot room, which was already filled with tobacco clouds and onion smell, was now also enveloped in powder smoke.

The czar sat down again at the table. Even in all that noise he wanted to sit and think, but he never allowed any one else to shirk the duty of drinking and become serious like himself. He drew Feodosova afresh to his knee. Poor, poor Feodosova! She sat there, a bit sunk together, with arms hanging and mouth impotently half-open, as if she waited cuffs and blows amid the caresses. Why had she not courage to pull the sword to her from the table, press her wrist against the edge, and save her honor, before it was too late? Over and over she might have laughed at my wooden leg and my disgrace, if with my life I could have preserved her honor. Nor had I ever before been so near her and seen so clearly to what a wondrous work she had been formed in the Heavenly Creator's hands. Poor, poor Feodosova, if you had but felt in your heart with what a pure intent a friend regarded you in your humiliation, and how he prayed for your well-being!

Hour after hour the banquet continued. Those of the Boyars and dwarfs who were most completely overcome already lay relaxed in the straw and vomited or made water, but the czar himself always rose up and leaned out through the window. "Drink, Wooden-Leg, drink!" he commanded, and hunted me around the room with the glass, making the Boyars hold me till I had emptied every drop. The twitching in his face became ever more uncanny, and when we were finally together at the table again, he moved three brimful earthen bowls in front of me and said: "Now, Wooden-Leg, you shall propose a health to be drunk all round and teach us to understand its meaning with your maxim."

I raised myself again as well as I could.

"Your health, czar!" I shouted, "for you are assuredly born to command."

"Why," he asked, "should the soldiers present arms and salute me if any other was worthier to command! Where is there anything more pitiful than an incompetent ruler? The day I find my own son unworthy to inherit my great, beloved realm, that day shall he die. Your first truth, Wooden-Leg, requires no bowl."

The pistols cracked, and all drank but the czar.

Then I gathered the fragments of my under-
standing as a miser his coins, for I believed that, if
I could catch the czar in a gracious and mild humor,
I might perhaps save my Feodosova.

"Well, then, Imperial Majesty," I continued,
therefore, lifting one of the bowls on high, "this is
Astrakan ale, brewed of mead and brandy with pep-
per and tobacco. It burns much before it delights,
and when it delights, it puts one to sleep."

With that I threw the bowl to the ground so that
it broke in a thousand pieces. Then I lifted the next
bowl.

"This is Hungarian wine. 'Drink no more only
water,' writes the Apostle Paul to Timothy, 'but use
a little wine for thy stomach's sake, and because
thou art so often sick.' So speaks a holy one to
weakly men and stay-at-homes. But go out on the
battle-field amid frost and wailing and tell me, to
how many of the groaning would this bowl of
sweetish wine give relief from pain and a softer
death?"

Therewith I threw that bowl also to the ground
so that it broke. Then I lifted the third bowl.

"This is brandy. It is despised by the fortunate
and the rich, because they thirst not after refreshment as the desert for coolness, but would only
gibe at the pleasure it gives. But brandy assumes
power in the very moment it glides over the tongue,
like a despot in the moment he steps across a

threshold, and the bleeding and dying draw comfort from a few drops. Therefore I call brandy the best, for I speak as a warrior, and to tell the truth is in the long run less dangerous than to lie."

"Right, right!" acclaimed the czar, and took the bowl and drank, at the same time that he handed me two gold-pieces, while the pistols cracked. "You shall have a pass and a horse to go your way, and wherever you come, you shall tell about Poltava."

Then I knelt yet again in the straw and stammered: "Imperial Majesty—in my pettiness and weakness—beside you sits a—a pure and good woman."

"Haha!" screamed the dwarfs and Boyars, who tottered to their feet. "Haha! haha!"

The czar got up and led Feodosova toward me.

"I understand. He who limps on a wooden leg may fall in love, too. Good. I present her to you just as she is, and you shall have a good situation with me. I have promised every Swede who enters into my service and is baptized in our faith that he shall become one of our people."

Feodosova stood like a sleep-walker and stretched her hands towards me. What did it matter that she had laughed at me? I should soon have forgotten that, and she would soon not have seen my wooden leg, for I should have cared for her and worked for her and prayed with her and made her home bright and tranquil. I should have lifted her up to my bosom as a child and asked her if an honest and faithful heart could not make another heart throb. Mayhap she already bore the answer on her tongue, for slowly she beamed up and became flushed, and her whole face became transfigured. Far away in a corner house on Prästgatan in Stockholm a lonely old woman sat with her sermon-book and listened and wondered whether a letter would not be left for her through the door, whether no disabled man would step in with a greeting from the remote wilderness, whether I never should come or whether I lay already dead and buried. I had prayed for her every night. I had thought of her in the tumult in the midst of stretchers and wailing wounded. But at that moment I thought of her no longer; I saw and heard nothing else but Feodosova. And yet I was angry and strove against something heavy which weighed upon my heart and which I did not understand, but was only slowly and gradually able to make out.

I bent to Feodosova to kiss her hand, but she whispered, "The czar's hand, the czar's hand."

Then I stretched myself toward the czar and kissed his hand.

" My faith," I whispered equally softly, "and my royal lord I may not desert."

The czar's cheek still twitched, and the dwarfs in their terror pulled forth the Zaporogean from his nook to make the czar laugh at his ridiculous figure. But then the czar's arms began to move convulsively. His face grew gray and he trembled in one of his dreaded fits. He went toward the Zaporogean and struck him in the face with clenched fist so that the blood streamed from his nose and mouth, and with such a hoarse and altered voice that it could no longer be recognized he hissed: "I have seen through you, liar, from the moment you came into the room. You are a Zaporogean, a renegade, who have hidden yourself in Swedish clothes. — To the wheel with him, to the wheel!"

All, even the drunken men, began to tremble and feel toward the doors, and in his terror one of the Boyars whispered: "Bring forward the woman! Shove her forward! As soon as he gets to see pretty faces and woman's limbs, he grows quiet."

They seized her, her bodice was cut over the bosom, and, softly wailing, she was supported forward step by step to the czar.

It grew black around me, and I staggered backward out of the room. I remained standing on the street under the stars, and I heard the clamor grow muffled and the dwarfs begin to sing.

Then I clenched my hands and remembered a promise on the field of battle to pray for a poor sinner's soul. But the more fervently I spoke with my God, the further went my thoughts, and my invocation became a prayer for a yet greater sinner who with his last faithful followers wandered about on the desolate steppes.

The surgeon ceased with an anxious glance toward the coffin, and the lady-in-waiting followed him forward to the catafalque.

"Amen!" said she, and the two again spread the covering over the wax-pale Queen Dowager, mother of the Charleses.

END OF PART I

THE CHARLES MEN

PART II

CONTENTS

Part II

When the Bells Ring

IN southern Småland, just where the stony road
to Scania branches into several village paths and
a dusty slope leads up to the parish church, there
stood a mill, painted red, and with the largest wings
that any one had ever seen in all that region. The
miller was dead long since. His widow, named Kerstin Bure, a woman who in her childhood had seen
happier days and eaten from shining plates of pewter, managed the mill after her own fashion. She
never made mention of her birth or of the love-
dealings that had enticed her from a well-to-do pastor's home to the narrow tower-room of a miller,
where the axle-beam groaned directly over her
sleeping-place; but then she did not speak of other
things either. The husband had been too poor to
possess a cottage of his own, and had instead built
a chimney straight through the roof of the mill.
There, year after year, with her sewing in her hand,
the wife had silently continued to watch the work of
the men. If at any time she was asked for advice,
she answered preferably with a nod or a shake of
the head, and she seldom went away further than
a stone's throw from the mill. In figure she was tall
and slim with delicate hands, and her face under
the starched cap, which was always of the same in-

variable whiteness, reminded one of Mary Mag-
dalen's on the picture at the altar, though it was
more yellowed and shrunken. She never took women into her service, and so women in particular
accustomed themselves to passing her in silence.
They did not rightly know whether she was proud
or meek, but most of them thought that she might
well be both. When the sexton appeared with his
spokesmen and in his best Sunday attire to solicit
the hand of this woman, who was already old and
gray, she became quite confused and abashed. She
blushed to the roots of her hair, and merely shook
her head.

One morning she found an infant boy on a heap
of twigs by the spring, and as no one knew anything about the parents, she took the little one in
with great tenderness.

"Nobody can tell whether there lies in that heart
good or evil seed," she said, "but the day may come
when I may find out. You shall be called Johannes,
because you are to become devout as an angel of
God. I have been sore afflicted, but for you I shall
lay by a pretty penny, so that your life-days may
sometime counterbalance the heavy ones I have
known."

The boy grew up, and when he prepared for confirmation, he surprised everybody by his pious and
godly answers. With his glossy flaxen hair hanging
over his shoulders, he afterwards sat by his foster-

mother on the mill steps in the bright midsummer evenings and read diligently in the books that he had borrowed from the pastor of the congregation. They sat always taciturnly and quietly, but sometimes he pointed out with his finger some line that seemed to him more beautiful than the others and read it aloud softly.

Hay-ricks and meadows were sending out their perfume of harvest and pasture, and so, too, though withered, did the clover- or trefoil-blossoms that lay forgotten here and there between the leaves of the books as markers. Even late at night only a single star burned, but that was large and radiant. Everywhere people were awake and talking, and the cottage doors stood open.

Many whispered to one another a dark rumor of how the Swedish army had been beaten at Poltava, and that now the Danes were to land and complete the entire overthrow of Sweden.

One Saturday night a rider stopped at the stairs of the mill and asked for lodging.

Johannes looked doubtfully at his foster-mother, and asked the stranger whether he would not rather go on up the hill to the provost's place.

"No," he answered, "I want first to see to-night how the people are getting on."

He managed to get his horse into the walled passage under the mill, and then settled down quite

contentedly among the others to a plate of beer-
soup and a loaf of black bread.

He had let his hair and his chin-whiskers grow,
so that he looked like a common peasant, but sometimes he pulled his mouth toward his ears and
talked harshly in the broadest Scanian, and sometimes he squeezed up his eyes and lamented in the
most sentimental Smålandish. He kept awake all
night, continuing his merry discourse. Once he took
a piece of charcoal and drew a speaking likeness of
Johannes on the wall. A little later he gave Kerstin
Bure shrewd advice as to how she should grease
the mill-axle. Or he would sing psalms and polka-
tunes, to which he himself set the words. In the
morning he took from his travelling-sack a suit with
bright soldier's buttons. When Johannes and the
old woman peeped wonderingly through the shutters to see whither he went, he was already standing
in the church square, and there was such a clatter
and hubbub among the populace that it echoed for
miles.

"That's Mons Bock!" clamored the crowd.
"That is our valiant General Stenbock. If we have
him with us, we'll go out and fight for our country,
every one of us, father and son, so help us God!"

"Johannes," said Kerstin Bure to her sixteen-
year-old foster-son, with a hardness in her voice
that he had never heard before, "you are meant to
keep devoutly to your books and some day wear

a pastor's surplice as my sainted father did, but not to lose your blood in worldly feuds. Stick your tinder-box and clasp-knife in your jacket and tie your leather coat at your belt! Go then out into the woods and keep yourself well hid there until we have peace in the land! Before that I do not wish to see you again. Remember that! You hear now how the men shout in the church square, but mayhap their mouths will soon be stopped with black earth."

He did as she bade, and wandered off into the woods by unknown paths. The firs became gradually more bristling and dense, so that for a long distance he had to push through backwards with the leather coat over his face. In the evening he came to a wide fen, and far out at the rim of a black lake lay an island overgrown with alders.

"There I'll build my den," he thought. But the quagmire of the swampy fen which floated over the twofold bottom, and the dark water where not a glimmer of daylight broke through, sank beneath his feet, until, exhausted and half asleep, he sat down on a ledge.

A rustling still sounded from the ridges of the wood, but the lake lay quiet, and the little yellow reflections of the fluffy clouds soon stood motionless. In the infinite distance beyond the mist of the fen a goat-bell from time to time struck a few short, unresonant strokes. Two herd-girls blew

quaveringly on their cow-horns, and on the forgotten and dilapidated sepulchre-mound in the dip
of the valley the glow-worms kindled their lanterns
in the grass.

"Are you one of those that have run away from
war service?" a voice asked him, and when he
looked up, a goat-girl was standing among the juniper bushes, knitting. She appeared to be one or
two years older than he, and her leather boots hung
on her back.

"That's right enough; but now the fen bars my
way, and berries and ferns get to be scant fare after
a while."

"It must be you don't know the woods. Nobody suffers want there. Since my ninth year I've
spent every summer up here in the wilds with my
goats. Trim and cut down a couple of fir saplings
and tie them to your feet with withes, and you can
go on the quagmire wherever you like. Thatch your
hut with fir bark and make yourself fishing-gear."

She carefully pulled a long basting-thread from
her jacket and tied to it a pewter pin, which she
had taken from her head-dress and bent into a
hook.

"Here you have a hook and line," she said and
continued on her way, still knitting.

That night he did not much heed her advice,
but when the sun again shone into his eyes, he
pulled out his knife.

As soon as he had trimmed himself a couple of skis of the sort she had taught him to make, he betook himself out on the fen to the island. When he stamped on the grass there, the whole island swayed like a soft feather-bed, but he opined that this was good, because if there was moisture in the ground, he would not need to go far to find angle-worms. Hardly, too, had he dug under the grass-roots with his fingers, before he found abundance. To be sure, the fishing went badly at the start, but after he had mystically laid two blades of sedge crosswise on the water, it became at once a differ-ent affair. As he carried a tinder-box in his jacket, it was an easy matter to broil his savory capture.

Afterwards he began to build his hut with such haste that he did not give himself leisure to sleep in the bright summer nights. He understood that it might easily tumble in on the swaying ground if he made it too high. Therefore he built instead a low turf-thatched roof-tree, under which he could not stand upright but had to creep. Every morning he fetched from the shore trimmed saplings, twigs, and pieces of fir bark. Finally he built a hearth of stones, where he let the juniper twigs smoulder and glow all night to drive off the midges. During his work he sometimes talked to himself half aloud, pretending that he was the overseer of a whole gang of workmen, and he called the island Wander Isle.

He met the goat-girl quite often. Her name was

Lena. She went about with her knitting, feeding her charges on clearings and meadows. She taught him to set nooses and traps. Eventually they met every morning to see whether the fortune of hunting had been favorable to them, and she made him a good friend to all the wild animals.

"Did you see that gorgeous bird?" she asked, pointing to a blue-black black-cock that roused the whole wood with his thunderous wing-beats. "Him I call the Rich Bachelor of Växjö, for he asks neither after his home nor his relatives, but just sits at the tavern in his fine dress-coat and greases his wattles."

"And just hark now!" she said one night when an owl hooted in the ravine. "Him I call the Tax Collector, who, when he turns his head in his white collar and rolls his red eyes or snaps his bill, frightens both man and beast. But if it's a question of the little white harmless eggs in his own nest, then you'll see. Then he has a father's heart in the right place."

But about nothing did she know so many traditions as about the cranes.

"Never yet," she said, "have I got a glimpse of the long-legged, bald-headed cranes when they set up their trumpeting from the bog and hold their autumn assembly before taking flight. Round their camp they have outposts that sit each with a stone in his one uplifted claw, so that it may tumble down and wake him if he falls asleep. But the most wonderful thing is that if any human being sees the ashen-gray birds go up, he himself begins to flap with his arms and longs to be able to fly with them so high that the lakes below on the earth are only like little shimmering water-drops."

"I want to see the cranes," answered Johannes.

"Perhaps you may get to see them in the autumn, but then you must first teach yourself a great deal. First, you must be able to stand so quiet that you look like a dry juniper bush, and to bend down so that you look like a stone, and to lay yourself flat on the ground so that no one can tell you from a pile of rotten twigs."

"All that I shall try to teach myself, but you must never go on my island. It is n't the way you think there. I have a high fireplace and hangings on the walls, and the floor between the rugs is so shining and slippery that you can't walk on it, but have to crawl."

The pretty stories he had read in the dean's books ran in his memory, and he wanted to show the girl that he was not inferior to her, but could in turn rouse her to wonder and curiosity.

"If you 'll let me get a sight of that house, I.'ll go down to the settlement and fetch you a musketoon with bullets and powder-horn."

"To my island you 'll never come."

"If you 'll let me get a sight of that house, I 'll

teach you in five days to feed yourself on ferns and roots and nothing."

"That's why I've come hither. Keep that promise, and you shall see my house, if you can really get there."

With that he fastened the skis on his feet and vanished in the mist on the fen.

"The enemy stand on the shore," he said to his imaginary soldiers on the island, "but they have neither axe nor knife for making skis. We may feel secure, if only we always remain upright and good."

But late in the evening, when he was about to lay fresh juniper on the hearth, he saw the goat-girl coming on the fen with the help of twigs and dry branches.

"The enemy thinks to take us by storm," he continued, "but there is a secret which I have long suspected. I shall make the whole Wander Isle sail to sea like a boat."

He pressed a pole against the outermost tussocks of the fen, and the floating island swam swaying further out on the water.

Then he laid himself calmly to sleep by the crackling embers, but when after a while he suddenly opened his eyes, the goat-girl stood straight before him and peeped in under the low roof on which fox-skins lay spread inside out to dry.

She asked him nothing about the high fireplace or the hangings or the slippery floor, but merely said, "A fresh breeze has blown up, so that the island has driven to land on the other shore. But why do you let the dry fox-skins lie on the roof instead of spreading them in here on the ground? And we ought to stick in juniper around the island so that people can't see either us or the hut."

He thought she spoke sensibly, and went ashore at once to collect the juniper. When it was already long after midnight, they still worked at the strengthening and beautifying of his island. They even made of birch-bark and pegs a door which they could set before the entrance, and when they finally shoved the island off from the land again, they anchored it out in the water with two piles.

"Now the drawbridge is raised," said Johannes, "and we must see to providing the new guests with entertainment such as is right."

"The cook-maids and scullery-maids are always so slow," she said, and turned the two fish upon the hearth.

The heather droned, and the lake splashed, so that the island and the sedge and all the closed water-lilies swayed. As soon as mealtime had passed, Johannes lay down inside nearest the hearth, but Lena, who did not yet feel that she possessed the right of ownership to Wander Isle, huddled together outside at the entrance with one hand as a pillow. She still heard the juniper sputter with heart's delight, and as she fell asleep she counted

the small sparks that sailed forth above the chink
in the roof like stars through the night air. That
was the fifth — that was the sixth — that was the seventh. So she was put in mind of one of her songs:

> *It was on the seventh morn of the week,*
> *When the prayer-bells rang, I ween,*
> *That the bitter tears ran a-down her cheek,*
> *Though her bride-wreath still was green.*

Next day she no longer thought of leaving the
island, and the third day, without noticing it, they
began to say "our island." Every morning they
landed at the rock, and then she went up to the
clearing with her goats or followed him to examine
nooses and traps. At last she began also to teach
him the art of feeding himself for many days on
berries and ferns and nothing, and she noticed that
he soon won even greater aptitude in this than she
had herself. He grew thin and dry as a blown-off
branch, and yet his sinews knotted themselves all
the harder. But he always remained quiet and taciturn, and when she asked him what weighed on his
mind, he went off on his own paths and remained
away long.

They no longer knew the names of the days,
but on the Sabbath the wind carried the distant
sound of the bells far into the wilderness, and then
Johannes put on his embroidered leather coat and
led her upon the overgrown sepulchre-mound,

from which they could see over fen and lake. With her hand in his he spoke then of God's love, which covered the wretchedest crevices with its fairest bounties, and often they knelt in the grass for long periods and prayed that He would likewise sow a few grains of His seed in their souls.

After such conversations, however, Johannes was always doubly heavy in mind and sought for solitude.

The nights became ever darker, and often when she turned back from her herd she had to light her way with a torch between mountain walls and the bared roots of trees. The yews, heaven high, were like tents, where black hands sprawled out through the ragged seams to seize her by the braids; but she felt no fear, she thought only of one thing. Wherever she went and whatever she busied herself with, she only thought that the summer would soon be ended and that no one could know what would then become of Johannes and her.

Then one October morning she was wakened by Johannes.

"Do you remember the cranes you spoke of?" he asked. "Now I can both stand so quiet that I look like a dry juniper bush, and bend down so that I look like a stone, and lie down flat on the ground so that no one can tell me from a pile of rotten twigs. I have taught myself more than that. I can feed myself on berries and roots, and if those are wanting, I can starve along on nothing."

She sat up and listened to a far-off noise.

"That is no crane."

"Then I 'll investigate what it is."

He washed himself in the lake, put on his leather coat as on a Sunday, and pushed her gently aside when she wanted to hold him back.

"Don't go, Johannes!" she begged. "I won't let you go from me without following."

In silence they came ashore with the island at the ledge and went down through the woods toward the settled land to a bare clearing, from which there was a free outlook over the mossy heath and meadows as far as Kerstin Bure's mill and the church.

"Johannes!" she burst out with almost a scream, and seized him tightly by the coat tail. "Come back with me to our place!"

He answered her meekly: "My conscience has pained me long enough. Do you see down there on the heath the gray creatures with thin legs? And the outposts that you told about are standing there too. It 's Mons Bock, who is out again on his recruiting. In that crane-dance I 'd like to play myself."

He walked violently away from her, so that the coat tail was torn off at the cracking seam, and began to run down to the heath between the ferns and the charred stumps.

She followed irresolutely after him, but when she saw how he spoke to the outposts, and stepped straight into the assembled crowd of armed peasants, she went at a warm pace to get to him.

When she came into the ring, he already stood before Mons Bock and was taking his recruit penny.

"Where have you stuck your knapsack, Smålander?" asked the general.

"I have no knapsack, but I can feed myself for five days on nothing."

Lena pressed forward between him and the general's dark brown horse.

"He, Johannes here, is no serving-boy, but we have a place of our own up in the woods."

"As to the marriage, I should much like to see the certificate in black and white," answered Mons Bock, and the hot color rose and fell on his forehead as he spoke.

Then Lena held out in her two hands the torn-off coat tail, and let him see that it fitted to the leather coat.

"I call that a parson's certificate on real sheepskin," he broke out. "The recruit money may therefore be yours, my good young lady, but the boy has been clean sworn in. And now, ye worthy yeomen of Småland, forward in Jesus' name! Drums we have none, but we can still in our poverty stamp with wooden shoes the old Swedish march that makes me warm at heart to hear."

Staffs and wooden shoes banged and clattered on

rocks and ledges. Even the riders had wooden shoes tied fast to their feet, so that they tried in vain to use their stirrups.

When the last farmers had vanished across the heath, Lena went on to the mill. She dared not relate that Johannes had gone along to the war, but told only of how she had met him in the woods, exhibiting the coat tail, which was carefully inspected and turned over.

"That's the right coat tail, sure enough," said Kerstin Bure, "and though I don't like to see women in my service, you may as well stay with me till Johannes comes. I really need a pair of strong arms, for I am well on in years and all my men have been bitten with madness and have run off with Stenbock. There is hardly an able-bodied man left in the parish, except the sexton, the fool!"

After she had said this she spoke no more to Lena of what had passed in the woods, and asked nothing about Johannes, but silently continued her occupations as was her custom. The mill stood with unmoving wings, because there was no meal to grind, and through the long snowy months of winter there was heard in it neither steps nor voices. Beggars who went past on the road supposed it was unoccupied and deserted.

When the spring began to reappear, and white trailing clouds swept across the heavens, there came one day a boy, hot and panting, who ran along the road and to each and all whom he met shouted a single word, until he vanished in the woods on the other side of the heather. Some hours later a rider came at a gallop and shouted in the same manner on all sides until he was gone. The women gathered in crowds on the church grounds — Sweden, Sweden was saved, and Mons Bock and his goatboys had beaten the whole enemy's army at the Straits of Öresund!

Kerstin Bure alone asked nobody what had happened, but sat every noon on the mill stairs in the glorious sunshine and carded wool with Lena. All at once, as they were sitting silent and busy, while the spring freshet purled in ditches and brooks, they heard that the bells were ringing in the neighboring parishes to the south, although it was Wednesday. Expectantly the people ranged themselves along the road on both sides, and from the wide-open door of the church advanced the tottering pastor of the congregation, followed by his chaplains and in full ceremonials.

Once more the well-known march of the wooden shoes clattered on ledges and stones, but now to bagpipes and shawms. It was the returning army of farmers. There were deep lines of shaggy beards and slashed sheepskin coats and honest blue eyes. With staves in hand, muskets in the strap, and wide hats over their flowing hair, the homeward-bound

troops marched back from their victory. Far in the
van the tidings-mace went from church to church
as far as the northernmost wooden chapels, where
the Lapps tied their reindeer to the bell-towers.
All the sunny springtime of Sweden was filled with
the song of praise that reëchoed from the bells.

Just in front of the hay-wagons with the wounded
rode Mons Bock in his gray overcoat with his
riding-whip instead of a sword. Calling down blessings upon their saviour, the peasants hailed him
with waving aprons and caps, but he turned to his
ensigns and shouted that they should sing.

When the voices ceased, Mons Bock went on
alone and sang stanza after stanza which he himself had put together.

Kerstin Bure had risen on the mill stairs and
looked and looked beneath her lifted hand, but
Lena, who had broken her way through so fear-
lessly in the thickets of the wilderness, did not
dare this time to wait and look about any longer,
but stole away and threw herself sobbing among
the empty meal-sacks.

Step by step, Kerstin Bure withdrew up the
stairs until she stood at the very top with her back
against the wall of the mill. Then she pressed her
hands like opera-glasses to her eyes. In the last
wagon Johannes sat on the hay among the wounded,
as merry and quiet as always, but paler and with
bandages around his arm and shoulder.

She pressed her hands even harder to her eyes.

"So after all he was what I thought him, though to prove his soul thoroughly I commanded him otherwise. Then, though he is Kerstin Bure's foster-son, he shall still keep for his life long her whom he himself has chosen, even if she is the poorest of goat-girls."

But at that moment she heard how the sexton and his ringer clattered at the trap-doors of the steeple, and the great bell gave forth its first stroke.

She knitted her brow and went into the mill, saying: "I 've no meal to grind, but if he lets his bell sound, though he has had no son in the war, my mill shall play, too."

Creaking, the dust-white axle-beam began to move and purr, and while the peasant army marched by singing, the empty mill kept turning its great wings faster and faster.

Gustaf Celsing

THE sultan, who was going about the streets in disguise with a fig basket on his head, talking searchingly with the populace and many of the Janisaries, met his mother in the seraglio garden.

She swept aside the veil from her wrinkled forehead and threw back her arms.

"The people are minded for war," she said. "When will you gather them again and help my Northern lion against the czar? Command your soldiers to bear Mohammed's banner above the head of the Swedish king and follow him to the combat!"

The sultan set the basket of figs on a stone table, and answered: "I knew but little of him when he came to my land as a fugitive. Soon men and women spoke of nothing else than of him. How, I asked myself, can a lonely, impoverished fugitive without authority conquer a whole people so by his mere presence? I hardly understood it, but wished to give him my hand graciously, although he was an infidel, and I sent my soldiers against his enemies. The people fired salutes of welcome and lighted lamps in the towers of the mosques. At the river Pruth the armies met. — But hearken to me! Peace was made. Then my grand vizier beheld far out in the stream a man on a swimming horse. It was the Swedish king, who had come

spurring with his cavalry from Bender. My grand
vizier has told me all very exactly, and his voice
still trembles when he speaks of that time. Without saluting, the king galloped to his tent and, wet
through as he was with the water of the river, sat
down at the head of the divan under the banner
of Mohammed. He required to have at once the
newly signed treaty of peace, so that he might tear
it to pieces. There, then, hundreds of miles from his
own provinces, sat the beaten fugitive with Mohammed's banner over his bald head, and, proudly
as if his realm had extended down even to the
Arabian deserts, he commanded my armies to continue the strife. It was a windy day. The tent-cloth
flapped and beat. Now and then the banner rustled,
and when he lifted his clenched hand, he struck
his gauntlet against the sacred green tassels.—But,
I say to you, peace was made. Other times have
come. Every day I have had money and gifts of
many sorts delivered at Bender to your hero. I
have treated him as my guest, but instead of returning to his own people, he remains year after
year. My grand vizier counsels me no longer to
lavish gifts on the uninvited strangers, from whom
we have little advantage to hope. They are too poor
to be capable of any great achievement. There,
mother, you have the truth."

It grew dark while he spoke, but that same night
the Swedish lords who had been sent to the city

of the sultan conferred together in the house of Thomas Funck. They spoke together in anxious whispers, and when it began to draw towards morning, Funck pushed the candlestick across the table to the military preacher, Agrell.

" Read something for us from the Scriptures before we disperse, for with all our deliberation we have got nowhere. The grand vizier did indeed conduct his soldiers to the firing line, but he set a higher value on a full purse and pretty slave-girls than on bullet-wounds in his white arms. At the river Pruth he had his turban brimmed with Russian bribes. Since then the Turks are against us. But Gustaf Celsing, with his readiness in their speech, might easily compose a letter of complaint. Still, who could bring it to the sultan's own hands? He does of course receive such letters when he rides to the mosque on Fridays, but we all know that he who has the foolhardiness to present such a letter is at once arrested, and if he cannot prove point by point the truth of the writing, he is executed without mercy. And who here has the proofs?—Therefore, I say, let us rather hear some words from the Scriptures, and then each and all may go home."

Herman Tersmed took the Bible from the wall-shelf and laid it before Agrell.

"I have a true respect for open dealing," he said, "but at this stage I must agree with Funck. If our king had owned the treasury of France, he would

have won far more provinces than he has lost. He
would by this time be the greatest and mightiest
among the princes of the earth. But poverty ties
our hands. What are we, in fact? a great power with
a beggar's staff in our hand."

During the whole conversation Celsing, the secretary of the commission, sat at the end of the table
facing the closed window-shutters. Unknown to
the others, he had already composed beforehand a
letter of complaint to the sultan; he could feel it
under his coat with his hand, but he did not yet
know to whom he should dare to entrust his plans.
The day that is now glimmering, he thought, is a
Friday, and the sultan will then ride to the mosque.
While the dawn comes, I will carefully note which
of those present is struck by the sunbeam from the
chink between the shutters, and I pray the good
God that He may in that manner point out the man
who is most worthy to become His instrument. To
that man I shall then turn in trust and confidence.

Engrossed in his thoughts, he could only momentarily follow the words that Agrell read in a
melancholy voice by the guttering candle.

"And the woman was clad in a mantle of purple and scarlet, and she shone with precious stones.
. . . And I saw the woman drunken with the blood
of the saints and of the witnesses for Jesus, and I
fell into a great wonderment when I saw her."

Celsing was inwardly ashamed at not being able

to listen to Agrell more attentively. He continued
to sit facing away, while he shaded his pale countenance with his hand. He heard how the city
awoke, how quick steps echoed over the streets,
how oars splashed, how the first breeze stirred the
chestnut trees around the house, how the criers of
the muezzin sent forth their song.

The chinks between the shutters already glowed.
He dared not shift his hand from his cheek or
move his chair.

From the middlemost crevice the first streak of
the sun fell, bright and radiant, full into his own
eyes.

He arose so violently that, stammering, he had
to seek for an excuse.

"My good sirs, I do not feel quite well and am
going up to my room to rest."

He understood that he was to seek no longer for
coöperators, but was himself to be the only witness
for truth. The morning light filled all his room.
This was situated above that where the others were
gathered,·and the walls and flooring of the wooden
house were so thin that he could still hear Agrell's
voice.

He opened the chest of drawers, where a multitude of Turkish costumes and cloths lay stored to
be used by him and his comrades at any time when
they wished to be unknown. The gold lace and
tassels glinted, and he slowly unbuttoned his Swed-

ish coat and vest to exchange them for the foreign habiliments. But when he saw them lying on the bed, when he saw the rents sewed up after a sabre cut on the sleeve, and when he recognized in the worn lining the stitches with which his mother had sewed in his commission and passport, he did not want to let the old suit go out of his hands. He threw himself prone on the bed and drew the clothes together in an embrace, hiding his face in the lining of the coat as against a pillow.

"God, God!" he whispered, "this is the mission Thou hast given the Swedes, that they in the midst of an evil world should show what poverty and an open brow can avail. Was it not through their poverty that they were beaten? Was it not through their poverty that they became honored among men? If they had money to bribe the serail and were not ashamed to use it, all the soldiers of the sultan would stand beneath their banners. Is it not Thy will that where the czar pays with money, they should pay with their lives?"

Through the floor he still heard that Agrell read from the Bible: "And the kings of earth who lived with her in luxury shall weep and lament over her, when they see the smoke of her burning, standing at a distance out of fear at her torments, saying: 'Alas, alas! woe for the great city of Babylon, that in one hour thy judgment has come!' And the merchants of the earth shall weep and lament over her, for no one buys their cargoes, their cargoes of gold and silver, of jewels and pearls, and fine linen and purple and silk and scarlet, and all odorous woods, and all their vessels of ivory, of costly woods, of copper, iron, and marble, their cinnamon and spices and ointments and incense, and wine and oil and fine flour and wheat, and beasts and sheep and horses, and chariots and men and slaves and bondmen—"

Celsing saw before him the great city and the sultan who approached on his horse, and he saw himself as he would present his letter. But with that it seemed to him that the turbans changed to chevril and dandelions in a garden, where bare-footed village urchins played with a boat of bark in a stream. On the bench up at the house his mother sat and showed him how neatly she had sewed his commission and passport under the lining of his coat. He rose, passed his hand over his brow, and burst out aloud as if he were speaking to her: "Rather than that the Swedes should become a byword and be hunted away like beggars, one of them might well lose his life."

"With whom are you talking?" asked Agrell, who at this moment was coming upstairs to the room. "You have locked the door on the inside, and left me no bed of repose."

Eagerly Celsing rolled up the garments in a cloth, and knotted the bundle firmly together again. At one corner he fastened a slip of paper, on which he wrote that he bequeathed everything to his servant, on condition that no stranger should wear his honest old Swedish uniform.

"Dear brother," he called to Agrell, "don't be annoyed at my oddness, but let me still remain alone with myself a few moments."

Meanwhile he pulled on the wrinkled Turkish trousers, thrust the slippers on his feet, and slipped his arms into the gold-embroidered jacket. As soon as he had hidden the letter of complaint in his girdle and put on the red turban, he cautiously opened the window.

Agrell sat down on the highest step, but jerked every now and then at the door-knob. Celsing is such a shy and reserved young man, he thought, that nobody can rightly know what he is about, but it would little suit such a home-keeping lad as he to throw himself into anything desperate.

He shook the door-knob yet again and said: "You were not born to undertake any fooleries, Brother Celsing, but in good time to settle mildly down and honorably cultivate your cabbage. But what does it mean that you are going back and forth across the floor without being willing to open the door?"

Instead of answering, Celsing opened the window and climbed quietly down to the ground on the branches of a chestnut tree, so that the warnings of friends or their parting hand-grasps should not rob him of self-command.

Among the trees a crowd of servants were going about in light blue coats with enormous gold and silver braid, so as outwardly to conceal the poverty of the expedition; but these were on the other side of the house. Without looking back, Celsing stole through the gate, and when at last he came out on the square between the church of St. Sophia and the serail, he stationed himself under the great tree among the beggars and cripples.

Here is the place, he thought, to which God has now assigned me. You poor fellows on crutches, you beggars who hardly have a stone to sleep on, learn from my countrymen the way to promotion!

He did not take his eyes from the Sublime Porte, where guarding capidgis held back the inquisitive with their sabres, and where, dripping after the heavy rain of the night, two severed heads were set on spikes in niches of the wall. Unused to the low slippers without heels, he felt himself shorter than usual, but when he rose on tiptoe, he could see over the turbans into the spacious Court of the Janisaries and beyond to the second gate, the Gate of Prosperity. There white eunuchs disclosed between the walls a path of gold-embroidered silk and swaying turban plumes. Bearded ulemas in violet cloaks and blue boots, agas with sky-blue mantles, and soldiers with high yellow caps leaned

forward and watched the still closed door. Through
this the sultan was to come. He knew it. He recited to himself from memory the final lines of the
letter which his fingers clutched under the fold of
the girdle: "This is written, not by any one's
request, but for the sake of the truth and his op-
pressed countrymen, by the Swedish subject, Gustaf
Celsing."

In that letter he had told of the venality of the
grand vizier and the officials, but now, as all the
gold and silk glittered in the sun, it seemed to him
that he had still said too little. He recalled the cart
with the sacks of straw on which his own sick king
had driven across the steppes. He recalled how in
Bender colonels and generals blackened the rents
in their worn-out coats, so that their deficiencies
might not strike the Turks in the eyes. And yet he
had seen powerful ambassadors bow before these
fugitives with a reverence more sincere than that
with which the trembling onlookers now sank their
turbans.

A silence of terror spread over the sea of men,
and on high the callers-to-prayer sang from St.
Sophia. He heard them hail the imperial descend-
ant of Mohammed from the church whose convex
canopy of stone had been built to the sound of
psalms as a miracle of Christendom, and where the
bones of holy martyrs were immured behind every
twelfth layer of tiles. He took hold of a beggar's

crutch so as to raise himself. In the Gate of Prosperity, as it opened, he distinguished the pyramidal head-dress and green kaftan of the grand vizier, the light blue stable-grooms, and the dark green agas of the sultanic stirrup. The red executioners came with their cords; coffee-bearers and water-bearers with their handcloths, trays, and golden pots; and finally, shaded by silken banners, approached the sultan, Achmed III, the lord of bridals and tulip festivals.

Celsing felt with both hands in his girdle and pulled forth the letter.

"God be gracious to the unfortunate!" murmured the beggars. "That is an insane man, who knows not what he does."

They grasped his jacket to hold him back, but they were too weak and infirm. Then one of the cripples began to beat him with a crutch, but he did not feel it, and with the letter raised above his head he pressed in through the Janisaries and placed himself in the path of the sultan.

The sultan, who sat somewhat bent forward in the saddle, was very pale, and his eyes were like firelight through misty panes. Without reining in his horse, he lowered his hand and received the letter, instantly hiding it in his pelisse of damask bordered with black fox.

The executioners now seized upon Celsing and led him across the Court of the Janisaries to a prison den which was situated under the Gate of Prosperity.

"You have dared to deliver a letter of complaint," they said. "May it be that you have also satisfactory proof for what you have written?"

He came to himself and said: "Proof? My word. Take my life, take my blood, as proof!"

Sighing, they shook their heads and left him in solitude, but on the prison wall fell a streak of daylight as warm and brilliant as the sunbeam that in the morning had determined him to sacrifice himself. This strengthened him in his resolve to await the consummation of his punishment with uplifted forehead.

He picked up a sharp piece of stone from the ground, and shortened the long hours with cutting words just where the sunbeam struck the wall. As the ray slowly shifted, he followed and worked out letter after letter. When the evening broke in, he had already engraved in his mother speech the following lines on the plaster of the remote death-prison:

> *I hungered, I froze*
> *For the hero I chose.*
> *Right gladly we bled,*
> *And the noblest are dead.*

When he had finished the word "dead," the beam faded, and it was dark. In the distance beyond the third and innermost gate, the Gate of Felicity, flutes and guitars sounded from the gardens of the serail.

Then unrest and anguish rose again in his mind, and he spoke half aloud, wringing his hands: "Women and gaieties I care for but little—and food and drink but little more. And all the bedizened satin of life that men long for? Vanity, vanity! What worth does it possess when once you get it? How well did I not sleep many a night with my old coat rolled up under my head! But out there in the world there is so much, so much that I went by coldly and indifferently. If I had my freedom again, I would be able to sit under the tree among the beggars and point to one of the small glittering lizards in the grass and rejoice at seeing it. O heart, heart, you that knock so heavily, why did you hang so empty in my breast when the light of day yet shone upon my path?"

Hour after hour he remained awake in the darkness, while all the more fervent grew his longing to see again his beam of light on the wall. Through the keyhole he could discern that pale moonlight lay over the earth, but around him all remained dark.

Then he threw himself down and proceeded to think out the verses that he would cut on the wall next morning. He believed that, if he became free, he would repeat and interpret the verses for the poor folk under the tree at the gate of the serail;

but if he never saw the open sky again, perhaps some one of his unfortunate countrymen would take comfort in finding the Swedish words on the wall. When he had got the whole piece finished, he sat up and sang with a loud voice to the tune of an Easter song that he remembered from his boyhood:

I starved and I froze
For the hero I chose.
Right gladly we bled,
And the noblest are dead.
His squadrons are taken,
The old and the young.
His stars may not waken,
With clouds overhung.
In alien places
His men of proud races
As beggars must crouch.
Of straw is his couch,
Though reckoned most royal.
Ye hungering ones,
Behold on the stones
Your monarch, ye loyal!

While he was still singing, all of a sudden a red gleam shone through the fingers he held over his eyes. He rose. Was that the sunrise at last? But the red beam shifted restlessly back and forth on the wall, and he heard ever nearer the sound of voices. Then it grew dark again, and a bunch of keys clattered a long time at the lock.

Two slaves entered with torches, and laid before him on the ground a knotted bundle. Thereupon one of them raised his torch and addressed him.

"The padishah greets you and says: So great is his respect for the Swedes and their king that he rather wishes to see you as his guest than as a prisoner. Your writing he will consider. Assume now the clothing that belongs to you, and go in peace to your house!"

Celsing knelt and opened the bundle, in which he found his Swedish garments. He lifted his coat up to the torch to see that it was really the right one. When he recognized the sabre cut on the sleeve and his mother's sewing on the yellow lining, he took off in the sight of the slaves the velvet Turkish costume and buttoned on again his worn but honorable uniform.

With his hat in front of him he stepped out into the moonlight, but when at the Sublime Porte he came to the beggars sleeping under the trees, he caught the nearest old man by the shoulders and kissed him.

"You do not know me," he said; "but if you did in truth, you would follow me to my people, and they would teach you the way to promotion. Often have I seen my king sleep as you do with a stone under his head."

The Stupid Swede

ON a certain winter morning the mists lay on
the Sea of Marmora like rugged islands of
snow, but all the yellow minarets of Stamboul were
already glowing as far down as their lowest balcony.
A eunuch, who belonged to the sultan's mother,
had betaken himself to the grave of his former master to pray. On the way home he bought at the market-place a white slave-girl who had attracted his
notice by her tall figure. He followed behind her at
the distance of a few steps, and from time to time
pointed out the way with his silver-ornamented
bamboo staff, but as often as not he kept shaking his
head and thinking: What they will say this time not
even a prophet could foresee. Why, she has feet
like a bearer of iron.

He conducted her past the haughty, indifferent
guards of the outer court in the serail, and turned
down toward the water. There he knocked at a little
insignificant garden gate which was almost hidden
with creeping vines.

"My child," he said to the slave-girl while they
waited, "the old man who is now coming with his
keys is called the Deposed Messiah, and you may
as well learn first as last that he is a dangerous and
peculiar man. In his youth, it is said, he was called
Sabathae and lived as a Jew in Smyrna. Then he
began to preach that he was the second Messiah,

but the governor ordered the bowmen to prove his
invulnerability, and with that he renounced his holiness, and instead became porter in the serail."

The lock creaked, and the door was slowly and
cautiously opened by an old man, who had a ragged
brown shawl knotted around his waist like a belt.

The eunuch condescendingly laid his black hand
on the other's shoulder.

"I will give you a coin of shining silver, you old
fellow, if before we go further you will tell the fortune of this new servant. Never have I brought a
newcomer over your threshold in more perplexity.
—Look here, woman, take my staff and draw a line
with it on the sand of the path so that this man can
interpret it and predict your future!"

As soon as the slave-girl had followed out this
command, the Deposed Messiah bent over the sand
and mumbled: "That is a straight line—it goes
crosswise over the path to the border where poison-
ous vermin slink about under the roses. It is altogether straight, I say,—not a bend, not a flourish.
Keep your coin, master; such a straight line has
nothing to foretell. This woman's fortune I cannot
predict."

"You may then take the reward you have long
deserved, old impostor," answered the eunuch, as
he took his staff and let it fall across the back of the
Deposed Messiah. "Do you remember when you
preached and taught that you were a prophet of

God, who would one day come riding on a wild
beast with reins of seven-headed serpents?"

The Deposed Messiah stood a moment on one
foot like a crane and scratched the inside of his knee
with the other. After that he took a couple of steps
back, and his little wrinkled face was distorted while
he raised his hands and hissed, "Cuffs and blows
I get on your account, unknown woman. Be you
accursed, and may serpents and scorpions cause
your death! Now I 've told your fortune."

When he had said this, he again carefully locked
the gate behind them, and limped off across the
pebbles by the water.

Meanwhile the eunuch had already taken the
slave-girl by the arm and led her up a steep stone
flight of steps between walls as high as those of a
fortress. They came up to a pleasure-garden, where
the paths were strewn with broken conch-shells
that crackled softly under their tread, and he made
a sign to her to walk slowly in reverent silence. Between the cypresses gilded cages with song-birds
hung on cords, small fountains plashed and dripped
into basins of Parian marble, and through a long
archway of sighing myrtle and boxwood he led her
out on a promontory facing the sea.

In a circle of plane-trees stood a white kiosk with
a fluted curving roof, and crescents and stars on the
spires; and on the rug before the door a couple of
nurses babbled caressingly in low tones with some

children whom they were teaching to walk. In the
middle of the doorway a white-haired woman in a
pelisse of sable that reached to her feet sat upon
cushions, knotting a white ribbon rosette around
the shaft of a child's rattle of pure gold. It was the
Bee of the Rosebuds, the sultan's mother, the wondrously beautiful Greek from Retimo, who in the
bloom of her youth, when her lips were still like the
dew of spring, had made Mohammed IV mad with
submissive love.

How well the elderly sultana remembered the
terrible hours when the torches of the Janisaries
shone over the courts, and her dethroned husband
retired to the innermost chambers of the palace to
prepare himself with prayers and meditation on
death for imprisonment and the grave. She could
still see herself in the long years when in the serail
of Eski, the gloomy home for superannuated women of the harem, she went sleepless back and forth
over the carpets and wrung her hands, while the
son of a rival, engrossed in theological discourse
with softas and astrologers, breathed out his chill
over the citadel of the earlier sultans. Best of all,
however, she recollected the morning when a son
of her own blood received the oath of allegiance in
the acclaim of the Janisaries, when once more she
saw from her portable chair the Gate of Felicity
rise to the cornice, and grasped the sceptre of authority with a hand as firm and tranquil as that

with which she now held the rattle of her grand-child. Her countenance was yellowish and sharp, but an infinite charm hovered over her melancholy smile.

The eunuch threw himself down prone on the rug, but raised himself again at a sign from her and began to speak:

"Once upon a time in Haivanserai a child found a great diamond of the fairest water. No one, noble sultana, no one knew how it had come thither, but a learned alim related that just in that place, on a day of triumph, the crown of the Emperor Justinian had been lost. You have doubtless also heard, noble sultana, that a poor man once found a splendid dia-mond on a rubbish heap close to the Gate of Egri-kapu. So little did he suspect the value of the stone that he exchanged it for three silver spoons, but now that stone holds together the tuft of plumes on your son's turban. Precious things of all sorts lie hidden from of old in the gravel heaps of this city and perhaps in the ground beneath us here, but when the treasure-seeker comes with his spade, he searches in the wrong place, and finds only bones and mouldered fragments of masonry. After that fashion, too, it often goes with me, your servant, when I am to buy slave-girls. For a whole year I have anxiously borne your command to provide a tall and yellow-haired girl. The freshest spring water has tasted brackish to me, and the softest

sleeping-rug has seemed to me harder than one
of the stone stairs in Seven Towers, because the
thought of your desire has not granted me any
peace. To-day for the first time—just when I had
forgotten my disquiet for a short period, and was
going to pray at your husband's grave—the gracious
God let me quite unexpectedly get sight of such
a slave as you wished."

He lifted off the plain shawl which the slave-girl
wore over her head, and there stood a woman with
fair, tightly combed hair and a clear, open expression.

The sultana laid the rattle on her knee and answered, smiling: "One night in Ramadan my son
dreamed that he saw me embrace and kiss a tall,
yellow-haired slave-girl. As there is no such in all
the serail, the dream made me inquisitive. I know
not well, though, what office we shall give to this
newly arrived servant. She is too tall and awkward
to become a dancer or to serve my son. Above all
things he loves small feet and small hands."

"Assuredly," answered the eunuch, as he noted
how little his purchase pleased the sultana; "but
as yet I have not by any means related to you the
most remarkable thing about this woman. I myself should indeed hardly dare to believe my own
speech, if the slave-dealer had not affirmed the
truth of it on his own salvation. I know him and
know that he is an exceedingly pious and righteous

merchant, who has never deceived us either in respect to the slaves' ages or places of birth. Furthermore, this woman already knows many words of our
speech, and has herself attested that the slave-dealer
speaks the truth. Hear me, therefore, noble sultana, and judge whether I have ever had a more
marvellous jewel to present to you! With what enthusiasm are you not wont to speak of your lion
at Bender, the great king of the Swedes! Now this
poor woman is a daughter of his people and was born
in his remote kingdom, where there is neither grass
nor flowers, but deep snow lies in the middle of the
summer."

The erstwhile indifferent sultana threw the rattle
aside and rose, full of confused wonder. She forgot
her own dignity and walked around the slave-girl,
scrutinizing her carefully. She took her hands,
raised them, examined them, and let them fall
again. She opened her lips and inspected her teeth.
She felt of her hair and skin, but during all this long
investigation continued to smile steadily.

"Everything about this woman," she said, "is so
large—the mouth and even the chin are large.—
Girl, show me your legs!"

The slave-girl made an uncouth, awkward gesture of sudden disgust and turned away, mumbling
in her own language: "Ugh, such foolery!"

"She is quite simple-minded," the eunuch observed conciliatingly. "I noticed that at once, and

the merchant, who would not give false testimony as to that either, admitted that he had never come to give her any name, but used to call her just the Stupid Swede."

"Then she may as well keep the name until she deserves a better. — My child, show me now your legs!"

The Stupid Swede became still more vexed and bashful and held around her the long brown skirt with both hands.

"Lawks! càn't you let me alone?"

"What does she say?"

"That I do not know, noble sultana. But — perhaps she would do to carry the linen to the washing."

"No, she shall be the caretaker for my parrots, because none of my other attendants is able to lift their cages. Evening Starlight, who now has charge of the birds, is too slender and graceful a girl for the task, and may have a great future to look forward to. Meanwhile let her at the start instruct the newcomer carefully in her office."

The sultana, who had sated her curiosity and wearied of the conversation, went back to the door and called to the nurses to lead forward the children.

So the days passed, and Evening Starlight showed the new slave-girl how to tend and feed the parrots. In the hour before sunset the two often sat whispering together in the pleasure-garden among the parrot cages that had been lifted down; and Evening Starlight, who was a little thirteen-year-old Circassian and the youngest in the sultana's service, became devoted to the Stupid Swede. Once the sultana commanded that they should carry the oldest and most elegant of the parrots down to the shore in his silver cage, so that her favorite bird, which was sick and pining, might inhale the salt breeze fresh from the sea. When they had sat down on a bench by the cage, Evening Starlight wound her arms about her friend's broad shoulders, and began to question her about everything imaginable.

"Tell of yourself, and I'll tell of myself."

"Little have I to tell. As a nurse girl I followed the wife of Major Eneberg from a city called Nyköping to a city called Riga. There I was married to a brave and God-fearing soldier who was named Andersson, but when the siege and famine came upon us, and Andersson tried to help some of us women to escape, I was captured by the Russians, bound and laid in a cart, and sold to the Turkish slave-dealer."

"Tell me one thing. Do you know the splendid story about the soul of the dance? No. Is there anything more blissful on earth than to dance?"

Evening Starlight arose, dancing softly, and turned around with eyes half closed so that her floating veil was like the blue-white rings of Persian incense.

"The Deposed Messiah has foretold that some day I shall get two hundred shawls and a kiosk carpeted with red damask. I truly believe that his words will be justified if I can but get to dance before the sultan. Do you know, I cannot sleep o' nights, but just lie awake and think of all that. Perhaps, I think every evening, perhaps even to-morrow I shall get to dance before the sultan. As yet he has hardly seen me.—About what do you mostly think? I mean, what do you long for, what do you hope for? For just nothing, you say? Can it really be any amusement for you only to go about and do your heavy and monotonous task with the parrots? I've never yet heard any one praise that enjoyment. I think it's a punishment to have to sit and feed those stupid wretches. You are a strange sister, and nobody rightly understands you."

The Stupid Swede sat stern and morose. She played with the ninety-year-old parrot in the cage, and tried to teach it some words in her native speech so as to hear a living creature utter them.

"Now do learn to say Andersson!" she enjoined.

But the proud and fastidious bird gurgled and shrieked, and would not do so.

Then she stared at the Venetian merchantman that, with gilded lanterns on its prow and surrounded by sea-gulls and caiques laden with garden-stuff, dried its loose-hanging sails in the sun. The pennants were so long that they reached down to the water, and the oarsmen scrambled to catch their tips, which were lifted by the sunset breeze.

For the first time she reflected upon her own fate. She thought that it was absurd and ridiculous, as if the sultana's hunchbacked story-teller had related it in jest, and while he spoke had shaken arm-rings, dry pods of rape-seed, parrot-feathers, and shreds of yarn in his cap. When she saw her own shadow stretched by the evening light over the glittering mosaics of the stone bench, she had to smile, as if in a sultan's mausoleum she had struck her knee upon Swedish settle-beds and chests of drawers, and had found a couple of cast-off Småland boots of goat-skin in the sacred prayer-niche. But to sink down in meditation with hands on knees was not her business, and she was suddenly aroused by steps on the paths.

There came the eye-doctor with wonder-working salve of collyrium in an agate box, but he himself was blind, so that he had to be led by both hands. There behind the hyacinths fluttered the light blue caftan of the Master of Flowers, and in portable chairs with carefully drawn lace curtains much-envied imperial concubines listened awhile to the plashing waves. With almost dismal menace that whole cloister, sanctified to earthly happiness, rose like a mountain, to whose uppermost heights only the boldest cliff-scaler of fortune dared to climb in order to pull to him its fruit or fall back a bloody corpse. Leafy plane-trees and oaks shaded the meadow-carpets along the shore. Above the nearest walls, behind hedges of myrtle and laurel bushes, extended the length of the harem building, imbedded in vines and roses, with wooden gratings before the little windows. But highest of all, where the all-powerful beings looked down upon their realm and mixed their ice-cold sherbet in bowls of roughly polished turquoises, the pines and cypresses soughed with the dusky green of a mountain forest, and the marble kiosks shone out like snow.

"The sun is sinking," said Evening Starlight. " Let us go out on the grass slope and play. Beloved sister, what are you pondering?"

" It is now almost a whole year that I have not heard a single passage of God's word.— But the air begins to be chilly, and it 's time to carry in the sick bird so that the poor thing may not take harm."

"Why should we trouble about the wretched beast? Nobody sees us. Come, beloved sister, take my hand."

The Stupid Swede sullenly lifted the heavy cage instead of replying. Step by step she carried it alone up the endless stairways to the top, and while the song of the callers-to-prayer from St. Sophia urged the faithful to kneel, she muttered to herself in her own speech: " One ought forsooth to think of one's duties, I trow, even if nobody always stands behind the bushes and glowers."

After that evening she was still more sulky and cross, and the other slave-girls stared after her, laughing, as she sought out her way through the innumerable corridors and long verandas of the harem, on which verandas eunuchs-in-waiting stood without thought and beheld the remote summits of Mount Olympus in Bithynia. Neither did little Evening Starlight any more throw her arms about her with the same childish fervor, but danced and hopped in her footsteps, or called to her out of nooks and corners: "Look after the sick bird!"

The Stupid Swede did not sorrow over her fate. She longed for nothing and hoped for nothing. She desired no more of the coming day than the past had given, but she went about in a constantly increasing vexation with all the alien and vain life about her. The parrots were soon the only creatures that with their chattering could entice her to answer, and in especial she took most tender care of the feeblest and oldest bird, which had seen nine sultans. She did this, not because it was the oldest and most distinguished, but because it was the most decrepit. The alabaster bowls and spoons from which it fed could never be sufficiently polished, and sometimes she sat up with her birds all night.

At last, however, the slave-girls noticed that

she found other things than parrots to serve. One night well on in the summer, for instance, the eunuch had forgotten to fill the water-jug that always stood beside her sleeping-carpet, and when she had slept very peacefully awhile, she awoke and began to feel thirsty. Then it occurred to her that not a single drop of rain had fallen for many weeks, and that the tulips outside the kiosk must be as thirsty as she. The more burning and dry her throat became, the more clearly she imagined that she herself felt the torture of the flowers. Finally she rose, took one by one the well-filled jugs of the other sleeping slave-girls, and went out in the middle of the dark night and watered the tulip-beds. There she was seized by the eunuchs, who at first thought she had slipped out to steal. All this was long talked of in the harem, but the sultana continued gracious toward her. At times she even entrusted to her the purse, which otherwise she kept constantly under her clothing.

Late and early the guards saw the Stupid Swede with the food-bowls of the parrots, and to all questions alike she answered harshly. But if from the wall she recognized the Deposed Messiah, who stood on one leg like a crane in the splashing waves beyond the sun-white beach of pebbles, a shudder passed through her body.

It happened one day that the High Stewardess of the palace ordered her to carry the parrot-cages to the Kiosk of Peris, the nearest one to the sea, and to be there herself at sunset.

She answered as usual by mumbling some angry and incomprehensible words. She kept this up while she fetched the cages. Later, at dusk, when the tulip-beds were illuminated by countless little glass lamps, so that the whole garden seemed to stand out in a glow from subterranean fires, she put on the wretched skirt which she had not worn since the morning she stood in the slave-market.

When she entered the outer hall of the Kiosk of Peris, all the sultan's dancers had already assembled, with small circlets of parrot feathers on their necks and parrot feathers scattered over their skirts of silver gauze. In the middle of the circle stood the fattish High Stewardess with gold-mounted, quadrangular spectacles. In her hand she held a great roll of parchment, for she possessed great learning, was at home in the art of writing, and composed prettier verses and tales than any man in the whole city of the sultan.

"Look here, my child," she said, fastening a little feather circlet on the Stupid Swede's braided hair, "we are now going to delight our noble sultana, the mother of the padishah, with an ancient merry festival that is called the Crowning of the Parrots. All these slave-girls are skilled in the art of dancing. You alone do not know it. For precisely that reason you shall stand in the middle of the ring and try to mimic the others with your long arms and large feet—that will be the merriest foolery of all."

"Yes," repeated Evening Starlight, mimicking the High Stewardess behind her back, "that will be just the merriest foolery of all."

"No, that I could n't do," answered the Stupid Swede. "But folks can dance with us, too, though we take each other by the hand like this—and then we dance like this—and then we stamp the time as hard as we can like this—and then we sing like this: The lads are coming and . . ."

She had caught some of the dancers by the hand and drawn them with her, but the High Steward-ess grew so frightened that the quadrangular spec-tacles slipped far down on her nose. She pulled from her pocket her short wand, which was com-pletely covered with silver flakes and had a seal carved in the end, and with it she rapped briskly on the door-post.

"The sultana may at any hour whatever occupy the room on the other side of that curtain with her most distinguished friends and eunuchs. The Chief Historian is already sitting at his place in there to record everything and describe the festival in the Bridal Book. Are you mad that you set up such a disturbance? Such trampling may possibly do for mules that have chanced to knock over a beehive ; but it is not dancing, for dancing is, before every-thing, beautiful."

The dancers laughed with their mouths full of sugared chestnuts and bullaces. They wailed and lamented and had to sit down on divans, and the eunuchs hid their white teeth behind the door-curtains.

Then the Stupid Swede no longer knew what she did. All the vexation she had buried for weeks and months ran suddenly together in a single flame of wrath, and a flood of words in her harsh native speech streamed forth unchecked from her tongue.

"Devil's in me if I care for you and all your ugly blackamoors. I don't care for you any more than that, you there that only live in surfeiting and wantonness and sin! You never talk of anything else than of the twelve lucky ones who get to wait on the padishah—lawk, the lucky ones, forsooth!—and of the seven imperial concubines who get two hundred shawls apiece. Is it right and decent to have a wife in every room around the whole house? Ugh, ugh, ugh! I am an honest woman; and an honest woman, look you, you've never seen before in this abode of Satan. Ay, and now, drat me, you're paid for calling me the Stupid Swede, you!"

"Very good!" said the High Stewardess, who without understanding a word had observed her slightest gesture. "Exceedingly good! You shall do just so when you come in and the dance begins. Only recite the verses in a somewhat lower voice. A little softer—and perhaps not quite so many

jerks of the neck. One may show oneself a trifle
pleasant even in the comic. Take this basket in your
hands now. In it there is, as you may see, a fresh
rosebush. I have myself had the Deposed Messiah
dig it out of the earth with his fingers and plant it
in the basket, because no one is more deft than he
in such a matter. As soon as the dance is done, you
are to step forward and with a kneeling salutation
set down the basket on the mother-of-pearl table
that stands before the most distinguished of the
parrots."

Stiff as one of the cypresses that stood before the
threshold of the kiosk, the Stupid Swede received
the basket, but everything around her grew dark
as she grasped it by the handle twisted with moss.
She had become a mockery and a laughing-stock
from the time when she had first been brought before the sultana, but she had heeded it little, and not
before now, on this starry evening, when she was
called to the kiosk to amuse the others by her mere
presence, had she felt profoundly her helplessness
and loneliness.

Pipes and drums began to sound on the other
side of the curtain, and after some delay the High
Stewardess rapped again with her wand on the door-
post. Then the curtain was drawn aside, and the
dancers marched into the cupola hall of the kiosk,
where the flower-crowned parrots stood under a
temple of starlike lamps. Then the troop humbly

saluted the sultana, who lay on a bed of cushions. The High Stewardess unrolled the parchment, and with much elegance recited her story.

"Noble parrots, ye who have received the beauty of flowers and human voices! This is the tale of the spirit of the dance. Not long since there lived a begging dervish who was called Turk. He slept on the bare ground, and went naked in the middle of the street without other clothing than a great turban. One day when he drank from a spring under an oak, he saw a boy who was playing music and dancing with a parrot, while he tried to fasten a ring of diamonds and rubies on one of its claws. 'Even if you are the son of a sultan,' said Turk, 'you ought not to think upon dancing and vanity. Learn that more precious than the dead diamond is the water-drop, because it can refresh your tongue; and more precious than the ruby is the drop of blood, because it bears the fire of life through your limbs.' The boy answered: 'Ungrateful and weary man! My father teaches me otherwise, for he says that the diamond and the ruby and everything fair upon the earth is as living as the blood in our hearts, and hangs like dew on the great tree that overshadows all the world and is called God's love. When I look up into that tree, I can neither sit nor lie, but the spirit of the dance comes over me so that I must arise from the ground.' When the boy had said this, he began again to dance so charm-ingly and softly that the begging dervish could not take his eyes from him, but felt that he himself must also dance. First, however, he wished to refresh himself with yet another draught of water, but when he bent down over the mirror of the spring, he became ashamed of his own ugliness and his unkempt beard, and sat there like some one paralyzed. Then the parrot flew to him commiseratingly, and sat on his turban with the sparkling ring on its foot and its white wings outspread like a wondrously beautiful tuft of plumes. The begging dervish again surveyed his image in the spring. Tremblingly he rose and danced with the boy, while he uttered a vow that his cloister-brothers from that day forth should thank and praise God with music and dancing. Noble parrots, it is in commemoration of that dance that we crown and salute you to-night."

As soon as the High Stewardess had finished this tale, the slave-girls, gently swaying, began to revolve and dance. They moved so quietly that their steps on the carpet were inaudible. Their costumes of gauze spread out around them in wide rings without making the smallest rustle, and the music sounded muffled and remote as a song from a galley far out on the sea.

With eyes closed, Evening Starlight raised her arms behind her neck, blissful that in the dance she could display and be herself conscious of her mild beauty. Her foot was no larger than a hand, and her hair hung to the bend of her knee. She knew nothing else of the earth than that it was sweet, and that the padishah might some day give her a kiosk with hangings of red damask and fountains of scented water.

In the midst of the softly whirling circle of human butterflies, the Stupid Swede had stood as it was commanded her, and the ostrich eggs and tassels that hung from the lamps grazed her hair. She did not know how tall and handsome she was as she stood there in her poor work-dress. She never once thought of it. She felt no happy gratitude to God because her expression was clear and open and her hair as soft as the silk of which the women at Brussa had woven the sultana's money-pouch. It never occurred to her that the earth was sweet, that the very rejoicing of the senses might be innocent. She had not received the spirit of the dance at birth. She could not raise her arms instinctively as she danced, like an inspired priestess. She could hardly sing thanks with her lips and still less with her limbs. God had not bestowed on her such a jewel as a christening present. She understood that all these Circassians and daughters of Lesbos were born in huts as she was, and were simple as she, but that still they possessed a knowledge which was not hers, knowledge of the mysteries of the dance. She looked obstinately down at the carpet, but she felt that the

High Stewardess was all the while surveying her over her quadrangular spectacles with impatience and displeasure.

For a long time she tried pretending to notice nothing. Then she started and remembered the command to mimic, to be the fool in the play. Swaying her hips a little, she took a couple of steps. Immediately she heard around her in the hall a rustling and whispering, as when a puff of wind from the doorway hurls dry winter leaves over a stone floor.

When she looked up, she observed that it was the onlookers, who were whispering and laughing suppressedly, with hands before their mouths, at her awkwardness. She had succeeded, and had satisfied the High Stewardess, but shame and vexation struck her again into immobility. The reek of the lamps and the perfume of the flowers went to her head. When the dance finally came to a standstill, and she carried the basket to the most distinguished parrot, which sat, sunken and decrepit, blinking on its perch, she hardly saw any longer the carpet in front of her. Her hands began to fumble, and just as, kneeling, she held out her offering, the basket slipped on the smooth mother-of-pearl table, and the rose plant fell to the floor.

Then a whole swarm of scorpions crept over the edge of the basket, and from the earth at the bottom rose a snake with a flat, broad head.

For a moment the snake swayed jerkily to and
fro, as if even it had become possessed of the spirit
of the dance. Then it drew itself together with a
swift, wavy motion, and lifted its wide and hissing
jaws toward the parrot. Flapping noisily, the frightened bird struck against the silver network of the
cage to get to its caretaker and find protection.
Through the whole kiosk, silent as the grave, where
the laughter paled away, and dropped crowns of
feathers lay strewn over the carpet, it uttered,
screaming, the single word that she had most
earnestly tried to teach it:

"Andersson! Andersson! Andersson!"

"There you said summat!" muttered the Stupid
Swede. She had risen from the floor, and in a dream
she saw that moment in the cool twilight when the
Deposed Messiah had hid the snake and scorpions
in the basket under the roots of the rose. But she
no longer remembered that the terrified onlookers
stood round about her, huddled up on cushions
and divans along the walls of the hall.

Cautiously she took hold of the basket and carried it to the open window. The snake turned its
head toward her and licked the air with its tongue.
But when she drew her hand back, the snake had
coiled itself about her arm. It struck her on the
wrist so that the blood dropped down, and only
let go its bite when she pressed it to the floor and
stamped its head to pieces with her large foot. She

took two or three steps to one side, and remained standing with her back against the wall.

Only now did whispering and talking begin again round her; but the proud, white-haired sultana, who had seen the Janisaries dismember the bodies of viziers before the serail gate, and had heard many a night the stealthy tread of "the dumb ones" on the shells of the garden paths,—she came forward, and examined the bleeding arm long with practised skill.

"My precious child," she said quietly, as she embraced and kissed the dying Swedish slave-girl, "you have saved with your life my favorite bird. But you have also given us a deep riddle to ponder. How, pray, could your duties and your tedious daily tasks with their constant monotony be so dear to you that all that we strain after seemed to you empty foolery and trifling? They have pointed the finger at you, because you did not understand the mysteries of the dance.—Alas! my child, they are easier to learn than it is to interpret your riddle. I would praise the God of our fathers, if He would permit such mothers to suckle our sons."

Afterwards, when the lamps were quenched, and the night was roaring outside, little Evening Starlight sat awake on her sleeping-carpet.—Was there, then, really something in the world that was worth more than shawls and jewels? Why had no one said so before?

"You would not miss the dead slave-girl so bitterly," whispered some of her friends, "if you had
not loved her and yet caused her sorrow. For such
things there is no remedy."

"You would not grieve for her so," they whispered the following night, "if you had before loved
a man. Now your whole heart is hers.—You are
so passionate, you Circassians."

But the sultana said, "You have dark rings under
your eyes, and I counsel you to begin coloring your
lips, for if the padishah happens to see you as you
now look, you are like to wait long for your kiosk
and your red damask tapestries."

Evening Starlight died, and was buried on the
slope above the cloister of the dancing dervishes
at Scutari under the same acacia as the Swedish
woman. The dervishes planted hyacinths around
the tree, tended it long, and called the place the
Grave of the Two Sisters.

"There lie two princesses," they would relate,
"who lived long, long ago. The elder believed that
God dwelt in pious employments and the younger
that He dwelt in the dance, but for this they were
called sisters, because they both contended in serving Him."

When on quiet evenings the small hand-drums
and wooden flutes played in the cloister, it sounded
as if a troop of boys were amusing themselves with
toy fiddles from the bazaar, but through the open

gate the pious dervishes now and again would come out in their white garments, barefoot or in stockings, and move about so softly and silently that they could hear the sigh of the acacia as they danced.

Bender

THE thinning ranks that followed the king over the steppes to the kingdom of the sultan had pitched their camp at Bender in a charming river valley. Many an officer continued to live in his cart like a care-free gipsy, but the king got them to build huts and dens in the earth against the winter. He received daily from the sultan a sufficient gift of money and the necessities of life. There was gay commotion in the camp when the trumpets and drums called to meals and divine service. The pasha and his Janisaries vied with one another in paying honor to the conquered champion, who never tasted wine, who despised residence in a city, and whose body-guards were never allowed to marry. When the tillers of the soil and their wives saw the blue horsemen gallop out among the vineyards, they hastened to meet them, and coins of gold and silver rained into aprons and baskets. At last, however, the sultan wearied of filling the hands of his prodigal guests with gold and their bins with hay. Ducats again became a rare Shew Bread, and even the Turkish guard of honor which had been stationed at the camp marched away.

The king stepped out from his tent only when the overflowing water of the river came halfway up on his jack-boots.

He took Colonel Grothusen by the arm: "We

have told them that we will not go back to Christendom before we have a following of fifty thousand Turks. To that we will stick. Now that they
deny us money, we shall work wonders. The royal
household shall be kept up three times as splendidly as before, and besides the king's table and
the table of the Court Marshal, there shall every day
be prepared here a plentiful board for strangers."

After that he went out and ordered the soldiers
to build on the high bank before the straw-thatched
huts of the village of Varnitsa a royal mansion and
a whole town for warriors with streets and stone-
paved walks.

This new town on the sultan's soil received the
name of Carlopolis. With hearty energy the scarred
warriors knotted leather aprons around their waists
in the midst of the gaping Turks and began to
forge the most elaborate locks or to fit the most
elegant doors and window-sills. Generals and colonels familiar with victory took command of carpenters, master masons, plasterers, stone-cutters,
and glass-makers in the hot sunlight, and in the
midst of them the limping king went about with
as rosy cheeks and cloudless forehead as if all the
misfortunes of the Ukraine had long since been
smoothed out of his remembrance.

Like a castle on the Rhine the royal mansion
rose, with its steep roof and red balcony overlook-
ing the rapid Dniester. Saddles of satin with rose

diamonds and turquoises on holsters and trappings
were hung around the tile-covered attic. Richly
carved doors with brightly polished locks of brass
opened from the entry to the two halls and eight
rooms, which were adorned with French tapestries
and divans furnished in brocade. The carpets were
so thick and soft that the heaviest soldier-boots
never awakened the slightest noise, and on the roof
at evening flickered reddish lamps, as if to illumi-
nate dancing slaves. Outside, streets extended between the droll little haphazard castles of the officers
and officials. A handsome wooden bridge in the
colors of the rainbow led over a deep ditch to Varnitsa, and around all the impudent-looking camp
were thrown up walls and entrenchments. All this
fortified town, then, did the diligent Swedes build
as soon as they were without money. The unwit-
ting beggar who went past along the river believed
that the kindly country-folk had chosen one of
their shepherds as king and had raised his capital
city there in the midst of a realm of vineyards and
cattle-calls and bird-twittering.

Outside the door of the royal mansion lay tame
deer and roes, gazing on the threshold, ready to follow the king whenever he went out, and large-winged
butterflies set themselves calmly to rest on the yellow
flag of headquarters, which with the strange three
crowns in its coat-of-arms stood stuck into the
ground in front of the drums and muskets of the

guard. In the shade of the mulberry trees on the slopes, which were overgrown with grass and flowers, naked and bathing warriors sat by the water without a thought of their former hardships, for they forgot the pain of their wounds on the same day they were healed and cicatrized. Others laughingly tried their muskets on snipe and hares, or strolled out around the plain among the cotton-plants and feeding herds of buffalo toward the rugged, far-stretching mountains that embraced the whole beautiful region with their dark blue wreath. Still feeling twinges of their severe wounds, Hård and Gierta lay in their shirt-sleeves beside a flask of wine on the greensward between the huts and played at *bête* with the noisy Axel Sparre. Kasten Feif hung up on the walls under his low roof the etchings of the new castle which had been sent from Stockholm. Without ever winning his point, he disputed there every morning with the king, who, more strict even than Tessin, would not hear of any statues or unnecessary adornments in architecture, but approved only noble lines and large surfaces. French Mons, who had now become so Turkish that only the most expensive tobacco was good enough for him, was sitting there with his pipe, but he had to hold and fill it with the same hand, because his left arm was shot away. The body physician, Skraggenstjerna, pounded powder in a kettle, while in the doorway above him hung jars and phials of plantain wood.

Captain Konrad Sparre, who with his comrades, Loos and Gyllenskip, had just come back from a pilgrimage to the Nile and Jerusalem, had all his hut filled with images, mummies, and stuffed crocodiles. At a gesture there had grown up a dwarf city with its collections and offices, but many palaces were of such a height that the owners could stand and lean their elbows on the roof. The inhabitants awoke and went to sleep to the blare of trumpets, and early every morning, when the mist lifted, appeared a kind-looking man, who in stiff braided uniform, with his shoulders raised and lips drawn together in an expression of importance, rowed out on the river against the stream. It was Hultman, who was going with a tall pewter pot to fetch the clearest drinking water for his royal master.

Just where in autumn the long streak of migratory birds was wont to pass stood the gloomy, grayish-yellow fortress of Bender, with its quadrangle of pointed tower-hoods, and from it streamed daily a train of Janisaries, Tartars, Armenians, and gipsies. They jostled among the earthen huts of the Zaporogeans down by the river, where Mazeppa had died with his head on the knees of his women, and when they had got their camels and asses safely bound to trees, they stared inquisitively into the cook=house and at Brandklipper's ice-gray flank in the foremost box-stall of the stable. They offered on all sides their bunches of grapes, their sheep and fowls, and were at times held back with bayonets when a foreign emissary arrived to pay the Swedish king his respects in the midst of his exile and mis-fortune. Now and then they met a courier with a mail-bag, or a poor shoeless Pomeranian peasant, who had voluntarily walked the long distance across Europe to deliver to his king a hundred ducats for travel money. Thickest, however, did the tar-booshes and turbans swarm below the royal man-sion, on whose balcony thirty musicians played on violins, lutes, and oboes. As soon as they were silent, the Turks below struck up with brazen cymbals, shawms, and drums. During all this the Janisaries embraced their Swedish friends or sat down con-tentedly and reflectively on the ground and stared at the open windows of the chancellery, where two odd figures bent, eagerly writing, over a table. Whenever the two gentlemen wished to look each other in the face, they had to turn their whole bodies, because neither had more than one eye. He who continually stuck his quill pen crosswise be-tween his lips was the nap-worn Court Chancellor von Müller. The other, on the contrary, who had his pocket full of tidbits and every now and then laid a bit of candy on his tongue, was Colonel Gro-thusen. He sat enveloped in a crimson dressing-gown of silk. His neck-cloth of French lace and his curling, raven-black wig swayed and swelled,

but on his feet he had a pair of heavy military boots,
for one night the king had stolen in to him through
the window and stuffed his satin slippers into a
heap of embers. His face was yellower than a dried
lemon, but his good eye glistened and blinked, and
as soon as he opened his mouth, Müller began to
bob on his chair and laugh.

Soon, however, clouds massed themselves over
the mountains, and the soldiers drove sleighs in
a merry-go-round with the Turks on the frozen
Dniester, so that the turbans rolled along the ice.
The windows were shut, and one lowering morning Grothusen threw his goose-quill pen from him
with such vigor that it was blown over the table by
the draught through the chinks and remained lying
on the floor.

"Müller," said he, "for lack of hay we have now
had to shoot nineteen fine led horses. If I can't
quickly get together the loan of a thousand more
purses, we're done for. In all Carlopolis there will
soon be not so much as a horseshoe nail that can
be called ours, no matter how I chaffer with both
Christians and heathens. Credit is finished. Good!
Away with the bank! We went off, not to gather
money, but rather to abolish its worth."

He lifted his wig and passed his hand over his
hot head, but Müller only wrote on, and inquired
in a plaintive voice, "And His Majesty?"

"At the present moment he is sitting in the din-

ing-room reading Corneille, but he has a trick up
each of his sleeves, and is holding in his sides, as he
always does when he has just come to some daring
resolution. He is so happy over it that he warms
one's sinful heart before one really knows what it
is about. There is one thing, brother, that vexes me
continually. The world is full of admirers who bawl
His Majesty's praise, because he can sleep on a
snow-drift and drink water from a wooden goblet.
And in truth he is such a man, and rouses our astonishment every day with such things. I would
only say that into the bargain he is something still
greater. There are not only soldier crotchets under
his hat. Listen to him disputing with Feif about
the fine arts or with me about philosophy! And
yet along with it are these—saving his honor—
veritable little slovenlinesses, as that he can hardly
scrawl a legible letter. Don't you recognize in all
this the spiritual gifts of the Swede in their most
brilliant form? A glittering web of the most gorgeous cloth-of-gold—with here and there great
dark rents through which one can thrust his hand!
Is it any wonder that the Swedes go to death for
such a man as for themselves? Don't ask him to
traipse home full of remorse like the prodigal son
to show his empty trouser pockets. Tell me, rather,
where the deuce are we to get money?"

Müller now stuck his pen behind his ear.

"The favorites both of Our Lord and our princes

are sore beset with the envy of their fellow men, and
you and your borrowing are discussed in the camp
here with greater heat than you suspect. You 'll find
out. Shut your account book in a hurry, hang your
dressing-gown on the nail, and put on your old
colonel's uniform, for in a couple of days we 're
going to have a row. Even day before yesterday,
when the pasha from Bender came riding up, cut the
air with his sabre, and ordered us in the name of his
great master to pack off home, I comprehended
that His Majesty would come to a terrible resolution. And have you noticed that his sword is always
three inches out of the scabbard exactly as in the
old days?"

"Well, then, we 'll slash and cut—that's the
only outcome. Hård longs for it so that his eyes
flash. — Come in, come in!"

Grothusen turned about, and saluted the three
men who crossed the threshold. One was named
Axel Roos. He was a slim, brown-curled dragoon
of the royal guard, and for him there was nothing
else in the world than the honor of his country and
his king. One of his comrades was Lieutenant Olof
Aberg. His whole face, which was of a manful ugliness, was scarred with sword-cuts, and a shell splin-
ter had broken both his front teeth. The last man,
on the contrary, was but a plain life-guardsman, who
was called Seved Tolvslag, but he was known as the
strongest and tallest soldier in Carlopolis, and he

could bend a horseshoe or squeeze together a pewter plate as an arm-cloth. Nobody had ever heard
him laugh. With his sunburned, almost black face,
he stood with equally terrible sternness, whether it
was a question of a psalm or a game, and his greatest enjoyment in life was to go on duty alone and
silent on cold nights with his hands stuck into his
coat-sleeves.

"I have had you summoned," said Grothusen,
throwing back his head, "because we consider you,
without distinction of rank, our three bravest men.
Go diligently about among officers and soldiers
according to your various ranks, and inspire the
wavering with courage. Soon we are likely to behold
an affair that is going to surpass everything we have
hitherto experienced. We have reached the bounds
of the possible."

While he spoke, he changed his clothes. When
he had hooked on his sword-belt in the most approved style, the window was darkened by a rider,
who tapped on the pane.

It was the king.

He sat there as radiant as if he had just emptied
a magic draught of eternal youth. His attire was as
simple as always, but spotless, and his thin hair even
was tied into a knot on his neck. The boy leaped
up in his eyes, and he tapped yet again on the pane
with his riding-whip.

"Grothusen, now we must go in to Bender."

The irresolute colonel ran out on the stone step.

"But Your Majesty has never before been able to ride in there, and just now the storm-bell is ringing. They have wearied of their distinguished guests, and it is all over with the old friendship. Look for yourself! There is hardly a single Turk in the camp any longer. They hope the time is coming to cut us all down and plunder us to the naked body."

The king smiled and nodded assent.

Then a merry light spread over the brow of Grothusen, and the next moment his charger reared beside the king's.

Contrary to custom, the king rode his horse away over the plain at a trot. Under the projecting thatch of the huts between the gorgeously painted wooden pillars threatening crowds were already standing, armed with scythes and muskets, but the king waved to them with his glove as to underlings. In the muddy, unpaved streets of Bender the hucksters had hooked up the shutters before their booths, and armed soldiers and merchants were walking back and forth. They recited from memory the sultan's letter, which gave them the right to compel the Swedes by force to return home. They shouted one another down with wild war-cries, but when unexpectedly they recognized the king in their midst, when his horse trampled on their mantles and caftans, they lowered their spears and threw themselves down with their foreheads to the earth.

"Haha!" jubilated the younger girls behind the grating of the harems, "his head is too small for his body, and his body too small for his horrible boots. Haha!"

But the wives and the older women pushed them aside angrily.

"Allah, if we had but such a lord!"

With that they took the dried festoons of leaves which since the summer had been fastened along the window-sills. They threw leaves and flowers over him, so that a withered rose remained lying on his hat. Meanwhile the tower bells were ringing to call the inhabitants to arms against the Swedes and their king.

Calmly saluting as on a pleasure ride, he continued up street and down street, till the open plain again lay before the two riders in the sunset light.

Grothusen pointed over a low stone wall.

"Look at that grass mound beside the sainted Bishop Malmberg's last resting-place! That is Mazeppa's grave. Two wonderful words! Mazeppa's grave. Thus may earthly greatness end."

The king bent sidewise, and laid his hand familiarly on his favorite's knee.

"Grothusen, my good fellow, if a withered leaf falls to the ground a hundred years from to-day, that event is a consequence of innumerable other small and unnoticed events. That moment is a link in a chain of happenings which goes back finally to eternity and the creating hand of God. If, too, a leaf now falls to the ground, it is because just that event and no other can occur at this time. If we might see all that has happened as clearly as a row of figures, we should also be able to reckon out all that is to happen up to the end of the world. We should then be able to foretell the day, the hour, that will be our destruction. Let us not therefore waver with anxiety!"

Half with the awe of a subject and half with the tenderness of an enthusiastic friend, Grothusen took the hand of the king. He had seen that with his last brave followers among the vineyard hills of Varnitsa, far from the small importunities of government, the king had celebrated perhaps his most fortunate years, the Sabbath rest of his days, that he had come ever nearer to his followers as a good comrade. The cold February evening grew starry clear and deep. By Mazeppa's grave Grothusen wanted to speak, but he had no longer power over his own voice.

"Journey home!" he whispered. "As true as I live, a Charles XII would become great as a peace king, and would accomplish what Christina never could do, because she was a frivolous woman. Journey home! There is a mutiny coming. Do not say I don't know the Swedes. They, like other men, have wives and children. If we got a great conquering Turkish army to follow us, then indeed we might found a Protestant confederation under a Swedish emperor. But it's the same with Turks as with pearls: they cost money. Soon I shall no longer have a single ducat for bribery. We must bow, we must bow before our own poverty, our ancient, heavy, pitiful poverty. It is that and not men which has conquered us. — Ah, to see the door wide open and be turned away because of empty begging-sacks!"

When the king remained silent, Grothusen leaned nearer to him in the half-dusk, then sprang back. His own words had driven away the happy moment when he had sat alone with his king in rapt conversation. The friend had vanished behind a cold, though still smiling mask.

Then Grothusen tried to joke.

"Yes, if we had money, we should strengthen our camp with heavy cannon and make a Jomsborg of it in the midst of the enemy's country, and like the guards we should all pledge ourselves never to marry. Then we should abolish all money there and eat at a common table, but invite Leibnitz and other great men to sit on the bench of honor. With them we should gather the various doctrines into one declaration, so that our royal fortress, though without either land or vassals, should be a perpetual temple of truth and reconciliation. All that we should do. — But as things are, it remains for us only to yield or fight."

"It remains for us only to fight," answered the king, giving his charger the spurs with such violence that Grothusen remained there with the empty glove in his hand.

He turned and looked at the large glove. At length he kissed it and hid it under his coat next his heart, as he whispered: "There it shall stay until my bullet whistles."

In expectation of a siege, the Swedes opened a well a few steps from the royal mansion, where a cool running spring filled it with crystal-clear water. The women of Varnitsa believed that he who drank of that water became proof against both love and shot. They could see that best in old Grothusen, they thought. He drank only wine, and never tasted a single glass from the well, and he was therefore so lovesick that whenever he met a pretty girl he lifted his braided hat to her and chucked her under the chin with his dexter and middle fingers. The others of the band did not do so.

Åberg's wrinkled and grinning face was often mirrored in the well. With his mattock under his arm, he drank away his thirst, and then hastened to the soldiers at the entrenchments. Around all the camp they threw up a breastwork of barrels, bedsteads, carts, and the spadefuls of earth that they could break out of the frozen ground. The king

himself stood and twined withes and ropes between
chair-legs and wagon-wheels. The country-folk fled,
so that the huts of Varnitsa became desolate, but
a great boundless host of Turks and Tartars drew
themselves up in a wide ring with their mortars
and field-pieces. Late in the frosty nights a tall
shape bent over the rim of the well and clattered
the chain of the tin drinking-can. It was Seved
Tolvslag on duty, after he had just helped some
Janisaries to smuggle in secretly their baskets of
fowls and sacks of hay. Close beside him in front
of a lantern stood Grothusen, who, with his pelf
borrowed from Englishmen, Frenchmen, and Jews,
paid for everything at three times its value, as if
he had awakened every morning with his jack-boots
full of ducats.

Sometimes the Swedish dragoons dashed out on
the plains in the bright daylight, and brought back
buffaloes and sheep right under the eyes of the
besiegers. Or, again, the king rode to the hostile
sentries and reviewed them, seeing to it that they
did their duty, as he taught them to shoulder arms
in the Swedish fashion.

In the royal mansion the windows were filled
to the height of a man with sacks of earth or barred
with palisades. Hultman and the lackeys carried
into the dining-room the long oaken chest with
the table silver, and they stowed away among the
soldiers in the attic the French tapestries and silken

cushions, and the most important books and documents. Regimental rolls, Tessin's etchings, and
French tragedies were embedded side by side under
horse-trappings overlaid with gold and precious
stones, and cartridge-boxes and muskets were dealt
out to the royal watch. All the little city of the king,
hundreds of miles from its native land, had hardly
the equipment for as many men as would be needed
to furnish a single full regiment. Even the ceremonious Court Chamberlain, Düben, with sweat on his
brow, had to drill and exercise his lackeys, scullions,
cup-bearers, and guardians of the silver. The chief
cook, Boberg, was forced to throw his ladle on the
shelf and tramp over stones with a broadsword on
his arm between Hultman and the panting kitchen
clerk. Bareheaded, hesitating, flurried, with coat-
seams worn bright and with ink on his fingers,
Müller marched at the head of his men of the chancellery.

"Look at His Majesty!" he whispered to Düben.
"Recklessness is a joy to the soul. Honor has become so precious to him that if he can only keep
it untarnished, then straightway no misfortune can
trouble him any longer. But I say this, that for my
part I will lay down my sword as soon as the brown
savages outside shall storm up. Is it sense that five
hundred men should fight with twenty or thirty
thousand?"

When the king caught sight of the Holstein

envoy, Fabrice, who for a last time rode out from
Bender to the camp to move him to departure, he,
as if by an accident, allowed his retinue to march
forward to the Holsteiner. The Swedish gentlemen
at once hastened to deliver into the envoy's keeping their pocket-books, snuff-boxes, and purses.
When Fabrice finally rode away, he had such a
plethora of valuables under his coat that he could
not button it. Then the soldiers, too, began to hide
their possessions. The last ducat, carried about for
years, was ripped out of the vest lining and, together
with a ring of silver or horsehair that had been
given by a first sweetheart, was hidden in a fig, a
tree trunk, or in the earth. Chamberlain Klysendorff himself stood with a spade in his hand among
the soldiers on the slope of the shore and buried by
a grapevine his old grandmother's portrait on ivory.

"I am far on in years," he said, "and broken
with gout and infirmity. I have a foreboding that
now I shall fall. Rather, though, will I entrust my
belongings to the dark earth, whither I myself shall
soon go down, than to greedy plunderers. Grass
will come to grow and be green above the little
love gifts and savings that we poor exiles conceal
here in the alien earth."

When he had passed on the shovel to the next
man, he heard the king's voice and turned around.

With burning cheeks like a boy of fifteen, but
commanding to-day like an emperor over princes,

the king sat on his horse at the outer entrenchments, and around him gathered the most distinguished of the Swedes. Gierta, who had risked his
life for him at Poltava, and Hård, chieftain of the
battle-loving guardsmen, were propped on their
swords. With coaxing whispers, the court preacher,
Brenner, leaned his full, cherubic face first to one,
then to another. His coadjutor, Aurivillius, twitched
him by the cloak, but General Daldorff tore away
the shirt over his lacerated breast and spoke to the
king without fear.

"Here," he shouted, pointing to his breast, "behold here the proof that we have always been ready
to give our last drop of blood for the land of our
fathers! We are ready now, too; but if we lay low
all the Turks that are here, we shall immediately
after have the whole might of the sultan upon us.
We all know that not only Turkey but also the sea
powers have offered to convey our king to his lands
with the greatest honor, and the way through Germany is still open. The Turks have heaped gifts and
friendship on us, but in return have gotten open
contempt."

The king answered: "The Turks sell themselves
to the highest bidder, and therefore they deserve
contempt. Of old we fought like valiant warriors,
but now you talk like poltroons. Obey, as is your
duty, and show yourselves hereafter such as you
were heretofore."

With that he clapped Daldorff on the shoulder like a good comrade, without the least rancor, and rode to the royal mansion as the enemy's field-pieces began to roar.

Klysendorff, who was a timid and retiring man, remained standing among the soldiers, speaking to them softly.

"I know well that the world will judge our gracious king harshly for what is now likely to befall and hold him for a madman. But the Turks are greater madmen when they fancy they can frighten him off by force. Even though all should abandon him, do you show, you lesser men in the ranks, where faithfulness lies deepest in the breast!"

Piercing cries now filled all the lovely region, and the enemy stormed up, but Grothusen in his laced parade hat stood at the entrenchment, and saluted the Janisaries with the friendliest greetings and the most whimsical bravado. He took from his knapsack at random ducats, Albrecht dollars, and bits of candy. He strewed these indiscriminately on all sides, and when he pointed toward the camp, there shone above the royal mansion a triple rainbow, and before the door the king sat calmly and proudly on his steaming horse.

"No, no!" murmured the Janisaries, and swung their sabres toward their own forces while they marched back into the town. "We will not attack that iron-head. We are his friends. Let him have time for thought until to-morrow."

.   .   .   .

It was Sunday, and in the king's mansion the Swedes struck up the first psalm of the morning service as if nothing were afoot. The sacks of earth and frozen water-barrels blocked the windows, so that the hall was like the dark corridor of a fortress. Two wax candles burned on the table, which was covered with a white cloth, and the minister bent far down over the Bible so that he might be able to read the text for the day.

"And when he went into the ship, his disciples followed him. And behold! a great storm arose upon the sea, so that the ship was deluged with the waves; but he slept."

The king stood nearest in front of the table with his fur cap in his hand. His resolution had been taken calmly and gladly, without debate, only with a longing. At Poltava misfortune had fallen upon him like a landslide in the dizziness of fever, and before he could raise himself from his sick-bed everything was devastated. Now he was once more master of himself. Year by year, day by day, he had seen the meshes breaking in the net he tried to weave, but which could be tied only with thread of gold. He burned with eagerness to be done at last with these stupid intrigues and in the full light of day appeal to the broadsword. Riga, Pernau, Reval, Viborg, Keksholm—each name, as it passed through his memory, pointed to lost cities and provinces. What more would it be if he fell? Earthly life was short, but the glory of battle deeds is everlasting.

The minister bent once more over the Bible.

"And his disciples went forward and wakened him, saying: Lord, help us! We perish."

At this moment one of the first cannon-balls struck the thick wall of the royal mansion, but remained stuck in the soft brickwork, and the minister proceeded.

"And he said unto them: O ye of little faith, why are ye afraid?"

An officer hurried forward to the king and whispered: "No one is likely to hear the words of the text any more for the noise, and now the Turks are storming."

The king answered: "We do not break off our divine service on account of shot, but each and all of us is likely to be needed at his post."

On the balcony of the royal mansion the musicians struck up with thundering kettledrums the Dalecarlian Polka and the Torch Dance. "Allah! Allah!" answered Turks and Tartars, and their white jackets fluttered, as they stormed in by thousands over the entrenchments, brandishing spear and scimitar. Some of the Janisaries, however, stuck

their blades under their arms and with brotherly
persuasion handed their tobacco pouches to their
Swedish friends and acquaintances. When the king
rode with drawn sword into the *mêlée*, he saw man
after man of his people lay down his arms, and he
reddened. He shouted to Grothusen and Daldorff,
but no one answered him. Then he noticed that the
strife had to do with himself alone, and those who
were not willing to fight were likewise unworthy
to do so.

"Those who still have courage and loyalty in
their breasts may follow me," he shouted.

Seved Tolvslag then gathered about him the
common soldiers and the scullions and lackeys
who had just been painfully drilled in the first
manual exercises. Fighting faithfully for life or death,
they surrounded the king, as he sprang from his
horse and ran his broadsword through the nearest
Turks. In front of him went Seved Tolvslag like
a swarthy berserk, presenting arms, but as soon as
the enemy pressed into his way, he made a swing
with his bayonet and cut a harvest for Death. A
pistol was levelled at the king's temple, but as if
moved by an invisible hand, he bent his head a
finger's breadth aside—and the ball only grazed
his face, but struck Hård, wounded, to the ground.
He saw General Axel Sparre bound and stripped.
Clashing swords and sabres cut deep notches in
each other's edges. In a struggle with his own life-

guardsman, Roos, and two Swedes, he was caught
about the middle with an iron grasp and carried
against his will into the royal mansion, whereupon
the door was barred.

It was not thus that he wished for sword-play.
The impatience of wrath and battle-lust kindled
fever in his blood. With eyebrows scorched away,
bleeding at the nose and ears, he mustered his band
of forty warriors in the Court Chamberlain's apartment and nodded pleasantly to old Hultman, who
with a great bandage round his head and a musket
on his shoulder stood in line beside Wolberg and
Groll and Friberg and all the bravest among the
faithful. With knitted brow and flashing eyes, his
long sword half raised, he rushed before his men
through the halls and rooms where plunderers had
already thronged in. Roos shot and fought by his
heart side. The begrimed and toothless Åberg
crouched under his arm like a grinning eunuch
and aimed his sword thrusts up at the bellies and
breasts of the Turks, but Seved Tolvslag went his
undeviating way forward, seizing man after man
by the beard and rolling him out through the window. He wrenched away weapons, broke them to
pieces under his foot, and then threw the fragments
out into the courtyard. Fire flamed and spurted
from priming powder and pipes. Oho! the song
of the crossed blades that sighed like harp-tones.

In the great hall, where the two half-consumed

wax candles still shone on the open Bible text about the Master who awakened and rebuked the winds, the Swedes could distinguish one another only by their spurred boots under the thickly rising smoke. With a howl so wild that many of the younger men shuddered, the slippers of the Janisaries and the yellow half-boots and white jackets of the Tartars suddenly began to mount, clambering up into the very smoke, as on a stairway, and to vanish. Swords vainly hewed and stabbed on all sides without longer hitting anything but empty air.

"These are witch-folk," murmured Hultman, taking his stand beside the Bible, but the king pushed a water cask from the window so that the smoke streamed out. Then they discovered the plunderers hanging on doors and mouldings, and anew the dizzy lion hunt roared through the apartments.

When at last all the enemy were driven out, the king stationed his thirty-two surviving battle comrades in small groups at each window and himself went round among the dead, emptying the bullets and powder from the wallets on their shoulder-belts. Still bleeding, he let his wounded hand be bandaged by Roos, who had just saved him by a pistol-shot in a hand-to-hand struggle with two Turks.

"I see," he said, "that Roos has not abandoned me, but where, I wonder, are all the others, who have deserted?"

"The greater part are likely to be dead or taken prisoners."

The king's glance blazed yet more at that, and taking Roos by the hand, he led him back to the great hall, from whose windows the muskets flung their fire against the ever approaching enemy. Deep dusk prevailed within, for it was already getting on towards twilight, but between the barrels and sacks of earth appeared the wide circle of baggage wagons, doors, and wine-vats, behind which the Turks drew nearer step by step, and the whole expanse of the courtyard was already covered with the fallen.

A keg of brandy was lifted down from the attic to still the grievous thirst, and he, the king whom no one had seen taste anything but water, went from man to man with the glass and enjoined them not to take more than a swallow apiece. But when finally the strong drink no longer gave refreshment, wine was fetched, and filling with it the same glass that had just gone from mouth to mouth among the soldiery, he drained it himself like an equal.

"It is better," said he, after another hour of raging strife, "that we should defend ourselves like valiant men to the last breath and so become immortal through our courage and our valor, than that we give ourselves up to the enemy so as to get a little longer time of life."

Along with the muskets' irregular rattle, cannon-balls and bombs rained on the solitary house, and arrows with long tails of burning tow bit themselves fast into the shingles of the roof. Meanwhile there spread for a moment through the smoke an unexpected scent of hay and fresh wood, as if the peaceful shepherd realm had sent a greeting from its fields and groves. Soon, however, a chief of the Janisaries came forward through the crowd with his men, like an executioner with his red-clad attendants. On their backs they carried bundles of hay and wood, but he himself held a torch of pitch. When all these combustibles had been laid on the windward side of the house, he threw the torch on the pile. Presently the fire leaped over the roof-trusses, and the valuables in the attic were enveloped in conflagration and smoke.

Alone and left behind among the dying, Klysendorff lay on the floor in a burning room, but every time he heard a new murmur of amazement, his pale countenance cleared. He could still distinguish far-off shouts from the Swedes in the courtyard. On the ice-covered ground plundered generals and colonels stood in only their shirts, with hands tied behind their backs. Tartars with laced guardsmen's hats on their necks and yellow or black wigs tied to their girdles were fastening the sons of Sweden's noblest families together on long chains and making slaves of them. They bound them to their wagons or drove them before with blows of the whip, and

Gierta and Konrad Sparre were led off to be fettered by a well and water cattle. A Janisary came up to Brandklipper and clasped his shaggy hand around the wrought hilt of the sword which the eleventh Charles had carried, and the pasha had already sat down with crossed legs on the cushions in his tent to await the end of the fight.

From the hills, from the farthest minaret, and from the fortress of Bender, thousands of amazed spectators stared at the flaming Hercules-pyre. They saw how the king and the guardsmen, with coats over their heads, pressed up among the saddles in the attic to thrust off the shingle roof, but had to retreat again because of the shot and smoke. From room to room the band drew back under the tottering rafters and stones, shot at from all the windows, with their clothes on fire, and their faces and shoulders bleeding. In their heated muskets the shots went off of themselves. The Janisaries shouted to one another that either the Swedish Charles was a salamander or else he wanted to burn in there with his men. The whole region murmured with joy, but it was the joy of astonishment, not of revenge.

Dusk had fallen, but the light of the flames illuminated the expanse of the house, and through the uproar sounded the clear voice of the king: "My dear Roos, let us now defend ourselves with the few men we have left, until all is over!"

He himself now fought at the window with a carbine. As if in pursuance of a silent resolve, he at last stepped forward to the shot-shattered bags of earth, and stood there alone.

Roos threw himself between and, stunned by a ball that struck the wadding out of his fur cap, sunk into his master's arms. Without stepping back, the king stood unflinching as ever with his noblest guardsman in his embrace.

Madly the Turks once again rushed forward at the window, but were felled to the ground, and the glowing sound-boarding illuminated the whole room as at a banquet.

"That Swedish Charles is having a festival," said the pasha. "Poltava was the people's day; this is his."

Then the door was unbarred. Wrapped in sparks, Seved Tolvslag stepped out on the stairs and presented arms.

"Make way!" he shouted. "The king, the king!"

At the apex in front of his men the king hurried straight out into the *mêlée*, and those who could not follow him defended themselves with backs against the wall. The dying and dead fell at his feet, and above his head the fighting broadswords met in a point like a tent of shining steel. Stumbling with his spurs, he was pressed to the ground and overpowered, so that the weapon could finally be wrested from his hand.

"The dance would have gone differently," he

said, "if all had stood at their posts. Now it has been nothing to talk of."

As soon as he had risen, the flashing glance in his eyes was extinguished, and as a reward he divided all his ducats among the Janisaries who had been able to disarm him. Blackened with smoke beyond recognition, with one of the skirts torn from his coat, which was hewn to shreds, he mounted a white Turkish horse with a purple saddle, and with a rustle of triumph about him as if all the banners of Islam had just been laid for a carpet under the hoofs of his palfrey, he rode toward Bender and captivity.

He never once turned to look back at the flaming pyre. All night the flames spread forth their light. On the heaps of ashes in smoking Carlopolis the Turks stood with their spades, but as early as the dawn the women of Varnitsa began to fill their pitchers at the Swedish fountain with the crystal-pure water, which in coming times they were to offer strangers, and which made him who drank of it proof against both love and shot. Round about under the mulberry trees and growing grapevines slumbered the buried last ducats of the homeless warriors, with the image of their hero king in the superscription; and even for a long time afterwards, when the herdsmen and their wives harvested the fruit in the stormy days of autumn, they believed they could discern a rumble of sword-clanging and battle-play coming up from the earth.

His Excellency

THE shrilling of trumpets between the houses of Moscow in their festal array saluted the returning czar. Before him, line after line, with faded and dusty uniforms, marched the disarmed Swedish prisoners of war. On triumphal arches of brick they saw pictures where the wrathful eagle of the East tore in pieces the Swedish lion, which was drowning or shot through with arrows. Every step brought them further into the strange barbarian city which surrounded them with its scaly ramparts. The towers were like heaven-storming mushrooms or oddly wrought celestial globes overstrewn with pointed gold stars. Tables with unfamiliar dishes and refreshments were spread in front of all the larger houses for the czar and his lords. Candles and lamps flickered before broad, black-bearded heads of Christ and unknown saints, but on both sides of the street the masses of people rushed about like water in runnels, mocking and scoffing at the vanquished. Widows, exhausted with weeping, and wives or sisters prematurely gray, who had long since been dragged off into slavery from the Swedish provinces by the Baltic, recognized from the windows their kinsmen among the prisoners. They shouted words of comfort from the Bible, but no one heard them among the cannon-shots, tocsins, and songs of victory that rolled over the city

like the unrestrained tumult of wildfire and carnival.

First went the soldiers. There tramped the gray
battalions of lean Finlanders, who so often, when a
comrade beckoned them to the watch-fires, grinned
in their red beards, shaking their muskets above
the snow-drifts and repeating obstinately their incomprehensible *"Saisumme tesse!"*

"You Finnish bosom-brothers," said the captive
women at the windows, "while your own home was
in flames, you have followed our men for life and
death and stood at your post like stunted little fir-
bushes. If we ever again drive out to a Christmas
morning service in Sweden, we shall point at the
fir-bushes that stand along the road in the snow and
say: 'Finlanders, Finlanders!'"

Then marched forward the officers, from the lowest to the colonels, and after them the captured
cannon with their spans of horses. On a long sledge
stood the kettledrums which on so many evenings
in the dusk had gathered the bleeding squadrons
on some field of battle. On another sledge stood
the drums. How often had they not in conquered
cities forced the plunderers with a sharp roulade
to thrust the sword in the sheath a moment and
range themselves in line behind a young and conquering king, who sat radiant on his charger with
the bunch of surrendered keys still in his hand!
After them came the standards and banners with

their provincial coats of arms, but they were carried in reverse under the left arm and dragged in the mud of the street. Fur mittens and hands frozen blue were clenched over the tattered folds that still carried spots of their defenders' blood. Snowballs, stones, and sand rained over the griffins of Söder-manland and East Gotland, the royal apple of Upp-land, the crossed spears of Dalecarlia and Närke, over the flaming mountain of Vestmanland, the goat of Hälsingland, the leafy tree of Blekinge, and the reindeer of West Bothnia. Ever more savagely the people thrust aside the muskets of the guards and shouted: " Filth and shame on the banners of these dogs!"

Then the Russian soldiers drew their blades, and now appeared the Swedish king's led horses, improvised litter, and empty blue-covered chair. Close behind followed the generals around the bent form of Lewenhaupt, and after them came the Field Marshal. But nearest before the horse of the czar walked His Excellency Piper, he who in the ze-nith of greatness had stood at the side of two Swed-ish kings.

He seemed to hear and see nothing. He, who was called the quickest-witted head of Sweden, had to-day no answer for the guffaws and taunts that saluted him from all mouths. It looked as though he walked in thoughts of quite other affairs and other destinies.

In the evening, when he was conducted to his quarters, and rockets pattered over the frozen river, he sat sleeping in an armchair, and never once awoke when the servants put on his nightcap and folded the coverlet around him.

Again it was morning, and again the bells played. Day followed day, and year followed year, but all were alike heavy.

The pious works of Francke and Arndt lay on his table. He induced the Field Marshal and Lewenhaupt to shake hands in reconciliation, and became a fatherly helmsman for the unfortunate people who dwelt with him in bondage. Impoverished Swedish soldiers often met him in the early hours, as he went along the streets with hurried step, followed only by a little barking dog.

Then it happened unexpectedly that he was taken away from his house, and when, after long and anxious waiting, some of his countrymen caught sight of him under the open heavens, it was far from Moscow, and he himself had become a broken old man.

It was a sunny day of spring. The rivers had already begun to burst their ice and all hearts to throb with homesickness. Petersburg had now grown up from the conquered Swedish fenland, and on the courtyard of the fortress of Peter-and-Paul stood a miserable wooden hut. In front of the cabin His Excellency Piper walked to and fro. After starving

for seventeen days on bread and water, he was there
able to get an hour's fresh air. His coat was worn
and hung in deep folds. The cane trembled and
tottered in the hand which aforetime had been
kissed by the king and queen of Poland, and which
so many times, before the name was inscribed under
a commission or an ordinance, had received silver
boxes or snuff-holders filled with ducats and glittering with diamonds.

At a few steps' distance stood the guards, and
His Excellency could never exchange a single word
with any one except Bredenberg, the battalion chaplain. He by special permission had just drawn near
to the cabin. He drew forth a letter from comrades
at Moscow and read it aloud to Piper:

... "The little dog which at his hurried departure His Excellency found himself obliged to leave
behind has been tenderly looked after, but it has
crept off with pitiful whining into all sorts of dark
corners without wanting to taste either food or drink
and has now died. Would to God that we prisoners
might, like that unreasoning animal, lay us down
in some retreat and be delivered from earthly life,
but it is our fervent desire that His Excellency may
now soon be ransomed or exchanged and be able to
return home to his wife and children. For all he has
been to us here as a fatherly guardian and Christian helper he shall ever be followed by our grateful
blessings."

Piper stood with his back to Bredenberg and gazed obstinately down at the sand. He did not brood on the severity of his guards, but his ear distinguished from afar the embittered reprimand of the king. Had not he, the Minister of State, ridden voluntarily into Poltava and laid down his sword? Did he not hear the execrations of his own people? At home in Stockholm the windows of his house were broken with stones. He saw his wife, Madame Kerstin, pick up all the jewelled rings and boxes and the many small silver ornaments in the ante-room where of old Swedes and foreigners, desirous of an audience, had stood and waited in every window-recess. He could see her in the dark of night driving away from the city on the road to Angsö. For long hours he could imagine that he himself was sitting in a Swedish pew and hearing the minister call down God's punishment on Piper who, bribed by foreigners, had misled the king, who had advised the last wars, and had built a road of men's bones over the snow-drifts of the Ukraine. His unfortunate fellow prisoners had become his only friends. Never would the land of his fathers own him; there was no land for which he might long. He alone knew the absurdity of the accusations, but he could not expose his master, could not reveal secrets of state. Broken, he stumbled to his cabin — a prisoner who was destined to die in silence under the calumnies of his countrymen and of strangers, as he had seen so many a nameless soldier fall in the ranks.

"Your Excellency," said Bredenberg, "many letters like that which I have just read get to Sweden —yea, to the king—and it is reported that he is already probably half conciliated. The czar in these days of hunger has empowered Your Excellency to request from the countess the payment of thirty thousand rix-dollars for your final ransom from captivity. Feel no regret at making the decision! If you refuse, evil tongues will say it is because of avarice. When you are at liberty, all may once more be well as in former years."

Piper answered softly:

"From early years I would not borrow;
I lay on Christ my weight of sorrow."

But in the same moment he turned, blood-red in the forehead, and cried in a thin voice: "What the thousand fiends and devils do you want, anyhow? I have secretly begged the countess to obtain the king's prohibition as to sending the money.— Enough of that! I have come here with my fellow countrymen, and with them I will also remain, seeing it was not granted us civilians to get a bullet."

Bredenberg smiled at the heat of the old Excellency, but bent his head and remained standing by the bench.

"They say the czar intends to conduct Your

Excellency to hard imprisonment in Schlüsselburg, and near to seventy the body is a frail vessel. Fervently I beg you in my weakness: turn back to your home, whither all our hearts long, even though revilings bow us to the earth! Do not lay the ineradicable disgrace upon us that the man who stood nearest to two of our greatest kings should perish in hunger and rags, a banished man, unreconciled to his people!"

Piper fumbled along the wall of the hut.

"Bow thine head before the altar and not before the discarded great ones of mankind! But if you are by me at the time of dissolution, see that the remains are laid on aromatic herbs or on salt, so that they may be taken home. My days are soon told. If I have served the Swedes under two masters, I may still serve them in meekness to the last where their most unfortunate sons now are."

When Bredenberg retired, troubled in spirit, a crowd of Swedish officers in sheepskin coats and capes emerged from the nearby senate house. Before them in a brown mantle went Norberg, the chaplain of the guards, easily recognizable from his lofty stature. They were to be exchanged and sent home, and their beggarly belongings had already been piled up amid sacks of meal on a ketch by the river-bank.

Upon the wall of the fortress the clatter of chains grew silent and the Swedish workman-prisoners leaned out over the wheelbarrows to gaze after their departing countrymen. Soon, however, the wheels began again to creak and the mattocks to ring. Those were the petty and nameless men, the living dead, who knew nothing of their people and who were never to knock at their cottage doors, but to stand and pine, building day after day the city of strangers.

Piper slowly raised his shaking hand and pointed to the wall: "There stand my brothers," he said.

Bredenberg, who went to meet the released officers, gently twitched Norberg by the mantle, and all turned toward Piper and bared their heads. They did not go to speak with him or take along a message, but Norberg stood still, so remarkable did the scene appear to him. He felt over his heart, and when he found his prayer-book stuck between his coat and vest, he lifted it and pointed to the cross on the cover.

"O God, thy course has been so directed," he whispered, "that this man has been chosen as one of the many among the martyrs of our people! Saved, honored be his injured name!"

The General of Papers

IT was still hardly four in the morning, but the yellow gleam on the grove of birches outside of Moscow foretold the dawn. General Lewenhaupt already sat in his accustomed place by the window, like an old owl on its branch in the woods. Two grizzled tufts of hair rose above his brow, and he meditatively opened and closed his great mournful eyes.

Roused by several scraping steps, he rose and turned toward the interior of the room. Before him stood a hunchbacked Russian Jew with drooping hair.

The Jew restlessly twined his one red lock about his finger. What legends had he not heard about old General Marchmarch, who, with a pinch of snuff on his thumb, had sent his psalm-singing soldiers against the redoubts and abattis in the wastes of Lithuania? Never previously had he stood before a hero who had commanded over armies. He thought that such a person must be a terrible man, who with an oath on his lips and hands crossed on his sword-hilt ordered in glasses and canteens and tobacco-pipes a yard long, until the smoke hovered so thick that it could be cut with a sword-blow.

"I am only a poor merchant from Tula," he stammered, "and I have come hither with a drove of oxen, but the Swedish prisoners there in the city

have requested me to bring their prayers for an
alms. Though they diligently manufacture wooden
clocks and snuff-horns, there is such need among
them that it cuts one's heart. But the poor men also
waste much time in foolery. For whole hours every
day they sit writing and scribbling. God help him
who drops the smallest speck of tobacco on their
paper. But it is just this that no man can comprehend: that they toil in that way when they have absolutely nothing to write about — and have scarcely
a rouble in the bottom of the chest. Warriors ought
not surely to sweat with the pen."

Lewenhaupt lighted a tallow candle, for it was
still very dark in the room.

"Look here!" he said with kindly melancholy,
throwing the light on the long, unpainted wall-
shelves, where thick volumes of papers stood stuck
into numbered holders.

The Jew twisted still more violently at his lock
of hair, and instead of glasses and canteens he
saw closely written paper wherever he turned. On
chairs and table and on the very crown of the stove
the paper lay. — A marvellous general this, he
thought. Is that the way he looks who wins
battles?

"A people," said Lewenhaupt, standing by a
shelf, "a state, my friend, means order. Here all
the prisoners are listed and their accounts duly
entered. This is our college of finance, our fiscal

bureau. Among the Swedish clerics on the other side of the street there is an equally long shelf. That is our church. Even in captivity we have remained a people. You, who are a Jew, you must understand that word."

He took down a volume and turned the pages, reading and ciphering half aloud. Then he went into the adjoining bedroom, and when he had set the candle on a hassock, he opened a chest and began carefully to count up the silver coins in various small leather purses. All the time he continued to talk half aloud — sometimes to himself, sometimes to the merchant.

"I have now reckoned out how much I have the right to send to Tula. But learn, my wise fellow, that ingratitude and jealousy are the only returns for effort. Jealousy, jealousy, that was the hand of darkness which divided us so that the enemy snatched the banners from our battalions. A fool he who in this sordid world cries out for friends and hearts! A comrade in arms embraces you when you rescue him from the bayonets, but he sighs because you did not at the same time fall transfixed, so that he might get your empty place. A fool he who presses toward other heights than the home of the Eternal Father! The foe have not smitten me with deeper wounds than my own countrymen have done. Yet God grant that I have served my heavenly as faithfully as I have my earthly king!"

His Bible lay on the coverlet behind him, and the sword, which had been returned to him, hung on the bed-post. For every filled purse he wrote a line in a book and then sealed the purse. The bed-room, too, was gradually being filled with papers, but every sheet always lay beside the others in good order. So the victor of Gemauerthof sat there by the candle with the smoking sealing-wax in front of his clear, mournful eyes, and while he was continually grumbling about the bitterness of fate, the dawn came softly on.

The Jewish merchant no longer understood his speech, but twined and twisted his red lock and mumbled: "A people, a state—even in the midst of captivity.—That is a noble vision!"

Lieutenant Pinello in the Apothecary Shop

LIEUTENANT PINELLO, the Italian, sat one
winter night in the prisoners' apothecary shop
in Tobolsk and drank strong waters. Behind the
counter an open door led to a dimly lighted barn,
where Ensign Kraemer worked as a tanner, turning over hides in a large vat.

Pinello was a good comrade, and between the
two white patches in his hair he had a long sabre-
scar from Poltava, where he had lain on the battle-
field among the dead for two days. But as he now
sat by his brandy tinctured with vermouth, he was
vexed at Kraemer's obstinate diligence.

"Yes, to be sure," said he, "be a stuck-up devil!
Stand all night at your tanner's vat! Don't think
of coming in and drinking a glass of strong waters
with an old friend! Perhaps I not do honorable
service as a volunteer in the Swedish army; yes, and
here in captivity even accepted their faith, which
is cursed by the Pope. What do you say to that,
giovane mio?"

"I keep still and tan ox-leather," answered
Kraemer.

"Yes, you keep still and tan ox-leather, you; but
I know an ox-leather that we foreigners have had
to tan, and that be the Swedish spirit. Just awhile
ago I take handsome Lieutenant Rothlieb up with
me on the mountain and say with my hands on his

breast: 'Rothlieb, bow your knee in this spot and thank the kind heavens that Rothlieb had been formed so comely and so fascinating before all women! Is n't he ashamed of going off and moping in the middle of the game?' Santa Maria! What do you suppose the fellow does? The big fellow begins to sigh, and I could feel how hollow the heart rattled in his breast. Then I go to Lieutenant Beck's wife. Though she is a saint and an old broom of fir-twigs where the needles prick harder the longer they stay, still in any case she be a woman. Her nose be a little freckled and her eyes two bright blue drops of water on a very cool day in the month of September. When I tell a how I hear all the good God's angels sing in the sigh of the west wind on the flower-plot, she answer with call Lieutenant Rothlieb a bad man. Then she snivel and get obstinate and hoity-toity, but that most likely mean nothing else but embarrassment. When I first swore the Swedish flag faith, the trumpet blare like the Last Judgment around the table and the *fontange*, and the excuse for the wig was that it concealed. Now the oven is heated hot for the poor prisoners with the quick head who play the commedia. Ah! comrade, I have seen in my land holy sisters breathing of lovely meekness and heavenly love. They speak of God's goodness, but not of man's wickedness. Ah! comrade, come and see the women in my land, where they embrace their children or sit with their wax candle and weep on the graves! That is to see the heart burn. What do you say to that?"

"I keep still and tan ox-leather."

"Yes, you keep still and tan ox-leather, you, but do you know why the Swedes remain a small people, why in the midst of their victory time they have never got to ten million souls? Do you know why Sweden and the Swedish speech have never swum like seething wine over the map of Europe and made an indivisible empire? I tella why. They have no claws of fire on their fingers. The Swedish spirit was from the beginning such a hard ox-leather that it could only be trimmed with the cold hammer of duty. The Swedes from the beginning could neither conquer nor fall for love, only for duty. They do not even love one another. The Swedes would rather be hanged than give full justice to a countryman. Their spirit from the be-ginning be a stony ground, but we Polish and German and French and Italian renegades have watered it with our adventurers' blood where the birds now start to sing among the leaves. Drops of such adventurers' blood hang on the branches of your proudest family trees like bitter oranges on an oak — yes, the orange often sits at the very root, look you! Juice of the orange flows in the veins of your own hero-king. My beloved Swedes, hearken what I say! When you come upon our ad-

venturers' names in your rolls, do not forget that
we have mingled blood in countless perils, that we
foreigners have been the gayest of soldiers,—have
been the flutes where you were the drums! For
love have I sworn the Swedish banner faith, and
for love I faithfully keep the vow to the last breath,
for—look you!—duty and love must at the end
become one and the same. Give your hand, comrade, to the little Italian and all his like! What do
you say to that?"

Kraemer dried his arms on his apron and stepped
out into the apothecary shop.

"I am not travelled and versatile as you are,
Pinello. Little I know what we were, hardly what
we are. But stay with us! Come home with me, set
yourself on the watch-tower at Brunkeberg and
shout that all those shall gather round you who
will risk their life for a deed—no matter what, no
matter if it has no meaning—no matter if you
have only to propose an emigration on ice but a
night old over the Åland Sea. Then you will grow
pale and note that you have thrown a torch. Dry
fir-twigs can burn, look you! and then there is a
smell as of oriental spices and incense."

His hands gripped in brother fashion those of
the swarthy foreigner.

"Why then work so hard at night?" asked
the Italian.

Kraemer answered: "I tan my ox-leather so that

as soon as it gets soft and ready I may deliver it to Dame Beck and her school children. They are to sew from it breast-pieces which we may wear secretly under our coats. There 's a conspiracy on foot among the prisoners all the way to Archangel and Kasan. With weapon in hand, men, women, and children mean to go back through the whole of Russia down to the king at Bender. Such have the Swedes become now. Will you follow us, guitar-twanger?"

The Prisoners in Tobolsk

ON one of the empty streets of Tobolsk stood an unpainted wooden house, and up in the gable room were gathered some of the Swedish prisoners of war. The table was spread with salted pike, pancakes, and gruel; and the pious Dame Beck, who had just helped Dame Morton instruct the school children in sewing, had been appointed as hostess for the evening.

Heavy steps shook the winding stairs, and the door was constantly being opened. Captain Vreech came with his prayer-books, and reserved Ensign Stjernflycht, who could never be tempted into a smile, and lively Lieutenant Kohler, — all of whom earned their scanty bread as school-teachers. Lieutenant Sprengtporten, who still bore on his wrist the scars from the chains in the tower of Kasan, talked so very loudly with handsome Lieutenant Rothlieb, the lady-killer, that Dame Beck gave them a questioning glance. Limping Captain Rubzoff, who had followed nearest the king at the Memel River, and Captain Vult, who even in captivity was as well groomed as ever, fingered and inspected the snuff-boxes, hair-bags, horse-hair wigs, and nightcaps which Cornet Ennes and his friends had made and were now displaying in a basket. Captain Stralenberg came, having just risen from the maps after he had drawn the first meridian over Tobolsk. Cornets Fries, Westfelt, and Toll, who had gone about and sung in the courtyards, came rattling their empty money-boxes. Major Hall, who had become a dyer, swung a cornucopia of sugar over a pancake. Major Riddarborg, who supported himself with embroidery, drew balls of silver thread from his knapsack and arranged them round a platter to make them look like pretty Easter eggs; but Lieutenant Beeth, who had become a goldsmith, laid a shining ducat on the edge of the table for exhibition—the first that any of them had seen for two whole months.

The younger men ranged themselves bashfully and stiffly round the walls with their hands behind them. Haberman, the worthy student from Viborg, who had worked as a servant and wore patched leather breeches, kept so close to the door-jamb in his embarrassment that Major Balck, who himself had but a damp brew-house for lodgings, was obliged to drag him forward to the table. Bergman, too, who had held the rank of cornet but was degraded because in the long wandering from Poltava he had threatened and cursed his own superiors, stuck by the edge of the stove with such diffidence that Dame Beck had to serve his food for him and hand him the dishes.

Vreech now clapped his hands and began to speak: "We thank thee, Heavenly Father, for Thy goodness towards us poor miserable captives, who may now every Sunday gather around a common table as in the old days. Next to Thee we thank the honest comrades who through the labor of their hands have brought it about that we may also sometimes feed our most needy and impoverished brothers and school children. Belau, too, our faithful doctor aforetime, who has just died in Moscow, has left us his silken dressing-gown, and it has been sold for a full seven roubles and twenty kopeks. Albeit captivity has given us a wholesome probation, we perceive every hour that Thy hand is still over us. We have recently heard that Erik Armfelt, who sat so long riveted in chains and the pillory, has now been helped to freedom; and we thank Thee that Piper, our old Excellency, has turned to a living faith and, purified from mortal weaknesses by a death of starvation, has now entered into Thy heavenly righteousness."

When Vreech was silent, Stjernflycht stepped forth and continued to speak : "Before we sit us down, we beseech Thee, O Father, for all our fellow countrymen who languish in the sulphur mines and stone-pits, and yet farther off in Tartary and in the valleys by the Chinese Wall, although they have not otherwise transgressed tHan that they have faithfully served their lord. Vouchsafe the cup of Thy favor to Ruhl, our comrade in arms, who for years has been lying in rags and filth in an underground vault, where he has already seen

his friend Taube perish in misery. Grant the release of death to Hermelin, if the rumor be true
that, hidden away in solitude, he is still pining in
a monastery at Astrakan. Strengthen with Thy consolation Seulenberg and Hay, who sit each in his
hut of earth far out in the wilderness, and Anders
Oxehufvud, whom a German merchant saw going
in harness before a plow. O God, our God! Doth
not Jeremiah speak, and say: 'The children of Zion,
they that were noble, that were valued as refined
gold, they are now despised in the streets; and
they that were borne upon scarlet, they embrace
the dunghills. Swifter were our pursuers than the
eagles of heaven. The soul of our body, the Lord's
anointed, was seized in their talons; he under
whose shadow we had thought to live among the
peoples . . .'"

The wind shook the panes and rustled in the
reeds outside the window.

"Worthy Dame Beck," whispered Stjernflycht,
as he moved forward chairs for the older gentlemen, "there is only one whom I still miss. That
is our charming friend Ferdinand von Kraemer,
the young cornet. A purer and more dutiful heart
has never beaten in a Swedish breast. When I look
at him, I have to think of a cool and clear summer night."

Before Dame Beck had found an answer, Kraemer
had already come in by the winding stair with his

coat collar up, and had fixed his blue eyes upon her.

"I have some one down below with me whom you would perhaps all excuse from appearing among you," said he with lowered voice. "It is Leiyon. I'm trying to entice him away from his lounging life at the taverns. If we only accept him with a little forbearance.—There's nothing bad in him at bottom."

"His light way is so different from ours," answered Dame Beck with a hard tone of voice and a mild expression.

"You mustn't be so severe, Dame Beck!"

She busied herself at the table and set out the plates. Then she went to the door and called down the stairs: "Kraemer is a righteous man, and none of us will lock out him whom he can bear with. Come up, Lieutenant Leiyon!"

Prematurely gray, with melancholy eyes and cheeks blood-red with frost and drink, Leiyon stepped across the threshold and was at once offered a chair, as if he had been one of the most distinguished of the company. At the beginning he sat perfectly still, but as the meal progressed, when the beer was poured out and no one remembered that he was there, he quite suddenly seized Dame Beck's reluctant hands, kissed them, and told with what unfeigned regard he loved her. He passed from chair to chair with his glass, embracing and pressing the hands of both known and unknown. Finally he went to the younger men, who were still standing along the wall, and prayed them to call him "thou," and when he came back to his place beside Kraemer, his glass was empty. Then he threw his arm about Kraemer's waist and tossed back his gray lion's mane from his brow.

After that he beat on the table with his free hand so that it rang: "What's become of the Swedish courage, my lads? I'm not asking for your Jesus. —If Leiyon is to amuse you, pass along a decent stirrup-cup! What do you say? Kraemer's honesty! I grant it, I grant it. But have you ever heard any one tell of Kraemer's cleverness? 'A man has his duty,' he says. Not to laugh in misfortune — or to do away with himself. Just to sit and wear out his breeches for five stivers a week. No, but do you know what? I'm thinking of doing like Stjernkors. I'm thinking of becoming Russian, swearing to the Russian faith, and amiably marrying a Russian woman. Just tell me this, my fine, good Madam Beck, just tell me this: Why should life be worse here than back at home? Is the grass there greener or the straw softer?"

"My dear friend and comrade," answered Kraemer mildly: "at bottom you've a good, childlike heart, and I'm very fond of you. But homesickness is the heaviest sickness of all, and my opinion only is that if we know we're doing our duty, then

we poor exiles have still something in this world
to rejoice at."

The yellow hair was brushed smoothly back from
his clear brow.

Leiyon nodded toward him: "Rejoice—I really
think we may. Do you know why even the Russian is fond of us Swedes? You there, it's not only
on account of our polite manners and because we
teach his children to read and write. Can you remember, on the examination day I went to the
school and described for the children Krokedum-
melum, the capital of Mesopotamia, where there
was n't a single sleeping-hall but only taverns and
hostelries, and where the wagons don't run on
wheels but on beer-barrels and kegs? And the
dragoons and Russian fur-dealers who sat on the
benches among the children to look on submissively and get to learn something useful laughed
so that Mistress Beck chased me out.—The deuce!
Therefore, look you, the Russians and the whole
world like us, because we here in the midst of our
misery can take both them and all Siberia to our
bosom and can be so merry that there is a radiance around us."

Kraemer looked him intently in the eyes. "Ah,
you old brother and hero of the beer-mug, I perceive strange emotions hidden under the gaiety of
the Swedes."

But on towards evening Leiyon began to curse

and thunder as if he had been the very field marshal, and Dame Beck's ice-cold hands quietly took the beer-mug from his.

"I keep no drinking-house," she said harshly; "and we have not come together to live in surfeiting and sin."

Kraemer immediately interrupted her, so that Leiyon might not catch the severe words, and managed to get the latter down with him from the room.

"I'm going to the churchyard," shouted Leiyon. "Alongside it is the best tavern. Prosperity and gaiety give health and long life."

"You can look down from here at the churchyard by the frozen river yourself. There isn't a single house near it."

"I'm going down to see if the grass we sowed over Raaf's little son has taken root."

Kraemer shook his head and took him under the arm. A biting norther whistled from the desolate marsh-land, and no wanderer was visible. The snow had whirled away from the road, and the two friends went on in silence. While still at a distance, they read in the twilight the white Swedish inscription on the wooden cross.

"Stop and read it aloud, Brother Kraemer! One of my kinsmen is said to be lying in the Ukraine and one at Bender. For fifteen years we have strewn Swedish bones from the White Sea to the Archipelago."

Kraemer plucked at his coat. "Come along, I tell you! This is nonsense."

"The grass has been frozen off. — Tell me, tell me, are n't the dead at home? Are n't they at home who lie already in the earth? Talk with me, Kraemer. You can calm the sea, you carry such a repose with you."

"Be still, be still, and let me alone! I won't listen to you. Don't brood on such things, but let us instead bethink us of our duties!"

"But, I ask you, shan't we even be at home when we dead sleep in God's bosom? Home, home—do you understand that word?—home! Shall we never, never come home?"

"You don't know to whom you're talking, Leiyon. I am weaker than you."

"Home—is n't it true that you, too, have brooded on that word? You have gone off and repeated it quietly to yourself—home, home! It begins when a child counts the nails and knots on the floor. A home, look you, is something that begins as a little seed and ends as a great tree. It begins with the children's room, then grows until it becomes many rooms and a whole house, a whole district, a whole country; and outside of that land the very air and water lose their refreshing taste. Can you not assure me that our comrades who lie here beneath us in the stony and alien earth are at home?"

Kraemer pulled yet more violently at his garments.

"Haha! Now I've just caught you finely in a
trap! But I myself.—Do you believe a jolly fellow
goes off and sorrows in earnest? Then you don't
know my beggar song that I've just composed to
sing in the courtyards, when I'm sometimes in need
of a farthing."

He walked more and more slowly off on the
driveway along the river, and Kraemer, who remained standing by the churchyard fence, heard
him strike up his beggar chant:

> *Near Uppsala lying,*
> *A cottage gleams whitely,*
> *Where daily and nightly*
> *The maples are sighing.*
> *So fast the days darted:*
> *But years have gone by now.*
> *A captive am I now,*
> *Who thence am departed.*

The song sounded ever more distant in the storm.

> *My voice is but broken,*
> *My tongue is unhandy.*
> *I sing when I soak in*
> *A throat-ful of brandy.*
> *Then let there be brought seven*
> *Glasses, red one of them!*
> *For my lion I've fought seven*

Years and am done with them.
Twelve times I was wounded.
I smiled, never swerving,
When icy winds hounded.
Since birth I've been starving.
My sword was the omen
Of death to twelve foemen.
But my sword's far away, sir,
Hilt-deep in the sand
Of the Dnieper's lone strand.
Twelve coins, then, I pray, sir,
Slip into my hand,—
Best wage of your labors
And spoil of your quarrels
Each day with your neighbors.—
Hurrah for King Charles!

The voice died away, and Kraemer turned back
alone to his meagre but well-tended room, where
hardly a speck of dust could be found on the table.
He undressed and went to bed, but could not sleep.
Time and again he jumped up and listened. That's
only the wind, he thought, and drew the coverlet up
to his forehead; but after a while he again sat up,
awake, in his bed. It sounded as if some one had
thrown sand against the window-panes.

He put out the tallow candle, which was still
burning, and went in his night-shirt to the window.
When he had opened it, he saw on the street below a little man, who beckoned to him incessantly.

He recognized by the sheepskin pelisse and half-boots that it was a Russian peasant.

"Little father," said the peasant, "I have often met you in company with the merry Swedish Lieutenant Leiyon. Never has that man caused me anything but joy. It's been a long time now that he has lived with my wife and me. Though he never paid for himself, we were heartily fond of him, and of evenings he told stories of how he and the Swedish king in the woods of Poland tore apart the jaws of leopards and heleophants and other animal scourges that had come up from hell. — To be sure he would sometimes sit in the cellar doorway and be silent, but if then he got only a glass or two, he became again directly the same kindly fun-maker."

"Ah, the Swedes!" muttered Kraemer. "Haven't I always said: I perceive strange emotions hidden under their gaiety?"

"Little father, when the lieutenant did not come to us this evening, I went to the barn where he slept. — And there he was lying, too. He had made away with himself. His great cheerfulness, no doubt, became at last too much to keep up."

The night was windy and dark. The following morning the prisoners wrote in their diaries of Leiyon's death. Next to that fact they made the entry that during the darkness Kraemer had left his quarters. No one heard anything of him afterwards, and no one found his remains, but the officers said to the soldiers: "He has got safe home to his people."

The Lion's Cage

NUM EDDAULA was the chief of the Truth-
tellers' Brotherhood. They lived each of
them by himself in their homes as merchants or ex-
pounders of the most ancient writings, but every
year at the first new moon after the festival of
Beiram they assembled at night by torchlight in
white robes in a remote gorge.

One night when Num Eddaula was returning
from such a meeting along the stony mountain
path, he said to the servant who bore the torch:'
" We have just sworn our brotherhood vow always
to tell the truth except in one thing; namely, when
it concerns our own good deeds. These we are to
suppress or prevaricate away, and we must aspire
to die forgotten. What better mirrors the silent
greatness of eternity than oblivion? On all the
earth there is no lodging so fair as a forgotten
grave. The grasses there sigh differently. The birds
twitter differently. Hearken to me, my friend! The
Truth-tellers' freedom of speech has so angered the
sultan that he has sworn to extirpate them with
the sword, if in recompense he does not receive my
head. That is easy to recognize from the birth-
mark beside the eye. I myself will be the man to
bear him the head. That, however, is a good action,
but will no longer remain good if it attracts re-
nown, and I have neither the desire nor the right

to reveal it. If our band suspected my intention, they would bind me and conceal and protect me to the uttermost. Therefore you are to follow me secretly, and when I have suffered my punishment, you are to bury me in silence in an unknown place and afterwards give out that I was seized against my will as a cowardly fugitive."

When the dawn appeared, the servant cast away the torch, and they descended to the blossoming plain by the castle of Timurtash, where the sultan had his pleasure-camp.

Num Eddaula was confused when he saw the splendid equipments and pavilions. He listened eagerly to a slave who related that the Swedish king lived at the castle with his needy court, half as prisoner, half as guest of honor.

"Let us go up thither," he said to his servant, "because I myself am a weak man, and the sight of a hero will lend me strength. Mine eyes, weary with age, will then close with joy."

They went through the garden, where the summer sun shone between the fig-trees and the mulberries. Along the path Brandklipparen was led to water. When they came to the steps of the castle, they encountered among the Turks who had just had a glance at the king the sultan himself, disguised as a Janisary. Num Eddaula squeezed himself against the wall and drew his loosened hair over the birth-mark beside his eye, but he felt on

his wrist the breath of the mouth which that evening was to command his death. A hero, he wanted
to see a hero before him, or else even he would
begin to waver.

A door was opened. Taking a few vehement
steps forward, he bent and through a hole in a
screen surveyed the king.

The wide apartment, where the sultan's dancers
often trod the carpets as they performed to the
music of flutes, was from floor to ceiling and along
the walls and windows so overspun with many-col-
ored arabesques that Num Eddaula thought he
was beholding a hall of leaves, where enchanted
spiders had fastened their golden webs among the
flowers and vines. By the farthest wall the king lay
on a small field-bed, with his shirt buttoned up to
his throat. Overmastered, without soldiers, without
power, and yet sovereign lord over a remote kingdom, he never had money enough for the bribes
and gifts which were necessary for an audience with
the sultan. He could not humiliate himself before
the foreign ambassadors and approach the sultan
as a beaten and destitute fugitive. He blushed at
the thought of having to show himself before his
lackeys and grooms as a disarmed prisoner who had
to fit himself to another's will, howsoever eagerly
they kept repeating that it befell by his own gracious command. Instead, therefore, he had laid himself on his bed; what had attacked him was not a

matter of health but of money. Ever since the
affair at Bender he had remained lying month after
month. He would not once set his foot on the
ground, but had himself carried in a sheet to a divan
when his bed was to be made. His two body phy-
sicians, Skraggenstjerne and Neuman, noted with
anxiety that his limbs were beginning to stiffen and
become paralyzed, as with a fakir who for the glory
of God has long endured in the same attitude
on a heap of rubbish. Vainly they begged him to
raise himself at least once every day and take a few
steps on the carpet.

So Num Eddaula thought he was beholding
one of those holy men who are wont to be reverently saluted beneath a leafy oak or on the sunny
side of some distant mausoleum.

Coughing, the consumptive scholar, Eneman,
had just been telling of his long journey. He shook
a couple of young crocodiles from two flasks that he
had with him and showed how they spat out green
and black poison, as they were burnt alive in a
heap of embers on a brazier by the bed. The king
propped his arms on the pillows and looked down
at the creatures that were twisting in the embers.

"Could a man fell a grown crocodile with only
a sword?" he asked. "A man *can* do what he
will."

The threadbare chancellor, Von Müller, who had
by now begun to serve as head cook, since there

was nothing else left, stroked his faded coat tail with a simper.

"Can one, when one will, fry pancakes without eggs and cream?"

"A man can get what is requisite—in necessity with his blade."

Grothusen lifted his dark nostrils into the air and drummed on his braided court-hat, while he addressed himself to Müller in a low voice: "In the very worst case a man can get what he needs at forty per cent."

"The noble pashas look so cheerful. Of what are they speaking?" asked Num Eddaula of the nearest lackey, but the latter became very much confused and answered conciliatingly at random: "They are talking about one of the most beautiful passages of the evangelists."

Therewith he accidentally gave the screen a push on the slippery floor. When the king caught sight of the venerable old man, he beckoned him nearer and commanded Grothusen to act as interpreter.

The king said: "Assuredly you are a wise man. Should you also have courage to stand where bullets are whistling?"

Num Eddaula lowered his turban, and reflectively stroked the white beard which reached to his waist. "I belong to the Truth-tellers' Brotherhood and may not attribute to myself any virtue. But do you that are a hero answer me this: If your first

teacher said to you, 'Do not kill, do not kill even
on a heap of embers the ugliest and fiercest of animals'—if the noble pashas around you and all men
should say every morning, 'Do not kill, for that is
a sin. Stay at home in your kingdom and watch
over the harvests, although you win no fame therewith'—should you have courage for that? Have
you courage in misfortune to humble yourself and
admit yourself conquered and to forgive your enemies and tormentors?"

The king knitted his brows: "Should not a good
soldier rather show himself staunch?"

"You that hate lying and never wished that
others should pretend you to be more perfect than
you are, high is your forehead and noble, large are
your eyes, but you have an evil line at your tightly
pressed mouth. People think that it smiles, but it
does not smile. It is something quite other that the
lips indicate. They tempt God. They say that your
will is His. You gathered your people, and they
were smitten. When God has smitten a people, He
rolls a heavy boulder upon the grave and ordains
quietness. He desires to see once more yellow fields
and playing children. But you continue the strife,
and against Him. The testifiers of truth—all the
steadfast ones who in prosperity are humble, in misfortune are proud—these have roused themselves
from their thoughts to see you; and now they turn
away. It may be that your land has brought forth

many great men and kings, but could any of them
from the beginning stand forth better fitted for a
warrior of light than you? You feared oblivion. A
star was to have been kindled on your grave to
burn for thousands of years. But fate was against
you, because God willed to smite you and your
people. Fulfil, then, your hero's task! Put away
vain reputation, as you have despised the wine-cup
and women. Do it humbly or do it proudly, whichever you can. Go forth and set yourself in the place
of the conquered and the destitute. Go forth and
set yourself, like Job, upon a heap of ashes. You
can control your countenance; control yourself
likewise. You are capable of more than you perform.
That is what God never forgives in a hero. Never
did He raise on His right hand a more transparent
pure jewel than you, and never did He in His
wrath fling His own handiwork so deep in the darkness—and therefore I love you, because you are
human. Of all the men I have met, none have I
loved as you, no one. Beware, beware! for there are
others, too, that love you and are far more dangerous than your worst enemies and traducers."

"And who are they?"

"The fools. They have observed the line at your
mouth, and interpret it in their own speech. Fools
never turn away; they fasten themselves to the garments. Fools demand a hero-fool, a laurelled arch-
fool for all time, and for that office they wish to

acclaim you with jubilation. The fools inquire not greatly of what nature you are. They love not men. They are like the little monkeys that sit huddled up on the stone images in the palm grove of Hedjaz and eat dates in the sun, but that leap from bough to bough, chattering and pursuing, when they hear a man's step. O king, death you fear not. God will give it you in compassion at the time when He remembers how your boyish hand wielded the sword of the cherubim. More heavily will fall His revenge. He gives you to the fools."

"You go far in outspokenness."

"I would but search how far your courage extends, inasmuch as you are a hero. Have you courage to die forgotten?"

The king's forehead became still more clouded, and he felt about for an answer. He sat sidewise in his bed with the cover twisted around his knees and feet.

Num Eddaula crossed his hands over his breast, and bowed: "There is much, then, for which your courage is too small."

Grothusen struck his hat against the brazier. "You that are a speaker of truth—who can say that you do not stand here and plume yourself on your humility? Who can say that it does not need courage to wish to die remembered?"

Num Eddaula closed his eyes, and with his lean fingers felt uneasily about him in the air. "There

you spoke truth, pasha. Fame is unclean slander,
unclean honor. It is an error and a delusion. The
arrogant man is called meek, the meek arrogant.
Among the world's famous men and women since
Adam, how much of clear gold would survive if the
misleading ashes could be sifted away? And you, O
king—who read your last thought in the evening
when you fell asleep? who saw you in the solitude,
in the darkness as you lay there awake? who beside
your bier could lay hand on heart and say: 'Such
he was'?—Only the fools shall dare to do that and
to say: 'Ask us, he was as we.' When they weary
of praising, they begin to throw stones, to bemock
you and point the finger at your heavy broadsword.
Your unrestful grave will be their favorite place of
resort. They will stand there packed so tight that
the clever folk can never come near your moulder-
ing bones. But this I say to you. Though the fools
acclaim you as theirs, if you can but rouse yourself
and gather about you the wise, the truthful, and
the steadfast—those who in prosperity are humble,
in misfortune are proud—then you have stood the
test. Then have you become a champion of God
even when you are but as a memory and a shadow.
Then have men weighed you with false weights.
Then are you he whom I will that you should be."

Num Eddaula cast himself upon his knees with
his head upon the matting: "I am a weak man who
have gotten strength from seeing you. Much have

I transgressed in my life, in many things have I
fallen short. If I have not scars on my head, I have
them in my soul. I want to be forgotten, forgotten.
I would sleep, would sleep. The famous man becomes a slave amid his fellows. According as he
suits his last master, he will either get a garland
woven into his hair or will have to endure buffet
and blow. No love has power to proclaim peace
over his dust. There, ever higher, is growing a tree
with wondrously gnarled branches and with un-
stinted restlessness and sighing in its leaves."

No one answered him. All was still throughout
the spacious apartment. Finally there was a bang
and clatter on the brazier, and the king held out a
shining doubloon to the white-bearded soothsayer.
He crept forward on his knees to the bed, and
pressed his face to the sheet that hung down from
it, but he thrust the coin from him. "You may live,
you may die," he said; "there will always be strife
around you. I go to rest."

Early next morning Num Eddaula was executed
before the tent of the sultan. The confident certainty of oblivion spread its tranquillity over his
last hour.

The servant buried his body apart between two
cypresses. When the grave was shovelled in again,
he strewed over it grains of maize for the doves,
which gathered in hundreds from grove and tree.
Soon bushes with white flowers sprang up from the

earth. Tired soldiers and herdsmen found there a shady spot and often lay down to rest awhile on the grass. It was a sacred place. There slept a forgotten man.

The King's Ride

ROYAL CHANCELLOR VON MÜLLER sat on a wooden stool before the fireplace of his room in the house of the Swedish king at Demotika and made pancakes. He raised one of the nap-worn tails of his coat to the fireplace and examined it.

"The braid is still holding on to the riding-coat," he remarked to Colonel Grothusen, who stood near him to warm himself, "but it 's disgracefully blackened. And the rest of the Swedish retinue are beginning—devil take them!— to look like a very pack of gipsies. I can say with Fabrice: 'I shall soon not remember how money-pieces look, whether they are round or square.'"

"They are so round that they roll away like wheels," responded Grothusen, rubbing his hands in high spirits. "A king, a court, a whole small army without anything but a little borrowed small-change in their pockets — and that in a Turkish market-town hundreds of miles from their native land! When did you ever see the like? God forgive me, but is n't it as funny a sight as can be, even if the sugar is sometimes too thin on the pancakes? We don't get a single purse from the Porte any more. Though I 've scarcely time to sleep at night, but am busy only with negotiating for travel-money from all the usurers of the world, yet I hardly comprehend how we can get decently away from

here. I have told His Majesty that we shall have
to take a whole train of creditors with us as a rear-
guard and quarter them at Karlshamn till they are
paid. Imagine little Karlshamn filled full of Turks,
who fall on their knees at the street corners and
call upon Allah!—Whew!—If we can only get off!
We must march away with drums and trumpets,
as befits the Swedes, you understand. Luckily we
have some finery left from the summer when I
went on the embassy to the great monarch. In
point of fact, there is neither padding nor lining in
the saddle-cloths, but outside there is that much
more of gilt thread and tassels —which is the main
thing. And I myself look like a full Excellency.
What more does one want? Lace ruffles, snuff-
spoon of pure ducat gold; in the wardrobe a court
pelisse given by the sultan, a pair of slippers down
at heel, a nightcap, and a silken dressing-gown
which Düben would be proud to wear even at High
Service. But that is the last, too, and let's see what
will be left of all the blessed stuff before we get
home!"

The longer Grothusen talked, the merrier he
grew. Finally he went to the window, and opened
it wide.

"What's there?" inquired Müller, buttoning up
his coat against the cold.

"It's a crowd of Turks that are standing about
waiting to get sight of His Majesty riding off.

There is a heavy rain, you see, and for that reason they know that he won't stay indoors."

Grothusen dug and searched in the skirt of his coat, and when he had found two or three large silver coins, he threw them out of the window and cried: "That's how money looks. Long live the Swedes and their great, mighty, bounteous king!"

"Is that your own money or the king's?"

"As if I knew!"

"Did n't you use to have your own money in your left coat tail and the king's in the right?"

"But the left coat tail has graciously consented to take a compulsory loan for necessities from the right. My dear fellow, I render an honest reckoning. That is, every evening I count up how much there is left in the total."

There was a murmur of applause from the crowd, but Müller lifted the griddle from the fire with a surly grumble.

"You keep your light heart, brother. I never believed, though, that you would become so important that you 'd get a freiherr and Royal Chancellor for your cook; but I 'm glad my pancakes please the gentlemen's taste. I 've often asked myself how we down here have been able to keep on all these years so willingly and joyfully."

"That I 'll explain to you. There is such a rare fascination for men in being daily and hourly with him who has command over their weal and woe, that one may inquire whether perhaps the bliss of heaven, too, may not turn out to consist in the same thing."

"That would be well, if such a diversion also made men nobler and better."

"Thank you, brother. That remark was for me. I know well enough that behind my back I am little spared here among you all. Call me a frivolous beggar, a—well, what you please! A skeptic, and philosopher such as I, who oversleeps himself badly at morning service, cannot expect much love among you Swedes. I may console myself, though, with the fact that the king himself is less dainty in such things than you. At home it's likely to be a question of falling on the battlefield, and then you shall see, brother, that the black wig of old Grothusen will not stand behind the line."

"At home, you say. Answer me honestly. Does His Majesty really hope to gather fresh troops there?"

"That he does—and he'll get them, too. That will make an affair in the realm such as the world never saw the like of. I've nothing against that. In the hour of need to call the money-lenders 'my dear fellow,' that's one thing—and it might happen that chevaliers would become scarce, if no money-lenders could be found. But one's honor and sword, that's another matter."

"And is he, then, for that reason, going to decamp at last? I thought I noticed that he was not quite clear as to the immediate future."

"The further he gets toward the north, the more clearly he comes to see it."

"You think of the ancient enemies waiting for him: Saxony, Russia, Poland, Prussia, Hanover, Denmark—six hostile peoples to fight!"

"Seven. You are forgetting the latest and most dangerous enemies."

"Whom?"

"The Swedes."

Müller arose from the stool, and the two one-eyed men stood face to face.

"God in heaven! don't talk like that. You used at other times to be of those who do not despair. This is a strange speech in your mouth."

"Since His Majesty has got certain knowledge that his subjects have begun to challenge and defy him, he has come to the point of riding home with the same fury as to a battle. What, besides, is one to believe after the latest news? The country is without government. The civil service is standing as still as a mill-wheel on a dried-up brook. The lords of the Riksdag and the Council talk of dethronement. We should get to see a flaming outbreak, if the Swedes were not such a law-abiding people—and it still happens that *he* is their prince. Don't wail and lament, my dear Müller, for all this is just your own old song—and don't be so damnably stingy with the sugar, but turn the whole cornucopia over the pancakes — and hold your head high! Adieu!"

Müller stood in the middle of the room, flustered and without an answer. The greatest astonishment was depicted on his face, for through the door he heard Grothusen call to a drummer-boy: "August, fetch a decent drum here! Hang it in front of you and come with me to the bazaar."

Müller shook his head, and sat down again by his pancakes. "In the name of the Lord Jesus Christ, what sort of absurdities will Grothusen commit with the drum?"

.   .   .   .

Next morning the Swedes marched out ceremoniously from Demotika, in order to begin at last their homeward journey to the shore of the Baltic. They had to struggle on for hundreds of miles through mountain passes and forests. In a long line behind them rode Turks, Jews, and Armenians with their sacks and bundles. These were their seventy-two most pressing creditors. The king was cheerful and brilliant, so that the citizens and their veiled women called down the blessing of God over the departing hero. Only Grothusen remained behind, for his Turkish friends held him back at the door. One of them stuck an ink-horn into his hand, another put a pipe of tobacco into his mouth, and the black attendants pulled at his coat. His large nostrils were raised aloft, and he emptied his coat pockets into the hands of the attendants with a magnificent flourish. He then opened the lid of his clothes-chest.

"My dearest, dearest friend," said he. "This exquisite nightcap I've had specially made for you, and have used it myself so that it should be a real memorial.—And you, father! These brand-new slippers—you wonder they are so down at heel. I myself have diligently walked in them so as to ascertain that they would not be too hard on your feet.—And you there, pray take this silken dressing-gown!"

He jumped up on his equipage like a fugitive, and ordered the coachman to drive on.

That evening, when the Swedes came to Timurtash, a pasha presented to the king as a gift from the sultan a silken tent and a sabre with a jewelled hilt.

"There goes my pelisse of sable," said Grothusen to the king half aloud. "No other return-gift can be raised, and Your Majesty yourself has absolutely nothing but a dusty coat and a half-dozen rough soldier's shirts."

"Lend me as well the ink-horn and pipe that you just got," returned the king with a roguish twinkle in his eye. "I must also present something to the chieftain for the escort of the Janisaries."

"Give the whole old fellow Grothusen for a eunuch in the great monarch's seraglio!" cried Grothusen jubilantly, rubbing his hands together and becoming more light-headed, the madder the jest became. At that moment he caught sight of his drummer-boy, who was marching despondently along the road with the drumsticks under his arm.

"Your drum has no tongue in her head. There's stolen goods in her," cried the boy's comrades mockingly.

When they examined the drum, they found that it was sealed with four seals; and big tears came to the boy's eyes.

"Strike bravely on your discordant drum!" ordered Grothusen. "It was I that sealed it, as Pilate the grave of Christ—and a little mournful music may come in well for all the Turkish creditors behind us, who are now riding into exile in our stead."

But in the evenings, when the Swedes rested a few short hours by the camp-fire, the musicians rapped and shook the drum, opining that it was full of money and securities embezzled from the king.

"He's a keen one!" they whispered. "It's no trick, is it, to empty the left pocket liberally, when one sticks such long fingers into the right?"

As early as two o'clock at nights the king had the trumpets blow for breaking camp. He galloped

forward between the cliff-walls by torchlight. When
at Pitest he found himself once more on the boundary of Christendom, the companies left behind at
Bender met him, and the last Zaporogeans, who had
remained faithful in so many perils, received, kneeling, his words of farewell. Afterwards he went to
Grothusen.

The latter had just halted to count the guldens
that one of the guardsmen had gone ahead and
dickered for in Transylvania.

The king said to him: "My passport is now
ready. I am to be known as Captain Frisk, and shall
ride at a gallop to Stralsund with Rosen and Düring."

Grothusen then lifted off his braided hat and his
wig and delivered them to the king.

"The slippers, nightcap, gorgeous pelisse, silken
dressing-gown — Seek them, seek them! All gone!
Now the wig and hat go. With this disguise and
a snuff-brown frock coat, Your Majesty is so unrecognizable and transmogrified, that if all the Rosen
family had not a knack with women, no tavern girl
— saving your honor — would ever proffer the gentlemen a glass of water. But for my part I'm thankful that there's no need to offer my flesh for the
king's ride across Europe."

Grothusen himself, however, took his place at
once in the travelling-carriage, so as to arrive first
and be able to meet his lord at the Swedish sea,

along whose coast the enemy were now building their fortresses and cities.

Day and night the king exercised in wild rides his two chosen companions and the two dragoons who were to follow after him at a day's interval. When at last the hour struck in which he was to assume his disguise and spring into the saddle, he gave his gelding the spurs with such violence that Düring and Rosen were almost at once a couple of horse's lengths behind. He looked as on the morning before a battle. He, who in fresh and sound health had endured months in a sick-bed so as to avoid a humiliating audience with the sultan, and who for years had trifled away the days in a small Turkish town in the hope of being able to gather a great army to follow him, now rode off impatiently with his two comrades and without a single servant.

The hoofs rang on the stones like those of a runaway steed, and the dazed vine-dresser sprang to the door of his hut.

"Who's riding there in such an alarm?" he asked. "If it's a poor hunted deserter, he may step in under my roof, and my wife and I will hide him and let him bed on the straw."

"Look out for the chevalier's sword, father!" answered Düring. "It is loose in its sheath to-day. He is an officer, who has been challenged by an unfaithful friend and relative, and who is on fire to meet him." But to himself he whispered: "That relative is the Swedish people. So that is to be our last fight!"

Meantime, with the sealed drum on the driver's box among baskets and canteens, Grothusen jolted toward Stralsund. His heart thumped like a youth's when for the first time he read the name of the city on a leaning sign-post. Soon he heard the hour strike in the church of St. Nicholas. He distinguished the solitary lights in the houses of wakeful and sick folks, and on the drawbridge he sprang from the wagon and shouted to the guard: "The king, the king! Where is he? What news?"

The watch knew nothing, and every morning Grothusen gazed from the wall in search of his home-coming lord. With the brightest moonlight on his face, however, the king arrived at Düker's house one night, and early next morning, after the boots had been cut from his swollen feet, into his room came Grothusen with the glad salutation: "Your Majesty, I 'm in love."

The king took him cordially by the hand. "Dearest Grothusen, we're likely to get other things to attend to than serenading demoiselles."

"But this is no demoiselle. She is assuredly both mother and grandmother. Further than that I know nothing about her. But now as before I beg most humbly that in all my fooleries I may retain Your Majesty as my secret confidant."

Grothusen laid his papers before the king, and sometimes pointed to a column of figures, but to make the work easy and merry he meanwhile told the story of his adventure.

"It was one noon just when I was to betake myself here to Düker. By the Kniper Gate, bathed in sunlight, stood a house that was so white it pricked me in the eye and forced me to glance up. There she sat at the window.—No, now Your Majesty is at the wrong column of figures. The two thousand guldens that are wanting here I have caroused away on my own account.—Yes, there she sat at the window under a curtain with white fringe. Her hair, too, was altogether white, but handsomely arranged, and her face was narrow and irradiated with an immeasurable mildness. She is certainly over seventy, but she's still a woman, just the same. There is nothing so refined and noble, my most gracious lord, as to adore an old lady. One does not long to draw near her. She stands up at the window like a memory, like a sacred legend. One only salutes her reverently with one's sword, as one goes past with one's troops."

"It is pleasant to hear you again, little Grothusen. My old passion for lively and crack-brained folk seems to increase with years. This Holsteiner Görtz, who is to come here soon, is said also to be a mightily agreeable and well-spoken gentleman, with great gifts of spirit."

"I myself have always recommended his services to Your Majesty, though I know that with his coming even I and Feif will have to crawl down nicely into the shade. Farewell, farewell! Such a little bungler in finance as I am avails no longer in these hard days when the whole realm is at stake. Here there is need of a great diabolical minister of the foreign kind. Görtz is bold and resourceful, a warrior in statecraft, and he got money for the administrator of Holstein like grass. He is more cunning than ten little Grothusens and fifty Müllers and Feifs. But what addles my wits is the question of how one should compose a *billet-doux* to such an elderly dame as my fair one at the Kniper Gate."

The king again got the look of mischief in his eye and handed Grothusen a pen.

"Stand there at the end of the table and write, and I 'll dictate."

The king pondered awhile, and then began:

NOBLEST LADY—A powder-stained warrior fellow, such as I, assuredly dares not beg for an audience with such a noble lady as Madame, yet still the noble lady might graciously send her likeness; but it must be done quickly, for my king says that soon we shall all go forth to fall, so that a hasty answer with the likeness—

Grothusen laughed and wrote and laughed, talk-ing in between of accounts and state affairs and Görtz. When the *billet* was done, he folded it, kissed the hand of his royal friend, and not long after went down the street toward the Kniper Gate.

Then it happened at last one day that Müller, who after a long delay had also arrived at Stralsund, was sitting at work with Grothusen in the king's ante-room.

A lackey opened the door and announced: "The Herr Baron Georg Heinrich von Görtz!"

One-eyed, in chevalier style, with a mother-of-pearl hilt to his court sword and his orders on a costly suit of velvet, Görtz stepped across the threshold. He took the hands of Grothusen and the confused Müller and laid them on his breast. After that fashion the three one-eyed gentlemen came to be standing before one another.

"Tell me frankly," said Görtz, pointing with his head toward the closed door of the king, "how long has it actually been since our hero has had a bath?"

Grothusen answered: "Let me see! He had his last bath last summer in Demotika. But he some-times has a douche of cold water. About such things Your Excellency may easily joke with him. But one thing I would advise. Don't talk unne-cessarily about the Swedes!"

Görtz shut his eye, nodded, and went inside to the king.

A slight shadow passed across the tanned forehead of Grothusen, and he muttered to Müller: "While His Majesty is signing himself over to the devil, I think I'll go down to the market-place and drive away my thoughts."

When Görtz had saluted the king, he came forward to him with polite negligence and without a single flattering word.

"It's remarkable," he observed, "that if you drop a coin in a big hall, it rolls over the whole floor till it hides itself under a cabinet."

The king, who was still half suspicious toward this foreign wooer of fortune, thereupon took a ducat from his purse, which happened to be lying open above the documents on the table, and threw the coin on the floor. It rolled in a circle and remained lying in the middle of the room in front of him.

"*Sapristi!*" said Görtz. "*Sapristi!* If one *wants* the coin to go under the wardrobe, it lays itself down in the middle of the floor."

At the same moment the king accidentally happened to strike his sword-hilt against the purse so that all the ducats tumbled ringing to the floor. Like a herd of frightened sheep they rushed with their rounded backs in all directions and hid themselves under the cabinet, the table, and finally even behind the stove.

Now for the first time Görtz began to bow deeply and still more deeply.

"Behold! I am weak in matters of faith, that I freely confess; but still I am superstitious in one particular. A bomb may fall in the midst of a tightly packed battalion without wounding a single man, but it has never yet happened in the world that a piece of bread and butter has fallen to the ground without lying butter-side down in the dust. There is in the air a race of small imps directed by the Evil One himself. If they were not invisible, they would appear like small brownish bees flying about. They for their part never cause any evil on a large scale, but only small vexations; yet when the vexations are many, the affair may end with a great misfortune. It is the invisible imps that are vexed and enticed by the shining Swedish weapons. If a flag be hoisted now, the cord breaks. If a soldier goes over a frozen ditch, the ice cracks. To put it more simply, Your Majesty is now pursued as assiduously by bad luck as formerly by good."

The king hummed softly:

> *Well, what can one do*
> *To plant a firm shoe*
> *On the mischievous crew?*

"He who will may be the architect of his own fortune. One scares them away. To begin with, one dismisses from one's neighborhood all petty people,

for such folk have as many invisible imps on them
as a baggage-horse has fleas. Then one draws one's
blade against all the world and follows the star of
one's will."

"The Swedish lords declare that at home there
soon will not be a single farthing to collect."

"Then one must coin new farthings. What is
money? Bonds secured by existent values. Has not
that bit of a kingdom that lies up there a value,
against which one should be able to write as many
bills of indebtedness as one chooses?"

"I have myself been long thinking of fiat money.
But would that be right? A sovereign should be
just. There must not be a stain on his honor.
Remember that!"

"Assuredly, assuredly! Fiat money, you see, is
a loan. In years of hardship one brings the genuine
money to oneself with it. In years of victory one
releases the genuine and throws the fiat coinage
into the furnace. He who would aim high must
not fear to let even Lucifer forge the arrow."

The king's bold thoughts burst out at once in
questions as into a hand-to-hand fight with artless
prejudices. He himself had never in the wilderness put his hand into his pocket without being
able to fill it with ducats. More indifferent than a
beggar as to his coat and his lodgings, he still had
never seen an object that he really longed to buy.
His ducats had never been used for anything else

than to encourage and reward others. Money was for him public funds. On the contrary, he observed daily that as soon as he ordered others to hand over their pelf to the army, they began to grumble and seek evasions. His contempt for these servants entwined itself serpent-like with his indomitable desire for redress, for revenge on the foes that had cast him down into such an abyss before the eyes of the world. Was not he a king, a lord over millions of men? Why, then, was he constantly trammelled and hindered by these small metal discs, in themselves worthless, which in one place were called rix-dollars and in another guldens? Money was an invention by which the base turned human worth topsy-turvy and betrayed honesty so as to live sumptuously themselves. Was it really a sin to change around some of the screws in such an invention? By rights money ought to be wholly done away with.

After meditating awhile, the king said: "And your conditions?"

"That I remain a subject of Holstein but free to choose my assistants and responsible only to Your Majesty. The civil service shall be remodelled for the greater advantage of the royal power. The army—"

The king straightway interrupted him: "But not a foot-breadth of the realm inherited from our fathers is to be surrendered to the enemy by peace treaty or bargaining. Rather may we all die and the whole of Sweden burn! I never began the war. My neighbors lay in ambush when I was still an inexperienced boy."

Görtz now knelt for the first time.

"The world can never understand the hero who would rather stand by the conditions he has sworn to than play the cunning politician, but a coward is he who shuns the service of such a firmness. Small of soul were the augurs who stood by Your Majesty's cradle. They saw, indeed, the constellation of the Lion, but they did not read in the stars that the conflagration of the Swedish Empire already stood foretokened there—irrevocably without mercy. The champion who stepped from the cairn to assemble the Swedes for the great conflict needs men. I am a stranger, but as true as I live, I speak with heart and soul. As long as my strength holds out, I will gather stuff from east and west for a bulwark of the sort that, alas, can be made only with nails of good ducat-gold."

"That game may be daring."

"The daring is the delightful. A good diplomat should every day be as prepared for the block as a warrior for his bullet. If everything goes wrong, well, then the bulwark, too, will become a pyre that turns the night around us to bright day and the enemy to mere shadows and supernumeraries. There will then remain for me only the honorable

madness of burning on the pyre beside my Her-
cules. Our good Luther's 'wine, woman, and song'
has always smacked too much of the tavern for me,
and I had rather make the words:

Who loves not woman, fame, and might,
A fool is he till death's dark night.

Fired by the sincerity of the moment and his own
warmth, Görtz had forgotten to cancel the word
"woman," but the king, not noticing it, went to
him with flashing eyes.

"My image must not be set on the fiat pieces."

"We may plunder all Olympus for deposed
gods."

The king stood a long time silent. He then
added softly and with faltering voice: "Neither shall
the arms of Sweden be set on them!" Over his
frowning brows settled a deep, dark melancholy.

Surprised, irresolute, trembling, Görtz rose from
the floor and, going to the window, pointed down
at the square. "If at any time bitter thoughts over-
take Your Majesty, do but go to the window and
look at the people. Then it is not hard to get a
hearty laugh."

"It has been long since I laughed from my
heart."

Down in the square, Grothusen was going back
and forth among the girls by the biscuit-stall, and

behind him stood a drummer-boy with a sealed drum.

"Rattle a gallant roulade and bring the girls!" Grothusen commanded.

The boy plied the sticks, and when all the girls ran up inquisitively and stood around, Grothusen broke the seals and unfastened the drumhead. Thereupon he took from the drum all imaginable sorts of women's gear which he had purchased at the bazaar the last evening in Demotika. There were small kerchiefs and veils and mirrors and flasks of attar-of-roses and neck-cloths with crescents and coins. He waved the kerchiefs high in the air. With head thrown back and drops of sweat on his pepper-brown face, he cried his wares and auctioned them off. For one trifle he demanded a kiss, for another an embrace, for the third a dance in the open square.

"Look, look," continued Görtz, "how our colonel forces his heathenish kerchiefs on the Christian women-folk! He is a gay fellow, our friend down there, but men of that sort are not of the calibre to serve a Charles XII."

The king now began to bow as a sign that Görtz should retire.

"Calumniators have also said that you, baron, are a sad rascal. One thing I will say. When we work together from now on, you, baron, will not speak ill of any one in his absence, for in that case I always take the part of the absentee. How much evil have they not tried to whisper into my ear about that drum down there! And what did it contain? Why, harmless toys and rubbish! If, too, Grothusen was an extravagant servant, he has at least never stuck away anything in his own pouch either. —I wish now to look over a few matters."

Görtz bit his lip, but when he came down he beckoned his friend Grothusen to the *porte cochère* with a lofty gesture.

"The sick and bleeding lion from the Ukraine and Poltava has rested his paws so long that the claws have grown longer and sharper than ever. Press your hat down on your head and button your coat, my good sirs, and keep yourselves in readiness. The autumn storms are beginning."

The small garrison of Stralsund soon heard the enemy's cannon making music before the walls. The tocsin called the men to the ramparts or to burning houses. Toward morning the king would lie down with his hat over his face for an hour's rest on the stone pavement at the Franken Gate. Awake, he stared into the dark crown of his hat, but the soldiers who lighted him with hand-lanterns discerned only his chin and lips, on which still remained the smile, though it was compressed and cold as if it merely belonged to his cast of features. Then they

whispered that they had never seen a more undaunted hero, but off in the starlight stood many
high officers who said that only his death could save
the Swedish realm.

He knew of what they spoke, although he pretended to notice nothing. The people for whose sake
he had dreamed his greatest dreams were already
looking for their salvation in his death. When did
fate fall upon a king more terribly? Had he been
born only to lead the Swedes in their last great conflict and then be cast aside like a worn-out tool? His
sister's husband was already glancing at his crown,
and the son of his favorite, now departed, sister was
lifting his childish hand toward it.

At the Holy Communion he humbled himself
and was bathed in honest tears, but he never wept
over his own misfortunes. Were they not out-and-
out foes, which he had to meet with an avenger's
wrath? He grew harder and colder toward his officers, and often spoke with his hands clenched, but
he also ruled more strictly over himself and his own
thoughts. To be sure, he neglected his clothes even
more than of old, so that he could wear the same
grimy shirt for fourteen days; but he controlled his
limping walk. His hair had already changed to silver, though he was hardly thirty-three, but when he
looked up, awake, into the crown of his hat, he repeated to himself: "This must be the will of God
that I am following."—Then he would rise like

a rested youth and hand his cloak to some frozen graybeard. But if any one named his homeland or the Swedes, he picked at his coat buttons and was silent.

One day Grothusen was drilling his soldiers with greater ardor than usual down below his fair one's window at the Kniper Gate. Motionless as a picture, the old lady sat behind the flower-pots, and when Grothusen lifted his hat, the new braids gleamed.

He beckoned to his drummer.

"Your drum still has not a full speech in her mouth. Let us open it. Here are a pair of the most delightful little gold-embroidered shoes. Go up to the lady and say that they are a parting gift from Grothusen. Now the drum is empty."

"Herr general! There is a Turkish gold-piece at the bottom."

"To be sure! It has come to a trembling situation there. It is the king's money. Now we are to go out to Rügen, where the Prussians and Danes intend to land so as to shut us in on the sea side. Go with the coin to the king, and ask him to accept it as a reminder of the years when Grothusen had the fortune to serve him in distant lands. May the gold some day be recast in the melting-pot during years of peace as an honest coin, on which the Swedes may again behold both their arms and their king! Say all that in humility from Grothusen."

When all was arranged for decampment, Grothu-

sen saluted with his broadsword before the seventy-
year lady. As he rode along the streets, he waved to
the inquisitive girls in the windows and shattered
booths, and, for the first time since Demotika, the
drum thundered with full voice. It roused such an
echo from the church walls that it was like the
rumble of the enemy's field-pieces. Fearless, elated,
Düker was consulting with the king by the bottom
of the stairway. Listening to the embittered whisperings of Bassewitz about Görtz, Daldorff rode up
among the generals, and little Cronstedt clapped his
major of artillery on the shoulder. Now he hastened
to one side, now to the other. He glanced at his fast-
shooting cannon as a good chief groom at his horses,
and sometimes he polished with the tip of his cloak
the newly discovered Polhem sighting-screws.

"It will be a hard struggle," said he, "and only
when His Majesty actually stands on Swedish
ground shall I say that the king's ride is ended."

The autumn storms roared over Rügen in the
twilight, wailing and moaning on beach and head-
land. No star told of God's goodness, and when the
troops were drawn up for prayers, the vengeful words
of the Old Testament sounded from the mouth of
the preacher. The Swedes were now so short of men
that they set out tied dogs as sentries, whose mournful howling could be heard through the seething of
the surf.

"It 's a foreboding of death when the dogs wail," said the soldiers.

The country folk were armed with axes and scythes, but the enemy, sheltered by the dense rain, approached the shore, and finally landed more than ten thousand men in front of the almost unguarded village of Stresov. The gale tore away the mist, and the moon rose bright above the desolate region. As early as three o'clock at night, however, the advanced scouts of the enemy crept cautiously back over the sand, and reported that the Swedes were approaching.

The king halted a moment to unhook his cloak. Turning to Daldorff and the Royal Guard, he said: "The years have flown. We have had the good together. Who knows when the lead that is to be our bane is seething in the casting-ladle?"

Grothusen drew a yellow gauntlet from between the coat buttons at his breast and answered: "I received that glove from my gracious lord at Bender, and no night of frost has been so cold that the glove has not warmed my heart."

Thereupon Daldorff bared his head: "When I get my bullet, if my poor wounded clay could still smile and speak, it would turn toward the departing troops and call down a grateful man's blessing on his true-hearted brothers in arms. Ah, that victory might yet once more shine on our way! As a farmer finds it advisable to leave an old field fallow and sow a new, so God dismembers and changes kingdoms and empires. When He has sown the new borderlands, He permits no one to bear the boundary stones back to their former place. We do not understand His will, we perceive only that He is against us."

The king answered: "God is *for* us. It cannot be His will that the Swedish Empire should be divided. If that be so, then may He give us the token by smiting us with death man after man!"

"That is a plain and true saying," replied Daldorff.

The officers who had whispered aside in the starlight before the city gate of Stralsund no longer remembered their dark thoughts. Instead, they pressed forward among the Royal Guard so as to march next to the king. It seemed to them that they recognized in his person something of God's own hard and merciless love for the right and for the accomplishment of His will.

The conversation died down. The trumpets ceased to play and the drums to beat; the banners were borne along lowered and furled. With sword drawn, the king went before his troops. He had barely three thousand men. They were now to fight three against ten, surprise the enemy, and chase them down into the sea.

He came to a standstill. "What can that be? Here are obstructions, and off in the moonlight I see a redoubt. The enemy has made good use of the time.— Forward!"

At the same instant a row of flashes spurted along the parapet, and the first volley broke through the night, but the Swedes thrust aside the obstacles and stormed up the rampart.

Cronstedt's cannon-balls soughed over their heads and cast up stones and sand where they struck the entrenchments. The ground trembled, and from all sides the fire of the musketry sent its lightnings. There was whining and shrieking, as if an army of hungry kites had sailed out over the shore. Clouds of smoke shot up so high that only in isolated places could the light of the moon break through and paint white expanses, as of snow, on the ground. When the din momentarily abated, the combatants could still hear from afar the howling of the fastened dogs, but soon the thunder grew so violent that the soldiers could not make out the officers' shouts of command. With hands clenched on their sword-hilts, the Swedes rushed forward like berserkers to the duel. It was no longer an ordered battle with leaders and obeying battalions. It was the last warriors of the army that had marched through Europe, who now in the autumn of their achievements offered up their blood for the last time south of the Swedish sea. It was a standing breast to breast in a hand-to-hand, life-and-death combat for eternal glory or shame.

Colonel Jacob Torstenson already lay fallen, but his brother, Karl Ulrik, burst in over the rampart with his guardsmen and fought his way into the midst of the foe's entrenchments. Forced slowly out, his back pressed against the earthen wall and the dying Captain Adlerfeldt between his feet, he shouted: "Hold on gallantly, dear comrades! My grandfather led a whole Swedish army, and I won't lay down my sword before any one but the Dessauer himself."

Bare-headed, with the flame of wrath and enthusiasm on his brow, the king hewed his way through blades and musket-butts. He went to meet the murdering sword-points with the autumn storms in his breast, humbled, indifferent before wounds and death. Again the toothless, masculinely ugly face of Ensign Åberg grinned beside him, and Seved Tolvslag shattered heads and weapons. Musket-flashes spurted from all sides and singed the king's tattered soldier's coat. He thrust and fired. He was seized round the waist by rude hands, he wrestled breast to breast with plain, swearing privates. A Danish officer, who recognized him, caught one hand into his thin hair and tried to wrench his sword from him, but the king snatched a pistol from his belt, and shot the Dane through the body, so that he fell dead. Then new foes leaped forward, and the Dessauer's cavalry and field-pieces fell upon the Swedes from the flanks, so that in the stormy

November night they were surrounded by a ring of stabbing swords and flashing lightnings.

Major-General Stromfelt gave the king his horse, but in the darkness the beast became entangled in an obstruction, was felled by a cannon-ball, and remained lying on top of the king. When he tried to work himself free, he was struck on the chest by a spent cannon-ball so that the blood gushed from his lips. Everything grew black before his eyes, and he sank back unconscious and half buried in sand, but with hand still clenched on his sword.

Lieutenant-Colonel Tranfelt fought in the midst of a swarm of Danes. He brandished a weapon in either hand, and beneath his torn coat and shirt three wounds gleamed on his naked breast. When he could no longer stand, he fought on his knee, until he fell and gave up the ghost.

Cronstedt, wounded and bleeding, had been lifted upon one of his field-pieces.

"It is the Romans of the north," he said, "who are falling to-night in defence of their last provinces."

Before him lay a dead artillerist youth with port-fire still burning, and in the midst of the roar from the battle and the storm came from nearby the sound of a voice in prayer. It was a chaplain, who was bending over the wounded and dying behind the fighters.

"Thou King of armies and of kings, cry not unto

us as to the children of Jeroboam's house: 'He
that dieth in the city, him shall the dogs devour;
and he that dieth in the fields, him shall the birds
of the air devour, for thus the Lord hath spoken!'
Wherefore dost Thou refuse us a sign that Thou
art yet with us? Wherefore grantest Thou not to
me to shed the peace of victory over our men that
bleed, so that their hard bed may be made soft for
them?"

Bassewitz had already been carried dying from
the *mêlée* on two muskets; and the veteran Daldorff who, bleeding in the midst of fallen guardsmen, had saved the king's life in so many struggles, and who had led his Småland horsemen into
the jaws of death at Holofzin, lay on his outspread
cloak with his brow pale as a corpse. The shells
threw their sudden light over the hacking and
crossing swords, and over the shadow-like fighting
soldiers. By the light from a field-piece Guardsman
Corporal Baumgarten finally recognized the king,
lifted him on his horse, and placed him in the midst
of the repulsed Swedes.

Then a persistent and violent drumming penetrated the ears of the king, and when he turned
sidewise to investigate it, he made out at a distance
in the gray of the dawn a drummer-boy, who with
drumsticks in hand still stayed behind, facing the
foe. Beside him an officer lay on his back with both
arms extended at full length. The large laced hat

still rested on his head with dignity and elegance. A neck-cloth of French lace, specked with red, fluttered in the wind, and round the skirt of the coat there shone all about on the dewy heath bits of confectionery and silver coins.

"Who is the fallen man?" asked the king.

Major Riddarstadt answered: "That is a gallant warrior before God, but one whom many men reviled. It is one of Your Majesty's cherished friends —it is Grothusen."

When Riddarstadt had given this reply, he himself went back into the *mêlée* and met his death.

It was on the darkest of winter nights that the king in his six-oared barge finally left Stralsund, which was smoking beneath cannon-balls and shells. During, who had so unweariedly shared the hardships of the king's ride, had fallen in his blood before the city wall, but his brother sat in the stern at the tiller. Many workmen with clubs and pickaxes walked on either side of the channel broken through the ice, and Rosen, who stood in the bow, was such a living likeness of the king that it was to him they waved their farewell.

Pursued by the enemy's shot, the barge drew near the open sea. Vainly, however, did Rosen look for the two Swedish vessels, the *Snap-up* and the *Swift Sven*, which had been ordered to meet them there, but had been driven back by the storms.

The king, then, with his two companions and a lackey, climbed on board of a heavy freight-galley with red patches on its wretched blackened sails, which hoisted anchor. Where now, forsooth, was the proud fleet swimming, on whose decks fourteen years ago, young and confident of victory, he had heard old Piper's glad hand-clapping? The threatening line of masts that Rosen pointed out on the horizon was the squadron of Tordenskjold. Only far out at sea did they meet the brigantine *Snap-up*, and with wrathful orders and gloomy eyes the king set foot on the belated ship. Was this the gracious master of whom the seamen had heard tell that he used to tuck his hat under his arm with graceful bowings?

He raised his hand to salute the crew, but it sank slowly, tight-clenched, and his first words under the Swedish man-of-war's flag were words of chastisement: "The captain of the *Snap-up* shall be flogged; but as for the captain of the *Swift Sven*, which has altogether failed to appear, he shall be shot!"

The storm raised the ice-floe aloft. The waves lifted white necks above the bulwarks like the ghosts of drowned men, but even when the darkness settled down once more, the king remained standing silently by the mast. Had he not been a prince, he might even yet have been able to turn and seek for himself a peaceful retreat; but as it was, men would soon have pursued him and dragged him with them.

He ought to have been permitted to keep a privateer fleet and to have lived out his years on it amid shot and cutlass, but as it was, his subjects commanded him to turn home to guard their manure-stacks and dairies. The nearer he approached to the shore of Scania, the more clearly it seemed to him that it was like a landing among the enemy. He remembered the early morning in the royal residence at Karlberg, when before his grandmother and sisters were awake, he stole along the stairs with Hultman and rode off to the war. He did not want to see the well-known faces again. He did not want to ride through the streets of Stockholm and see the people welcome with pine torches a king driven in by wind and weather. He saw, to be sure, that these Swedes continually gave up their lives for him and for the bit of land that was still theirs, but he knew also that in their silent prayers many of them called upon God to give him a speedy death. He saw all that as clearly as his eyes had previously been darkened. He did not think of peace and reconciliation. He could not forget that the thousands who had followed him had got their bullets, that the tears and blessings of his people had made soft beds of their overgrown graves, that they had become holy men, whose sins were forgotten and their virtues glorified. For a warrior there were but two ways of reconciliation with God and man, and they were victory or a death-wound.

When he stepped ashore on the plain of Scania in the streaming night-rain, he did not kneel, and he drew no sigh of sadness or joy. Hurriedly, without a single word, he went to a great stone that was called the Staff Stone. He, the rider from Demotika, the soldier who had lain down to sleep untroubled on the snow-drift, forgot himself so completely at that moment that he sought shelter in the lee of a stone from a few harmless drops of water. There he remained standing.

No bells rang in the churches. There was no sweeping and lighting of fires at the Crown estates. While the night-rain splashed in the roof-gutters, the Swedes slept in their homes and had no premonition that, after fifteen years of saga-like victories and nameless misfortunes, their king was now treading the soil of his realm with the wrath of failure in his soul, received and greeted by no one. He no longer looked back, only forward. Revenge!—that word swung his thoughts like a hammer. Revenge on the perjurers, revenge on the world that had made of him a fugitive weakling without money, without power—but a great and royal revenge! He knew that next day many of his subjects would rejoice, but also that many tremblers would seek to divine as to the gallows and the block. He smiled at the thought. His exasperation came from diffidence and wounded love. It was because of this that in his last years he spoke of

Sweden so evasively. He wanted to punish and conquer these latest enemies, but not on the place of
execution. Calmly and commandingly he meant to
tread the earth which they were almost ready to
pluck away from him. He wished to place himself
among the gloomy faces. Careless as a shepherd
amid the bushes of the wood, he wished to sleep
among the conspirators, if there were any, and compel them yet again to lower their flags and go where
he went. He wished to conquer his Swedish enemies by showing them that they were still faithful
to him.

Day began to glimmer, and some tillers of the
soil came out on the plain, but all the colors shone
so hard and strong! Everything seemed so còld
and strange!

"Is this Sweden, then?" muttered Rosen behind
his turned-up coat collar. "I hardly recognize it
any more."

"Your eyes are red with the wind," answered the
king. Later he added: "What if we do not recognize everything here at home, as long as others
recognize us?"

He got one of the laborers to show them the
way to Trelleborg. With the most tranquil countenance he spoke of his desire to meet the learned
professors at Lund, and the great Polhem, who
was to help him build a canal across Sweden. In
the lowest corner of the realm the three gentlemen

walked between the fences and slumbering cottages of the small town like shipwrecked adventurers who had become strangers in their own land, and under the hat which he had drawn down over his face, Rosen wept like a child.

When the king was to give the guide his fee, he noted that all the ducats had been given away on the journey. He found only the Turkish coin that Grothusen had carried along in the drum and sent him with the wish that some time, in peaceful years, the gold might be melted into an honest Swedish coin. It was the king's last piece, and even that was not his, for it had been borrowed of a Turkish Jew.

Without a word, he laid the foreign coin in the hand of the Swedish peasant.

Among the Swedish Skerries

THE returning Swedish soldiers tramped from inn to inn with dusty clothing and worn-out shoes. On the cart in front of them jostled the Finnish women whom the king had ransomed from the Turks and married off among his soldiers, and beside them on the straw beneath the wagon-seat stood the cage of chameleons that Professor Eneman had fetched from Asia. The cart with the women was soon left behind, and the animals died, but between the sun-browned soldiers and grooms was still led Brandklipparen, though he was weary with years, stiff in gait, and no longer bore any conquering hero in the saddle.

A tall, thin man with restless eyes and knitted brows always walked a trifle in front of the others. His cheek was dusky as bark, but his teeth gleamed from the midst of the grizzled beard which he never took the time to cut off, since he had neither knife nor shears. The wretchedest vagabond would have scorned his bedraggled coat, but he carried with him all he owned,—which was a sack and a cudgel. At the start of the journey, to be sure, he had been sent around to borrow money, but it had long since been strewn to the winds. So that strangers might not point their fingers at his poverty and his country, he called himself a plain private, but he was a royal guardsman, and was named Ehrensköld.

In his youth he had, one October night, stabbed a certain Ensign Gyllenstjerne, and his wits still fluttered so uncertainly that, although he was the merriest with the ale-can, he lay awake at night with restless thoughts. Hardly did the dawn brighten before he thumped on the floor of the hostelry with his wooden staff to waken his comrades.

At evening, when the exhausted band gathered round the table in the hall of the inn, he remained standing and cheerily raised the can toward all the inquisitive folk who climbed up outside the windows.

"Look, look!" whispered the beholders. "Every scar on that man's face and hands is a saga of some exploit. These are the heroes returning from Ilion!"

Later, when they saw Brandklipparen's rigid pace in the courtyard, they added: "And they have brought along the wooden horse."

But when Ehrensköld had told that it was Brandklipparen, while high-born countesses stepped out of the wagon with bread and sugar, so that they might be able to tell their descendants that Brandklipparen had once eaten out of their hand, he emptied his can to the dregs and beat on the table as a sign to his comrades that they should disperse.

"You don't let us either sit or sleep, with your homesickness," his comrades grumbled. "If a meal is laid out, you at once shout to us to get up and go on, even before the meat is carved."

Then he grew mistrustful and rancorous toward his former friends, and one morning he stole off ahead of the others.

He hardly needed to read the sign-posts or to ask his way. He knew that he went toward the north, that he always turned in on the most direct road. For year after year his homesickness had become more and more overpowering, and now that at last every step brought him nearer to the places of which he had never spoken, but on which he had always brooded, his longing only increased in strength. At times he would stand with hands crossed over his staff and stare at the road, but without himself being conscious of it, and he would then begin to walk on and on. If, on a rainy night, he happened to be turned with harsh words from a door where he had humbly called himself a poor Swedish baggage-driver who prayed to be given a piece of bread by the warm blaze, he forgot that he was no longer in military service. If, then, in the light of the embers, he saw through the window loaves of bread and a bowl of milk on the table, he bent the strips of lead, pulled out two or three small panes, and took for himself as much of the viands as he could reach. But as soon as he had appeased his thirst and stuffed his sack full of fragments of bread, he remembered that he was a good warrior, and before he departed he thrust in his stick and brought it down on the table with such thundering violence that the bowls and loaves leaped. Then the people of the house, who ran in on all sides, understood that it was not a common thief.

He got to Stralsund before the others, but the city surrendered to the enemy, and their fleets barred the Baltic. After many adventures he at last found in Amsterdam a Dutch smack, which lay ready to sail for Bohus, and into which he was received on such terms that he had a bed on the straw in the cabin under the skipper's patchwork quilt.

But as soon as he heard the anchor-chain rattle, he struck his stick against the roof of the cabin and called to the skipper: "Good father, when you get in sight of the Swedish skerries, you are to let me know, so that I can fix my beard and clothes, and go on deck."

The skipper promised to fulfil this request, but hardly did he get on deck before there was another knock on the cabin roof.

"Homeward, homeward bound," stammered Ehrensköld, taking the captain by the hand. "You have sailed the seas and experienced many things, father. Tell me, whence comes this delusion of the mind which determines that a man must know himself at home in order to be at peace with himself? Down there among the Turks, when poor Funck died of the fever, I had charge of the watch at the burial; but trust me, I could hardly hold my blade or remember the word of command. The stones lay so white — the cypresses stood so indifferent! If I myself had been laid in that place, I could not have slept in peace. I should have torn through the earth over my head and begged the Lord God for pity."

The skipper answered: "Has not the same Father's hand formed every part of the earth and even the frail boards that now bear us in the storm? Turn over to the wall and take a good rest! You warriors of the land are bad sailors, and we 're getting stiff weather."

The first thing next morning, when the captain was standing by the steersman, he heard fresh rapping on the cabin roof.

"I have a bullet here under my ribs, and I have never rightly understood whether it is that or homesickness which has so exhausted my strength that now I can't hold myself up straight without pain. Just this time of the morning, when it is half light, but the sun has not yet risen, is the hour of homesickness."

It was a restless passage, and the seas thundered. One night the captain came upon the cabin stairs with a horn lantern and threw the light on Ehrensköld. He sat awake on the straw with the staff beside him and the sack as a pillow, and his hair was now so long that it hung over his ears.

"My good sir," began the skipper, as he fastened the lantern to the hook in the roof, "we are now at the Swedish skerries outside Uddevalla, but the storm holds heavy, and the night is misty and dark. We must turn and make to sea and wait for clearer weather."

"Yes, turn the smack, you there!" shouted Ehrensköld, so that the cabin rang. "I don't want to go home. No, no,—what business have I at home, to be sure? In Kalmar church lies my father, and his scutcheon is on the wall. My brother is in captivity. My little sisters have become tall and married and old. They are no more the same. There are no little sisters any more. There is no home any more."

With such words he replied to the captain, but when the latter was about to go, he held him fast by the coat-sleeve.

"Don't listen to me!" he said. "Stick bravely to the same course as before! A good soldier mustn't come home like a coward after long and honest service with his king."

"But the smack, my good sir! It is my only property, and on it I command. I'm fairly sure I see the beacon-fire in the northwest, but the coast is dangerous here and full of pirates, who set out false lights."

Ehrensköld was no longer an enfeebled man. He sat straight up with one leg out of the bed and seized the captain in an iron grip.

"If you 've any respect for an officer's will, then sail ahead. It 's true I 've nothing else to give you but the wretched rags that I shall still wear with honor when I go ashore; but by Kalmar Town I have a little estate, if it has n't been taken from me. That you shall have in requital, if the sloop goes to wreck."

The skipper thought that homesickness had quenched his wits. He well knew that if the helm was not put down in time, they would be on the rocks. He wrestled to free himself. His coat-sleeve tore at the shoulder-seam, and with naked arm he sprang to the ladder.

A blow shook the ship so violently that the candle in the lantern fell over and went out.

"Jesus! There, master, you have the Swedish skerries!"

"Then may this moment be blessed! Not since I was a child have I sprung from bed in the morning with a lighter heart."

Ehrensköld heard shots and a struggle. He took the sack and stick and clambered up to the icy deck. The seas burst over him, but the dawn broke through the snowy mist, and he saw that the boat had stranded on a rocky isle and that a swarm of men were disarming the crew.

"Give us what you 've got!" demanded a red-bearded man, raising his musket. "Stranded wreckage belongs to the folk on the shore."

Ehrensköld clenched his hand on the shaft of his stick and slung the beggar-sack in front of him.

"Take it, take it! The peace of mind that I 've just found, no bullets of yours can take from me; but if you had n't a gun, a game of this sort should cost you dear.—I am an officer of the Crown."

Cautiously Red-beard lowered his musket.

On the summit of the island glowed a false beacon that had burned down low, and behind the cliffs lay a galliot without a flag. Beside the extinguished stern-lantern sat a sickly, sallow young man wrapped in a splendid fox-skin pelisse and with two crutches on his knee.

"What 's this, Norcross?" he cried, with a voice that was thin but shrilled piercingly like a whistle. "Hurry up there, hurry up there!"

Red-beard answered, "The man here says that he 's a Crown man, and in that case we might do better to give him a bullet than to let him slip ashore and carry the tale. Come, fellow, tell us who you are! I see your rags well enough, but no Crown uniform. Have you been away so long that you have n't heard tell of Lassë of the Highway? There he sits on the galliot. That 's Commodore Gatenhjelm, look you!"

"My name," said Ehrensköld, " you may know if you first get me clothing according to my rank, but I care little for the harm you can do me, if only I may tread the soil of Sweden once more in this earthly life. I clearly see that ye are godless free-booters, and I recognize clearly another land than the bright and happy one I left—but in any case I am now home. I'm home! My life I can give up freely, but don't deny that I may first step down on the Swedish island!"

"That's reasonable," answered Gatenhjelm. "But hurry up there, hurry up!" He rapped still more impatiently on the railing with a crutch.

Ehrensköld threw his staff on the deck like a surrendered sword and stepped down on the island. He walked forward slowly several paces, as if the ground had taken fast hold of his feet. Then he knelt, stroked and caressed the cliff with his hands and bent down his cheek to it.

"Praise be to Thee, Heavenly Father," he whispered, "who hast led home Thy wandering son by such long and strange paths. Thine, Thine be the glory!"

With that Gatenhjelm gave a sign, and Norcross laid the musket to his eye and from the railing shot Ehrensköld through the head.

When the day arose, the pirates had already steered in with their prey to the coast of Bohus, but out on the island lay the dead warrior with his arms round the cliff.

In Marstrand's Church

RESTLESS burghers were talking together in the square at Marstrand, and a fisherman stated that Tordenskjold intended shortly to make for the island with his ships and seize the fortress.

Martin Rosengård, the sexton, came across the square with his bunch of keys and went his undeviating way to the church through the midst of the throng without speaking to any one.

"He is old and hard of hearing," said the folk.

Martin Rosengård answered softly to himself: "But he's good of memory is old Martin. He is mickle good of memory. He never forgets the day that gave him gladness and courage for a whole lifetime. He never forgets Baggë, though by this the man has lain five years in his grave with a commission from Bender under his pillow. He was our teacher, and even from the mould shall he teach us. Therefore it is that to-day we ought to remember him. He belongs to us, even though his deeds adorned past days. In our heart is a fortress that no enemies can take from us. Wring your hands! It is Sunday morning, and old Martin has his affairs to attend to."

His withered figure became a head taller, and he nodded with inward content, when he had locked the church door behind him. He set blue-and-yellow irises in the candlesticks and folded up the altar-cloth of Vadstena lace. A recollection from his youth so occupied his thoughts that he almost believed he heard voices and the clatter of spurs in the empty church.

That had also been a Sunday, and Gyldenlöw, who with his Danes had just conquered the island, had ordered the pastor, Fredrik Baggë, to offer the *Te Deum* and read the customary Danish prayers for King Christian and his victorious army. Gyldenlöw himself sat in the commandant's pew with his officers, and in the aisles up to the door stood foreign soldiers, so that Baggë's mass-robe looked faded and shabby among all the glittering uniforms. The Swedish men and women in the farthest pews stared fixedly ahead, and many among them whispered bitingly, when they saw his tranquil face in the sunlight of the open window, where sparrows flew in.

He intoned with a clearer voice than ever before. When mass had been celebrated, and he stood in the pulpit, Gyldenlöw softly interrupted: "Baggë, Baggë, see that you preach well for us!"

He proclaimed the magnitude of the victory with such flashing zeal that the stern soldiers' eyes grew moist, but when he came to the prayer for the king, he clasped his hands high above his brow, and prayed his old prayer for the king of the Swedes.

Then Gyldenlöw sprang from his pew, and in

the little church there was such a din and cursing
and such a ringing of spurs and weapons as if there
was a hand-to-hand fight, but rising above the
clamor all the while was heard Baggë's quiet prayer.

Soldiers thronged up on the pulpit steps and
led him down, but he kept on to the last word of
the prayer.

"If you have nothing else to say," shouted
Gyldenlöw, "then expect a sentence of death or
life imprisonment."

"I have still something to add."

The sobbing in the farthest pews became still,
and the Danes held themselves back, waiting.

Then Baggë began to pray for the Swedish
army, for the humblest men in the ranks, and for
victory, victory for the Swedes, so that they might
return and set free his island.

Gyldenlöw took several violent steps to the altar
rail and snapped his gloves in the air.

"Fetch the handcuffs that hang in front of the
church door by the penance-stool!" he commanded.

Two soldiers went out and returned dragging the
chains, which clanked against the pavement. Gyldenlöw stopped in front of Baggë.

"I am ready to believe that you are a worthy
shepherd and that you have acted from mere zeal.
Therefore I'll extend you pardon this once more,
as soon as you show repentance. But by God! if you
rebel again, you have nothing else to expect than

court-martial and sentence. You have a house and home. Consider well! I shall wait patiently, while you examine your own mind. Release him, soldiers, and let him yet again mount into the pulpit! And you, good folk behind there on the benches, you have heard my words."

Baggë straightened his mantle as if to obey and betake himself to the pulpit. But then he turned again toward the congregation.

"I have something to repent. That is rightly said. But I can impart it here where I stand and do not therefore need to enter the pulpit."

Gyldenlöw pushed the nearest officers back, and set himself in his place, but his fingers played impatiently with his sword-hilt. All the audience by this time stood either in the aisle or at the doors of the pews.

Instead of clasping his hands, Baggë stretched them out before him, and no one knew rightly what he meant by this.

"I repent," he said, "that I have too long delayed with the prayer which perhaps lay nearest my heart."

With that he began to pray for the crops and the weather, for the lumber rafts on the river and the hay-wagons by the cottages, and for all the Swedish land, to which he vowed his loyalty even if in future days he should pine in the deepest and darkest dungeon.

Then the soldiers understood why he had held out his hands. While he was yet speaking, they screwed on the clamps, and afterwards, in the midst of their drawn swords, led him from the church and up to the fortress.

Katerinushka, Little Mother

IT was a winter night with the cold starlight that
causes a lonely man to weep without knowing
why. The crowned King of the Revels, who had
just been carried through the streets of Moscow,
had been acclaimed by the people more silently
than of old, and in the midst of the disbanding
holiday processions there was whispering about hate
and conspiracies and imprisonments. Whenever two
men met where they could not be overheard, they
execrated the czar. The priests muttered by their
censers that he ate meat on fast-days and worshipped
the gods of the Romans instead of the saints. The
Boyars lamented that they never got a chance to
sleep in peace at night, but had become toiling
slaves, who had to rebuild all Russia from the cellar
to the cap of the tower. They related that he had
gone mad. If he did not sit in his travelling-coach
or at his microscope, he cured diseases like a doctor, made boots like a shoemaker, boats like a ship-
wright, and ivory chessmen like a turner, or even
cut off heads like an executioner. After such a
day's work, they had sometimes at table seen him
go off and sit down among the musicians, where
he beat the drum with such skill that in that art as
well no one could surpass him. The merchants
at their counter grumbled about the long wars,
and the serfs pulled at their thick coats in bitter

mood and hid their sacred, shorn-off beards in their pockets.

The later the night drew on, the more sharply glinted the stars. Alexei, the son of the czar, sat alone in his vaulted room, which was wholly painted in scarlet with green festoons of leaves. Round about him on the floor lay theological works with pious legends of the saints. He held his pen still poised over a half-written letter to his Affrosinya, the red-haired Finnish thrall; but the exertion wearied him, and his pen sank. He forgot that they had taken from him his sword and his right of succession to the realm. In the stiff silken pelisse of the ancient czars and small boots studded with turquoises, he imagined himself to be in his secluded castle examining the work of the court goldsmith and conversing with learned monks. Then he dreamed of going down into the chapel and performing his devotions under the staring Christ head in the crypt, but far about him spread a realm of the ancient days, where the village bells rang, and where men arose late from bed and early put out the light. With that, Czar Peter's blood leaped to his brow, and he imagined himself ending the evening with a drinking-bout and hurling empty pewter pots at the heads of Boyars, who raised thankful shouts of joy.

The door opened behind him, but he supposed it was the servants and remained sitting in his meditation. Only when he heard steps and laughter in the corridors did he turn his lean and grayish-pale face with its hollow cheeks and crafty eyes. It was his father. It was the czar, who was coming with his guests of the night, and between them they carried a long table on which stood ten burning waxlights fastened into a like number of buns. How often had Alexei taken medicine to make himself sick and avoid appearing at his father's banquet! With what anguish had he gone in disguise with his Affrosinya as far south as the vineyards of Naples, in order to hide from this father, who was now lifting the cane above his head! He moved back toward the recess.

"Alexei," commanded the czar, "you shall be host to-night. Sit down opposite me!"

At the same moment that they all sat down, the czar gave his neighbor a resounding box on the ear, and shouted: "Let that go on round the table! Nobody knows how well such great gentlemen as sit with a prince deserve a box on the ear."

The cuff proceeded heartily around the table with blow after blow as far as Adjutant Vyasemski, who was the czar's nearest neighbor on the other side. Being a very young and as yet inexperienced officer, he grew pale, with hand half raised, and stared at the czar. There was no one in the party to whom the czar had taken such a liking as to this golden-haired youth; but a rumor had been whispered to-night that he had joined himself to the son and the rebels. The czar therefore wished to test him, and with the fury of Ivan the Terrible in his look and the good nature of a Muscovite artisan in his laugh, he said to him: "Vyasemski, my lad, soon no one will dare to name my name in my own kingdom without cursing me. Here is my cheek. By God and His only begotten son I enjoin you to sincerity. If you believe the slanderers, then strike away! In that case I deserve no better than the others. What I require is truthfulness—and I shall thank you."

Vyasemski rose and moved his chair aside in order to kneel, but with that he fixed his eyes on the light of the candles, and whispered: "My hands are unclean. Let me wash them first!"

The czar assented with a melancholy nod and gazed after him.

"He, as well! I had expected otherwise."

He held up the empty beaker in front of him, and the czarina, who had secretly watched him all day, entered in a simple blue dress and sat down on the vacated seat. He laid his hand on her arm, and turned toward Alexei.

"Well, why don't you fill up and drink to us? That is good. Again! And yet again! Fall into position! Quicker! No, ye others are to sit, but *you* shall stand. You shall stand up to answer. Is it true the monks have told you that you are the darling and hope of all the nation?"

On the other side of the table stood Alexei, shaken by ague, and his wrinkled face grew ashen and old. The czar looked as if he were the son, and at every new question Alexei twisted the long lace neck-cloth harder about his finger, but answered never a word.

"Is it true that you hate me, the author of your being, that you wait with longing for the hour of my death so as to overthrow the labor of my days and nights? Is it true that your father confessor enjoined you to become a martyr for the people? Ah! there are other martyrs in the world than those who pour out their blood in the market-place for the sake of the people. I would fain be a father and benefactor to you all. — But who can say he has fetched down a golden tablet from heaven, on which it stands inscribed that his work was the right one? Perhaps ye shall one day shout that this ninny, in whose veins my blood is disgraced, is the man whom ye needed for your salvation. But ye shall shout in vain. The life that I kindled I can also quench. Katerinushka, little mother, what have I done to be so lonely?"

With closed eyes he leaned his face on the czarina's arm and laughed sobbingly, so that one by one the guests at the table began to rise and steal aside behind the czarina. His laughter was so genial and warm that they had never heard anything like it unless in some honest hut in the country, but they knew from of old the mirth that brimmed up ever higher with despair and scorn, and they feared for their lives.

"Katerinushka, my child, wherever in all of Europe they strike a medal or print a pamphlet, there they dress me up as a fool. What have I done to be so lonely? There is a like lonely man, who is now gathering his troops in Sweden to lead them against the Norwegian mountains. Strange, we should have both come to the same thing by such different ways!—Why does the adjutant delay? I long to see whether among you all there is not *one* who is honest enough to show me openly whether he loves me or not. May he strike heartily!"

He raised his tear-stained, laughing face, but the czarina stroked his curly hair gently and caressingly, while in a thin voice, long since broken, she chanted to a folk tune:

The great, with their servants and guards to attend them,
Are lonely as beggars that roam on the moor;
But the humble—at twilight the angels befriend them
And lull with soft music the sons of the poor.

"I am concerned about Vyasemski, the adjutant. Is he a craven who has gone off because he dares not strike the czar? Or is he hesitating outside the door? Or perhaps—does he love me?"

Menshikoff, who had remained sitting, arose with his great powdered wig and his orders.

"In the old days, when I was only a confectioner's boy who carried my tarts about the streets of Moscow, I could make you merry, little father, when I talked. I could so dress up my stories that you imagined you saw horrible owls and owlets fluttering before you or absurd dwarfs walking on their hands. But we have become old; both you, my benefactor, and I. I must obey your imperial command."

He went out into the corridor in front of the room, and the czar called after him: "Why does the adjutant tarry, I say? Were his hands so unclean that he needed to wash them so long? I should like to see the water."

When Menshikoff came back, he carried a large tin basin half full of a red fluid that was like frothing wine.

"Your Adjutant Vyasemski is dead," said Menshikoff. "He washed his hands in his own heart's blood."

The czar again closed his eyes and leaned against the arm of the czarina. While she stroked his hair and combed it between her fingers, she heard him whisper: "He loved me not—he only feared—Katerinushka, little mother!"

The Dark Yule Service

IT was Christmas Eve. The parson's widow sat in the parsonage at Undenäs with the account of the deceased on her knee. Her bodice was made of his worn and much weathered cloak, she had tied his starched handkerchief about her head with a knot at the nape of the neck, and her thin fingers, blue with cold, lay stretched on the paper. In figure she was taller and leaner than other women, and every one hated and maligned her for her avarice and spitefulness. Even in good times no tallow candle had ever been lighted in the parsonage. She drove the servants from bed at three o'clock on winter nights, though they could not see by the scanty light of the torch or the fire, but sat down to yawn and gossip in the loft. In the middle of the road between the cow-house and the stable she would say to the man that he must hang his wooden shoes on his back and save them for Sunday, and if any one was condemned to penance, she was always supposed to be the secret informer.

It was already dusk, and through the panes, which were half covered with snow, she stared indivertibly at the shingled wooden church and the steeple. Beside her stood a man with a thick curled wig and a reddish but ever smiling face. It was the manager Trulsson from the mill below.

"Do you think he'll come?" she inquired anxiously. "He was my only man, and he has stayed away since he went into the city. Three days he has been gone. Thrashed he ought to be. Surely he was caught at the tavern on Monday and therefore taken as a soldier according to the new proclamation."

"I feared that it was going ill here in the house of sorrow," answered Trulsson in a friendly tone. "For that reason I rode up here. Don't complain, Mother Ingebritt, because at bottom there's not such a great difference between happiness and misfortune as we think. Both of them are what we make them. You should only see the fine old fellow, Soop, my gracious master, when he stands by the dinner-table in the hall, erect and without saying a word, counting up the great heaps of money for his yearly taxes. Six hundred dollars of silver coin in luxury taxes for the women's imported silks, sixty dollars for lace, forty for sable cloaks, twenty for special hats and clothes, four for tea and coffee, forty for the gilded fittings on the coach, forty for all the tobacco-smokings and such trumpery, parade tax and quota tax for property and dependents. Think of it, that the iron must be offered to the state, which has nothing to pay with, and that in all the mill there are scarcely three able-bodied men to send down to the forges! And yet old Soop stands there so grand and fine, shaking Görtz's copper idols out of his purses. You are too greedy

after this world's goods, Mother Ingebritt; that's
what everybody thinks."

"Poverty begets thrift," she muttered harshly.
"Never has such want come upon a people. We
have eaten bark bread since November, and in order
to support a dragoon, poor Vibelius himself went
out into the fields like a farm-servant, until he sank
down and gave up the ghost. I can hardly get a
pound of sugar for five dollars or a cask of herring
for fifty, and salt costs over a hundred. To-morrow
we have Christmas Service, but no tallow for a single
candle. We have no clergyman to read the Lord's
Word and no sexton. The horses are taken for the
baggage-train; and if the man does n't come back,
I 'm lost, for there stands the place without a man.
For God's mercy, tell me he 's coming!"

She pressed her brow to the panes, faltering and
irresolute.

"He 's coming," replied Trulsson. "I hear steps
out in the snow."

At the same moment the door was pushed open
with much clatter and noise. Several loud-mouthed
soldiers in tattered uniforms staggered across the
threshold, and behind them followed a crowd of
gaunt vagabonds, mostly young men and boys.
They were uncannily black and distorted in countenance from eating bark bread, and they had strips
of sheepskin tied around their legs and feet. She
recognized her servant in the hindmost youth, and

comprehended that he had been taken for a soldier and carried off with the rest.

"Serve up what the house has to offer!" commanded one of the soldiers, and blew on his stiffened hands.

"Here there's nothing, absolutely nothing," she answered without moving.

"What isn't offered must be taken. For seven hours we've wandered about in Tiveden Forest from one deserted farm to another."

Spurs and broadswords rang, voices murmured, and Mother Ingebritt swayed back and forward, and plucked with her hands at her apron. She gave her servant a questioning glance. For a long time he listened to the quarrel, stroking his neck with an awkward gesture.

Finally he looked down at the floor and uttered very softly: "You were always hard and stingy, mother. Therefore last summer I stole four loaves of black bread and hid them in the chest of drawers in the porch corridor. Those I'll divide with the others right before your eyes, because in such need there are no enemies."

The soldiers noisily snatched the bunches of keys from Mother Ingebritt's belt. Chests and cupboards were opened. Earthen bowls were filled with hidden delicacies, and amid swearing the soldiers thawed out a piece of ham, where the maggots lay frozen along the bone.

"Just be quiet, my good men!" admonished Trulsson in a fatherly and friendly way. "As the winter frost killed the maggots in the meat, so the misery that is now passing over our country is killing many evil maggots that were eating at our heart."

While he spoke he was looking at Mother Ingebritt, as though he had directed the words particularly at her, but she tried to silence him and looked away.

Then he spoke in a pastorly, sermonizing tone. With back to the fire, he stood in front of her in the middle of the room, while he folded his hands and continued:

"Just be quiet, my good men, and let us not eat without praying first. Such a night of misfortune as this is given men by Almighty God to make them good and great, and so that a little people may come to appear more beautiful and glorious in their poverty than all the others in their gilded splendor."

She went away to the opened cupboard and clattered the cups back and forward, so as to escape hearing him, but she turned toward him again.

"Trulsson, I thought you had a kindly disposition—"

"You rule with a tight hand in the cottage, mother, but no one can take our grace in bad part."

The wild lads ranged themselves along the wall and folded their hands.

Surveying Mother Ingebritt with his tranquil eyes and dwelling on every word, he began with a strong voice: "Our Father—"

She plucked painfully at her apron, trembled, and tried to look away, but with his gentleness he forced her to meet his look, and every time she breathed more heavily. When he came at last to the words: "Give us each day our daily bread," she involuntarily interrupted him.

"No more!" she muttered.

"What? Shall I not recite the Lord's Prayer?"

"Not to-night. To-morrow we'll recite it."

She caught him by the arm, and drew him with her into the entry. "You called me stingy and hard?" she inquired in a voice so remarkable that not her tongue but her very heart seemed to speak.

"I did."

"And you said that want such as this had come upon us to make us good and great?"

He nodded.

"Follow me, then!" she whispered, and they stepped out into the winter night.

The crust was so hard that it bore, and the stars flickered over the dark stretches, where no cattle lowed and no sheaf was set out for the sparrows. A thundering norther swept around the corners of the house. They pressed close along the walls of the cow-shed on account of the wind, and when they entered the wood, they held tight to the fir branches.

Terror has robbed her of her wits, thought he, and he called after her through his hand, but in the storm she did not comprehend his words. She only peered in front of her and kept on walking. He mistrusted that she had no good purpose and began to be afraid, but he was ashamed to leave a woman alone in the night, for he knew that wolves are more plentiful after men have become fewer.

Chilled through with cold and uneasiness, he hastened his steps, so as to seize her around the waist and hold her back. Then he saw that they were come to an abandoned and dilapidated house, whose proprietors had died in the plague and their son on the battlefield. The granary had collapsed into the snow-drifts, and the snow whirled between the slats of the house porch. In the wide-open doorway the windows of the opposite wall glistened through the empty rooms. Overcome with dread, he stood still.

Leaning against the cottage wall stood a frightful apparition, a gigantic shape like to a man wrapped in gray furs and with a great pointed crown full of snow. Was it the peasant that had died of the pest, who had risen from his hastily shovelled grave to keep Christmas in the house where in the days of Charles XI of blessed memory he had so often bidden the loving-cups be filled and the hurdy-gurdies resound?

Mother Ingebritt shook with apprehension, and pressing her hands to her eyes so as not to see, she sprang into the cottage.

The man's heart stood still, and he bent slowly forward toward the apparition. He saw that it was an elk, frozen to death. Led by the memory of other winter nights, when it had found shelter and radiating warmth by the same wall, it had leaned against the deserted dwelling, where no sleeper any longer breathed in the deep shutter-bed, and no embers glittered through the pane.

"God have mercy on you!" stammered Trulsson, and stepped into the room. "Not only men but even the beasts of the woods are perishing."

But Mother Ingebritt did not hear him. She had already lifted several boards from the floor, and in the pallid light of the snow had laid bare a chest, which was about half an arm's length across and two arm's lengths between the ends. The chest was painted blue with white scrolls and leaves, and it had handles of iron.

Mother Ingebritt dared not turn her back to the alcove and the empty shutter-bed, but always placed herself so that she had Trulsson close behind her. He still understood nothing, but when she grasped one handle, he grasped the other. Then, continually looking around them toward all the corners and recesses, they carried the chest out of the cottage and home toward the church. They set it down in the corridor of the church several paces within the porch.

"Go to the dwelling-house," said Mother Inge-britt, "and sit down at the table as host for my un-bidden guests! I myself must stand by the chest and ponder much and hard, for when we gather here early to-morrow, it's I whom God will likely choose to hold the Christmas Service."

He obeyed her and went across the churchyard to the parsonage, but he thought that misfortune had quenched her understanding and that next morning he should have to conduct her to an asy-lum.

When it was morning, and the storm had abated, no bells rang as heretofore, and no well-to-do par-ishioners came up on pack-saddles over the un-shovelled roads. From the mile-wide expanses of gloomy, dilapidated, and abandoned farmsteads was heard neither shout nor whip-crack. A couple of lonely torches shone between the trees, and a few women and infirm old men with crutches and canes assembled in the vestibule. Of other men there were none, and the church-goers were in all but twelve souls. The graves were more numerous than the mourners, and no Christmas Day had dawned amid deeper quiet.

They put out the torches under their snow-covered wooden shoes, and when they saw Mother Ingebritt sitting on the chest, but not a single can-

dle lighted, they saluted hesitatingly and wonderingly. When she remained sitting with her chin in
her hands without nodding or giving them a word,
they felt that they hated her more bitterly than ever.

Gradually now the drowsy guests from the parsonage assembled, but no ringing was heard across
the moors, because the steeple bells had long since
been cast into a field-piece that lay disabled and
silenced at the bottom of a bog in Ditmar. No pastor mounted to the pulpit. No sexton rapped with
his tuning-fork, but the servant-girl who had long
been performing his duties was already waiting at
the doorway.

Then Mother Ingebritt arose and brushed the
locks of hair from her forehead, but it was so dark
in the church that she felt with her hand to steady
herself against the pew-door. Neither the hanging
candelabrum nor the baptizing font could be discerned, neither paintings nor panelling. Only the
copper candlestick on the distant altar shone in the
snow-light.

"Yesterday," said she, "we closed our prayer with
the words: 'Give us this day our daily bread.'"
Thereupon she added softly and quietly: "Forgive
us our trespasses!"

At this moment a spectre-like, sallow little boy
came to the church threshold with a burning torch.
By its light she opened the chest and knelt before
it on the flagstones of the graves.

"Misfortune works wonders," she said, and it seemed to all in that dark Christmas Service that there was kindled over the corridor of the church a glow more bright than that from a hundred arches of the fairest wax candles.

Lifting out six silver cups and six silver spoons, she divided them evenly among the soldiers and their destitute fellows. She emptied out four big purses of fiat coins, and counted an equal number into each outstretched hand, so that none of those present was neglected, and in every apron she laid bread and salt and many finger-rings and other articles, until the chest was empty and the torch went out.

Fredrikshall

THE governors of the provinces now called the people together and counted out on the table fifty dollars to every one who volunteered as a cavalryman and a hundred to every one who became a foot-soldier. Many refractory men hewed off their fingers or cut themselves with knives so as to be incapable of war service, but these were sentenced to thirty lashes or were set to hard labor for life at Marstrand. Bands of deserters went through the country, quartering themselves by violence. When the peasant heard their voices at the road gate, he left his keys in the lock and hid himself under the hay bales or fled to the wilds with his household and cattle. In Stockholm the councillors barred themselves in their rooms to keep from being seen and interrogated. Inspectors, accompanied by guardsmen, roamed from port to port and broke into cellars and larders, and wolves even ventured in on the streets. There were no goods in the shops, no grain in the mills, no hands that raised a hammer, no happy voices, no cozy winter evenings around the home firesides.

Then the whole people shuddered with a premonition. At the church doors or in the barred rooms it was said that God, who had set the crown of martyrdom upon them, would soon let the thorn-spikes fall away and the leaves bud in the

green beauty of a new spring, and that the king
would now die. Day by day, folk awaited the tidings that he had fallen, wondering only that they
were delayed. All knew that he fought in single
combat at gates and fences like the meanest soldier.
Most people suspended their daily occupations,
and went about in fear and gloomy expectation.
An alderman in Stockholm was already lamenting
that he did not know where they would get mourning cloth and money for the funeral. Even Görtz
was lying sleepless one morning, when his servant
came in with wood for the stove. Sweden was like
the collapsing house of the king at Bender, but
over this burning city of ruin, where the lamentation died away into waiting silence, glittering plans
for the future harmony rose like meteors, of which
distant prodigies the soothsayers foretold that only
after hundreds of years would they be realized and
understood.

At this time there lived at Uppsala a begging
scholar, who wished to become a clergyman, but
could never succeed in anything but gambling and
fighting, or in making Swedish and Latin verses
at weddings and funerals. His name was Tolle
Orasson. His hands and feet had always been
too slender and delicate for his large stature, and
however much he starved, his beardless boy-face
always bloomed equally round and pink. He did
not want to harm any one, if only they let him live

as free as a bird, go his own ways, and sleep in peace o' mornings; but his comrades opined that he could not distinguish between good and evil.

One fine Sunday, when the recruiters began their hubbub in the town, he all at once became thoroughly pious and stuck himself away in a pew with the empty covers of his Latin grammar. It was in the Church of the Trinity. In the midst of the service the recruiters pressed in, threatening and clamoring, with a bunch of handcuffs on their shoulders, but Tolle Orasson bent over his empty book-covers. He swayed back and forward, singing with such devotion and fervor that nobody thought of seizing him, although he belonged precisely to the useless students who, according to the royal proclamation, were to be taken out for the army.

From that moment, however, he found it most advisable to hang his wallet on his back and go on adventures. He gazed about him with terror in the dear land of his fathers, which war and pestilence had so ravaged and transformed. Was this Sweden, the realm his fathers had made and guarded as the apple of their eye, the mighty empire of the north, beloved and feared? On the roads he came upon lamenting peasants, who were forced to convey their grain by long journeys to the headquarters in Norway or as far up as the redoubt of Järpe in Jämtland. Overturned loads and dead horses lay on every slope. Up in the deserted forest region

tattered vagabonds peeped from the cottage windows, and he always carried his money hidden in
the leg of his boot. Lined up on the grass plots
by the peasants' houses were settle-beds, wagons,
and domestic animals, and amid weeping and shouting the thump of the auctioneer's mallet rang on
the door-jamb. In the kitchens of the gentry the
servants related that the master and mistress had
buried their silver, because Görtz had commanded
that not only all genuine money but also all utensils of precious metal should be delivered up in
return for the fiat money, so that the king got the
entire property of his subjects. Tolle Orasson
found out that not even the princess at Stockholm
had enough silver for her table, and that the king
himself ate off of sheet iron. In the abandoned
smithies, outside some of which the streams rushed
unimpeded to the ocean past standing wheels and
open sluice-gates, he spoke with the single remaining smith, who was too old and infirm for army
life. There he came to know that, if any iron was
forged, it had to be stored at once in the government warehouse against the payment of certain
bags of fiat coin. For preference, however, he sat
and warmed himself in the parsonages, where his
Bible learning and Latin caused him to be well regarded, and the pastor would sometimes converse
with him until daybreak. There it was whispered
that there was a question of taking the appropri-

ations for the school and the poor; yes, even the very bank; and that there were no pens and paper, but all official work had to be suspended, if the gentlemen were not willing to dip their fingers into the ink-horn and write on the bare table. One grizzled parson told him that the governors of the provinces had been deposed or put under supervisors, so that nobody knew any more which of them should command or obey. The old man described how he himself had had to pawn his Bible and surplice and pour small-beer into the Communion chalice.

After this fashion Tolle Orasson wandered from district to district, and sometimes earned a copper for conveying letters and official reports. The postmen, it seemed, had been ordered to the army, and the unruly innkeepers became postmasters. These did not understand their business, but mothers and orphans daily thronged about them in vain, crying for letters from their relatives in the wilds and mines of Siberia. In the midst of grumbling peasants in the church of Slätthög he got the privilege of running his fingers over one of the sultan's gold-embroidered coats of honor, which hung there as an altar-cloth. In the town of Kalmar he became sworn brother to Artillerist Edstedt, who had just married a servant-girl, but who himself was no man but a Miss Stolhammar in disguise. At Visingsö he diced with the ragged Russian prisoners; in Karlshamn he tussled

with Polacks, Armenians, and Jews, and twitched the
turban tassels of the solemn Turkish creditors.
He even beguiled them into drinking wine, but
thereupon shattered the defiled glass, so that the
stone pavement resounded. In Lund he listened
among the armed students to the rebellious talk of
Professor Ihre, and shot at Professor Rydelius,
who wanted to allay the tumult. After roaming half
around the kingdom, he was finally standing one
evening in Göteborg, where during his journey the
king had been received as guest by the pirate Gatenhjelm in his house on Stigberg Square. Dusty
and athirst, Tolle Orasson sat him down in Dorotea
Ek's coffee house, where the loudly weeping and
guffawing citizens embraced one another and related that the terrible Madagascar pirates were now
to have permission to come with sixty richly laden
privateers and settle in the city to improve trade
conditions.

Then he could no longer keep his tongue between his teeth but let his light shine, relating the
experiences and adventures of his journey both in
Swedish and in Latin. Soon he noticed that two
men, who had sat next him with the collars of their
cloaks turned up, were themselves silent in order
to listen to his talk, and this made him even more
communicative.

"The Swedes are going to feel the iron glove as
never before since heathen days," he said, survey-

ing his shining nails. "The king has carried his sword against nation after nation, and now he is turning it against his own. Could it possibly end otherwise? But dark forebodings are being whispered about in the land. He leaves no son behind him. What indeed would such a man want with a son? In the councillors' desk there lies already the outline of an English constitution. Never shall we bear from another what we have now voluntarily endured. Perhaps to-morrow — perhaps this evening, while we converse here — a weary soldier is sitting before a heap of embers, melting lead in a casting-ladle. Perhaps at this very moment he holds in the bullet-shears the heavy drop that shall put to sleep forever the greatest among heroes."

A merchant, already weighed down by years, with the whitest of hair and the most melancholy eyes, tapped him on the hand.

"We human beings judge everything according to the pain in our own wounds, but now let an old man speak! Even if our hard, iron-souled king had never been born, our neighbors, who are ever growing stronger, would none the less have begun to dismember the Swedish Empire. Slowly, year by year and day by day, our children and children's children would have compromised and been humiliated and given up province after province. There would never have been quiet, and yet never glory either. It's a stupid spectacle to see a bound lion

whose blood drips away in little thimblefuls. So I'd
rather once for all see the flame in the clouds and
a man in front of us. When did he order us to
offer more than he has offered? Has n't he hun-
gered, has n't he been cold? And now there spreads
over us the foreboding that he shall also fall with
us."

Tolle Orasson changed his tone. He did not wish
to dissemble, but it became even more firmly fixed
in his mind that the man who had spoken last was
right.

"If I did n't value freedom and a good bed, I
could steal away after the king to press my lips to
his footprints in the Norwegian snow. Soon it may
be too late and the bullet be cast—"

At the moment he uttered these words, the two
men who had sat next him rose at a secret mutual
sign, and his fear of a soldier's coat was so great that
he grew pale, for he noticed shining brass buttons
under their cloaks.

"My fine lad!" they cried at his ear, and led him
out by both arms as a prisoner. "If you can talk so
elegantly, it won't be much for you to stand near
where the bullets whistle. We 've now got a fat bird
on our twig. We are recruiters, we, monsieur! Do
you understand? And now, march to Norway!"

"All my days I 've longed for nothing else than
to become a warrior," he answered at once, with such
a gentle and friendly firmness that even he himself

believed his words. "Put your pretty recruiting penny in my hat!"

So at last he had to put on the blue coat for which he had entertained such fear, and every day he experienced new and unlooked-for adventures in the midst of the land where of old the plough had peacefully cut its furrow in the earth. Scarcely had he gone a short way beyond Strömstad, when he caught sight of great galleys on the dry ground. He himself was yoked to the bow with peasants and horses and oxen to drag the vessels two and a half miles farther over the promontory to Idefjord. Inch by inch the ship was pulled over corduroy roads and heaps of twigs; by night in the light of pine torches, and by day in the heat of the July sun. A little man in a coat of lilac satin and a bushy wig, with broad gold buckles on his shoes, went back and forth among the men to encourage them. It was Emanuel Swedenborg, for Polhem had commissioned him to execute this unusual task.

When he caught sight of Tolle Orasson, he shaded his weak eyes with his hand and said: "That fellow has the most robust and blooming health I've seen in many years. My worthy corporals, don't go too hard with the man, for I see well that he has not full strength in his limbs!"

That was the first word of sympathy that Tolle Orasson had heard since he had clinked glasses with his comrades at Uppsala, and he was straightway impelled, with tears in his eyes, to stick out his chubby hand and beg.

"I am an unlucky wretch," he whispered in a mixture of Swedish and the most scholarly Latin, "and I shall bless and thank you for a single pinch of snuff."

"Snuff is one thing and serving the king is another," answered Swedenborg seriously, and went off. But the very same evening, when the relief was blown, he came up with his snuff-horn.

"Take the whole snuff-horn, keep it, and say no more about it!" he whispered, and was off again like a wanderer suddenly met on the road.

People are good, Tolle Orasson thought at once, and made an effort to come to himself in his loneliness. Soon, however, he used up the last copper he had saved and all the contents of the snuff-horn in bribing his way to an occasional extra hour's sleep in the morning. He was then immediately of the opinion that people were bad.

When the last ship, with her gilded god of victory at the prow, finally glided out over the dark waters of Idefjord, he was again ordered to march. Many foreign and native officers gradually united themselves to the band, and the long march of the country's last conscripts went from farm to farm.

One noon at a posting-station it happened that Tolle Orasson was sitting asleep behind a wagon-shed with his hat on his knee. When the drum rolled, and he awoke, a bright rix-dollar of hard money lay in his hat on a piece of folded paper.

It was an unexpected sight, and he rubbed his eyes and wondered whether he was dreaming. He smote the coin with his knuckle and weighed it in his hand. Finally he unfolded the paper and read:

"In Tistedahl by the miller's Cottage stands a weeping birch called the Candlestick, because it has three arms on one trunk. If His Royal Majesty falls before the Enemy's Shot, you will on that same night bear witness to the Wonder that a Purse with 50 Ducats lies in the earth close to the Candlestick."

"Some foreign devil has written that Swedish," burst out Tolle Orasson, almost wailing and moaning, as he tore the paper into little bits and strewed them about him. He put earth on them with his foot and trampled them down. Then he stuck the rix-dollar into his trousers pocket in order to go to the others, but hardly had he taken a couple of steps, before he snatched out the coin again, as if it had burned his body and clothing. He threw it far away from him into the bog.

When he had tied his baggage on his back, he began to march again with his usual boyish smile, as if much in the world was quite wonderful and yet of no consequence at all; but next night he dreamed about the white birch with the three uplifted arms.

The wooded mountain ridges became ever more
enveloped in clouds, the roads ever steeper, the
sutler's pots ever emptier, but no hardships could
take away the flesh from Tolle Orasson's round
cheeks and limbs. The boots fell in pieces from his
feet, and the regulation trousers, which had been
cut out for a starving army, were so inadequate for
him that he had to fasten them together at the
belt with a string. His well-conditioned and shining
forehead irritated his emaciated comrades so that
they vowed to thrash him, but because he was also
a head taller than any one else, no one finally dared
come too near him.

Although he betrayed no sign, he brooded from
morning to late at night over the strange writing.
Why did evil men wish to choose just him as their
tool? He could think of nothing else. When at last
the dusty band marched in among the tents and
brushwood huts of the headquarters at Tistedal, he
came to a halt, and without any longer knowing
what he did, pointed to a leafless weeping birch.

"The birch, there's the birch! That's the Candlestick! I'm sure— it must be called that."

"Here you're to be quiet and obey," returned
the corporal, and stationed him directly in the line
as fugleman to be inspected.

When the corporal thereupon gripped him by
the arm, he felt that the sinews were soft and that
the tall recruit swayed powerlessly in his grasp.

"This fellow we'd be better without," averred the corporal. "He's all soft and tender."

.   .   .   .

One November day several detachments of troops made a halt in a mountain pass, and though the clock only pointed to three, twilight prevailed. Tanned by the sun of the steppes, with a Turkish tobacco pouch at his breast, many a veteran officer wondered at the wintry realm into whose wooded wildernesses the army now marched to new adventures. Captured sharp-shooters told wild stories of trolls and shrieks of wood fays; and women with flaxen hair, as tall as men, came to the camp-fires by night and cut down the wearied and sleeping Swedes with their axes.

It was snowing, and far below the ravine the sun cast a yellow light over the stunted woods and overhanging crags of the mountain wall.

The army consisted of pallid fifteen-year-olds, of half-grown boys, who stood with their weapons in the drift.

The little West Gotlanders, with their sharp noses and shifting eyes, whispered to one another: "The king will probably say that, if we don't want to starve, we can dig food from the Norway mountains."

"We may as well dig, then," answered the Smålanders in mournful, long-drawn accents.

The Dalecarlians and Bohuslanders propped themselves sullenly on their musket-barrels, but the battalions of Södermanland began to grumble. Then Colonel Rutger Fuchs reined up his horse and came to a stand before the front ranks. One foot was askew in the stirrup, for at Gadebusch, where he was carried from the field, his leg had been shattered by a bullet.

"For shame, you Söderman fellows!" he cried in his Scanian dialect. "If you don't get plums in your cake, you butter boys, you begin at once to grumble. I hear you are all down-hearted, but now it's your duty to bear up bravely, for I tell you that never again in time will Swedish men get to serve such a hero as our royal master, and gladly would I shed my blood for him. Look at me! What am I called? Come, out with it!"

"Rika Fuchs," answered all the soldiers with one mouth, and their expression brightened.

"That's correct. All my days I've been called Rika Fuchs. Well, now, where are Fuchs's riches? He who can step forward and answer gets two farthings."

No one dared to advance.

Then Rika Fuchs drew his pocket-book from his breast, opened it, and turned the leaves, while he kept up the following discourse:

"What the devil is this talk of being rich? It's a matter of book-keeping, lads. Do you think,

maybe, that all property pays interest? Well, try
it! Listen to what I read. Debts: nil. That's the
first half of Fuchs's riches. Here we have the departed Schlippenbach's dressing-down. Have you
quite forgot the departed Schlippenbach, your former colonel, who bequeathed to me both his dressing-gown and his regiment, the two dearest possessions he had in this world? That dressing-gown
is so precious to me that I should n't be willing to
sell it for less than five thousand rix-dollars. It is
therefore worth exactly that sum to me. Listen,
furthermore! Assets:

The departed Schlippenbach's dressing-gown, five
thousand rix-dollars.

The Södermanland regiment, ten thousand rix-
dollars.

My beloved wife Greta at home, seventy thousand
rix-dollars.

A cur from Holstein, a thousand rix-dollars.

My royal master's favor, eighty thousand rix-
dollars.

The tavern, Golden Ass, two thousand rix-dollars.

Deuce take me if that is n't all reckoned too low,
but then, too, it's all I have in life. Well, what is
the tavern of the Golden Ass, anyhow?"

"That's the gracious colonel's sackcloth tent,"
murmured all the soldiers confusedly.

"Just so, right! At that tavern any one whoso-

ever may breakfast gratis, for there is not a crumb
to get. Now let us add! Total assets, one hundred
and sixty-eight thousand rix-dollars. But as the nil
for debts is the half of my riches, that half of my
wealth must also then be a hundred and sixty-eight
thousand rix-dollars, too. Accordingly and demon-
strably, I have all together three hundred and thirty-
six thousand rix-dollars. Look you, boys, that 's
what Görtz calls finance; and such an art is useful
to master, you understand. Do you but learn book-
keeping and to set a right value on everything, and
you 'll get to see that you are finely rich and don't
need to hang your head, even if your belly cries out."

"Hurrah, hurrah for Rika Fuchs!" rang along
the line. But at the same moment all swords flew
from their scabbards, muskets were presented, and
drums thundered. In the gleam of the mountain
range strode forward the tall, magnified shadow of
a limping man, with a round fur cap on his head
and a gnarled stick in his hand.

It was the king.

He walked between the pines, followed by dragoons who came in a long line with broadswords
drawn, leading their horses. He himself was first,
and tramped the path in the snow. His scarred and
compressed features had become darkened by sun
and frost with the years, and between his eyebrows
lay a deep furrow. When he stuck the fur cap
under his arm and answered the salutes of the men

in all directions, the snow fell on the bald crown of his head. Gradually the generals collected about him, and the guardsmen cut off a few fir boughs with their swords and spread them on the ground. The whole time he stood bare-headed in the snow-storm, and the grizzled wisps of hair brushed back along his temples were like a garland of frosted leaves. He ordered the soldiers to stack their muskets and light fires of branches, but the musicians were placed by the cliff-wall with orders to play until sunset.

"These Norway goats are a merry set to butt against," said the king. "Such men as their Kruse and Kolbjörnsen ought to be buried in gold coffins when they fall."

Field Marshal Mörner answered: "We have just captured some Norwegian spies who were lying hid in the bushes here to shoot Your Majesty. Shall we string them up?"

"No. Give each of them a ducat for his wasted time and tell them not to bungle in the soldiers profession any more."

Mörner lowered his voice. "There are, besides, other more highly trusted bush-rangers. I have just got from Provost Brenner a new letter of accusation as to secret conspiracies against your crown and life. If one might believe him, there are dangerous enemies standing here even now scarcely five yards away."

"They may stand, then, unless they choose to sit. War days are no time to investigate."

Mörner's dwarf, Luxemburg, now advanced with a water-flask. When the king had drunk, he handed the dwarf his juniper staff, which was worn shiny, as if to arm the little man, while he said to him: "A Turk predicted that I must beware of fools. You can try now whether I am afraid."

Luxemburg took the staff and made as if to twang it like a guitar, while he struck up a French love-song.

Mörner stepped near to the king, and whispered behind his hat, "The men are starving."

"A full soldier is slow at his duty."

"But a dead-hungry soldier drops his musket."

"If one melts snow, it becomes water. If one chews on a fir twig, hunger can be much dulled for a long while."

"The people we at least have under our eyes— but the brains at home—They say the parsons in the pulpits are openly calling down vengeance from heaven. They believe that, after God has smitten the Swedes and given a sign that their empire must be divided, Your Majesty is fighting solely for your own honor."

"Have their honor and mine become two separate things? They were insolent, and I answered. I will force them to hold out to the uttermost. Is it not as much for their own sakes as for mine?

They say that I tempt God. I answer that I follow Him. That is my royal word! In the name of righteousness, that is my vow! Who is the arbiter?"

With these words the king put on the fur cap, turned up his cape-collar, and laid himself down calmly to sleep on the fir boughs, as if no enemy had existed in the world.

Düker energetically shouted his commands to the officers. Mörner dozed as he stood leaning against a Scotch pine, without being able to listen further to little Cronstedt's quips; and the cunning Stjernroos, who had been out spying, came disguised in a sheepskin jacket and wooden shoes with a keg on his back. The king himself was already sleeping, motionless, without a thought of letters and menaces. He had entrusted himself to his soldiers.

But there were two eyes that followed him. Tolle Orasson, who on the preceding day had been assigned to the Södermanland regiment as corporal and leader of the wood-choppers, could not force himself to look away from the sleeper. The words of Rika Fuchs still lay in his heart.

I ought to keep an account book, too, maybe, he thought. Fifty ducats in the earth by the Candlestick Birch!

With his clear and friendly eyes he stared off at the king so fixedly that he did not notice how Rika Fuchs came close up to him.

"What ails you?" said Fuchs, clapping him heartily on the shoulder. "Here's a communication for Tistedal, since we are now to go up to the fortress of Fredriksten and open fire. Take two men along and a bundle of torches to light you — and run fast! A man with such a splendid food supply under his skin does n't need either to bivouac or eat oftener than every third night, if he only understands rightly how to husband God's gifts."

Tolle Orasson now betook himself off into the woods with two soldiers, but still when he was a long way off among the firs, he turned and looked at the king.

At daybreak, when he came to the village of Tistedal, he stood under the Candlestick Birch, and stuck the last torch into the earth with the burning end down.

"I have wandered about widely to study and teach," he said to the soldiers. "I have met both good and evil men. It may be, too, that beasts and trees can be good and evil. At every noon rest, when I 've been out with the wood-choppers, I 've laid me down to sleep here, but never got a wink of sleep. There 's a curse on this tree. Look! I 've driven an axe into one of the boughs up there. There will be a morning when I 'll set that axe to its root."

He remained standing while he surveyed the expiring torch.

"Good and evil men, I said.—Never did I see a more glorious man than our great king, but the years make him ever stricter and harder. He has tenderness for the wailing of neither beast nor man. Even a cry of agony cannot induce him to turn his head. His winter is come, with its gradual death. How we should have wept for him, if he had chanced to fall in his youthful years! No age would have acclaimed a greater or purer name than his. See that torch, how slowly it's dying, how it reeks and poisons the air with its stench of burning! Why not rather with a little motion of the hand press it deep down, quickly, without hesitation—so that it goes into the earth while it is still glowing brightly?"

The soldiers did not understand him, but merely answered, "May no evil befall our beloved lord and king!"

He took a couple of steps to follow them, but the Candlestick Birch spread its limbs above him imploringly, and he remained standing and talking to himself.

"Who is thinking of evil? Tolle Orasson takes his musket, he the despised, the outcast, who has had to go from farm to farm and beg for charity bread. He takes his musket and lays his finger on the trigger. That shot will call whole peoples to reconciliation. Even if all the cannon of Fredriksten thunder that night, no one will hear them. The

soldiers will think that it 's as quiet as on a distant,
frozen mountain lake. They will only hear the
single shot. It will echo from night to night as long
as men live on the earth. When I have dug up the
fifty ducats, I will go forward to the generals, throw
all the gold-pieces over their hats and wigs, and say:
'Bring out your handcuffs, good sirs! There 's
drink money for your pains. Drink my health in
real wine! It is I who have shot His Royal Majesty. Of you nobody will speak, but as long as *his*
name lives, so long will mine live.' And so the
handcuffs will be screwed on. I shall be set on the
tumbrel and drive up the Götgata at Stockholm,
but there will not be a window, a doorstep, a roof,
that will not be black with eager folk who want to
see Tolle Orasson. And at the gentlemen's houses
where I 've had to eat at the kitchen table, and at
the parsonages where I 've had to bow for a plate
of beer-soup, it will be: 'In that chair Tolle Orasson sat, that was the pipe Tolle Orasson smoked,
on that door-knob he held the finger that fired the
shot.' The students of Uppsala, the proud, the false
friends, who finally considered themselves too good
to house me over a rainy night—they will become
old, their heads will grow white, but they will never
weary of saying: 'We knew Tolle Orasson, we
called him by his first name.' So it will always be.
As often as a coach drives into Stockholm Town,
one gentleman will point through the window

and say: 'There's the gallows!' There may be a
hundred executed men in the graveyard, but he'll
only say: 'There lies Tolle Orasson, the miserable
wretch!' And then the other gentlemen will answer:
'The liberator of his people!'"

Tolle Orasson raised his arms to support himself, but at the same moment he laid his hand on
the smooth, cold bark, he snatched it back with a
suppressed cry of terror.

The soldiers stopped and turned around. He motioned them to go on and followed them, but he
had grown as pale as a corpse.

.   .   .   .

By a trench in front of the fortress on the mountain ridge the king had had built for himself a hut
of boards; and thither a bed, table, and chair had
been brought. No soldiers were posted with loaded
muskets at the door, and the adjutant of the watch
was often sent away on various errands. The king
even overcame his former nervousness in the solitude of night and no longer allowed any page to
sleep by his bed. Wearied by the exertions of the
day, he sometimes slept on the rampart between
the enemy's cannon and the soldiers working in
the trench. Any one might have stolen out in the
dark and extinguished his life with a sword-thrust.
The sleepless and tortured nights in the Ukraine
after the first crushing blows of adversity remained

only as scars in the lines between his eyebrows.
Had he not hardened his soul in misfortunes, as
he had his body in privations? He never brooded
a minute on danger, but he knew that its heavy
cloud hung closer than ever above his head, and
this filled him with the confident repose of his vanished youth. His voice had grown hard, but a mas-
terful composure kindled its rejuvenating gleam in
his eyes. All, all the gloom that misery and defeat
concealed rose around him, and, propped on his
juniper staff and often cursing impatiently, he directed the soldiers' work.

Occasionally he surveyed the heavens and
searched out the constellations he knew, but when
the mist had spread, and darkness fell deeper, he
sometimes shut his eyes and counted on his fingers:
"Three hundred, three hundred and eighty-five,
ninety, ninety-four, four hundred thousand rix-
dollars. Will Görtz really be able to collect as much
by December? How, indeed, can the army be kept
up otherwise? And would Görtz be able to get here
within two days? Was it not his expected arrival
that spread such unrest in the camp? What, though,
is to be done about it now?"

The king knew no scruples, for he had become
a highwayman who despised money and property.
Had not the Swedes called him a madman and
reached their hands toward his crown? Ah well, he
forgave it them, since he had given them their an-

swer, but he wanted to hold them together to the last, even if house and foundation should burn. Was not that the duty, was not that the divine mission, he had sworn in his soul to fulfil? It was no time now for ease-lovers, no matter who might prefer to be at home in a shutter-bed. And Görtz's proclamation, which let his royal name be flaunted under perjuries about peace and the good of his subjects? Where in his campaigns had he ever seen princes act otherwise in time of necessity? And yet had they not been called wise and good as long as they succeeded? When the storm was over, he would hold an inquiry and straighten things out. Severity he had commanded, never conscious dishonesty. The matter was now to conquer the fortress of Fredriksten, which, standing before him on the mountain ridge with its gray walls and pointed battlements, barred the road up to Norway. Had they not already taken the outwork of Gyldenlöw with sword in hand?

With sword in hand! He shut his eyes, as he used often to do when he was unseen, and softly repeated the words. "They think that I tempt Thee, O eternal, wondrous God, Holy Spirit, my delight, my joy, my refreshment! They ever say: 'Stand halfway up, where we stand, otherwise you are presumptuous; sit down when we grow weary, otherwise we shall no longer call you our Gideon.' Thou, who art the arbiter, before Thee I humble myself in my need—I, a contrite sinner. If I have gone astray on the earth, strike me down dead!"

"The king has gone to sleep at his post," said the soldiers, when they saw him with head sunk and hat pulled down.

He heard them, looked up, and answered: "Not yet."

On the first Sunday in Advent the king mounted his horse and rode down through the mist to the miller's cottage at Tistedal. He was heavy at heart, and to overcome his melancholy he sat on a bench by the fire and looked over his papers. They were petitions and old letters and cancelled accounts from as far back as his sojourn at Lund. His eyes at last paused at two half-sheets, which were fastened together with a brass pin and written full in his own almost illegible hand. He read:

Anthropologia Physica. The natural tendency of all living things is that which is called passion, or the enjoyment of pleasure. Pleasure is of two sorts, namely, corporeal or spiritual pleasure. That is called spiritual pleasure wherein the body may have no part. But that is called corporeal pleasure which the body feels alike with the soul. The three parts of the body are: the material structure, wherethrough the form of the body with its outer and inner parts is shaped; the liquid matter, which consists of the blood with what thereto appertains; and the material *spiritus*

or breath, which is, as it were, the finest part of the
material being, is the strength and life of the very
blood, and receives life and feeling from the vital
breath or soul, while it conveys this throughout the
entire body. It also dies of itself, as soon as any
body or limb dies. — The reason why the soul par-
ticipates in both sorts of pleasure and that the body
only feels the pleasures of the flesh is this: that life
is in reality a property of the soul, which the body,
being itself a dead essence, receives through the
action of the spirit. — That which is commonly
reckoned under the name of the five senses consists
only in one, which is called feeling and is an effect
of the spirit, and which (according to the nature of
each and every one's bodily structure) exhibits itself
in five sorts of ways. . . .

He rose from the bench and grasped the incom-
ing Field Marshal Mörner by the belt. "If Mörner
were not as bad a philosopher as he is a good econo-
mist, he should here get a hard nut to crack. No,
don't read the writing — that is only some nonsense
I put together one evening down at Lund. I always
observe that when after an interval I see again a fab-
ric of thought which I endeavored to build, I enjoy
disguising myself as an enemy and storming my own
redoubt myself. Does the pleasure of thought lie in
the mere fighting?"
Mörner answered: "Your Majesty is a hard du-

elist in learned disputations, and never do I hear my gracious lord so well spoken as in such combats, but I cannot offer my sword-point as could the departed Grothusen."

He unbuttoned his coat hastily, and handed the king several sealed letters. "Bethink, Your Majesty, that even the stupidest accusation *may* be true and *may* strike the scythe from the hand of Death for many years."

The king knew beforehand these communications in printed characters without signature, which blackened those nearest him and foretold a sudden death. The threat of death alarmed him no more than the whine of a bullet. Had he not since his very boyhood days wakened nearly every morning prepared to lie on the field among the fallen before dark? He threw the three letters into the fire unopened, one by one, and stood in the lowly miller's cottage as tranquil as if his last army of tired and starved youths had brought all the crowns of Europe with them on a baggage-wagon.

"Answer me frankly!" he said after a short silence. "On how many may I still depend? I don't mean in an engagement, but if everything goes against us?"

"Must I answer? Is it a command?"

"Yes. On how many may I still depend?"

"On none."

The drums rumbled in front of the cottage, where

the soldiers were marching up for divine service, and Hultman, entering, said, " I have to inform you humbly that morning service is now to begin. The text for the day treats of our Lord Jesus Christ's entry into Jerusalem."

The king now washed off all the grime from his face and hands, besides which he put on brand-new clothes of blue broadcloth and new yellow gloves of elk-skin. While his hair was powdered by Hultman so that it became white as an old man's, he supported one foot on the wood in the fire and said very softly, as if mainly to himself: " That text is very dear to me. — But the people spread out their garments on the way, and others cut branches of trees and strewed them in the way. And the people, both they which went before him and they which followed after, cried out, saying, Hosanna to the son of David! Blessed be he that cometh in the name of the Lord! Hosanna in the highest!"

"Yes, yes, most gracious lord," answered Hultman almost in a whisper. "So, too, will the saints cry whenever a righteous hero of God rides into the heavenly Salem."

The king then turned from the fire and went out to the troops. With bared head he took his place under the Candlestick Birch. The soldiers, who were accustomed to love his juniper staff and stained uniform, hardly recognized him.

He spent all day in the camp, and only after

evensong, when the mist began to descend, did he
ride his horse, Engländer, up the woody ridge to
the hut of boards by the trenches.

Tolle Orasson and his soldiers worked in the
outermost trench. Commanded by the Frenchman
Maigret, the Swedes crawled forward with their
spades, rolling fagots and gabions in front of them
step by step as a protection against the shot from
the fortress. The echo of the enemy's firing thundered in the mountain like the clatter of bolts and
bars, like the blows of clubs upon iron doors to
subterranean dungeons and vaults.

In order to direct their fire and protect themselves against surprise, the garrison set out long
stakes with burning hoops of pitch, and the fire-balls
that were hurled about cast their sudden light over
the crags. Fire and smoke spurted from the battlements of Fredriksten, and above the turf-covered
Swedish rampart Tolle Orasson recognized the
king's large hat and small head.

Hidden in shadow down in the trench, he pulled
a fallen comrade's musket to him and, stooping,
went back for some distance toward the rampart
of earth. Only when he had come so near that he
heard the king's words to the officers who stood
in the ditch on the other side of the rampart, did
he make a standstill.

Wonderful! he thought. Here in the approaches
many soldiers fall nearly every night. Whence, then,

comes the power to compel hundreds of men to stand and fall here without daring to shout to one another the simple three words — We won't obey?

He wanted to kneel and pray heaven for forgiveness and to persuade himself that his deed was righteous, but he could not. He did not know what he himself wished, and if a child had called to him to throw down the musket, he would have obeyed and commended the advice. But no one addressed him, and no one saw him, so that he feared only to delay, to prolong his own anxious uncertainty. He cocked the musket. He laid it to his eye. He sighted at the man for whom he had seen his countrymen fall and bleed submissively — but his finger lay trembling and paralyzed on the trigger.

Steps approached. It was the gray-haired Hultman, who in buckle shoes and white stockings, his hat respectfully stuck under his arm, was coming over the rocks amid the whistling bullets. In front of him he bore, covered with a napkin, the pewter bowl which contained the king's supper. As soon as he had come up to the rampart, he spread the napkin over his hat and then placed the bowl on top while he offered it to the king, who ate standing and every now and then took his faithful servant by the coat buttons.

Tolle Orasson lowered his musket and heard him say, "Hultman is beginning to get as stiff in his gait as Brandklipparen was in his last days. But no one has more faithfully followed me wherever I went, and therefore I nominate him to the place of chief cook. With the years we get ever further away from the good men of old times."

"God, merciful God!" muttered Tolle Orasson, swaying back and forth with his musket in his grasp.

He saw how Hultman went his way again through the rain of shot, and the king leaned over the rampart with his chin supported on his left hand. The moon, which was at the full, now rose large and bright above the pine woods.

Nearby Swedish, German, Italian, and French officers conversed in their various languages, planning how they might be able to lure the king down from his exposed position. Maigret, who had also joined them by now, plucked him gently by the cloak and said: "This is no place for Your Majesty. Canister and musket-balls have no more respect for a king than for the meanest soldier."

Then Tolle Orasson once more lifted his musket in both hands.

He threw it on the ground so that it went off, and the report was lost in the crash of the enemy's fire.

"Never," he stammered, "never! A Swedish-born man can never do it, though fifty ducats awaited him under every birch in Norway. Better desert or fall one's self. What do I care for the ducats? It was his *life* I wanted to take—and I can't do it. I should never be able to do it, until I shut my eyes. Isn't there any foreign marksman that can shoot a king blindfold?"

Tolle Orasson did not notice that the moon was already shining into the trench and threw his own shadow with its thin limbs and smiling boy's cheeks high up on the slope of the rampart.

"What are you doing here, my lad?" asked the king. "Go forward, straight forward toward the enemy!"

Tolle Orasson gave a start, turned on his heel, and began to march ahead toward the fortress. Behind him he heard the officers still urging the king to step down.

The king answered, "Have no fear!"

Then, without knowing any more what he was doing, Tolle Orasson grasped the crown of his hat and began to leap over gabions and fagots straight onward toward the enemy, always onward. Many Swedish soldiers, who saw him, rose to follow and desert. He stood and struck at them with his hand, and every time he turned, he recognized the king on the rampart. Why did he never take a spade and start to dig? That, to be sure, was what the king had meant. Instead he ran ever more violently and blindly, and at last he no longer knew whether he did so out of obedience or to desert. He took shelter behind stumps and in clefts, but he kept always

getting nearer to the fortress. His soft limbs already
bled from three wounds, yet he did not heed the
warm drops that ran down under his glove, but recited prayers and psalms, calling himself an evil-
doer eternally lost, who had been meditating a way
to sell his soul.

He came to a shattered outwork of small size,
which seemed to be abandoned; but when he heard
voices of Norwegian soldiers, he hid himself in
among the gabions.

A few paces from him, on splintered wheels,
stood a field-piece, red-brown with rust, which was
aimed at the king's rampart. It was loaded with
gravel and old iron slugs. In it were corroded musket-balls, which a hundred years back a drunken
pirate had shaped in his bullet-scissors, while he
hummed a bawdy song for his trollop. In it were
twisted keys and nails, which had long since fallen
from a peasant's barn, and farthest inside lay a
bent clapper, which had once rung in a cowbell on
the sunny mountain top to the call of the milk-
maids.

Long, broken clouds hurried white across the
moon, and Tolle Orasson lay in among the gabions,
bleeding and with folded hands.

"This is a night," he stammered, "when heaven
stands wide open, and God surveys the earth with
such deep thoughts that men feel His gaze. They
may flee away, they may hide themselves, they may

be wretches such as I or leaders of armies, yet they perceive His glance. A hero—what is a hero? He is constancy to the end; constancy toward adversaries, toward friends. But Thou there above, Thou art the avenger both of Thyself and of men; and when the hour-glass of Thy mercy is run out, Thou raisest Thy finger in omnipotence, and the hero bows his head to the earth—and lies reconciled."

Tolle Orasson bent aside the withes of the nearest gabion and heard the Norwegian corporal talk with the soldiers.

"Boys, there 's no use wasting men and artillery on this entrenchment; but seeing the old field-piece is too rickety to be dragged hence, the commandant has ordered me to fire it before we go. The shot may very well do the Swedes some harm still, if the gun does n't burst all to bits."

While he spoke, he carefully laid the slow-match on the field-piece, and, followed by his men, turned thereupon to the fortress with brisk steps—and singing.

Tolle Orasson followed the yellowish flame of the match with his eye, as it coiled ever nearer to the touch-hole. He thrust aside fagots and sacks of earth to burst his way through and pluck away the match, and he spoke aloud as if to the night: "I wanted to kill the man—and now I want to save him, only because I have just seen him and heard him speak. It 's so, then, that he makes us all his servants with a look. My wit is going out, and I can think no more."

He hewed apart the withes with his clenched hand, but the palisade barred him out, and all the time he saw the flame at the touch-hole. Sometimes it dwindled away and was nearly blown out, but then it leaped up again, bright and large.

That was a sign, Tolle Orasson thought, that men should try no more to act that night, and he stepped down into the clefts that descended toward the valley and the black chimneys of the burned town of Fredrikshall. Even at that distance he saw the flame. It burned bright for a long time over among the gabions, but he went down still deeper behind the rocks. Then he heard the crash of the shot, and the cliff trembled.

His strength was exhausted, and his understanding was befogged. He no longer remembered why he had gone toward the enemy. He only feared darkly that he might be seen and seized. He stared up into the night, where the thunders of the fortress rolled over the peaks like the chariots of Thor.

He did not know how long he tottered about among juniper bushes, nor did he know where he went. At last he perceived the tread of heavy, iron-shod boots, and heard gravel and stones rattle. Twelve soldiers of the guard were coming down the steep slope with a litter.

He kept quiet behind the junipers and waited.

On the litter lay a fallen man, enveloped in two plain soldiers' cloaks and with a white curled peruke pulled down over the face under the braided hat, which was pressed down over the forehead.

"Who is it that has fallen?" he whispered, so low that Colonel Carlberg, who supported the tilting side of the litter from in front, noticed nothing.

"The colonel says it's a gallant officer," answered the nearest bearer, but as in so doing he turned his head to look at the solitary night-rover, he stumbled and sank on his knees under the burden.

The borrowed peruke and hat slipped from the dead man's head, so that the moonlight fell bright on the face with the temple shot through.

"The king! Our great beloved king!" the bearers murmured, and were about to set down the litter.

The dreaded monarch, to whom it had just been whispered that he could no longer rely on any one, lay there disarmed; and old warriors, stained with mud and grime, twisted their rough, frost-bitten hands over his corpse, wailing and groaning: "Our great, our beloved king!"

The colonel had to threaten them with hard words that they must be silent and not betray what had happened by their lamenting.

Heavily and slowly they bore the king onward again upon the same unplaned bier where during the previous nights he had seen so many nameless soldiers, already forgotten, who had obeyed his will and died.

Midnight was already past when the bier was set down on an open sward among the cottages in the lonely village of Tistedal. After the bearers had got three fiat coins for drink-money, they all went off. The officer remained and sat down, brooding and sighing deeply, on the single pole of the bier. Volleys still rang in the distance on the wooded ridge, but elsewhere all was hushed, and the mill-wheel down by the river stood motionless. All the panes were dark, and the same full moon that had lighted the disguised horseman through the city gate of Stralsund and to the dismal conflict at Rügen shone to-night over the grass where a lonely warrior kept watch by his fallen king.

Step by step, Tolle Orasson had stolen after and had only come to a standstill close by the sward under the motionless, drooping branches of the Candlestick Birch. Talking to himself half aloud, he went around the white trunk in ever narrowing circles, shaking over the tussocks the big drops from his wounded arm, in order to conjure into eternal sleep and oblivion the evil ducats that lay buried there.

"Sleep and be accursed!—Why don't the drums beat? The bier stands off there so lonely. No women are weeping there, no children, no faithful friends. Ah! you moon, that have come and gone and beheld so much, never shall I see you above a Swedish forest without remembering that bier."

He pulled out the axe which was stuck in one of the branches and which he had pointed out to the soldiers several evenings before. Chips of wood pattered down, and his strokes on the Candlestick Birch resounded far through the stillness.

With that he checked his hand again, and a new glimmer of comprehension passed through his soul: "Almighty, avenging God! He before whom assassins threw down their weapons, he who went smiling to meet innumerable deaths, — he falls as quietly as a trampled ear of grain, when Thou hast filled the measure of his fate. He falls nearly in solitude one night on the ramparts, like a petty soldier at his post. He dies by a shot from a condemned and rusty field-piece, on which a few soldiers, indifferent and singing, have thrown their match. Or—whence, forsooth, did the bullet come at Thy bidding? What do I know, a simple man? I only know what I have just now witnessed and therefore must believe. But there were so many strange voices up there in the dark."

All this time the officer sat on the pole of the bier by the dead man wrapped in the soldiers' cloaks, and ever more wearily in the repose of night the axe-blows fell on the thick trunk of the birch.

When the tree finally plunged to earth, the un-known wood-chopper sat down in silence on the trunk.

The hours grew long. It was already getting toward morning, when a couple of servants, who had been sent for him, drew near to carry back their fallen lord. Between them with the king's sword walked a captain, who related that in the moment of death the hand had clasped the hilt so vehe-mently that the blade was half drawn from its sheath.

Listening to every word, Tolle Orasson bent aside the branches of the Candlestick Birch.

"The sword—" he asked of himself. "Was there a hardened man, a man prematurely gray, who drew that sword against the memory of the prince of light who once bore his name? Or may—"

He stepped forward straight in the captain's way and inquired in a suppressed whisper: "The sword—against whom was the sword drawn? Under my blood-covered corporal's clothes there is a like man, one perhaps cleverer than ye, though sunken deep from the sight of men. Don't motion me away, then, but answer in pity's name!"

"My friend, I don't understand your question."

"Against whom, I say? Against whom was the sword drawn?—I know it myself now. Against whom, do I ask? Against all. Is n't that answer

enough for us? Is n't it so that a hero must die?
He believed in the righteousness of his own conduct. — Such defiance God forgives. — Such defiance even men forgive."

Capture Görtz!

TO capture Görtz was to beat a fox at his own
game, but the Prince of Hesse had at headquarters an incomparable lackey by the name of
Pihlgren, who afterwards in his old age used to
relate how it came about. Many years after Pihlgren's pious and altogether edifying death, an old
manuscript was preserved in one of the parsonages
of Värmland, where it was all recorded and described. Nobody rightly knew whence the manuscript had come, but the dean, who had read the
yellowed sheets carefully, used to tell it as follows:

The night when the king was shot, the Prince of
Hesse sat at table with several officers at Torpum.
Then the Frenchman, Siquier, stepped in and
whispered into the prince's ear, and the prince whispered into the ear of the man who sat next him.
When the whisper had gone round, the prince
dropped his knife and fork. He then ordered up
a horse and a lackey. Pihlgren, who was on guard
at the house of the prince that night, packed his
cloak in his saddle-bag with great haste and rode
behind the prince and the officers to the trench
where the king lay fallen.

The litter had just been fetched, and the prince
ordered the officers to lift their glorious master upon
it, but the incomparable hero had seized the broad-

sword-hilt so hard in the instant of death that the
generals had great difficulty in unclasping his fingers. When the Swedish gentlemen had finally disarmed the great dead and gotten away the sword
which he let go so reluctantly, his hand clung a long
while to theirs, and all who stood near believed that
in that hour God Himself had sealed the hand-
clasp forever.

As soon, now, as the litter was carried away, the
prince summoned the officers to a council of war
on the spot where the king had fallen, and thirty
soldiers with torches stood round about at a little
distance.

Bomgarten, who was colonel of the Nobles'
Regiment as well as a chamberlain, finally went
aside with Lieutenant-Colonel Björnschiöld, while
all the time he gazed furtively at Pihlgren. Thereupon Björnschiöld came to Pihlgren and praised
his clever understanding and many accomplish-
ments, as he requested him in the prince's name to
come with him on a long ride, concerning which he
would get instructions only when they were well
on the way.

Pihlgren became quite at a loss, but as he rode
in company with Bomgarten and Björnschiöld next
morning, they said to him: "Now we 're off to capture Görtz."

"In that case," said Pihlgren, "we must needs

be nimble both with tongue and hand; but for my share, I shall do my duty faithfully, as the gentlemen surely know. Where, then, is the sinner?"

They said, "He is supposed to be not far off, but if he reaches Tistedal, he'll be the cause of a pretty spectacle."

When they had travelled the roads another night and day, at five o'clock in the dusk they met Görtz, as he came riding in his red cloak on the plain at Raballse.

When Pihlgren pointed to the plain, Bomgarten and Björnschiöld ridiculed him, crying gaily at his ear, "Do you think the great man would be on horseback?"

But Pihlgren answered, "Devil take me if it is n't Görtz. I recognize for sure his servant Petter Berg, who is riding by him, and is my honest old friend and crony."

When they had come nearer and noted that Pihlgren spoke the truth, Bomgarten dismounted and greeted His Excellency very humbly, while he assured him that His Majesty had never been better than he was at that moment.

"And whither do you mean to turn now?" asked Görtz.

Bomgarten, who hated Görtz for all the evil he had done him, bowed lower and lower with great cheerfulness, so that he scraped the road with the hat in his hand, and then he made up a handy lie. "I 'm journeying to Göteborg to buy boots for my regiment," he said.

Görtz now turned to Björnschiöld, whose German wife was a relative of his: "And you, cousin?"

Björnschiöld grew red in the forehead and bravely grasped at the first lie that came to hand: "Oh, I 'm going to Göteborg about a stranded ship on which the prince has effects."

Bomgarten now began again to bow and scrape and be so glad that his eyes shone, and with that he contrived a new fib: "The remarkable thing is, that just now we 've got to turn back. But we must get us fresh horses first at Raballse. Perhaps there 's a question of some assault. The prince has sent this foolish lackey here after us and ordered us to return."

When he had spoken after this fashion, he gave a wink to Pihlgren, whom in his heart he considered a fellow as honest as he was sharp, a man worth more than ten others. Had the colonel not had such an artful lackey with him, Görtz would perhaps have gone free to this day; and who can tell whether that denier of God, who was so much at home both in the black arts and every sort of forbidden thing, would not then have known how to lengthen his worthless and sinful existence so that he neither grew feeble with years nor departed this life? It was therefore surely by God's dispensation

that Pihlgren was on the alert, though the reward
he got afterwards was ingratitude.

Because Pihlgren was a crony of Petter Berg's,
he came near to riding forward and honorably
betraying the whole plot, but in a short time he
began to hear so many untruths that he had to smile
within himself, and soon he grew as crazy as the
others.

They dared not seize Görtz out of hand in the
open, but he inquired of them with much affability,
" Where do you think to make your quarters for
the night? Will you not come on to the deanery at
Tanum and eat supper with me?"

That was water to their mill, and they accepted
with feigned gratitude, pressing their hands to their
breasts, but between themselves they thought that
they would be the guests who knew how to get the
tidbits of the goose.

Görtz now rode forward to the deanery at Tanum,
but a cornet and an adjutant followed him stealthily
at a distance to observe if he kept the road he had
said and did not turn off toward Glomm, for in that
case they were to shoot a bullet through his head.
Bomgarten and Björnschiöld rejoiced meanwhile
at the good turn the affair had taken, notwithstanding that they could not get any fresh horses at the
hostelry in Raballse, since they were all bespoken
to carry Görtz's heavy baggage. Only Pihlgren
adroitly managed to find himself a horse that had

stood in the stall for three days. The fact was, he
accosted a servant-girl and stationed himself as if he
wanted to entice her round the corner of the house
to chat with her. When, unable to withstand such
an invitation, she followed him out into the rain, he
became quite serious all at once and promised her a
pretty penny if she could immediately find him a
rested horse.

Bomgarten and Björnschiöld were sorely amazed
when they saw Pihlgren come leading along a
white-faced nag, which was so lively that it reared
and snorted; but they were now so tired out that they
straightway ordered Pihlgren to gallop off ahead to
the deanery and there in all secrecy beg the dean
for a room with a fire on the hearth and a light on
the table.

It was cold, and a pouring rain fell all night.
When Pihlgren came to the deanery where Görtz
had taken quarters, he happened on the cornet and
the adjutant, who were keeping out of sight in the
dark wagon-shed. They could not believe their own
eyes when they saw his steed, which was so frisky
that they could hardly hold him, and they praised
Pihlgren, rejoicing to have with them such a clever
lackey.

There was a long delay before the others came
up with their hard-ridden beasts. Silently they fastened all the horses in the wagon-shed, so that no
one in the house might discover them. Light shone

at all of the windows, but deep darkness prevailed outside, and before they went up to the room which Pihlgren had, with much foresight, engaged in a side-building, they each and all got ready their pistols.

They were wet through to the skin, but were so much excited that they did not notice it. When they entered the room, whispering and walking softly, Bomgarten said to the dean, "Our errand here is that we wish to arrest Görtz, because King Charles has just been shot dead."

The dean, a small, slender man with a most cheerful countenance and thin white hair, took a turn across the floor, which was covered with fir twigs, stroking and shifting his skull-cap: "God bless you, colonel," said he, "if you will cut short the power and authority of this wicked plague of our country. He is an Achitophel, and who knows whether the devil himself, imitating in mockery an exalted model, has not taken human form in his person, and so is sitting and eating this evening in my own humble dwelling? Ever since that abandoned villain came riding through the rain, the kitchen fire blazes and roars so that the sparks come out of the chimney, and yet it's as if the flame could not warm one's forehead, but was always cold as ice."

Bomgarten then answered, "Be easy, my good dean! You must now station your servants under the window with axes, and then Pihlgren, who is a more cunning fellow than all of us put together, will quietly entice Görtz's servants in here, one by one, till we have them all under lock and key."

Pihlgren then went softly out and found in a shed his old friend and crony, Petter Berg, whom he requested to follow him and take a secret letter to the little Duke of Holstein. Berg, who had some business in the shed regarding the many flasks that Görtz had brought along, offered Pihlgren a glass of good wine and thanked him for his true and faithful friendship from ever since they were little. But when Berg came into the room and saw the cornet and adjutant at the door with pistols and naked swords, he began to weep and exclaim, "Never should I have believed such a thing of Pihlgren."

Meanwhile Bomgarten inspected Berg's pockets and found a hundred ducats in specie, but when the poor fellow assured him it was only drink-money that he had received when he served with Feif and carried letters of appointment, he was allowed to keep them in return for confessing whatever else he knew.

" Well," he then related very softly and charily, "there's really both French and Hungarian wine in some of the flasks in the shed, but the others are filled with Görtz's chinking money."

With that the dean stopped short in the middle

of the floor, and smote his hands together, while
Bomgarten, rapping and drumming on the corner
of the table, shook his head and never ceased ex-
claiming, "We're making a better haul here than
we ever could have dreamed."

Pihlgren now returned into the dark to catch
more fish with the same lie that he had just used,
and soon all Görtz's lackeys were shut up in the
room, with the exception of the valet, who was in
with his master. Pihlgren found him the hardest to
get on his lime-twig, but he relied on his skill and
stationed himself before the kitchen window, which
faced the courtyard.

It was raining in torrents, and he saw that the
girl who was cooking Görtz's dinner shifted the
saucepans back and forth over the fire without
ever getting the strongest flames to heat as they
should. By great good fortune the valet soon came
out into the kitchen, but as he was mightily
haughty in all his ways, Pihlgren understood well
how to handle him, and went no further forward
than to the open kitchen door.

"My good sir," he began, bowing, "I would
humbly ask whether you will be so gracious as to
follow me across the court and speak a few words
with Colonel Bomgarten?"

"Why, it's raining," said the valet.

Pihlgren now no longer knew what device he
should trump up, but stood out in the deluge and

stared. "My good sir," he said at last, "it's surely
something about His Excellency's flasks."

Thereupon the valet at once made haste to follow him across the court, but when he came to the
room and saw the naked swords, he wished to turn.
He burst out in wrath at Pihlgren, but the latter,
now no longer using the words "my good sir,"
went close up to him and said, "Be quiet, will you?
I 'm a remarkably honest man, and perhaps a finer,
a better, a braver — perhaps, too, a smarter — yes,
a better servant has never waited on a master.
That 's enough! "

"A bragging groom, that 's what you are," retorted the valet.

"Yes, the varlet is insufferable," the dean said
of Pihlgren.

But Pihlgren had not meant to boast, but had
only said that of himself which was right and fair,
and Bomgarten, who had seen what he was worth,
struck the valet on the mouth with the back of his
hand, and said aloud so that all heard it: "Pihlgren is a much stauncher fellow than you, and if
you don't keep good and still, I 'll beat you to a
jelly. — And now, worthy sirs, keep good watch and
ward over these chaps, so that they don't slip out,
while we others get to business ! "

Thereupon Pihlgren followed Bomgarten and
Björnschiöld across the court, and they saw that

the light shone in the dean's apartments, where Görtz was sitting alone. A blue cloth was hung in the window. The candle-light fell steady and quiet, and no shadow moved on the cloth. The whole deanery lay as still as if it were already late at night, and the only sound was a subdued clatter, when the maid now and then shifted the pans above the heatless flames.

Pihlgren thought of the many remarkable adventures which he had shared in his time, and it seemed to him that this last was the most noteworthy of all. Only now did he feel that his clothes were wet through, and all warmth departed from his body so suddenly that he began to freeze, and his teeth chattered.

When they came into the entry, they stuck their swords in the sheath and in that fashion went in to Görtz.

"Good evening!" began Bomgarten.

Görtz, who sat deep in thought with his spectacles on, only moved his large nightcap without lifting it off. There was a fire on the hearth, and on the table burned two white wax candles.

Bomgarten stood in front of him in the middle of the floor. "I order His Excellency, the privy councillor, under arrest!"

"Whom? me?—Indeed!"

Görtz's very fair and delicate countenance

changed hue, he snapped his fingers, and moved his lips: "King Charles is dead! Does the king still live?"

Bomgarten answered, "When I last spoke with him, he lived."

But Görtz, who was no less crafty than Pihlgren himself, stuck to his inquiry and asked: "Did you see him?" To this Bomgarten replied: "I saw him as recently as when he sat, shy and embarrassed in times of good fortune, in conquered Thorn with his hat in his hand."

"I mean," said Görtz, "when did you see him last?"

To which Bomgarten replied, "In the dusk of misfortune, when he never took off his hat except before his hungry army or at divine service."

Görtz then cried, full of foreboding: "The king of the Swedes is dead."

Bomgarten stepped forward to the table, tied together a large red handkerchief full of documents, which Görtz had just been reading, and handed it to Pihlgren at the door. Björnschiöld, meanwhile, was seeking for Görtz's sword, which he found at last behind him on the bench where he sat and gave to Pihlgren. It was a sword with a large infantry hilt of pure ducat gold.

As soon now as Görtz had risen from the bench, Bomgarten began to examine his clothes to see if he had any papers, any vials of poison, or any sleeping-powder for the watch, because he was of opinion that such a bird would need to be caged with great precaution, if it was not to fly straight off again. He turned his breeches pockets inside out, but found nothing except a gold penknife case, an antiquated dollar in specie, and one and a half ducats. But when Görtz came to the fireplace, he suddenly tore a document from under his clothes and threw it on the fire, where it would at once have become ashes, had not Pihlgren plucked it from the embers with such haste that he burned his fingers.

"Stop, fellow!" thundered Bomgarten, seizing Görtz by the shoulder. "You are no longer he whom you have been. You were my worst persecutor in the realm of Sweden, but now I am your master."

Görtz, as he came to hear so many unaccustomed compliments, bit his teeth, changed color many times, and looked straight at Bomgarten with his single eye. The dean, who was host in the house, then came to the threshold and, touched by the transformation he beheld, addressed Görtz in a mild voice: "Your Excellency is a denier of God and cares far more for the heathen philosophers than for the unhappy Swedes, whose souls may be likened to a sword laid on an open Bible. But in the hour of misfortune it becomes every servant of the church to offer his consolation."

Görtz now straightened himself up to his full height and stood proudly, as he said, "If I do not believe in God, yet I believe both in the Bible and the sword. Ye rancorous and simple-witted Swedes, little do ye understand what I believe or do not believe."

The dean said: "Your Excellency has built on the favor of his earthly prince."

Görtz replied: "He who lived in a strange country far from your absurdities has honored me with his favor. If you would preach, my worthy dean, pray wait until Sunday! Man is in life a bubble, in death food for worms."

"Then I have nothing further to say," declared the dean, "but will only inquire whether Your Excellency graciously commands that dinner shall be brought in."

Bomgarten interposed and answered curtly in Görtz's stead: "Yes, I am right hungry. Have the dinner brought in at once!"

When the dishes, which might well have beseemed the greatest king, had been laid on the board, Bomgarten and Björnschiöld sat down to table with Görtz, but, not venturing to let him use a knife, they cut his food for him on his plate. The word "Excellency," which had been used in the plain at Raballse, had been forgotten, and Bomgarten inquired: "The privy councillor has perhaps some wine with him, too?"

Görtz became wholly dismayed: "Wine! Yes. Both red and white. Both — yes."

Bomgarten whispered to Pihlgren in Finnish, which no one else understood, that he should fetch in a couple of flasks of wine and likewise flasks with Görtz's money, but aloud he said: "Fetch in red wine and white. A glass of Volnay will taste splendidly — and then a little golden with our sweetmeats."

The dean and Pihlgren now helped to lift in the heavy and odd-looking flasks. They set them on the floor by the table, and Bomgarten beckoned to Pihlgren, "My good Pihlgren, be sure to give me a good glass of wine, because I surely need it, and have surely deserved it, too, most particularly to-day. And you shall take a glass yourself as well, comrade, for without you I hardly know how things would have gone."

Görtz, who sat at the end of the table without knife or fork, could touch nothing, although the best tidbits had been cut up on his plate. Then Bomgarten again beckoned Pihlgren from the door. "My good Pihlgren, come here with you, sit down, and eat. You are probably as hungry as I, and I know you have n't had a blessed bite since Torpum. Let's see. *Petit-salé à la choucroute* — does n't that fall in with monsieur's taste? Or a piece of capon? Or a prune tart? Oh, that's excellent. A regular little French *souper* for starved lads such as we. Not for two years have I eaten as well. Dear me, don't stand there scraping and shilly-shallying!"

"I must very humbly decline such an immense honor," answered Pihlgren, who saw that Bomgarten spoke in that way only to humiliate the haughty Görtz yet further. "To boast or to make much of myself is not at all in my mind, but the colonel surely knows that in a question of behaviour and knowing his place, there is no lackey in all the army — no, not in the whole of Sweden — no, not in·. . ."

"Hold your gabble, you arch-prater, and sit down!" yelled Bomgarten.

When Pihlgren, too, was treated in such a fashion, he found nothing else for it than to obey, but he smiled contentedly in spirit, for he had often before in his time waited upon Görtz and never had he dreamed that he himself would come to sit at table with such a potentate.

On account of his cousinship, Björnschiöld at the beginning was somewhat abashed and silent, but as none of them had had anything to eat for two whole days, they ate as much as they needed of the delicate fare, and straightway drank to their hearts' content. Görtz said not a single word, but stared at Pihlgren, who had tied a cloth about his injured hand. However,·Pihlgren was little inconvenienced and knew very well how to manage knife and fork and how to hold his glass.

At last Bomgarten gave around the sweetmeats, and Görtz took two or three pieces, one of which he dropped in a glass of Hungarian wine which stood before him; but when he took the morsel into his mouth, he had to lay it on the plate again. He thereupon drank half the glass. That was all he consumed that evening.

Bomgarten then got Pihlgren to open the heaviest of the flasks and took it in his hands. "My dearest sirs," he said, "we must not forget now at the conclusion to thank the privy councillor for this capital French meal. This which I have here is a heavy wine that gives a big appetite and easily goes to the head, but in our impoverished and unfortunate land it is now unusually rare, and is reputed to be assuredly the favorite drink and daily medicine of our privy councillor."

While he spoke in this strain, he began to tilt the flagon, and all the bright ducats ran down into the glass, glittering and clinking.

Görtz held his hands under the table without answering a single word and looked straight in front of him into the darkness between the two candles. The dean still stood at the door, kneading and rubbing his fingers, and the maid who had helped Görtz's valet to set the table stood behind him in the entry with pinned-up skirts.

Björnschiöld, however, could no longer remain sitting pale and silent, but sprang up and grew red to the roots of his hair. He seized all the glasses, and threw their contents back into the flagon. "Accursed be that wine," he cried, "and accursed each and all that taste of such a drink!"

"Amen, amen!" said the dean.

With that they all rose from the table, and the dean took one of the candles and lighted Görtz to the room where he was to lie. Last of all came Pihlgren with the costly sword and the papers wrapped up in the silken handkerchief.

Görtz walked with a lordly air, but threw his wig and vest on an armchair and was then about to lay himself in his spurred boots on the dean's bed, which was covered with the fairest bed-clothes. With that the dean was ill-pleased and he therefore made as if he would pull off the boots, but Bomgarten prevented him, saying, "You are too just a man, my worthy dean, to pull off such dirty boots. But if you will have your maid come here and pull, she is welcome to."

"Fetch in my valet!" ordered Görtz.

"I am an honorable Swede," answered Bomgarten, "and can get along without either valet or groom, if need be. You may thank the dean that he will allow his maid to pull off your boots."

The girl came at once, but could not get off the boots, and Bomgarten again forbade both Pihlgren and the dean to help her. Finally she had to sit down on them and ride them off, but that went very slowly, and Görtz grimaced and looked more and more savage, but again did not say a single word.

"If the privy councillor would now like to read his evening prayers and give thanks for a good day's work, there is nothing to prevent," said Bomgarten, pushing to him on the coverlet one of the heathenish Cartesian Latin books that he had come upon among Görtz's belongings. He, however, did not touch the book, but only whispered very softly to himself:

> *Le rideau descend. Je sors,*
> *je sors d'une grande tragédie,*
> *le héros et sa belle patrie,*
> *les amants malheureux, sont morts.*
> *Allons nous coucher, c'est fini!*
> *Allons nous coucher, c'est la nuit!*

"Yes, now the game is ours," said Bomgarten. "Early in the morning the dean's men shall help the servants of the Crown to convey the man to Uddevalla and then on with cavalry to Stockholm. But before all else we must compose a report of the affair and send it directly to-night to the headquarters in Norway. There is no one but Pihlgren to whom I dare entrust the letter."

"The colonel knows," answered Pihlgren, "that if ever a servant faithfully took upon himself every difficulty, and honestly and discreetly, and perhaps boldly as well—"

"Can no one get that self-righteous man to keep quiet?" whispered Björnschiöld.

But Bomgarten, who was more sagacious, winked at Björnschiöld and said, "Such another fellow as you, Pihlgren, is n't to be found. Get a horse now — and good-by!"

Although Pihlgren was wet through and so tortured and tender that he could hardly hold himself up straight any longer, he now mounted again to the saddle and rode back in the dark night to Norway. Bomgarten afterwards received Görtz's great gold sword as a recompense for his trouble, and Björnschiöld was given a horse with full equipment; but Pihlgren, who, so to speak, had captured Görtz and all his retinue, never got so much as a single farthing.

A Hero's Funeral

ON the gallows hill in the outskirts of Stockholm, a man stood outside the executioner's cottage in the winter twilight and tapped on the window. When nobody answered, he turned about in the direction of the city and listened with hand to ear. Then he walked forward a stretch toward the verge of the wood, where Görtz's foreign servants stood with their spades, whispering.

"Good evening, comrades!" said he. "It's only Duval, the chief cook. Bring forward the lantern without fear. The executioner is away. All men are now gathered into Stockholm to behold His Majesty's funeral procession."

One of the servants brought out the lighted lantern from under his cloak and threw the light down upon a coffin, which stood without a lid beside the secretly opened grave. There upon the fir twigs, which were still green, lay a corpse in black velvet clothing with the severed head between the feet.

Duval shook his clenched hand toward the city and muttered between his teeth, "Ye vengeful Swedes! These, then, are the earthly remains of the proud Baron Görtz, our gracious master. But remember, remember, he went to the block like a philosopher and a knight, shrugging his shoulders at your bloody sentence. The tool ye broke asunder, but the king who held it in his hand, him ye bear at this moment under a velvet canopy to his last resting-place. Do ye suppose that his sleep will be tranquil?"

"Now the funeral knell is beginning," said the servants, threatening with their spades the city, where the glow of rush-lights already tinged the nocturnal heavens. "Hark how vainly the bells are calling down peace!"

Duval replied, "They cannot call down peace upon a grave where men are still disputing. Last night I disguised myself as a groom, went into a tavern, and said to the people, 'Throw stones on the funeral pall to-morrow! Are not your bleeding wounds still open? Did he not bear the sword against his own subjects? Shout his right name over the funeral sledge, oppressor of the people that he is — King Heartless, King Tempter-of-God, King Dolt!'"

"And what answer did the chief cook receive?"

"'Do you hate him, then?' the men answered. What, forsooth, was I, a foreigner, to say to that? Is it not a wonder about this prince that nobody can hate him? Two embittered men cannot meet and find fault with him without beginning to doubt their own words when they separate; and the next time they meet, they speak of him with bared heads. Are we, then, fools ourselves? Thousands of men are standing hushed along the streets to-night, but there is not *one* who hates him. At the first threaten-

ing word, they would gather about the funeral sledge
and defend it, without themselves rightly knowing
wherefore. Look you, comrades, we sometimes lay
a man in one scale and all our cunning in the other,
but yet we note that the beam stands as still as
ever. Do you know what that means? That means
that there is in this man a drop of the eternal righteousness, because that drop is heavier than gold and
lead, and we have no weights to weigh it. Though
we pile on all the offences we believe this man com-
mitted, the drop still lies bright on his forehead
—and the beam does not move. I spoke of the
funeral pall. Should I myself have the heart to
throw a stone on that pall? What I hated was the
severity of fate against my own unhappy master."

The servants now took off their hats, and began
to sob, "Our poor unfortunate master! Who, then,
will ring the bell for his soul?"

"Good brothers, it's a sorry spectacle when the
skipper dies, and all the rats jump out to gnaw in
full daylight. We will now hide our master's earthly
remains in a portmanteau, and so convey them with
us secretly to our country. In case of necessity we
must cut off the legs at the knee. Afterwards we
will cleanse his face and lay his orders on his breast
and bury him in the grave of his fathers. There will
then be found some pitying hand that will ring for
him the bell for unhappy sinners."

While the servants of Görtz were weeping beside their spades, the fallen king lay in the midst of waxlights at the royal abode of Karlsberg. Like the poorest of soldiers, he lay in a clean white shirt of rough material, but on his head with its gray hair rested a laurel wreath. The smile had even in death become fixed on his lips, so that the teeth were slightly visible.

A cushion with spices was laid over his face, and when the coffin was closed, twelve weather-beaten colonels carried it down the steps and set it on the black-draped sledge under a canopy of royal velvet. To the right of the head walked Gierta, and thirty dark and solemn guardsmen surrounded the sledge with drawn partizans. Close by, among the long black cloaks of the court servants, old Hultman still attended his master, as he had followed him over the snows of the Ukraine and the ash-strewn fields of Poltava. It seemed to him that all that was holy and great in the world had got its death-blow, and when the night-wind roared in the leafless lindens, he recalled the hour when, kneeling outside the barred chamber door, he had heard the king as a boy recite his evening prayer. Everything grew black before him, but at the top of the funeral pall he recognized the crown of the realm, which he had ever seen wave in the air above the head of the king amid the soldiers' coats stained with earth and blood in the trench.

When the funeral procession passed through the

gate of Karlsberg, all the rush-lights along the Drottninggata and the bridges as far as Riddarholm had already been lighted, but the February night brooded over the city, starless and cloudy. Last among the guardsmen marched a very young man. His rosy face with its severe brow had such a resemblance to the picture of St. George in the Great Church that his comrades called him among themselves Brother George. On the previous day he had dined with Councillor Tessin and had heard many whispers of the malcontents, so that he looked about restlessly at the spectators.

They stand hushed, he thought. It must needs be so. It is an unfortunate whom we bear to the grave, a solitary, abandoned by God and men — a hero!

When the foremost heralds became visible on the Drottninggata, where the townsfolk on foot had formed a hedge, the royal household stepped out from Wrede's house in long cloaks, led by Düben. He walked as stiffly as when, at Bender, he drilled the lackeys with muskets, but when he made out in the distance the banner, against which the wind tore with such violence that it nearly sank, he bowed his head. He walked so stoopingly that his relatives at the windows did not recognize him. After this the knights and nobles stepped out from Cronhjelm's house, and the crown marshal, Per Ribbing, who went with difficulty down the slippery stone

stairs, turned half round and said, "I am resigned
at being childless, for otherwise I should be thinking to-night of the sons fallen in battle who could
not steady my faltering arm."

But when he recognized about him the families
which were thinned like a wood where every other
tree has fallen before the axe, he added very softly
as if to himself, "If I had had sons fallen in battle,
perhaps my lonely steps would feel less heavy. *Dulce
et decorum est pro patria mori!*"

The light shone on folk in windows and on church
towers, where the ringers bent forward out of the
open shutters. Step by step, the train moved onward to the rumble of discordant drums and kettledrums, and the funeral sledge rocked in the snow.
Around North Bridge foamed the black waters of
the river, where once Little Karin's betrothed lover
had been cast, sewed up in a sack, and where mud
covered the sunken barges and shallops that had
formerly anchored under the oaks at Agnefit. At
Riddarholm churchyard, where the hundred-men
of the land in the old days had paid fifty marks ster-
ling to get their burial-place under the flagging,
the newly raised life-guard was drawn up. By every
seventh man was a dark vacancy with a taper, as if a
light were burning there for the fallen and missing.
The people whispered about it, but softly and sub-
duedly. No one wept, and no one threatened. All
the Swedes divined that thousands of years would

gaze back at that night. They felt that now they buried half of their own being.

The wondrous church, around which every age has built its various temples to departed great men, shone as at Christmas Morning Service, and from the tower sounded the metal which before had swung above the highest gallery in the Three Crowns. Brother George, who had long since forgotten to spy about over the mass of people, seized the nearest courtier by the cloak.

"Never did I hear a tolling that affected me so. There is pleading joy in every tone, as if it were for a coronation. And perhaps it is. Does he not return to his capital to-night after eighteen years? Isn't it the expected, the longed-for triumphal march?"

"And the victory?"

"The steadfastness of his will conquered on the night at Fredrikshall when God struck him down dead."

"That steadfastness he turned as a scourge against us."

"Are not your eyes opened yet, so as to see that it was our own secret will and desire which he preserved against our own indecision, like a banner against a rebellious guard?"

It no longer seemed to Brother George that he followed to the grave a solitary and deserted man. He discerned that, when the hero lay fallen and the duel was ended, they who had suffered worst beneath his inflexibility lifted him up on their arms.

When Brother George stepped in through the church door, he was blinded by the five hundred wax candles which, borne by gilded figures, burned in a pyramid in the choir. He no longer remembered that it was a funeral ceremony. He thought that the music played a Christmas song, that it was the Christmas Service, that it was the Midwinter Festival for home, for country, for the dead or absent kinsmen. He thought of the fallen, of the prisoners in Siberia, and of all that which had been.

On the black tablet to the right were described in golden characters the nine years when fortune had attended the Swedes, but on the tablet to the left one might read of the nine years when fortune had continually shrunk away. Here the last surviving warriors were now assembled.

The courtiers arranged themselves according to their rank behind the illuminated shrine where Magnus Ladulås and Karl Knutsson lay motionless with their sceptres of stone. Hark to the clangor of knightly squadrons and gay tournaments, hark to the mournful murmur of the rushes at Foglevik!

The gallant Axel Roos and his friend Åberg, who was now so ill and weak with gout and wounds that he supported himself on a crutch, stood on the oldest gravestone of the Vasa race. Behold the hotheaded lords, proud, honor-lusting, well-spoken, quick to threaten and to offer their hands again!

Every slab in the floor, every tile in the wall, was illuminated by sagas as lanterns by their flame. How the cope-bells tinkle through the church, when King Albrecht, his fingers in his beard and his red-lashed eyes half shut, surrounded by thick-legged, swaying brothers of the cowl, speaks in German with the Swedish Lord Constable!—But who comes in the doorway before the banner with the leopards? It is Queen Cristina of Denmark; and her servants, emaciated as skeletons, carry chests of garments, tapestries, goblets of silver, and all the precious things that cannot quiet hunger. Trumpet-blasts shake the windows. Pale, her hands before her eyes, she mounts on the highest of the chests and from the choir gazes up at the city, where, like a spring flood of melted ice and snow, Sten Sture's army billows down with its round morions—and all the while the windows rattle.

The banner stood on that side of the choir where the knight Karl Nilsson Färla fell transfixed in the gray long ago with a fragment of the altar-rail in his hand, but the crown was set on the other side, where King Gösta gave Laurentius Petri the pastoral staff, and where the bones of Torkel Knutsson rested. Hark to the song, hark to the murmur in the wilds of Karelia, where the banner of the cross flutters over soothsayers and sorcerers and over the blood-smeared gray-stone images of Jumala!

Along the aisle on both sides the partizans of the guards were pointed at the floor under which the pious father confessor of St. Birgitta slept. *Salve regina!* Behold the city of Jerusalem, where thy penitent in pilgrim's weeds hears the harp-notes of the angels of heaven!

The heavy ring of footsteps and spurs struck out echoes under the slab where Göran Persson's uncanny blood was entombed with his sons. How the crows of the gallows hill peck the hand of the priest's son which pushed the two royal brothers away from each other!—and yet do they not sit together in bliss? Gray of hair, gray as to his hanging rags, the fool stands by the prison grating, but back and forward through the castle chapel of Stockholm goes John with ink on his nails and a manuscript in his belt. He is alone, and it is night; but the master musician sits in the gallery, and the organ plays and plays.

The white gleam of the wax candles shone over the darkened, the almost black visages of the warriors, and above in the broken plaster of the roof were red, ominous streaks as of scourge-blows on a human head. They were the old monkish writings,—self-menaces, judgments, scarred upon the foreheads of the Swedes. Six have been, are, and remain the causes of Sweden's misfortunes: Self-interest, treacherous hate, contempt of the laws, indifference to the common good, short-sighted inclination toward strangers, obstinate envy of fellow countrymen. — The last words glowed blood-red, only the words about contempt of the laws had faded and were almost wholly obliterated. Might it be that some day all the words would be erased?

The candle-light made its way between the black mourning tapestries to the banners and armorial bearings above, to the blood-red horn of the Oxenstjernas and the blue lion of the Lewenhaupts. There the dead listened to the flutes and kettledrums. Torstenson remembered when he sat on his litter with his battle chart, and Baner when he rode along the front with his bride, a child who looked down at the pommel of her saddle in fear before the glances of so many men. — And enveloped in that swathing of cloth of gold, which women's hands, wet with inconsolable tears, had arranged for the last time, lay their king with closed eyes, and in the psalms he heard the mild rustle of the summer wind over laurel woods. They all realized that to-night once again a Swedish prince was descending to their dwelling-places.

In the darkness before the church, where the treasurer Råfelt scattered among the silent people the memorial coins which had with difficulty been procured, Cronstedt's field-pieces thundered, and the powder smoke penetrated in through the windows.

Thus now was ended the hero saga of the Charles men, and every soul was conscious of a void that nothing could fill. Before the doors the servants already kindled their torches to light home the court to the royal house.

Brother George stood with wide-open and dreaming eyes. He moved his lips and, unheard of others, whispered, " May we celebrate his memory with torches on stormy winter nights! Where have I seen an epitaph as great as that which our beaten folk is now inscribing over him: He did not make us fortunate, and yet we weep for him as for no other."

The guards presented arms.

The organ and flutes and kettledrums were now silent. It became so still that the slightest rattle of a weapon was audible. With harsh and choked voices the warriors raised the last funeral psalm, and slowly, heavily, step by step, the councillors of state bore the coffin to the vault.

The stairway to the tomb of the Charleses descended at the side of the choir. Golden sceptre in hand, with golden crown, golden apple, golden key, golden sword—so accoutred lay the tenth Charles, victorious and mighty. The eleventh lay without adornment. Behold the girls with wooden shoes dancing at Mora, hear the quiet words of law and right and harvest and peace!—Whither did they depart hence, those golden days? Where now were the locked barns?

In the same space where the coffin was now set down, Pater Hieronymus, bare-footed and followed by a long row of the gray monks, used aforetime to bow before the altar of St. Francis. Early before the dawn, ever faithful and ever quiet, he invariably came through the icy church. But one morning he remained away. He had gone to Rome and set the papal crown on his head. Hark to the silvern clang of the Lateran's bells, hark to the rustling palm boughs of the congregation!

In such wise had tradition already hallowed this chamber. Where the altar candles had burned before St. Francis, who preached evangelical poverty and renunciation, and who had the earth and the cave for his couch, there now slept the lord and monarch who had made the poverty of the Swedes their adornment. Oh, ye shades of what has long passed away, of what has descended unto the earth, of what sleeps in the starlight! Ye echoes of a saga sung! Do ye hear? Do ye hear who it is that knocks to-night at your dwellings? It is a king— that ye divine. But did ye note the yearning with which he has long been knocking? Saga, he loved it—that which sleeps under the great stars. He longed to become the echo of a sung saga.

Two slabs were lifted by their iron rings, and the grave was closed.

The Ship

LUCIDLY the summer night spread its shadow,
but far out among the islands at Korsö gathered armed country-folk and islanders from Sand-
hamn and Harö.

A winter had snowed itself away since the Sunday when in Tistedal the muskets had been presented the last time before the king. Many of the
oldest Charles men and those most broken with
gout had already retired with their scanty pensions
to their little farms, where they knotted their fish-
nets by the window or looked over their old diaries. Serious, God-fearing, respected, they met at
the church on Sundays; and generals and colonels,
without regard to rank, embraced with moist eyes
their brothers in arms of the long campaigns. The
terms of peace had not yet been signed. When the
cannon of the Russian fleet thundered once more
among the islands, the veterans buttoned up their
worn blue coats as tightly as before and unbuckled
the broadsword from the bed-post. Then they each
and all went out to defend hearth and home to the
uttermost.

Captain Resslöf had appointed himself leader of
the band that was assembled on Korsö. Already
weary of his room, he stood among the people with
a confident bearing. His razor and scissors had
rested all winter in the drawer. His hair was so

long, his beard was so white, and it was such a pleasure to look at him, that even the sullen and heavy islanders brightened whenever he turned toward them.

After the day's tempest, the surf was still rolling against the rocky seaward shore of the island, but in the hollow by the shining sound hardly a puff of air brushed over the pines under which the men, restless and expectant, counted the distant cannonshots.

With shaking voice a pastor's son from Djurö stepped forward. He held his cap squeezed in his hand, and his pallor was grayer than ever in the nocturnal light:

"Captain, you have sent the sloops that brought us here to the inner islands to fetch more people. Two leaky rowboats are all we have to save ourselves in, if the enemy lands, but we are more than forty men. Conceal the truth no more! Our little band can no longer accomplish anything here. We have heard, of course, that Rika Fuchs with his Södermanlanders has already marched to Södra Stäk to beat the enemy or lose his life, and that Düker with his Dalecarlians and Westmanlanders is following soon after; but we know, too, that at Boo and along all the coast of Värmdon and Södertörn there will soon be nothing to look for on the cliffs but black ashes. Forgive my words, but we have all heard that Trosa is sacked, and that Nyköping is burning, so that

the glare is visible away up toward Stockholm. In
Norrköping Swedish peasants and soldiers plunder
the wagons of the fugitives in the open street. At
Vikboland the peasantry give signals to the Russian ships with sheets and bleached cloth to show
that they surrender and swear loyalty to the czar,
and at Marstrand Tordenskjold has hoisted the
Danish flag. Whichever way we look, the air is full
of conflagration and smoke. It's all over with Sweden, our home, our home."

"I conceal nothing," answered Resslöf, "but
rely upon it that the Swedes always get help at the
eleventh hour. They seldom get it sooner."

The pastor's son smiled with a sneer, as he departed: "It is night now, and the tenth hour has
just gone by. Let us be hopeful!"

The men pressed close about Resslöf in great
uneasiness. The cannon-shots were still thundering, but more faintly and farther out to sea.

Then the pale son of the pastor came once more
across the rocks. He stumbled and slipped. He
leaped. He pressed in among the crowd without
letting himself be checked.

"Here's an uncanny thing, good people. Out at
sea there a ship is coming with a lighted lantern in
the bow, but with neither mast, nor sail, nor oars.
And not a man can I make out on deck. Nobody
is standing at the tiller. But the ship goes on just
the same, though it moves slowly, slowly."

A murmur of superstitious fear ran through the peasants, but the taciturn islanders followed Resslöf to the topmost cliff by the inlet. They thought that the pastor's son had seen the ship in a vision, for they could not discover anything on the wide sea, around which glowed the nocturnal heavens.

Suddenly they all uttered a cry of astonishment, and the others, who followed them at a distance, began once more to murmur. From behind the rugged cape there drove forward heavily and slowly in the surf a brigantine, without sail and rigging, but with port-holes painted white, and at the stern under the lighted lantern stood a golden lion with paws raised as if to spring.

"That's a ghost ship," muttered the peasants.

Hesitatingly Resslöf ordered some of the bravest islanders to take their muskets and accompany him in one of the rowboats.

They neared the ship cautiously with noiseless strokes and raised muskets, but when they hailed, they received no answer. Some of the small panes in the after cabin gleamed, but that was the reflection of the night, and soon they all became equally dark. Only the bow light burned and flickered.

"God have mercy on us!" whispered Resslöf, pointing to the long strip of cloth which trailed in the water from the stern. "There are our colors. And now I can read the name. This is the brigantine *Swedish Lion!*"

"Yes, yes, it's the brigantine *Swedish Lion*," murmured the peasants on the island.

They shipped the oars. They lay to by the helm and climbed up on a rope of the fallen rigging, but when they entered the empty cabin through a broken window, they had to feel their way forward in the darkness with their hands.

"Is n't there a crew of a single man here?" inquired Resslöf, raising his voice. No one answered, however, but all remained as quiet as before.

He then shoved up the hatch to the deck. Ship rats ran freely back and forth over the planks, but along the gunwales on both sides lay pale and motionless sailors, who had fallen at their post. He went from man to man, bending down to convince himself that they were all dead.

Thereupon he said to his followers, "The eleventh hour is come. Bring the people on board now and make the two rowboats fast at the stern, before the surf and current drive the brigantine ashore. We can both bring ourselves safe to the inner islands and salvage a vessel of the Crown that has gone bravely through its fight."

The old man went off across the deck and sat down at the highest point of the stern, alone and apart from the others.

As soon as the people had been conveyed on board, they towed the brigantine in between the islands. Under the softly gliding prow the bays

and sounds, illumined by the summer night, reflected the golden lion.

The reports of the cannon no longer rolled in
from the sea. More slowly than a broken veteran
proceeding to his cottage on a crutch, the ship
glided between the rocky islets. Women and children, who had hidden there under bushes and roots
of trees, stepped out of their concealment. Joyful
at hearing the words of their mother tongue from
the deck, they flocked upon the beaches and piers
with countless importunate questions.

"This is the *Swedish Lion* coming back from the
fight," answered those on board.

With that the old Charles man by the flagstaff
roused himself from his melancholy and stood up.

"It is more than that. Give me your hands!"
he said to the younger men, drawing them close
to him. "Hats off, good people, hats off! This devastated ship is like Sweden, who conceals herself
behind her islands with her last troops and her
dead. How the prisoners longed for her, those who
have gone hundreds of miles away beside the rivers
of Siberia! Lonely, in disguise, they stood on the
deck of their whale-boat with the illimitable expanse of the Arctic Ocean before their sight, calling upon God every hour in their anguish that He
should not quench the flame of their life till they
were under the roof of their home. The roof of their

home? It lies charred upon the ground. Beaten, beaten is our people, divided is our empire, and on our coasts the ruins are smoking. O inscrutable, eternal God, will the dawn never come? — Be silent, be silent, good people: the dawn is coming. The captives in Siberian cities, as they sit dumbly at their handiwork, shall one morning leap up and see in the square a rider waving a white flag as a sign that peace has been declared. Thirsty mouths shall drink from Frederick's and Ulrica's gold-rimmed goblets, and the Christmas board shall again be spread by women who are not in mourning. Yet again the hay shall diffuse its fragrance in Sweden. The church bells shall ring. For a whole year they shall ring every noontide for peace—and for the fallen. Where, indeed, are the old battalions with Grothusen's drum and the banners of Turkish silk? And he who held us together in the great strife and never would believe the sign that God had forsaken us, he in whose heroic nature all our yearning was concealed,—where does he dwell? Ask the children that sing. Alas! they go hence one by one, the old brothers in arms. Wherever we fare through the country, walking or by post-chaise, we shall recognize in the mists of night the small white churches where eight or ten strong sons have laid the slabs above their graves. And where does there blossom in an alien land a field so remote that we may not sit down on the sward and whisper: 'Is this perchance the place where one of ours, one who fought and bled, is slumbering?' In their poor garments they loitered a short while before us by the bivouac fire, and then went away and fell. Such they were. So I recall them. So, too, they live in memory and say amid a grateful land: 'Beloved be the people that in the decline of their greatness made their poverty to be revered before the world!'"

THE END

www.ingramcontent.com/pod-product-compliance
Lightning Source LLC
Chambersburg PA
CBHW032253020726
47495CB00001B/88